# AIR BASE

**Leonard Henry Le Blanc III**

**SEATE BOOKS**

Published by SEATE BOOKS. Distributed by ASIA BOOKS. Please contact with the author for a signed copy at: PSC 720, BOX R68, APO AP 96502-0001 USA.
E-mail: leblancleonard@gmail.com or leblancleonard@hotmail.com. Tel: +66 (0)65-524-2900. All rights reserved.

Printed by the Tanabutr Co., Ltd. 931 Rama 1 Rd., Wangmai, Pathumwan, Bangkok 10330, Thailand. Tel.: +66(0)2-215-0105-8, +66(0)2-216-0309-14, +66(0)2-215-0318-21, +66(0)2-216-2901-5 Fax. +66(0)2-215-1713, +66(0)2-216-2906-7. E-mail: info@tanabutr.co.th

Cover designed by Cordi Grebler, Dresden, Germany, grebler@arcsign.de

"Eternal vigilance is the price of liberty."
Wendell Phillips (1811-1884).
Speech, Boston, MA, 28 January 1852.

"The price of freedom is eternal vigilance."
Attributed to Thomas Jefferson (1743-1826).
(Informal motto of the USAF Security Police.)

"Quis custodiet ipsos custodies?"
"Who watches the watchers?"
Juvenal (d. 127 AD).
Satire 6.346-8, late 1st/early 2nd Century AD.

"The three greatest threats to the security of the United States are ADM Hyman Rickover, the Soviet Navy, and the US Air Force."
Attributed to ADM Elmo R. Zumwalt, Jr., USN (1920-2000).

This book is dedicated to the men and women who have honorably served in the Air Police and Security Police of the United States Air Force. It is also dedicated to the men and women who now have and will honorably serve in the Security Forces of the United States Air Force.

This book is also dedicated to those who inspired me to write: CAPT Edward L. Beach, Jr., USN (Ret.), (author of 'Run Silent, Run Deep'); Raymond Chandler, (author of 'The Big Sleep'); Len Deighton (author of 'Funeral in Berlin') and Michele McCormick (author of 'Polishing up the Brass').

**INTRODUCTION**

It is 1975 (or *B.E.* 2517). America's involvement in the long Vietnam War is over. The US has withdrawn its forces in frustration and defeat. The North Vietnamese and Viet Cong finally conquered South Vietnam, thus unifying the country and completing the lifelong dream of Ho Chi Minh. Over 50,000 US troops are dead in an ultimately futile effort to prop up an intensely disliked, weak, and corrupt regime. But over 10 times that number of North Vietnamese and Viet Cong combatants also lie dead. These soldiers have again fulfilled the pledge Ho Chi Minh first made to the French when they returned to Vietnam in 1946 to "Reclaim our inheritance." "You can kill ten of my men for every one that I kill of yours," Ho Chi Minh had told them. "But even at those odds, you will lose, and I will win." Ho was ultimately proven right again, although interred in Hanoi for the past six years, unable to live long enough to see the victory he had long led and inspired others to wage.

However, if all US forces have been withdrawn from South Vietnam, not all US forces are gone from Southeast Asia. There is another type of conflict being waged there. This does not involve armed combat. But it is a conflict, nevertheless. It involves US forces and a local population. There will be no medals awarded for bravery, outstanding service, and courage. But there will be medals awarded for cowardice, treason, and treachery.

*U-Tapao* Royal Thai Naval Air Base still exists. However, this is a work of immersive historical fiction. The characters, military units, events, and conversations are from the author's imagination, and any similarity between real people and events is purely coincidental. However, the Thai and English profanities accurately reflect the words spoken at the time. My apologies if anyone is offended. It was what you would have heard if you were there. When the first National Geographic Magazines in the early 20th century showed photographs of bare-breasted women overseas some prudish or puritanical readers wrote in and  complained about the nudity. The editor replied it was what you would see if you visited these countries. There is an abbreviated dictionary in the back for those who do not speak Thai, Navy, and/or Air Force.

**SOI SUKHAN, OFF OF NATIONAL HIGHWAY #3, *BAN CHANG* VILLAGE, *RAYONG* PROVINCE, THAILAND, 0015, 01 JAN 1971.**

The massive cold front had bulldozed in off the high Tibet Plateau from the northwest bringing sub-arctic temps (for Thailand) straight down from the Himalayas. The Thais were all bundled up like Eskimos. The front decided to take an in-country, three-day vacation. But it brought bright blue, crystal clear, cloudless skies as payment.

He was freezing. Constantly moving helped, but not much. He could see the Thais walking around during the day, all wearing heavy coats, scarves, gloves, woolen hats, extra socks, and as much clothing as they could, even though the daytime temps were in the mid-60sF, light windbreaker weather to him. And this was the tropics, he thought! Who could have guessed it would be so cold this close to the equator!? It was at least in the low 40sF at night! This was crazy. All the Thais incessantly said: *"NOW MACH!"* or *"NOW MACH-MACH!"* He was hearing both phrases 100 times per day.

He rarely took his eyes off of the side *Soi* entrance, about 100 meters away, waiting in anticipation for his informant to show up. He stood in the black shadows to be safe. They had agreed to meet at 2300 sharp directly across from Charlie's, the O-Club bartender, gated house entrance. He explained he'd be standing under the elevated large community water tank by one of the concrete legs. He could see but not be seen. He arrived at 2200 to be early and on the safe side. But now it was 75 minutes past the rendezvous time. Typical damn Thais! He mused there was *farang* or 'normal' time, which meant 'on time.' Then there was 'Thai time,' or one hour late. He should have never come this early, he ruefully thought. He was dying for some hot java. Maybe soon.

He'd been working as an OSI agent at Det #7 for three months. They'd hand-picked him at OSI HQs for this special assignment. He knew he'd been selected because he was razor-sharp, very perceptive, and highly intelligent. A real 'fast burner,' groomed to go higher in the organization as far as his talents and connections would take him. He had a string of successes in the past with tough cases (his specialty), so he was quickly getting a good reputation for cracking the hardest ones. But this was his toughest case yet. It would take subtlety and diligence. The ongoing investigation of the massive stealing on *U-Tapao* had already been assigned to another agent. The standard joke on *U-T* was: 'Everything on base is stolen, but the Thais hadn't gotten around to picking it up yet.' He must have heard that a thousand times to date.

He was assigned to new, very routine cases, being the Det's 'newbie.' However, OSI agents made their reputations on solving cases: the tougher, the better. That is just one of the reasons you got promoted. But the other agent wasn't doing much on this massive theft case if anything. He pulled it out from the filing cabinet during a lunch break (without telling anyone and waiting until the office was empty) and reviewed it at his desk. He saw it had been 'going-through-the-motions' fluff from years back. Earlier OSI investigators had all come to the exact same end. Something was not right here. No real investigation had been done: all inconclusive, scant evidence, nothing substantial, little could be pinned down. All nebulous speculations, rumors, and suspicions.

But the level of thievery was titanic, catastrophic. Everything was flying off the base in some way, shape, or form: a/c units, B-52 spare parts, furniture, spare tires, radio equipment, vehicles, and lubricants by the barrel-load, JP-4 and bulk fuel oil. Even a fire truck with siren blazing had blown right out the front gate. Anything not nailed down was fair game. And even if it was, the Thais would somehow manage to steal it, then come back with claw hammers and steal the nails too. He just needed one break. If this kept up soon there'd be nothing left of the base.

Three days ago, an informant, a local Thai *poo-chai,* speaking excellent English and working in the NCO Club, one he'd been secretly developing over time, unexpectedly promised he'd explain how everything worked, how all the pieces fit together. Or so the informant had furtively told him. This might just be the big break he needed to crack this one wide-open.

That was his real 'undercover' assignment: find out why no progress was being made on this investigation and solve it.

He set the meeting up for tonight. A good 'cover' move on his part. There'd be Thais and GIs everywhere celebrating the Thai New Year. No one would notice another *farang* out and about at this hour. All the Thais (and most Americans) were cheerfully saying *"Sawasdee bee-mai!"* to each other.

At Midnight a cascade of heavy, continual weapons fire commenced for about 10 minutes; then it slowly settled down to scattered single shots and short bursts afterward. He could hear the occasional stray ricochets in *Ban Chang* village nearby. He was startled when it began. The intense firing sounded exactly like some US ground-pounding/grunt battalion had accidentally collided with a hard-core NVA regiment in the SVN Central Highlands and were having a furious lead toss. An old Thai New Year's tradition, he imagined. But it was as silent as the grave just then; not even the insects were making sounds.

Suddenly he thought he heard someone rapidly walking down the *Soi* toward him. Yes, he could hear the footsteps now echoing faintly on the tar-pebbled roadway. The *Soi* was dark, only barely illuminated by one light from a mostly closed window in a house halfway down. The footsteps were coming much closer, finally, almost next to him. Then someone softly called him:

"You there, pal?"

"Right here, buddy!" he replied in a low, anticipating tone of voice.

The bright flash and the sharp report were simultaneous at that range.

The AF coroner determined the cause of death was two .38 caliber rounds fired, one in the head. Just to make sure.

-

**SIDEWALK, OUTSIDE BUILDING #837, 8300TH SPS HQs, MAXWELL AFB, MONTGOMERY, AL, 1300, 14 FEBRUARY 1975.**

Things were quiet. The day was cool, and bright, with a robin-egg blue, sky and not too humid. It was too early in the pecan, black walnut, hickory, and magnolia blossom season for the military wives in the on-base housing areas to start trading jabs, uppercuts, and roundhouses over who was snagging the rich harvest of assorted nuts lying in (or just outside of) their yards. The problem stemmed from when the ripened nuts all fell outside the single housing unit fenced-in yards. Most wives held as a given that anything falling off their trees belonged to them, no matter where they fell - fences or no fences. Other wives, neighbors or not, said anything that fell outside their yards was 'fair game,' fences or no fences. Every year there were more than a few dustups and knockdowns, with just as many bruised egos as knuckles and faces. (Didn't anyone ever hear of 'share'? It wasn't like we had a nut shortage on base; or they were too expensive.) But we had to send two SP patrol vehicles out to every prize fight to function as referees and send the lady pugilists back to neutral corners every year. At least it was better than investigating armed robbery and arson.

I walked out of Building #837, the original compact, square, stucco, red-tiled roofed two-story firehouse. It dated from when the base was built back in 1920s; then later converted to the 8300th SPS HQs. It being lunchtime, I headed towards the BX snack bar across the street. Both buildings were near the junction of the flight line and a large parking apron off to one side. I was of average height, average build, average looks, brown hair, green eyes, and one-each military-trimmed mustache. I was as unremarkable as your US Post Office mailbox.

I was dressed in USAF Class 'A's' with a garrison cap. Toss in three pretty-much-everybody-gets-them ribbons, one SP Identification Badge, a standard-issued blue USAF nameplate with white lettering that said 'Legere', and two 'butter bars,' one on each shoulder. All worn to complete the disguise as a total 'Greenhorn,' relatively clueless, still wet-behind-the-ears, 'just-out-of-the-cellophane-wrapping,' 2LT 'shave tail'. I'd been the SPS Ops Officer for the past 20 months, my first assignment. There was no chance of me making AF Chief of Staff, or even full-bird COL, in this career field. But my assignment was quickly coming to an end. I'd been FIGMO for a month: 'hard copy' orders in hand, headed to *Osan* AB, Korea, with a report-no-later-than-30-June-date; leave-in-route authorized. But I was first leaving in about two weeks for USAF Air Base Defense Training at an old WWI/II US Army base called Camp Bullis outside San Antonio, TX.

Walking out of the BX snack bar towards me was the SPS Supply SGT, SSGT 'Marty' Martinez. I liked Marty. However, few officers or enlisted personnel on the base did. He was relatively short, somewhat dark-complexioned (Is swarthy a good word?), not exactly rotund, compact is a better, black-haired, and a motor-mouth of endless fascinating chatter and base-wide gossip. Always center-of-the-bull's-eye. His political commentary on current national events was unmatched, in my opinion. When you heard it from him, you heard it here first. From an old 'Centro Californio' Valley family, he once said. SSGT Martinez also knew more about everything than anyone I'd ever met, or at least he said so. And I believed him, from the spot-on commentary he never lacked to endlessly expound or promulgate.

SSGT Martinez had several natural disadvantages working against him for further and future advancement up the NCO ranks. First, he was extremely sharp; that was strike one. Second, he was always right; strike two. But what always caught him flatfooted and looking at a third letters-high, hard, lightning-fast one for the strikeout was he had no compunctions at telling you (or anyone) both those facts and opinions, depending on how you viewed him. He must have spent every waking hour, when not at work, intensely devouring the latest national publications and academic periodicals. Martinez had been a SSGT too long and was not destined to see TSGT for many more years in my book. (Not exactly a 'Cassandra,' but you get the idea.) It was the source of his endless griping. He was too brilliant, too self-assured, too knowledgeable for his own good, but from all accounts, he was a crackerjack Supply SGT.

"Hey, L.T.! Howsit' goin', sir?"

He had a grin on his face, which always meant he knew something good. He didn't forget to salute this time. (No, he always saluted.) I saluted back. He spoke fluent English, of course. But he liked to mimic a total 'hayseed' manner-of-speaking to officers he didn't like just to mock them (virtually every commissioned and warrant on the base was included). I knew about it and didn't mind. It became a private joke between us.

"SSGT Martinez, good to see you. What's the latest?"

I was always interested in the hottest 'Scoop-from-Group.'

"Heard ya' gunna' to be workin' for the railroad, L.T."

The look on my face offered him my answer. He might as well have said I was going to Mars on a spaceship. I could only guess at what he was talking about.

I replied with friendly patience. "You know I'm going to *Osan*."

I WAS going to Korea but didn't want to. I wanted to go to Thailand. Well (to be completely honest), I actually wanted to go to Vietnam. But that wasn't in the cards. I could have volunteered to join up and trudge off when I was 18 after high school. But I had dreams of going to college first. I would also be the first in my family to attend, no small feat in my tribe. So, I vowed if the 'Big Southeast Asian War Games' were still on when I graduated, I'd volunteer and go. But the US stopped sending troops to Vietnam in late January 1973, and I was commissioned upon graduation from Kansas State's AFROTC unit that May. Plus, the USAF had a strict personnel policy not to send anyone straight to Vietnam unless they had at least one stateside tour under their belt first. So, I had a better chance to fly to Mars than *Bien Hoa* or *Tan Son Nhut*. Thailand was as close as I could come to the 'Big War.' But the whole effort in Vietnam was rapidly taking on water now and sinking beneath the waves for good. It wouldn't be much longer before the final curtain dropped on the whole fiasco. I volunteered for Thailand over a year ago on my 'Dream Sheet,' but orders had poured in from AFMPC for Korea last month. I was slightly disappointed. However, you just roll with the punches with going overseas. And I loved to travel. All I had seen so far outside the USA was on one quick day trip to New Brunswick where my distant relatives and ancestors had long hung out.

"Nope L.T., ya' gunna' be workin' for the railroad!"

If I could have increased the puzzled look on my face, I made a concerted effort. He then presented me with a thick slab of printed papers he'd been holding along with his biggest grin. I looked down at the stack. My name and SSAN were on the top. I looked up, showing even more puzzlement.

"Layin' Thais!"

It was a change of orders. I was officially being re-assigned from *Osan* AB to *U-Tapao* AB in June. I was going to Thailand.

-

**USS *BERKSHIRES* (LCC-21), FLAGSHIP OF THE US SEVENTH FLEET, AT ANCHORAGE IN THE GULF OF THAILAND OFF OF *PATTAYA* BEACH, *CHONBURI* PROVINCE, THAILAND, 0900, 10 MAY 1981.**

I would always remember that day. Not only for what transpired, but for the day itself. The air had a special visual clarity. As if every object in view was sharply focused, like a Karsh photograph. The sky was a rare, bright, pristine 'Wedgewood' blue. It was that special kind of perfect day when picture postcard photographers look out their windows, lick their chops, then grab their cameras, knowing they'd need no filters for some top souvenir postcard sellers. The temperature probably wouldn't have melted lead, but at least it wasn't humid as befitting the traditional 'hot' season. In a few weeks, the traditional 'rainy' season would start when the monsoonal winds shifted from the Southwest across the Indian Ocean, then it would be hot, humid, rain-drenched, and nearly unbearable every single day until the end of October. Daytime temps would match the humidity, both in the high 90sF. However, today was a great day. It was also a good day to die.

I was the only one in the liberty boat to the beach in uniform: summer whites, ENS Line Officer black-and-gold shoulder boards, and four ribbons. I knew I'd be the only one to wear it all through the four-day port call. Not even the *Berkshires'* CAPT would be in uniform even one time. Only those assigned to Shore Patrol duty each day would be so attired. But I would. I had to. Or she would lose endless 'face.'

*Noy* was waiting on the beach. She said she'd been there since dawn. We sat at a café and talked, then strolled along the *Pattaya* beachfront road until it was time to depart. She had already rented a taxi for the trip to the restaurant as I had written her. *Noy* said it was a 20-minute ride south. I guessed it was somewhere along the beach. We were meeting a RTN CAPT *Thanachaibitirungma,* for lunch.

-

## OUTSIDE TABLE, PATIO, *TOOK LA DEE* RESTAURANT, SOUTH OF *PATTAYA* BEACH, *CHONBURI* PROVINCE, THAILAND, 1300, 10 MAY 1981.

Lunch was an unmitigated disaster. It made a major Swiss Alps avalanche looks like a beach sandcastle collapsing. *Took La Dee* Restaurant was the exclusive 'feeding trough' for the most senior RTN and RTMC Officers stationed down in *Sattahip.* I saw RTMC officers use the same RTN officer ranks and insignia, something I hadn't realized until now. The Thai food was delicious and plentiful; the lay-out impressively ornate for being in the middle of the jungle (and near the beach), plus the servers were all Junior Miss Thailand contestants. CAPT *Thanachaibitirungma* treated *Noy* if she were as welcome as a scruffy panhandler outside a millionaire's resort on the French Riviera. Basically invisible, and unwanted. He spoke fair English and asked me about my earlier time in Thailand. But he didn't even say a word of English (or Thai) to *Noy*; not even acknowledging her existence. He inquired how I got to know his name. I didn't exactly lie; I just didn't tell the whole truth.

Earlier last year I was dating an older Thai *poo-ying* (named *Bunsue* or 'Suzie'). Suzie worked as a bartender at one of the many downtown watering holes frequented by Seamen Recruits training at NRD San Diego. I met her one evening out at the 'WESTPAC Wives and Widow's Club' at MCRD, also in San Diego. I was going through SWOS at NAB Coronado then. I accompanied Suzie when she went to visit her best (Thai) buddy's

14

home in Chula Vista on a Saturday afternoon (the typical Thai noisy bash). Later her buddy broke out a small mountain of photo albums. By a strange twist of coincidence (or fate), Suzie's 'fren' had worked on *U-Tapao* in one of the jewelry shops ('Little *Sattahip*', she said) for a number of years but departed to the US right before I arrived. One of the photos in the first album she showed me was of *Noy* in full color: blue top and ball cap; white pants, gloves, and tennis shoes with a small plastic '#1' badge pinned to her blouse. Her hands were blurred as she was 'snapped' waiving them while managing the *U-Tapao* O-Club Girls' Softball Team against some unknown USAF officers one sunny day. 'DEC 1969' was printed on the photo's bottom.

This was my first trip back to Thailand in five years. I had asked the CAPT if it was possible to visit *U-Tapao*. He explained it couldn't be done without the 'Official' Thai government, Royal Thai Supreme Command HQs, and RTN HQs approvals. And that would have to have been granted well in advance. I silently swallowed my disappointment and dropped the subject.

I told him I got his name through his favorite 'niece' in San Diego last year (I assumed it was true, what she told me), and left off the more 'detailed' explanation. I added his 'niece' urged me, if I ever returned to Thailand, to go down and see her favorite 'uncle' in *Sattahip*. She printed his name, address, and phone number down, pressed it into my hand and made me swear a holy oath to visit him if I went. I explained to him about seeing the photo of *Noy* (no other details), but that didn't mitigate her quickly rising temperature (or fury) one single iota at being royally 'snubbed.' I probably would've been OK at the end, but the CAPT made one fatal, unforgivable, monumental mistake.

After we finished our *sappalote* slices for dessert, he casually pointed to the most knock-out, dolled-up, pneumatically chested (but youngest) waitress in the place (looking all of about 15 years-old) standing almost next to our table, and offered:

"If you like to bring her back to *Pattaya* with you, I can set it up ENS!" He beamed at me. I was a dead man. A corpse waiting for interment. My last day on earth. I was going to die in milliseconds. *Noy* was going to completely annihilate me. I was totally embarrassed. I glanced at her. She was wild, super-heated-volcanic-steam-pouring-out-of-her-ears, furious. *Noy* must have bitten her tongue off in humiliation. We all sat there in complete silence. We both had lost endless 'face.' This was the end - eternal darkness awaited me.

Then *Noy* suddenly sat full upright and brightened. She beamed a wicked smile at the CAPT in a heightened state of rapidly expanding self-awareness and total comprehension. Like an acolyte who finally grasps the hidden truth of the revealed word. Her downcast persona completely changed to one of perception, understanding and impending triumph. She finally spoke in excellent English, with a light, medium-high, sing-song Thai accent (for the first time):

"CAPT *Thanachaibitirungma*!!!! I know who you are now!!! You wife working at the *Nipa* Lodge in the *Pattaya* as Assistant General Manager! You 'num-bah' one *mia-noy* working in the *Sabailand* Massage Parlor in the *Pattaya*. You 'num-bah' two *mia-noy* working in the *Talay Tong* Seafood Restaurant in the *Sattahip*. You 'num-bah' one *tee-lock* working in the tailor shop over in the *Ao Udom*. You oldest daughter graduate student in the UCLA.

*Noy* went on to intimately detail the CAPT's whole extended family, their whereabouts, education, and activities, plus his previous *poo-ying* conquests and proclivities in graphic, X-rated detail.

-

## MAIN GATE, NATIONAL HIGHWAY #3, *U-TAPAO* RTNAB, *CHONBURI/RAYONG* PROVINCES, THAILAND, 1430, 10 MAY 1981.

CAPT *Thanachaibitirungma* personally drove us down to *U-Tapao* in his POV. We headed south to where National Highway #3 (also called *Sukhumvit* Road) turns east at the *Sattahip* port spur. *Noy* was quietly, self-righteously, and triumphantly beaming with her unexpected victory. The CAPT was silent all the way. As we turned left above *Sattahip* at the major intersection, the old familiar landmarks came into view. I felt a strange, uneasy feeling as we got closer to the base entrance, riding past the excavation of one large pup tent-like mountain not far from *U-Tapao*. It had spewed out half its side in rocks and stone for the foundation of the base's 11,000-foot runway that had seen tens of thousands of sorties land and take off, all headed for Southeast Asian air space and the 'Big War'. Now all ancient history. The runway originally was built for the RTN Air Wing over a small stream through a large swamp. It was greatly expanded back in 1965. We sped past the Swan Lake Hotel, no doubt long closed, then the moribund Kilo *Sip* market. Not much had changed in these past five years. It appeared the area's population was a fraction of before. Many houses stood empty, with the jungle reclaiming large parts of the landscape that had previously been inhabited and thriving.

I first picked up we were getting near the Main Gate when I noticed an eight-foot high, white-painted, long cinder block wall started on the right-hand side. So they must have finally pulled down the old cyclone fence, I thought. Then suddenly, there appeared on the left the row of dilapidated, wooden, two-story shop houses, seemingly unaltered by time's passage, right across from the Main Gate. There we were: *U-Tapao*. Turning right into the Main Gate area, only slightly changed in my mind's eye, we parked in the long-abandoned lot in front of the old Pass & ID building. CAPT *Thanachaibitirungma* spoke for the first time, cryptically saying:

"There is still one American on base from the time you were here."

We walked through the open doorway with the same USAF-issued gray filing cabinets, battered gray metal desks, and seen-the-worst gray padded chairs from five years ago. The upright gray medical scale, black rotary telephones, and window-paned offices were unchanged by time, all collecting more dust, rust, and cobwebs. We exited out the back doorway and headed towards the Main Gate guard shack. The CAPT spoke to the armed RTN First Class Petty Officer Main Gate guard (now stiffly at attention). He asked to use the phone and called someone, speaking briefly in Thai. He then said for us to wait a few minutes; someone was coming and did not speak again, no doubt due to the total embarrassment that Noy's revelations had caused him at lunch.

Less than two minutes later, a used, but serviceable, O.D., open-top US Army jeep raced up to the gate and screeched to a halt, the tires grabbing the few final inches of sand-covered concrete. The driver leaped out and thanked CAPT *Thanachaibitirungma* profusely in fluent Thai, while shaking his hand with undiminished vigor. Then he said to me he'd take us from here on out. The CAPT smiled and responded in English that he'd wait for us at the nearby RTN O-Club, obviously still in operation, and strode off.

From my first impression, the man, who introduced himself as Dave Doble, might have easily been an older, beefy (but still in fairly good shape), ex-pro football halfback settling into a comfortable retirement several decades after Sunday games days were a fond memory. I couldn't precisely place the man's accent (Jersey-side of the Hudson?), with some harsh 'New Yorker/Brooklyn/ Bronx' words thrown in for good measure (spoken in a gravel tone). The harder edges probably ground down by some higher education. But Doble (call me 'Dave') was extremely happy to see us, to the point of exuberance. He couldn't stop grinning. He picked up the guard shack's old black rotary telephone on the windowsill (another USAF war souvenir left behind) without asking a to by-your-leave of anyone and dialed three numbers.

"Guess who's coming to visit? 1LT Legere and Ms. *Noy* from the Club!"

*Noy* granted him her brightest, highest-wattage smile.

I assumed he had called his wife and thought that was strange. I was in my summer, short-sleeve, white US Navy uniform. How did this Dave possibly know what rank I held before in the AF? I had never stated it or said a single word except hello. But I had the immediate, uneasy feeling that Dave knew far more about me than I could have ever known about him. All down the main drag Dave couldn't stop talking how happy he was to see us, and how thrilled his wife would be too.

We barreled down 'C' Avenue at high speed into the base. Past my old BOQ, the AF O-Club, and 'COL's Country.' The wide wooden-slat and cyclone fenced-in area of trailers for assigned O-6's and VIPs above that pay grade, all on the right-hand side. On the left, I saw all the wooden hooches, trailers, and temporary buildings were histories, long gone. Turning right three times on the side streets to box around, Dave quickly went through the 'COL's Country' compound entrance gate. We quickly came to a screeching halt in front of the old SAC Air Wing Commander's 'hooch' (actually a long, double-wide trailer), the largest in the heavily jungled, tropical plant, flower, and tree-jammed enclosed compound, all now overgrown from the years of benign neglect. Dave ushered us into the living room. *Noy* and Dave's wife quickly embraced (apparently old friends) and then quickly evaporated into the trailer's kitchen, rapidly chattering like magpies in sing-song Thai. I followed Dave into a small office space off the living room.

It was completely jammed with papers, books, old magazines, stray US military gear, Thai souvenirs, some spare jeep parts, files, and cardboard boxes filled with whatever. I sat in a military-issued gray metal chair across from his hopelessly cluttered military-issued gray metal desk. Dave plunked down into the seat behind and inquired what I wanted to drink. *Sunee* brought a Thai iced tea for me (with milk please, thank you) and a *Singha* beer for Dave, after he happily bellowed out the drinks order through the thin metal walls.

We discussed what I'd been up to since I joined the Navy almost two years ago: the ship, port calls done and port calls still to go. I pretty much covered the last five years of my life in a nutshell. Dave listened intently, asking a few questions.

He suddenly stopped his banter, but not his wide grim, stared and said simply:

"We've met before."

I pondered this. A half-formed, vague impression was starting to coalesce in the back of my mind. Yes, I did remember meeting Dave now, at least one time on base previously. But where and when I couldn't quite place him; like, unexpectedly meeting an old, long-forgotten grade school buddy after decades.

"NCO Club," Dave prompted.

BANG! That was it! I had known him or actually had met him once, very briefly. The first time was one afternoon back around September 1975. I got a radio call to quickly repair to the NCO club over an incident. The LE Desk SGT said staff members there had caught a *gigolo* - a rare occurrence on the base back then. My Assistant Shift Supervisor for LE, MSGT Wozniak, joined me on the trip since I was already outside LE talking to him. We pulled up to the back of the Club in my jeep. Three burly, obviously older 'NCOs' from their haircuts and demeanor, but all in mufti -open-necked, casual 'two-Chinese-dragons-catching-the-fireballs-in-their-mouth's' printed Thai polyester shirts, dark slacks, and black dress loafers, were keeping one slender, very unhappy, young-looking Thai man in their close company. One American, obviously their leader, spoke to me without giving me his (or his cohorts') name.

"Caught this *gigolo* red-handed *ka-moying* some spare a/c units out the back door," the big man said perfunctorily in equal parts triumph, agitation, and determination. He didn't use my rank or name.

I clearly remembered now it was Dave who was speaking to me then. I also remembered offering to take the thief off their hands.

"NO!!" the big man said in a deliberately hard tone of voice. "You tell Sprayberry if he wants this *gigolo,* he can come down right here now and take custody of him himself!"

That was unusual. SPs always took custody of suspects. That was their job. Like plane mechanics fixed aircraft, bomb loaders loaded bombs, or chow hall cooks cooked chow. But I could see the man would not be cowed, swayed, or awed by any officer, even one with legal apprehension powers. I quickly figured these three were 'bouncers' at the NCO Club, undoubtedly some TSGTs or MSGTs 'moonlighting' for beer-and-party-hearty spare change. So as not to let their wives suspect anything (as they would have) had they dipped into their salaries, no doubt all being sent home. It was a well-sought-after job for anyone wanting to supplement their pocket money, especially for some of the more senior, experienced NCOs with regular jobs along the flight line and with the time and energy to take a second full-or-P/T gig. But something told me in the back of my mind, with my limited police training and against my better judgment, not to get involved in this one. I now felt this incident was going to be much more than met the eye and was also going to get me planted in the middle of something far more complex that I firmly believed I didn't need or want. I was going to need this caper like a big gorilla needed banjo lessons.

"OK, if you want to keep him - keep him."

"You just tell Sprayberry to come and get him if he wants him," the big man said with a determined finality. But now he gave me a broad smile and displayed a much friendlier manner, knowing he had won whatever battle he feared might have taken place over the destination and ultimate disposition of the in-custody *gigolo* had I pushed the issue hard about my authority on the shift, or base, up the chain-of-command as back-up.

MSGT Wozniak and I turned, got into our vehicle, and left all four men standing there curbside.

I now re-counted the whole incident to Dave. Then I suddenly remembered one other time we had met. Just outside the old SPS HQs, wooden hooches, where we exchanged routine pleasantries sometime after the previously mentioned incident. I remembered the same broad smile too. I told Dave about remembering the second, brief meeting. Dave grinned and nodded with satisfaction at both recollections and waited for me to continue.

I could have said a million things then. But I was suddenly struck by over-whelming melancholia, an indescribable, deep sadness. To bring up anything to do with the previous events connected to *U-Tapao*, now that I was back on base, made my heart heavy with grief, reflecting on a great loss in one part of my life.

"You know, I never got along with my bosses."

I thought Dave's smile couldn't have gotten any wider. I was wrong.

"I know," he simply replied.

You knew? I thought in amazement. Did you know? No one could have known.

-

**GROUND FLOOR, HQs BUILDING, ELECTRICAL WIRELESS COMMUNICATIONS (NIGERIA), LIMITED, *EBUTA-METTA* DISTRICT, LAGOS, NIGERIA, 1400, 22 JANUARY 1979.**

The *Harmattan* winds were blowing at full strength again today, as they had been for more than eight weeks. Usually, the winds in West Africa blew in from the west or south, bringing the two rainy seasons. However, come winter, the winds shifted and blow directly from the north. That meant blowing over hundreds of miles of the Saharan Desert, bringing millions of tons of fine dust, dead organic matter, and tiny sand particles to Nigeria. Respiratory ailments were as common as roadside beggars and chewing gum pack sellers. The landscape appeared more like London in winter than Lagos. The scenery was enveloped in a moderately heavy, but constantly drifting, khaki 'fog.' Sherlock Holmes would have felt right at home, except for the dusty palm trees, the endless mounds of trash, the 'go-slows', and a lack of cobblestoned streets. Sand and dust were everywhere, plus on and in everything. They found their way into every nook, cranny, crevice, bodily orifice, and hole. It played hell with the radio equipment and electronics. The only good thing about the problem was it blocked the sun's intense rays. So, the temperatures were cooler, plus one other small consolation - no flies.

People returning from leave brought the always eagerly anticipated mail bag, provided they transited through the Rochester, MN, main office. Or the new hires always did. One old timer, a telecommunications engineer, had arrived last night.

I looked at the pile and separated it into stacks by name. Most guys had their wives or sweethearts oversee their mail back home. A few got letters here, but it was never much. I always got more than half the bag, occasionally almost every piece. That inevitably drew comments, kidding, and asides from the others. I was Project Site Manager and one of three non-engineers and telecommunication techs, out of 30 people, on a large multi-million-dollar telecommunications project for the Nigerian Army Corps of Signals.

The firm, Electrical Wireless (Nigeria) Co., Ltd., (or EWN Company; we were all 'seconded' from International Telecommunications, Inc., a big corporation in the US) was putting in a large tropospheric-scatter and UHF/VHF radio communications net to cover the whole country. The engineers joked it would allow the Nigerian Army to plan coups more effectively, something they had done repeatedly since Nigeria was granted its independence in 1960.

I tossed aside the bills to be opened later and glanced at the few personal letters. One was from a faithful pen pal. We used to trade USAF military patches. Now we traded letters. Another was from my oldest pen pal, still stuck behind the 'Iron Curtain' in Dresden, East Germany. The rest was junk mail, advertisements, and unwanted circulars.

At the bottom was a large, thick brown envelope. It was from my oldest friend from Danbury, CT, and sometimes my 'legal counsel,' 'Don' Beschle. Or precisely, he'd given me free off-the-cuff legal 'advice' periodically over the years. We had remained buddies from grade school. Now over 20 years had passed since we'd first met. We'd remained in off-more-than-on contact ever since. Legal polymaths were unique. Don had effortlessly graduated first in his class from grade school through high school, BA, and JD degrees to his LLM, a legal 'Einstein' if there ever was one. As my favorite Aunt always told me you never know when you'll need a good lawyer.

I once reflected there were four types of friends. One group called and wrote. The second group called, but never wrote. The third group wrote, but never called. And the fourth group neither called nor wrote. Don led the fourth group. I didn't mind. A friend of Legere was still a friend, no matter what the passage of time. But he had never written before. I occasionally called him when I was stateside. But this event was of singular, even great, significance. Like hitting the state lottery or collecting an unexpected inheritance.

I sliced open the envelope and read what he had written on his personalized stationery memo attached to the top of the inch-thick stack of butterfly-clipped papers.

"I don't know what this is, but I think. . . ."

-

**IN THE LANDING PATTERN OVER *U-TAPAO* RTNAB AND THE GULF OF THAILAND, *CHONBURI/RAYONG* PROVINCES, THAILAND, 0655, 04 JUNE 1975.**

The military-chartered Trans International Airways 'stretch' DC-8 came around on final after doing the upwind, crosswind and downwind legs of the holding pattern. That gave me a panoramic view of the base, the surrounding Thai countryside and the Gulf of Thailand. I didn't know what to expect of the landscape. I half expected seeing thick jungles, somewhere like equatorial Africa in old Tarzan movies, or in TV clips of American soldiers fighting in Vietnam. But the undulating, strange topography was different than anything I'd ever seen in any book, TV show or photo. Randomly scattered, sometimes irregularly shaped, occasionally long, tall, pup tent-shaped mountains and hills with a lot of foliage were about. Similarly, the irregularly shaped rolling surface extended to the horizon. All the strangely shaped, large mounds had protruding and jumbled piles of pale-colored rocks around them. But mainly it was open spaces. Some farms had wide plots with evenly spaced palm or coconut trees, some others had planted crops, plus plowed lands, some roads, and fewer buildings in eyesight. But I saw no rice paddies. There was no question there was greenery everywhere, but Thailand wasn't the intense, heavy-foliaged, tropical rain forest I'd envisioned.

The flight had originated at Travis with brief refueling stops at Hickam and Andersen. We RON-ed at Clark, arriving well after sunset and departing before first light. Not even the hardiest 'party-hardy' types were up for the local night life after flying *beaucoup* hours. But they couldn't have done anything anyway since everyone was bussed right off the flight line directly to Billeting for room keys and then straight over to the TOQs and

TEQs. We were ordered to stay there until we departed the next morning. By then the chow hall, clubs and BX had all closed.

Check-in at Travis was a complete fiasco. I had arrived there in plenty of time (noon, in my summer uniform and blue lightweight, zippered jacket) and checked in at the boarding counter for tomorrow's 0230 airlift out. Although it was 01 June, I nearly froze to death. (I had forgotten the famous quip attributed to Mark Twain about summertime in San Francisco: "The coldest winter I ever spent was a summer in San Francisco.") Every question the TSGT Lautenschlager asked me (who was standing behind the check-in counter) except for a copy of my original orders, was answered with a 'No.'

"Shot card, 2LT?"

"No, TSGT. Didn't know I needed shots for overseas. No one said anything to me about shots."

"Dog tags, sir?"

"No, never issued any, TSGT."

"Proof of a Pre-overseas Briefing, sir?"

"No, no one at CBPO told me anything about a briefing, TSGT."

This was going about as well as when the local priest in the confessional knows exactly who you are on the other side of the screen after you've admitted to a basket load of sins. That kind of sinking feeling in your gut.

"2LT, CBPO was supposed to give you a check-out 'Check List' prior to you getting your personnel files and made sure you'd done everything before they released you from your last assignment, including a Pre-overseas Briefing."

"Honestly, nobody said a word to me about a 'Check List.' They just handed me my records in a sealed envelope on my last day at Maxwell and said to turn it in to CBPO when I got to my new assignment."

"Class-A uniform to board the flight, sir?"

"No, TSGT. It was already sent on to Thailand in my HHG pack-out over two months ago."

And so forth.

He finished asking the rest of the standard slate of questions. He cocked his head, gave me a knowing smile, and sighed as if he had done this ten-thousand times before. He leaned over the check-in counter and spoke conspiratorially in a low-voice, afraid that someone might overhear our conversation. I could see from his face he had decided to take a great deal of pity on me, like a small, cute, stray puppy caught in a bucket-dumping tropical hurricane.

"Look 2LT Legere, I'd really like to help you out here. We can waive all your problems like your missing dog tags, uniform, briefings, and the rest, but you must have at least two inoculations in your shot record, smallpox, and cholera, to board the aircraft to fly. Go over to where you see the 'Base Shuttle Taxi' sign and ask them to take you over to the Base Hospital to the Emergency Room. They'll get your shot card taken care of and get you all fixed up. Report right back here for your flight no later than 0030 tomorrow morning with all your baggage, shot record, and original orders in hand. Good luck 2LT."

I got the one shot, cholera. I was told that they'd also mark the shot card as my having gotten a smallpox inoculation at some previous date, since it was deadly to give both shots at the same time. But they confirmed what I was told. I couldn't board the plane without my shot card showing both had been administered. He made me swear my holiest oath I'd get the smallpox shot within 60 days.

We walked single-file down the rolled-out, aluminum landing ladder to the tarmac. Even this early in the morning the climate would have made a broiling Turkish sauna bath seem like a ND ice locker in winter. The hot, sticky air and bright sunlight assaulted my senses along with many different scents, smells, aromas, odors, fragrances, and stenches, both military-manufactured and civilian tropical types. The air was overwhelming with a rich, strange admixture I couldn't fully describe. In front of me was a large double open-faced, aluminum barn-like structure with a large sign announcing:

WELCOME TO U-TAPAO RTNB

DET 6, 66<sup>TH</sup> AERIAL PORT SQUADRON
PASSENGER TERMINAL

I assumed the Thai lettering painted below it passed the same info. I waited with everyone else inside the open-bay hanger for my green duffle bag and suitcase to be off-loaded onto long metal inspection tables by the APS staff. The SP Custom's checks and a quick once-over by SP-leashed German Sheppard's were efficient and perfunctory. I lugged my duffle bag and small suitcase to the curbside and waited for someone, hopefully, to show up and collect me.

I hadn't been standing there more than 10 seconds when a green US Army jeep with no top rocketed in from stage left. The driver slammed the brakes hard, screeching to a halt right in front of me.

"JUMP IN, SPORT!" the camo-clad, no-hat, burly-looking driver yelled.

I heaved my bags in the back seat and hoisted myself in the front. We blasted off with tires nearly smoking from the acceleration, even before I had settled in. We probably didn't reach escape velocity from earth on this launch.

"WELCOME TO THAILAND, SPORT!" he yelled over the engine noise. "EVERYTHING ON BASE IS STOLEN, BUT THE THAIS HAVEN'T GOTTEN AROUND TO PICKING IT UP YET! THE THAIS WOULD HAVE STOLEN A B-52 IF THEY COULD GET SOMEONE TO FLY IT FOR THEM!"

I hard gripped the side handle to hang on and looked at an old 'compadre' in the driver's seat: 'Railroad Tracks' Garri T. Guillory, late of Mather AFB. About community college football team-sized for a second-string linebacker, late-20's, FL 'cracker' accent I'd guess, broad-chested and excessively energetic, like a weightlifter on steroids at Muscle Beach. I knew he was completely aggressive, fiercely ambitious, and sharp as a finely stropped cut-throat razor blade. We had attended an AF-sponsored education 'boondoggle' together, three compact graduate courses in Corrections and Rehabilitation at the University of GA in the fall of 1974. He told me then he was going to be the first all-in-SP-career-field one-star. At least I had a familiar face and someone I could trust here.

He waved his foot over the brake at every stop sign (California-style), but at least gave the courtesy to look both ways as we blasted though the intersections. The stop signs were all written in Thai. But there was no mistaking the three-lettered, red-octagonal-shaped traffic markers for the universal meaning of 'whoa.' Fortunately, there was little traffic this time of the morning.

"How's the flight, sport?" He actually slowed down to slightly less than 100 MPH so we could hear each other talk without screaming our lungs out.

"I survived. Long. And I'm totally frazzled." I was. I slept poorly on the plane and got little sleep the few hours we RON-ed at Clark. I was dying for shut-eye.

"Take you over to meet the Ops Officer first; then we'll get you sorted out so you can finally get some rack time, sport."

The base looked even more expansive close-up. White-painted concrete, or cinder-block buildings were neatly scattered and widely spaced, with assorted aluminum, or sheet-metal trailers, block-long rows of wooden hooches, large three-story, white-painted masonry barracks buildings, and assorted little wooden ramshackle Thai concession stands all about. There was an abundance of foliage and trees, dense in places. Large, empty gravel-covered or plain dirt parking or empty lots were between most buildings. What really struck me were the deep, wide, grass-sided, or concrete drainage canals lining both sides of every street. The torrential rainfall must have been measured in feet. There were colorful flowers, neatly trimmed bushes, and exotic flora near many buildings. *U-Tapao* was as neat as a Manhattan, KS, old spinster's parlor.

However, the most noticeable, prominent part of the landscape was a tree-vegetation-and-rock-encrusted, small, angular mountain off in the near distance. Maybe you could even call it a very large hill, just northeast of the landward end of the runway. It was the most dramatic topographical feature in sight.

"What's the mountain called?" I said loudly.

"Buddha Mountain," Guillory shouted.

We turned right and headed down what must be the base's main drag. The grass-sided drainage canals on both sides were even wider and deeper. Short, stocky women in matching dark blue work pants and tops like simple cotton 'pajamas' wore wide-brim, conical, rice-straw, or rattan-woven hats. They also had their faces completely obscured by head-and-face covering, wrap-around checkered scarves. Only their eye slits showed. Squads of four on each side were grass-cutting the slopes. They swung shoulder-high poled scythes with one arm extended straight out, mowing down the tall blades in continual, fluid, and pendulum motions.

"How much do they get paid for doing that?" I screamed.

"Eighteen *Baht* a day, for eight hours of work," Guillory yelled back.

"How much is that?"

"About 90 cents!"

Within a minute, we pulled into an open parking spot on a side street in front of some long, low, wide-slatted brown wooden clapboard, corrugated metal-sided and roofed hooches that were sandbagged around the entrance and along the sides. There were a half-dozen protruding, furiously working a/c units. We walked down a few steps from the sidewalk and entered. We walked single file through the slightly claustrophobic long central passageway. Metal-and-clear plastic partitions and desks were jammed along both sides. Moving to the office in the back, I saw everything was tightly shoehorned into spaces made for a third of the business. Ebenezer Scrooge himself would have appreciated the layout for parsimonious efficiency. Everyone, except the Thai secretaries, was male and in jungle cammos. No one glanced at us. We entered through the wide-open doorway without knocking. It was the only 'room' in the building. On the metal desk was a large, light-brown wooden name holder with carved, crossed Thai and American flags displayed on the one side and a silver-colored SP Badge on the other proclaiming: 'CAPT A. J. Dentonville, Operations Officer, 365th SPS, *U-Tapao* RTNAB, Thailand: 1974-75'.

Dentonville was tall, maybe mid-30's, didn't get hit with the ugly stick, was athletic, and would have been described as a 'fair-haired' boy. He was sure of himself to the point of cockiness. Maybe he had a manic energy (as evidenced by the disheveled appearance of his desk and office, like he needed a thousand different projects going all at once) to keep himself either amused, engaged or both. But he might have just been overwhelmed (or simply lazy) too. Papers, files, reports, and documents were haphazardly piled high everywhere including the floor. It didn't look like much was getting done administratively on his ticket. He was probably on the B-T-Z list for MAJ from his apparent age and current assignment.

After introductions, Dentonville explained to Guillory what we needed to do.

"Take him over to Supply first and have him draw his alert bag with 'the whole nine yards.' Then the base tailor shop. Get him measured and fitted with tags and patches on one set of cammos for wear tomorrow. Stop off at the Armory and get his signature on a .38 and GAU weapon's card. Shoot him over to CBPO to drop his personnel files and get him signed in. The last stop is Billeting. Anything else can wait for tomorrow."

I headed out the door with Guillory. SPS Supply was next door in an exact same-looking hooch. Gear issue went fast: solid dark green web belt with metal stays and eyelets, O.D. poncho with hood, flashlight (with batteries), canteen, emergency medical kit, flak vest, helmet with liner, 'official' aviator sunglasses in a hard navy blue plastic case (the Supply SGT explained anyone working the flight line was authorized to draw them), web belt harness, multiple ammo pouches for M-16/GAU clips and .38 rounds, etc., and an alert bag to carry it all in.

"Sign here and here and here's your receipt. Thank you very much, sir! Welcome to Thailand!" said the Supply SGT. Then he snapped: "NEXT CUSTOMER!"

I heaved the now heavy alert bag into the back of the jeep. We rocketed over to the base tailor shop in probably under a minute. Guillory did his very best to set a new world land speed record. He probably came close in the attempt. The shop was in the middle of a stand-alone strip row of slap-dash cinder block and wooden shops that included a jewelry store, snack bar, embroidery business and souvenir-and-trinket store. All in a spacious, large block square, of an otherwise empty, dust-covered, dirt lot.

"*Sawasdee kup!*" Guillory shouted at a small, older, slender, but sturdy, Thai woman as we entered. "I got another customer for you! Fix him up *mach-mach lay-o, lay-o!*"

He woman smiled sweetly and replied: "*Sawasdee, ka!* Can-do-easy-GI, CAPT 'G.' I fix you fren' up, no sweat."

Two young female assistants scurried into the tableau, one with a cloth measuring tape, the other with a pad and pencil. One started to size me up; the other took down my measurements.

"I want one uniform ready by tomorrow morning, the rest in two days, *chai-mai?*"

"*Mai, ka!* Tomorrow one, rest two day, can-do-easy-no-sweat. Come same-same noon?"

Guillory asked: "What hat size do you wear?"

"Seven."

"Boots?"

"Nine regular."

The girl with the notepad wrote that down.

The woman brought over two navy blue berets for me to try on. Guillory was wearing a fairly stiff cammo Boonie hat with one side snapped up, Australian 'digger' style.

He told her: "Give him two Boonie hats same-same to try."

"You can wear it one of three ways sport," Guillory explained. "One, Aussie-style, just like mine; two, cowboy-style: with both sides up and three, jungle-style: both sides down. It's up to you."

Guillory had me hand the shop manager a USD$10.00 bill as a deposit. We moved out smartly after goodbyes.

The rest of the morning went like clockwork: signed for my weapons at the Armory; dropped my records off at CBPO (officially signing in); then checked Billeting to get on the waiting list for the next open BOQ room. I was lucky. One would be ready for occupation tomorrow morning;

someone just PCS-ed out. I had to stay in the VOQ for only one night. And I was totally out of steam now, having been awake more than 40 hours straight.

Guillory glanced at his military-issued watch, snapped his fingers, and pronounced:

"Lunch! 'Green Latrine!' Let's roll out, sport!"

I struggled mightily to keep my eyes open. As we shot past the flight line, I saw signs marked 'To Beach.' I could smell the salt air, sea, and sand even before I could see the water. A stiff onshore breeze was blowing. The day had shaped up to be intensely bright blue, blisteringly hot, with sharply defined white cumulous clouds forming everywhere, piling up high and moving fast.

The 'Green Latrine' turned out to be a large, two-story, rambling, ramshackle, green-painted, long wood-board restaurant at the high-water mark, just at the edge of the sand where the low beach vine-like foliage started. The sea was sparkling green blue, the sand dazzling white. We climbed the stairs and walked out on the open patio, now half-filled with mainly military and a few civilians. Guillory went straight to a white-and-red-checkered tablecloth-covered, wooden picnic table with four hand-woven, dull green cloth placemats. Two cammo-clad SP officers were already seated. He introduced them to me.

"MAJ Shellenbarger, CAPT Anderson, this is 2LT Legere. He just arrived today. I'm getting him squared away, sir. He'll be taking over Jake's place on Swings."

"MAJ Shellenbarger is the CO," he explained. "CAPT Anderson is the Admin Officer."

Neither of them nodded.

The rest of lunch consisted of three weird things, when I thought about it well afterward: One, I did all the talking. About me, my experiences, my family, Maxwell, the long flight from Travis, inane stuff just to have a conversation when all three of them mysteriously withdrew into a deafening silence as soon as I started on my narration. If the trio said a word amongst themselves, or to me, I didn't hear it. I knew I was simply exhausted and fighting it off hard now. I probably kept mindlessly talking in an effort to keep myself awake.

In fact, Guillory just gave me a 'Cheshire Cat' grin all during lunch and watched me intensely for some strange reason. Shellenbarger and Anderson also grimly stared at me. Like prim, spiteful, spindly, old New England parsons who held singing, dancing, and similar evil cavorting like handholding in league with the devil.

Two, this was the worst meal I ever had. To be on the safe side, I ordered a grilled-cheese sandwich and potato chips. I didn't want to get 'Delhi Belly' (diarrhea). What finally arrived consisted of two slabs of bread that were totally fried in deep oil, then left to drain dry with a faux piece of tough dull yellow melted something between them. It was horribly crispy to the look and hard-crunchy to the touch. I had a nibble to assess it and left the rest on the plate. The side of 'potato chips' wound up to be gossamer-thin, large, rice paper-like orange-and-green round pieces of an indeterminate tasteless 'substance' that snapped at the touch and hit my tongue like stale cardboard.

And three, it almost seemed the trio was judging me for some strange reason like they didn't trust me or wanted to validate their opinion on what sort of person I was. I probably was either just simply brain-dead tired, out of the loop with exhaustion, or my mind was hallucinating. We left with nods.

I was asleep as soon as my head hit the pillow. I slept for 18 hours straight, only waking up abruptly at 0215 to check the bedside alarm clock time after a long, deep dream of being in a plane to somewhere.

-

**BETWEEN 'C' AND 'D' AVENUES, 7TH STREET, OUTSIDE THE VOQ, *U-TAPAO* RTNAB, *CHONBURI/RAYONG* PROVINCES, THAILAND, 0800, 05 JUNE 1975.**

Guillory was waiting for me in front of the VOQ after first rousing me with a hard door knock at 0745. I quickly showered, shaved, dressed, and was out the door pronto. The day was already getting toasty and humid. The high, bright azure sky was half filled with individual bright, plumply puffed, sharply defined, billowing white clouds, all quickly on the move to somewhere inland. We drove to Billeting to drop one key and grab the other so I could move into my new BOQ room. We drove back to the BOQ closest to the O-Club and parked in the small blacktop lot next to it, not far from the VOQ. Guillory led the way and I followed, lugging my green duffle bag and suitcase and in my hands with my alert bag on my shoulder, with clean linen from Billeting tucked under my arm. We stopped six doors down on the inside face of BOQ #1, ground floor. This BOQ was one of five identical BOQs forming a square U-shape around a grass quadrangle, all the doorways facing inwards. The open end of the quadrangle was along the base's two-lane main drag, 'C' Avenue.

"See that wooden stand over there?" said Guillory. "Called the 'Bob Hope Pavilion'."

Right in front of the farthest BOQ on the left was a white-painted, nondescript, large, simple plywood stage with a backdrop and awning. There were wooden steps along both sides leading up to it.

"Came in with his USO show a few times; always played to packed-to-the-rafters houses. Shows were all televised back home. One time, or so the story goes, some lame brained, randy LTC pilot pinched Joey Heatherton right in the ass right on stage. The stupid guy got caught and immediately shipped off to Vietnam by the one-star Air Division Commander in the audience," Guillory added.

"Guess he 'bought the farm' that day. His chance to remain a 'fast-burner' went to zilch," I replied. "The proverbial 'kiss-of-death'."

Guillory chuckled and nodded in agreement.

I unlocked the door. We entered. The room was narrow, with dimensions slightly larger than a prison cell, as austere as a monk's cubicle, and with a very high ceiling. There was a metal frame bed with a mattress, a dark wooden dresser, simple metal clothes rack, a black rotary phone on the dresser, a small refrigerator, and a dark wooden nightstand with a goose-neck gray metal lamp by the bedside. A neatly folded Army blanket was sitting on the bed with a white pillow on top. The package a/c unit over the bed was set at 'arctic' and running full blast. I could have kept ice cream frozen inside the room. As the heat and humidity of the day was quickly kicking in, it would be a welcome respite after working hours.

I noticed three or four flesh-colored lizards on the ceiling and high on the walls, sitting immobile, probably waiting for a passing bug to provide 'lunch.'

"What are those?" I pointed and asked.

"Geckos," he replied. "Thais think they're good luck, so don't kill them. They eat mosquitoes, flies, and insects." Then added:

"*Hong-nam* and shower units are on the outside hallway end, sport."

I had heaved everything on the bed and was surveying my new home when a noisy clatter of things being set down outside sounded. We both turned as someone appeared in the doorway. Obviously it was the hootch maid.

"Ah, *Sawasdee, kup!*" Let me introduce you to your new 'customer' 2LT Legere. He's taking over from *Loi-to* Davis."

I nodded to her. The woman was short, stocky, dark-brown skinned, time-worn, round-and-wrinkle-faced, and sturdy of indeterminate age. She could have been anywhere between 40 and 120 years old. It was impossible for me to guess her real age. Her hair was jet black, so that didn't give me a clue. But it was readily apparent she'd cleaned a lot of BOQ rooms over the years.

She grinned broadly and nodded her greetings back.

Guillory explained: "Every day she'll will clean your room, spit shine your boots, wash, starch and iron your uniforms, make up your bed, get you bottled water and put it in the frig. You pay her USD$10.00 cash at the end of every month. Anything else like sewing buttons or mending rips is extra. Isn't that right?"

The maid broadly smiled, nodded, and started cackling in good humor at her new 'customer.'

"Ten Do-lah'!" she happily replied in broken English. "*Loi-to* Davis 'num-bah' one," she added. "Hope you 'num-bah' one too!"

"OK, we'll see you later. *Kop khun mach, kup.*"

"*Sawasdee, ka!*" she replied and continued to cackle in merriment as she grabbed the cleaning supplies and buckets she had left outside and waddled off happy at her good fortune once again.

The rest of the morning was spent doing minor errands: having my dog tags finally made; getting a mail box (P.O. Box 137, APO AP 96330); stocking up on toiletries, authoring paper and envelopes, plus some blousing bands from the BX; exchanging some dollars into Thai *Baht* paper money and coins at the Chase-Manhattan Bank; finally getting (and wearing) my cammo uniform, hat and jungle boots; then having my other uniforms re-fitted. I begged off lunch and spent the rest of the afternoon sleeping. The jetlag was pounding me hard like a muscular blacksmith working a bent horseshoe.

-

**BETWEEN 'C' AND 'D' AVENUES, 8TH STREET, USAF O-CLUB, *U-TAPAO* RTNAB, *CHONBURI/RAYONG* PROVINCES, THAILAND, 1715, 05 JUNE 1975.**

I walked over to the O-Club for the first time. It was directly across the street from my BOQ. It was a one-story, non-descript, simple ranch-style building done in white stucco. It had a well-manicured lawn, with angled palm trees, colorful shrubbery, and tropical flowers all around with a short circular driveway that led to the covered walkway entrance. Just inside were assorted oil paintings for sale from local artists along the corridor on both sides of the wall (expensive from the attached price tags). The whole interior was white painted sheet rock with dark teak wood trim. Designed to be a very simple, minimalist combination-faux-Polynesian/Japanese décor all from the early-to-mid-1960s, it was probably done up by some American interior decorator with a small budget. I walked past the vertically barred window of the cashier's cage on the left-hand side. There was a small, black-lettered, yellow background sign painted on Lucite, framed in wood, on the right of the cashier's window:

PLEASE COUNT YOUR CASH BEFORE YOU LEAVE THIS WINDOW. THE CASHIER CANNOT MAKE CORRECTIONS AFTER YOU LEAVE. THANK YOU.

There was another paper sign with the current exchange rate: US dollars to Thai *Baht:* USD$1.00=THB B20.50.

Straight ahead was the main dining room. It was still early. I could see through the open doors the evening diners hadn't congregated yet, but the tables were ready to receive customers. A dozen very comely, long black-tressed servers dressed in white blouses and navy blue (or black) short skirts scurrying around to make final arrangements for the evening's chow invasion. The servers sported small plastic badges on their blouses with different numbers. I saw they held a series of national beauty contests to hire the winners for the waitressing jobs. I turned right and headed towards the bar lounge. Both doors were wide open. On the left-hand thick, heavy, brownish-black, teak door was a large rectangular, black-lettered-on-yellow-background sign, words painted on quarter-inch thick clear Lucite (screwed-in down at knee-level) that read:

HE WHO ENTERS COVERED HERE BUYS THE HOUSE A ROUND OF CHEER. HE WHO RINGS THE BELL TO HEAR ALSO BUYS THE HOUSE A ROUND OF CHEER. JAY-PEE.

I'd never seen a sign like this before. But in the few O-Clubs I had been in that was the standard, unwritten 'rule.' Walking in the O-Club bar in uniform with your hat on would cost you a round of drinks for everyone, as did ringing the small brass bell, always somewhere close to the bar's countertop.

It took some seconds for my eyes to adjust to the interior darkness. I was the only one in there. I picked a comfortable spot in the middle and plunked myself down. Three cocktail servers were standing at one end of the bar clutching round metal serving trays. One small, fairly attractive, but older woman was behind the bar drying and stacking beer glasses.

I immediately concluded that if any of the three got less than five serious marriage proposals every night then it was going to be a damn slow evening. All had Ebony-sheened hair straight down to the small of their backs with minimal jewelry. All were dressed like the other main dining room servers, but with hems cut to barely cover their frilly skivvy shorts. They were ready for any action the patrons could throw. The three couldn't have been over 4'10", maybe 90 pounds soaking wet, very curvy in the right places, and looking all of about 16 years-old. They were stunning, turn-every-noggin-in-the-bar, permanent-Full-Nelson-head-lock-gorgeous, breath-takers. They sported light golden honey skin, Siamese Cat-like eyes, and 'I'm-not-taking-no-shit-from-anyone-but-I'm-friendly-if-you're-friendly' attitudes.

One cocktail waitress glided over, smiled, and asked in melodious, little-girl, high-pitched, Thai-accented, singsong, decent English:

"Wat' you like to drink, 2LT Legere?"

I stared at her in total amazement.

"How did you know my name?"

She gave me a knowing smile and a slight shake of her head like I was trying to tease her about my real age or pulling her leg with a silly joke she'd heard 100 times already.

"You 2LT Legere. You come morning one day sa'go from 'Land of Big BX.' You take *Loi-to* Davis place on Swing Shift. He go August. You stay BOQ 'num-bah' one, room 'num-bah' six. You here one year PCS same-same *Loi-to* Davis, no be TDY. You get promotion five more day be same-same rank *Loi-to* Davis. *Loi-to* Davis be 'su-pah num-bah' one."

How-in-the-hell does she knows all that I wondered? I kept staring at her, completely floored. She kept her sweet-as-honey smile planted firmly.

"One beer, please. Anything that's local."

"One *Singha* can-do-easy-no-sweat-GI." She laughed sweetly.

I was sure I'd remember her.

She smiled again and glided back to the bar with the order.

I finally looked at my surroundings. It was still very dark in there, even with my pupils adjusting to the dimness. But it was discretely lit around the bar. The lounge area itself was slightly longer than wide in a rectangular shape. There was a small recessed, but slightly raised, platform for a band to perform. It was all done in dark teakwood, with large round tables and comfortably easy-to-sink-into vinyl-upholstered chairs. There was a small parquet Teakwood dance floor in front of the bandstand. The rest of the lounge was durably green carpeted. But what grabbed my attention were the 12 wooden, painted unit insignia mounted on three walls, about three feet in diameter, hung about a foot above head high. Apparently, emblems of the entire major tenant units assigned to *U-Tapao,* and the higher organizations they belonged to were the 444th RED HORSE Squadron, 365th Combat Support Group, 18th Air Force, 703rd Strategic Wing, 31st Air Force, 71st Air Division, 103rd Strategic Wing, 66th Reconnaissance Squadron, 117th USAF Hospital, 89th Air Refueling Squadron, PACAF, and SAC. I was impressed with the detail and artisanship, even in the subdued lighting. I vowed when I left *U-Tapao* I'd take them along with me if I could. One *Singha* was it for me. I slept through most of the next day, still fighting off the jetlag. I had also remembered earlier to tell Guillory to leave me alone for tomorrow.

-

**CORNER OF 'A' AVENUE AND 9TH STREET, PARKING LOT, OUTSIDE CSC, 365th SPS, *U-TAPAO* RTNAB, *CHONBURI/RAYONG* PROVINCES, THAILAND, 1245, 07 JUNE 75.**

CAPT Guillory was delivering me to 1LT 'Jake' Davis after lunch. As I wanted to be early to Guard Mount, he dropped me off first before he went to pick up Jake. The on-duty shift supervisor, he explained, picked up their reliefs as a courtesy. I drew my weapons, ammo clips, and a radio from the Armory cleared my .38 and GAU in the barrel, and stood well away from everyone, starting to do the same thing. I went over to the sandbagged emplacement protecting the CSC emergency generator (across from the Armory), dropped my alert bag and leaned against the sandbags to watch the unfolding events before Swing Shift's Guard Mount.

A lanky, curly-haired SSGT sauntered over from a knot of SPs and spoke.

"How many days you got left in the 'Big War' sir?"

"I just got here on the 4th. A year's tour-of-duty, less three days now, 362 days there, SSGT."

"GOD-DAMN, 2LT! IF I HAD 362 DAYS LEFT IN THE WAR, I'D JUST GO SHOOT MYSELF! A DAMN 'THREE-DIGIT MIDGET'! HOLY SHIT! TOO BAD, SIR! A 'BROWN-BAR' FNG! Where you comin' in from, sir?"

"Two years at Maxwell."

"MAXWELL!! GOD-DAMN, 2LT! THAT ISN'T THE 'REAL' AIR FORCE AT ALL! JUST LIKE YOU WAS NEVER EVEN IN THE 'BIG WAR'! LIKE YOU JUST ENLISTED YESTERDAY! TOO BAD, SIR!" He chuckled and sauntered back to a group he was with before to report on the 'newbie.'

I stood back and watched the weapons, ammo, and radio issue. I could see things were moving slowly, primarily because of the men in line. There were two issue windows in front with quickly growing lines of men waiting to draw their items. Everything had to be signed out on temporary US government receipt forms, so the names, SSANs, weapons and radio serial numbers had to be written in by the issuer and receiver, and then signed. That took some time. However, the Black troops who were standing in line, in twos and threes, were doing some elaborate greeting or ritual, mainly involving their fingers and hands, with some arm and elbow touching or twisting and finger-snapping. They quickly grasped and re-grasped each other's hands and fingers in a continual fluid motion, the ritual becoming more and more elaborate as they continued. Some of the White troops started to complain, telling them to knock it off, as some of the Black troops were now at the head of the line and kept the ritual going. The Armorers inside waited impatiently to continue the issue. Finally, they stopped, and the lines started slowly moving again.

About 10 minutes later Guillory roared up in the shift supervisor's jeep and slid it in next to me with 1LT 'Jake' Davis riding shotgun. We were introduced, and then sealed it with a firm handshake. At first glance Jake was of medium height with a hard muscular, but compact, build. He had dark, close-cut hair, sported dark, sun-roasted skin and looked like a USAF recruiting poster in his uniform. I later found out he rarely had his sunglasses off and was a chain-smoking fiend.

-

**CORNER OF 'A' AVENUE AND 9TH STREET, GUARD MOUNT FORMATION, PARKING LOT, OUTSIDE CSC, 365th SPS, *U-TAPAO RTNAB, CHONBURI/RAYONG* PROVINCES, THAILAND, 1345, 07 JUNE 75.**

"Let me introduce you to 2LT Legere," Jake said to the formation of about 45 SPs. We stood side-by-side in front. "He's relieving me so I can get back to the 'Land of the Big PX' and fly my plane. So don't everybody applaud at once."

Everyone laughed uproariously and a few clapped. I could see from their faces everyone liked Jake. That was rare. Few, if any, enlistees liked officers.

"He'll be here two more months learning the ropes. Then I can finally airlift out of this dump. Give him the same support you did me and you'll be OK. Understand people?"

Jake paused to see if anyone said anything. No one spoke.

"Anybody got anything?"

No one did.

Jake turned to me and asked if I wanted to say anything.

I shook my head no.

"OK, MSGT Veeres, they're all yours."

I noticed that everyone was dressed smartly in cammos. Most were wearing camo ball caps, the rest had Boonie hats in various stages of flaps snapped up or down. More than a few had their names tags embroidered in English with the Thai translations right below it. Some of the men had harnesses on to carry their gear, but most wore plain web-belts.

MSGT Veeres did roll-call and gave them a briefing on firearms safety; what to look for with signs of heat stroke, heat exhaustion and heat prostration; proper water intake (too much water meant you were flushing electrolytes, as bad as not drinking enough water); VD prevention; excess alcohol consumption; a reminder that getting sunburned enough to where you couldn't work was a sure-fire guarantee of getting slammed with an Article 15 and busted a rank, and finally vehicle safety. He asked for any questions or comments. With none, the formation was dismissed. Everyone broke smartly into a mad scrum of bodies mounting-up in their vehicles to relieve the people on Days.

Jake and I walked over to where the TSG Shift Supervisor was holding his own formation of about 80 TSGs close to the SPs. It was behind and offset to the SP formation, more towards the back of CSC. The TSGs were all in solid O.D. uniforms and ball caps. I noticed they had matching round O.D. shoulder patches with three black diagonal interlocking rings with the letters 'SPS' on the upper left half and 'RTG' on the lower right half.

Jake addressed the Thai guards in Thai. I assumed Jake repeated the same things that he had just said to the SPs and turned them back to the Thai Shift Supervisor. Then we both walked into the CSC to relieve Guillory on Days.

Jake quickly showed me around CSC. There wasn't much. Four offices, two on either side along a short white-painted, cinderblock passageway with battered acoustic tiles glued everywhere with 'been-in-the-war' eggshell dropped ceiling panels. First left office was for the on-duty NCOIC Security Shift Supervisor. First right was for the on-duty Officer Shift Supervisor. Someone had a radio tuned to AFN in another office. The announced was saying don't keep your lights on during the day to scare the '*Klong* Monster' away. At the end of the passageway was CSC itself. Jake opened the large metal-sheathed door that had several large warning signs printed in over-sized black and red letters about 'Restricted Access' and 'Security.' We entered.

Inside was fairly dark. There was dim, back-lit, clear, thick Lucite, grease pencil-writeable maps showing every defensive position on the base on the walls; a smaller map showing the whole general area, including a larger scale of the base. Several sets of tables and chairs were in the back for anyone running the base's defense so they could see the maps. There was a bank of rotary telephones, a few IBM Selectric typewriters, an old, large, black manual one in use, plus various O.D. radios on the side. Half a dozen NCOs were inside either doing minor tasks or sitting. A young, fairly round-shaped, tall, crew-cut SGT was standing by a large radio set in front of the maps animatedly talking into a black radio mike in a mock-pseudo, high-clipped, British military accent:

"LOOK HERE, MATE!! THE HUNS ARE POUNDIN' THE 'ELL OUT OF US UP 'ERE ON THE FRONT LINES, SO JUST GET THE BLOOMIN' WINGCO ON THE BLOODY BLOWER AND SEND US UP SOME 'EFFING ACK-ACK AGAINST THE BLEEDIN' FLYIN' CIRCUS, CHOP-CHOP! HEAR ME MATE?!"

"Slow afternoon, SGT Perryman?" Jake dryly commented.

"YES, SIR, 1LT DAVIS, SIR! DAMN PEOPLE DON'T ANSWER WHEN I CALL THEM ON THE RADIO FAST ENOUGH, SIR! GOT TO GET THEIR DAMN-LAZY REARS IN GEAR! Then he added: "SIR! PROBABLY ALL ASLEEP-IN-THE-GUL-DAMN-BUNKER AND NOT PAYING ANY ATTENTION TO BUSINESS, SIR!"

"OK, SGT Perryman. But the CO actually listens to the radio net on rare occasions. Remember the last time you got yourself in the deep *kimchee* with your celebrated on-the-air comedy act?"

"YES, SIR! OK, SIR! NOT EVEN A PROBLEM, SIR! I UNDERSTAND FULLY, SIR!" He snapped to attention and saluted in the

British style, palm open and facing forward. We turned and started to walk out.

"PSSST! 1LT Davis!" Perryman said in a loud stage whisper. "Know what, sir?"

"What, SGT Perryman?"

"African girls think White guys have bigger *schlongs*!"

Jake just grimaced. As we walked out the door, he turned to me and said in a droll tone:

"Ten thousand comedians on the job and Perryman's trying to be one too."

Jake and I mounted up in the jeep outside CSC. We immediately rocketed out of the CSC parking lot and over the little concrete sloped ramp entrance spanning the drainage ditch, made a sharp left turn and went to the corner T-intersection a few meters away. Blowing right past the stop sign we made a hard right onto the street that paralleled the flight line.

"Everything is stolen here on base, the Thais just haven't gotten around to picking it up yet," Jake explained with a bitter-sounding tone in his voice.

"If the Thais could've gotten someone to drive a B-52, they'd have stolen one a long time ago. Only God-damn thing they haven't *ka-moyed* around here yet," he added. "But I wouldn't put it past them to at least try."

I nodded sagely and hung on for dear life. Jake was driving fast and recklessly, well over the speed limit, taking every corner hard, the tires squealing in protest. Maybe he had aspirations of driving in the 'Indy 500' one day. I knew he'd win every race.

"I'd love nothing better than to bust these damn Thai thieves, but we never catch any of them! Like fucking God-damn ghosts around here! They must be invisible! How they get away with *ka-moying* shit is driving me totally fucking crazy!" Jake deeply lamented.

I figured that's what must be driving Jake and driving Jake's driving, catching the Thai thieves.

"But I'm 'short'!" Jake animatedly exclaimed. "Shit! I'm so God-damn 'short' I'm ALMOST 'next'!"

"Where're they shipping you off to?"

"Malmstrom! God's own country! So, I can get back flying my airplane again after this damn shithole. I'm FIGMO and getting down fast to be a 'One-Digit Midget.' Only 63 days and a wake-up! Getting a real 'short-timer's attitude'!"

We paralleled the flight line for a while. Further down the runway there were dozens of different types of military aircraft and helicopters with SVN markings neatly parked in rows, a real grab bag.

"You should've been here for the fall of Vietnam in April then Cambodia in mid-May. Totally FUBAR! A real, complete, damned goat-rope, max balls-to-the-walls complete disaster. Most of the aircraft came in on 25 April; more flew in over the next few days. Last ones out arrived when Saigon fell on 30 April. *Ba!* Planes were landing on both ends of the runway. The sky was filled with them. Every plane had people inside jammed to the gills. The SPs had their hands full. All the control tower guys were going totally nuts. I'll tell you about it later."

"Then afterwards the NVA complained to the Thai Government, said the planes were all their 'property' and wanted them back. The Thais shipped back any planes they didn't want, useless junk, and kept the rest. The Thais might've even deliberately sabotaged some of the ones they wanted, just to keep them from being flown off, in case the damn NVA came looking. Then they repaired them later on. Hell, who knows? Just a 'rumor-from-rumor-control' I heard back then."

Jake headed south on the road I remembered Guillory had driven me to the 'Green Latrine.' But he banked hard left before we hit the beach turn-off and followed the paved roadway until it eventually turned into a not-too-bumpy sand track. There was nothing on this end of the base but low rolling sandy landscape. Dark, green-painted steel watch towers were strategically scattered around to the north.

"Perimeter road," Jake added.

Jake finally slowed the vehicle down to 15 MPH and his staccato speech. He seemed to become more relaxed in his posture and less agitated in his intense manner of talking. Perhaps it was due to the open terrain, greenery, and sand dunes as we left the cantonment area behind. We rounded a low ridge end and came across a vast US Army tent camp. You could see the Gulf of Thailand now. There were hundreds of large tents arranged neatly in rows. Every side and front flap was rolled up. There were hundreds of people in sarongs and light clothes either sitting on the edges of the tent wooden platforms, or in small groups strolling around the huge area.

"Called 'Camp Swampy,' mainly South Vietnamese refugees," Jake explained. "Everyone's been through screening and processing up-country. It's their last stop before boarding the big 'Freedom Bird.'  Only one rule: Don't cause a problem and you have a free ticket out to the 'Land of the Big BX.' The place is run by the JCRC 'Green Beanies' who were supposed to go into 'Nam to hunt for MIAs this past April after Saigon fell. But they got side-lined because of 'politics' and didn't go. Since they're already here twiddling-their-thumbs anyway, they got 'shanghaied' into running Camp Swampy. We'll drop-by later."

We paralleled the Gulf of Thailand then turned 90 degrees north. From east of the flight line and revetment area and north from the Gulf of Thailand the base was a gentle, undulating slope upwards. Jack pointed out the massive bomb dump area which seemed to be as large as the whole cantonment area. More slant topped, O.D., steel guard towers were scattered around. The whole perimeter area was overgrown with dense low foliage, chest-high grasses, and tropical greenery. It badly needed trimming.

"See the cyclone fence? Damn, slanty-eyed, Thai *gigolos!* Always *ka-moying* perimeter fencing every damn night. We never catch them. They run up to the concrete posts, snip the restraining wires, cut the fence section they want down both sides, drop it and roll it up like a rug. It takes at least a couple of days for CE to get off their dead asses after we submit the paperwork and come out to fix it. I've even been over to see the CE Commander personally. He wants to help us out. The COL says they move as fast as they can with the other thousand projects they have to do, plus all the red tape to get it done in the first place. But that's always too damn slow for me. So, we have all these God-damn gaping holes in the fence line. I'd love to shoot just one *gigolo* bastard, that'd stop them. Fast!"

I thought no doubt that would do it immediately.

"But the TSGs in the observation towers and bunkers rack-out as soon as they get out here, stupid lazy-ass bastards! Christ almighty! What a God-damn mess!"

As we drove along for a few minutes Jake lost his irritation and changed his tone of voice.

He started in on an overall briefing that sounded like he had memorized or given before.

"I don't know what you know about Thailand, so disregard anything you've heard before. There were seven ABs here: *U-T, Don Muang, NKP, Ubon, Takhli, Khorat* and *Udorn,* but three have shut-down already. We're roughly 150 kilos southeast of *Bangkok,* maybe 10 kilos east of the big RTN Base at *Sattahip.* The RTN started flying out of here about 1960. But the Americans started expanding *U-Tapao* back in October 1965. Base 'officially' opened for business in April 1966; runway extension was finished that July. But they didn't start flying air ops out until August with KC-135s. B-52s started missions against North Vietnam in April 1967.

"*U-T* is the largest air base in the free world. The whole perimeter is over 30 miles long, takes almost two hours to drive around it. The runway is 11,000 feet and can manage anything in the inventory. There're between 7,000-7,500 permanently assigned Americans, down from 10,000 during the 'Big War,' maybe 3,000 Thais."

Jake continued in a more relaxed tone.

"The major units are the 703rd Strat Wing and 103rd Strat Wing, with the 71st AD and 18th AF running them. Except for the SAC units, the 365th CSG is part of 31st AF and PACAF. There's also the 117th Hospital, a separate Commo Squadron and a Search and Rescue Det with an HH-53, call-sign 'Pedro'. There's a Navy P-3 unit assigned, and the US Army has units over at Camp *Samae San* running the deep-water port by *Sattahip.* They're just west of *U-Tapao.* Plus some U-2s with the 66th Recon Squadron.

"Just in-country training flights, I'm sure. And I can neither confirm-or-deny the existence of nuclear weapons in my BOQ room."

"Yah, right!"

"SAC" I dryly commented. "Just great." Then I started a cadence:

"'STRATEGIC AIR COMMAND! To err is human; to forgive is not SAC Command Policy.' 'When you have 'em by the balls their hearts and minds will follow.' 'SAC would supplement the Bible.'"

Jake replied:

"Speaking of religion: Everyone here has a girlfriend, and the Chaplains are strongly thinking about it."

I'd remembered the witticisms about SAC from the ex-SAC people at Maxwell. I'd also been fully briefed about 'wild' Thai women and their ready 'availability' for anything. So, I was looking forward to seeing it myself - soon.

"Jake, I need to ask. What's the *Klong* Monster'? And why do people keep their lights on to scare it away in the daytime? I heard it on AFN in CSC."

Jake grunted, shook his head and grinned.

"I think it's a myth, like the 'Loch Ness Monster' or 'Big Foot.' Supposedly there's a 10 to 12-foot long, nasty-badass, alligator-sized, huge, lizard-like 'monster' living in the *Klong* over by Buffalo Village. No one's ever seen it. But AFN uses it in their radio ads to remind people to shut their lights off during the day if they go out to save energy and not on to scare off the *'Klong* Monster.' Ads have been running for years from what I was told."

"Days are set-up for an eight-hour shift, but Swings and Mids overlap by two-hours from 2200-2400, so both Shifts work 10 hours. Mid Shift was called 'Tiger Flight' before. Swing Shift was called 'Cobra Flight,' but neither is said much anymore. You get one day off a week, so we'll have different days off. Come in early, draw your weapons at least 45 minutes prior to Guard Mount. But 30 minutes prior is the absolute minimum because of the long lines and slow issue rate at the window, 60 minutes would even be better. SP HQs recent changes made this new Shift Supervisor set-up mean there's an officer on-duty for each shift and responsible for everything plus Security and LE NCOICs."

I vowed to be at least 60 minutes early, if not the first one, to draw at the Armory window.

He continued.

"The CO you've met. The Ops Officer is a royal-pain-in-the-God-damn-ass. He won't make any decisions until they're forced on him, and even then, he'll stall. The bastard's squirrelier than the Mad Hatter."

I took it they weren't getting along. I doubted they'd be exchanging Xmas cards anytime soon.

"In fact, Dentonville's so squirrely he bragged he wanted a double-waiver to take the AWC course by correspondence as a CAPT!"

That was actually true. I was in the AWC Commandant Secretary's office back at Maxwell last Christmastime getting some document when she had to take a call from a CAPT so-and-so ringing up from Thailand. The caller said he wanted a 'double-waiver' to take AWC by correspondence. She explained that LTC was normally the minimum rank that could take the course, either in residence or by correspondence. And even then, only rarely were 'fast-burner' MAJs permitted to take it and ONLY if they were first on the B-T-Z promotion list to LTC plus the AF Chief-of-Staff called the Air University three-star about getting them admitted.

"He's out of here shortly, so I'm 'next'."

Jake grew serious and animated.

"We know exactly where the bastards are funneling all the stolen goods off the base. Right through God-damn Buffalo Village!"

Jake explained that virtually in the middle of *U-Tapao* (in a cul-de-sac area that led out to the main highway by a small road) was a small collection of bamboo-and-grass thatched huts named Buffalo Village.

Jack continued:

"The King personally gave the village headman a Royal Charter for the land ownership long before either the AF or RTN Air Wing started operations. So he's entitled, in his name only, to personally control the area. We've always had to ask his 'permission' to enter, but it's never been granted to my knowledge. And for damn good reason, we'd rip the place apart. The RTN could do it if they really wanted to. But no one's got the *cojones* to ask the Royal Family's permission to override the Charter or get an exception."

"Can't we just post guards around the entrance or the perimeter and cut off the in-flow of stolen goods?"

"No, I suggested that several times; got turned down cold by the back office. And so did my predecessor. It wasn't even considered. I don't understand why, but nothing ever changes. Even if a cyclone fence were put around the area it'd get sliced to ribbons and stolen. So, we just leave it be. Wouldn't matter even if we had a fence around it or not."

Jake thought for a second and then continued.

"Dentonville's PSC-ing out shortly. Good riddance! Not sure who's coming in to replace him, but anyone would be better. On Days it's 1LT Crowley and Guillory. Crowley PSCs out in August with me, Guillory's only a few months into his tour. On Mids it's two 1LTs. One is a 'short-timer.' Think he bails out with me too. The other 1LT is also a 'short-timer,' not sure when. CAPT Anderson is the Admin Officer. He was enlisted for a long time; then got a degree and a commission through OTS. He's been in 25 years, but the guy has a few face cards missing short of a full deck. He's got an assistant. Don't know anything about him."

"OK."

Jake continued. "On our shift you have MSGT Veeres as Assistant Shift Supervisor for Security; TSGT Bernardo's his back-up. Veeres takes over when both of us are off-duty, on-leave, or for whatever reason. He's outstanding, knows his shit frontwards and backwards. A sharp, professional NCO. He's how I get to cruise around on post checks all the time; he 'rides herd' on everything in Security so I don't have to get involved. On LE it's MSGT Wozniak. He also runs a tight ship, so I don't spend much time there either, unless there's a serious incident. His back-up's TSGT Reinhardt. You'll meet the other NCOs on Swings and Mids later. But the NCO with the most time on *U-T* is MSGT Boatwright, Assistant Shift Supervisor for Security on Days. Seems Boatwright's spent the last 10 years right here 'homesteading'. Guy never leaves. He must have over 30 years in the war now. You'll see him. In fact, you can't miss him."

"Jake," I suddenly remembered. "What were the Black troops doing in the issue line before Guard Mount? I've never seen that before."

"Called *DAP*. Started a few months ago over in the Post Office line and spread over here. It delays the issue, so we have people come in earlier than normal to draw their stuff, just to avoid any 'racial' problems if I shut *DAP* down. But I may have to put a time limit on it because it is starting to really get out of hand. People are getting pissed. Even the White guys are trying to learn it!"

-

## CORNER OF 'A' AVEVUE AND 9TH STREET, PARKING LOT, OUTSIDE CSC, 365TH SPS, *U-TAPAO* RTNAB, *CHONBURI/RAYONG* PROVINCES, THAILAND, 1330, 08 JUNE 75.

I was leaning against the sandbag emplacement protecting the emergency generator when a sextet of NCOs came over to check on 'Jake's replacement.' I could see SGTs were all motivated by curiosity. No one asked me how many days I had left in the 'Big War.' We exchanged pleasantries, hometowns and last bases stationed at. After about 10 minutes of BS-ing back-and-forth on nothing important about anything, one of the SGTs suddenly piped up and said to the man standing next to him: "Show the 1LT your Buddhas!"

The SGT reached inside his shirt and pulled out a long, thick steel-link chain (with twelve, plastic-covered, gold-framed little 'Buddha' statues attached to it by rings) from around his neck. I'd never seen anything like it. I intently stared at it as he explained where he got every little amulet from. I was impressed. I vowed one day to wear the same thing. Then everyone started to form up for Guard Mount. So, we broke and headed to our respective positions.

-

**'C' AVENUE AND 1ST STREET, OFFICE OF THE COMMANDER-SECURITY, PASS & ID BUILDING, MAIN GATE, RTN AIR WING, *U-TAPAO* RTNAB, *CHONBURI/RAYONG* PROVINCES, THAILAND, 1430, 08 JUNE 1975.**

Jake slid the jeep in a vacant parking spot marked 'SP ONLY' just outside the rear of Pass & ID. We dismounted and walked in. Turning left, we passed a few offices down a very short corridor and stopped in front of the last open door to the left. Inside through the big office windows you could see the whole Main Gate area. Jake knocked on the door jam, and then a booming voice in excellent, precisely spoken (slightly Thai-accented) English from inside exclaimed:

"JAKE, MY FRIEND! LONG TIME NO SEE! COME IN! COME IN!"

Jake had given me a briefing on CDR *Sawasdiyothin*, RTN, prior to our arrival. (How could I start even trying to remember all these long Thai last names? I barely was remembering their first names. But nicknames seemed to be easy. I just had to practice. I was not very good at remembering names right off. It took me a while to get the hang.)

CDR *Sawasdiyothin* was Commander of the U-Tapao RTNAB Security Section. In the overall *U-T* RTNAB/RTN Air Wing 'power structure' (or 'pecking order') it was the RADM of the RTN Air Wing; then the RTN Base Commander, a very senior RTN CAPT; then CDR *Sawasdiyothin*. Regardless of how many more senior ranking RTN officers there were on base, those three controlled everything on *U-Tapao*.

Jake also told me CDR *Sawasdiyothin* had attended various military schools, training courses and official conferences over the years in the US, plus finished the US Navy War College (Junior Course) as a LCDR in Newport, RI. That accounted for his excellent English and knowledge. The CDR was of medium-height, light-brown skinned, barrel-chested, and muscular. He wore a very tightly fitted, khaki uniform with stack of a dozen and a half ribbons, maybe half a dozen US and South Vietnamese-issued (standard 'Nam Era 'fruit salad') and had closely-cropped, going-to-gray hair.

Jake also said he strongly believed CDR *Sawasdiyothin* was no mere RTN O-5. He added the CDR was thought to have many uncles, older brothers and other male relatives who were big Thai Army generals, and big Thai National Police generals, plus an extensive ancestral genealogy that had served the previous Royal Families in the Grand Palace complex for decades. In Chicago, he would have 'clout;' in ancient Rome 'gravitas;' in short: 'very well-connected.'

We walked in, saluted, shook hands all around and sat.

"Jake! I never see you much anymore," CDR *Sawasdiyothin* grinned. "You never come to see me! And you never bring me any more presents!"

I noticed Jake squirmed and acted slightly embarrassed.

Jake replied: "Ah. . . .Maybe next time, CDR *Sawasdiyothin*, if I don't forget."

The CDR roared with laughter and slapped his desktop.

"Jake, you're one very funny guy! Who's your new friend? Can you introduce me?"

"I was going to do that," Jake replied. "This is 2LT Legere. He just arrived from stateside. He's my replacement in August."

"Jake! You just got here! Leaving so soon!?"

"My year's almost up; time to go to another assignment, CDR *Sawasdiyothin*."

"That's too bad, Jake. I'm very sorry to see you go. Believe me."

The CDR sounded quite sincere.

We spent the next several minutes in polite conversation. CDR *Sawasdiyothin* inquired about my service to date. When he found out my previous assignment, he told me he had attended several conferences some years back at ACSC and AWC on the AF's Thailand air operations supporting the 'Big War.'

"CDR *Sawasdiyothin*, we have to go," Jake said finally. "I just wanted to stop by briefly, say hello and introduce you to my replacement, 2LT Legere."

CDR Sawasdiyothin smiled, looked at me and said:

"2LT Legere, my office is always opened to you as it is to Jake. Come to see me any time with any problem, no matter how big or small. Please feel welcome to visit me. Also please be welcomed to *U-Tapao* and my beautiful country."

With hand-shakes and *Sawasdees* we left.

When we got to the jeep, I asked Jake: "What's the comment about never bringing him any presents? (I'd already forgotten how to pronounce the CDR's last name.) I didn't understand that."

Jake tightly grimaced: "I left my radio in his office twice. People on shift called me for something. I pulled it out, responded, and set it down on the floor. I forgot to take it with me both times. Now he never lets me forget it."

"Jake, you're lucky he didn't sell it."

"No, he's got bigger fish to fry. A radio's peanuts to him. He's just having fun. All Thais have a sense of humor and love to joke. But we need him 100 times more than he needs us, and he knows it. Don't let CDR *Sawasdiyothin* BS you with friendliness. He tracks where every single bug crawls on this base. Whatever's going on here, he either knows all about it or knows who does. And you can bet a paycheck it's either him, or someone higher-up on the food chain through him, who controls it all. Always remember it's their 'sandbox,' not ours. No matter what the big people in the Group back office, or Wing 'Head Shed,' thinks. We're just 'invited guests' here."

"Do this. Go down there at least once a week, grab the jeep, make a courtesy call. I seriously doubt you'll do him any favors, but he may be able to do you some in the future."

I said I would remember his advice.

As we backed out and drove away from Pass & ID, I could see large sections of the fence paralleling the main highway were missing. A large pack of mangy dogs were prowling about, perhaps 20-30 of them, darting in and out of the gaps. None looked like they'd been fed much, and all had scabies. Several had no fur. They were all lean, mean, tough scavengers, probably rabid and vicious. I remembered seeing other small packs of dogs, in twos and threes, plus a few single stray mutts moving between buildings. I asked Jake about them.

"Christ, another pain-in-the-ass problem. We have hundreds of wild dogs everywhere. Every month several poor Thais get bit and have to go for rabies shots, once or twice a year some American gets nipped. These fence holes don't help. As soon as they see an SP jeep appear, they run. We never get close enough to shoot them. I wanted to use an M-16 to kill them, but the base CO said we could only use shotguns. The problem's unfixable."

"I don't see any solution, Jake."

"There's none. For some reason Thais love dogs, even mangy ones. But they hate cats - don't know exactly why. Thais consider them 'dirty,' typical Thais. Even the poorest family will have a dog. Great for keeping *gigolos* away at night, but noisy as hell if you're trying to get some sleep."

-

**BRAVO SECTOR, PERIMETER ROAD, *U-TAPAO* RTNAB, *CHONBURI/ RAYONG* PROVINCES, THAILAND, 1900, 08 JUNE 1975.**

I determined Jake had a Midwestern 'twang' to go along with a staccato rat-a-tat-tat spew of conversation, a constant machine-gun-like patter; a lean, mean, fighting machine to boot. A total 'Pruning-Hooks-Into-Spears' kind-of-guy: in short, a real warrior. A man to shove you right out of the way and jump on the grenade to save your sorry hide.

I later learned that Jake was also nuclear fissionable material about to explode, constantly throwing off bolts of kinetic energy at all hours of the day or night, like a huge Tesla coil in discharge over-drive. Never idle, always nervously in motion, but deliberate in movement and thought. If you didn't know where you stood with Jake, or didn't understand any of his strongly held, direct like-it-or-not-opinions-on-every-subject imaginable (whether-you-asked-him-or-not), he'd be happy to help you out and tell you straight to your face (whether you liked that or not too). I liked Jake immensely from the word go. I always knew I would. Although I learned Jake always talked about other people's ignorant BS. But in a rare exception from everyone else, there was never any BS coming from him.

"Stay mobile, be constantly patrolling," Jake explained. "Always change your route, keep moving. Don't be at the same place at the same time every day. And show up unexpectedly on post checks, do different ones randomly, keep your eyes open."

He continued.

"The three fastest forms of communications in the world are telephone, telegraph and 'Tell-A-Thai.' There're NO secrets in Thailand. These people are totally incapable of keeping anything to themselves. Two Thais couldn't keep a secret if BOTH were dead. Everybody knows everything about everyone. Gossip, along with cheating the *farangs*, is the 'national sport.' They just do it with a smile."   Jake added:

"A Thai's 'social status' is tied into how many friends they have. The more they have, the higher their social status. In fact, the American military also has a 'social status' here, although we don't realize it. If you're in the Thai military that's very 'prestigious,' you gain big 'face.' Competition in their society is high to join and serve. And being an officer is very good but being a Thai Army officer is best since they're 'de-facto' running the country and have been for decades. So Thai military people have both a 'social' rank and 'military' rank simultaneously. The higher up they advance in rank the more 'social prestige' they get. Same thing happens with us in Thai society, or that's how Thais view us. Just remember that."

Jake asked: "What do you know about Thailand?"

"Just what I read about it in the 'CIA Area Handbook' in the Maxwell base library. The book was printed about five years ago. Don't remember much. Thailand is Buddhist and has a constitutional monarchy. They're the world's biggest rice exporter and have an ancient civilization."

He continued:

"If you want to survive your tour-of-duty here without going home in a body bag then pay close attention. Thais will joke, tease, and laugh with you, or anyone, about nearly everything under the sun - that's why it's called the 'Land of Smiles' - except never, ever joke about the King, the rest of the Royal Family, the Buddhist Religion and Monks. Say anything derogatory about them and you'll get yourself either killed, tossed into some nasty-ass Thai jail forever or, if you're lucky, just get immediately deported and permanently banished from the country."

"Sounds serious, Jake."

"It is! Last year one screwball, dumb-ass MAJ wanted to show the Thais out in town he had money to burn. So, he whipped out a five *Baht* note, took his lighter and incinerated it. All Thai paper money has the King's picture on it. He was on a plane out the next morning. He was lucky he lived; the Thais almost killed him."

"That's really serious Jake!"

Jake grimaced.

"Plus, don't bad mouth the Thais to their faces. It's another way to get your ass into serious trouble. If you don't like something about them, or Thailand, just keep your mouth shut, or keep it to yourself."

"Jake! You 'bad mouth' the Thais constantly! How come you aren't in trouble?"

"Because I NEVER 'bad mouth' them to their FACES! Sure, they all know I don't like them, or Thailand. But I save their 'faces' by not saying anything in public, only in private, and only to other Americans with the Thais out-of-earshot. Thais know not everyone likes Thailand - that's accepted. What isn't accepted is saying so to their faces. But I follow all the Thai customs; understand the culture and know how things work here, way more than anyone else on base. The Thais know and respect that. Plus, I'm honest with them, something they never get from anyone. I tell them what they need to know, not what they want to hear."

Then he added: "'Face' is everything to Thais."

"I'll give you a good example," Jake went on. "Late last year this CAPT named Maggiano, who hated Thais even worse than I do, was loudly trash-talking about Thais and Thailand big-time every chance he got, all over the base. But he was smart enough not to say anything bad about the Royal Family. Out near *Ban Chang* one day he got off a *Baht* bus next to a smelly, nasty ass *binjo* ditch. Another *Baht* bus came out of nowhere and clipped him into it headfirst. He was OK, except for some bumps and bruises. But he never left the base after that and kept his mouth shut until he boarded the 'Freedom Bird' back to the World. Thais have very long memories. You can push Thais really hard up to a certain point. Past that things can get fatal, real fast."

He started talking more evenly, changing the subject:

"The King was born in Cambridge, MA. That makes him a US citizen. He's married with four kids. An oldest daughter, her younger brother, and two younger sisters. The brother is heir apparent. The King has an older sister too. The oldest two are about our age if I remember right. The King is absolutely revered by all Thais, never forget that. You'll see his photo, or the King and the Queen together, or the whole family placed in every home and business in the country, but always hung above all other pictures or photos. Before the start of every movie, they play the King's anthem. Everyone stands up - even *farangs* - to show their respect while the music is playing and remains standing until it ends."

Jake let that sink in first, then continued:

"He's also a jazz musician, saxophone, or clarinet, wrote songs for a Broadway musical, likes photography, have a glass eye, used to race fast cars around the streets when he was younger and hasn't travelled outside of Thailand since 1961 if I remember it right. The whole Royal Family constantly travels around the country doing charitable works or making donations. They're always helping Thais out with humanitarian or development projects. That's one reason why they are held in the highest regard by everyone in the country. All except the oldest Princess who got disowned by the King."

"Why's that?"

"Ran off and got married a few years back when she was going to college stateside - some *farang*. No one knows exactly who she got hitched to. It's the only subject I've ever heard of that even the Thais don't know what happened. That's unique. Some say she married a classmate, or her professor. Others say it was to some guy from New Zealand. Someone said it was to some Army guy who went off to 'Nam and got wasted, dozens of other stories. Take your pick. It's all whispered anyway. I heard she didn't like the gilded court existence and was itching to have her own life. Who knows? When she was small and living in Paris with her parents, the French nick-named her *La Poupee*: 'The Doll.' She's a total fox if you ever see her picture."

"I'll remember to avoid the subject."

"Smart move. Do exactly what I told you, you'll be OK."

Jake changed subjects:

"There're many other important 'taboos' here. Don't touch or pat anyone on their head, back or shoulders, like we sometimes do with children. Don't point your finger at anyone, especially in their face. Pointing at something is OK, not a person. It's considered very rude. Don't crook you index finger and use it like we do to motion someone to come towards you. Thais do that to call a farm animal or dog over. Put your palm down and make a squeezing motion using all your fingers, that's how Thais call 'humans.' Also, don't put your arms on your hips when talking. Don't point your foot at anyone or cross your legs with your foot pointing towards a Thai while seated. The head is where the *Kwan*, or soul, resides. It's the highest part of the body. The foot is considered dirty and the lowest part of the body. Always take your shoes off when entering a *wat* or temple. And don't screw with the Buddhist monks. They have clean-shaven heads and are dressed in bright saffron robes. You'll see them walking around. Oh, by the way, if you see two guys walking together and holding hands, they aren't queers, just good friends. Women do the same thing. So don't get the wrong idea."

"Got it."

"I'll tell you another story about Thai customs," as Jake continued. "One 1LT I knew back at 'Frankie Warren's Rocket Ranch' worked over in the 703rd MMS. We used to grab chow sometimes at 'Grunt's Grove' sandwich place over near the unit's Electrical Shop. Anyway, he takes this taxi down to *Ban Chang* one day. The driver was speeding like a maniac and nearly killed someone crossing the street. The local Thai Police showed up, arrested the guy and threw his sorry ass into jail. Base JAG went down and bailed him out, got sent home on the 'Freedom Bird' the next day.

"Jesus Christ, Jake! That makes no sense at all! It wasn't his fault!"

"To you, no. To the Thais, yes. It makes perfect sense."

"How so?"

"If he hadn't been assigned to Thailand that one day, hadn't flown into *U-Tapao* that particular hour, hadn't left the base that minute and hadn't picked that particular taxi that second, the accident would've never happened. So it's all HIS fault, even though the taxi driver was driving like a total idiot."

"How-the-hell do you get out of that situation?"

"Easy. Throw the correct change on the rear seat, then bail out as fast as you can, and run like hell. Now the taxi driver is responsible for whatever happened. You did your part; you paid him for services rendered. Now the taxi driver gets arrested. You're clean."

"What a place!"

Jake changed subjects again.

"You don't have to *wai* when meeting anyone. There's a very complex system to it. I guarantee you'll totally screw up *wai*-ing to anyone being a *farang*, so forget it. But the Thais will appreciate the gesture anyway. Thais don't expect any *farangs* to even try and learn anything about their culture, customs, or follow them. But if you make any effort, even the smallest one, you'll gain enormous 'face.' The Thais will greatly appreciate you tried, even if you screw it all up. Try to learn as much Thai as you can. It's hard because of the five tonal changes, I know. But it's worth the effort to gain big 'face.' Thais will be impressed."

"OK."

"Now there are three levels of prices here. First is the 'stupid' *farang* price, the first price offered. Second is the 'smart' *farang* price, you bargain the first price down 40-60% if you're lucky or good at it. Third is the 'Thai' price, you'll never get that. It's what Thais will pay for anything. It'll be 1/3rd the 'smart' *farang* price. Bargaining is easy. If the Thais offer you a price on anything, just cut it in half or 40% if you like it a lot and give your price back to them. They'll always say no. Then turn and walk away. If they want to sell it for your price, then they'll chase you down the street and grab you. Otherwise, they'll let you go."

"Sounds simple enough."

"It is. You can have a lot of fun with it."

Jake continued.

"Although nobody else does this, I'm always the last person off shift. I wait for all the troops to get properly relieved by the on-coming shift; make sure the vehicles, weapons, equipment, and ammo are all accounted for and everything's clear before I turn-in my own stuff. I don't depart until that's done. Every other Shift Supervisor bails out right after they get a briefing from their relief. Not me. It makes for a late night sometimes, but the men on the shift know I got their backs."

I knew I would do the exact same thing.

I soon confirmed the 365th SPS, as Jake explained, was one of (if not the) most unusual SP units in the entire USAF. Normally there's a great shortage of experienced junior and senior SP NCOs AF-wide. That meant A1Cs did the work of SGTs, SGTs managed the duties of SSGTs, TSGTs filled billets normally rated for MSGTs and so on. Sometimes even SGTs had to fill jobs rated as TSGTs, or even MSGTs, in some units. Part of the demand was due to the Vietnam War surge. The AF greatly needed more security troops, especially for the huge ramp-up of air support in the war and the huge bases built in Thailand. The other was simply the extraordinary high turn-over rate of personnel. People got into SP, did their time, and then bailed out. In fact, the largest cohort of AF airmen was SPs. Many people didn't know that. Plus, majority of SP troops were stuffed up on the 'Northern Tier' in AFBs all strung out along a broad arc from ID to up-state NY. The standard jokes were: 'Ten months of winter and two months of bad sledding' and 'The only thing we have going for us here at Ellsworth is it isn't Minot.' And the oft-repeated proverb, said in a perfectly honest voice, by all who were sent: 'Only the best goes north.'

These SP units were composed of over 1,000-man Wings or Groups which were formed from three SP squadrons of about 350 men each. Normally the SP rotations went: Northern Tier-Europe-Northern Tier-Southeast Asia-Northern Tier-and then one final 'Homestead' assignment and retirement. Not everyone could manage the isolation and rigorous climate; not all marriages could stand the heavy strain of separation. The people who did relish it like 'God's Own Country':  hunters, anglers, campers, hikers, outdoors people - kept their homes outside their favorite bases there, all knowing they could volunteer and be guaranteed to return between assignments to Europe or Asia.

But not everyone was a backwoodsman or sportsman. And all it took was one screw-up, even a minor one, to get your security clearance yanked and you were booted out of the SPs.

One old-timer, a MSGT back at Maxwell, said when his service started at the beginning of WWII, during the Army's enlisted job assignments, when millions were processed into the service with him, that anyone with some talent or skill got selected first and assigned to some specialty. Whoever was left got assigned as either MPs or cooks, in other words: the bottom of the barrel. But I'd the strange feeling only some things had changed in nearly 30 years since the USAF was formed.

However, I knew there were SP officers who wanted to change that. Two of them were my former bosses at Maxwell. They, and others, were working quietly, persistently behind the scenes, fighting for better recognition, support, equipment, treatment, vehicles, awards, manpower, respect - anything to have the AF treat SPs as 'professional warriors' instead of unwanted, bastardized stepchildren. It was a long, up-hill fight.

But if I'd ever wanted to find out what being a 'third-class citizen' was, then being an SP officer was it. I quickly learned there were over 1,000 ways to get fired in the career field, especially as a mid-to-senior grade SPS commander. You never got any respect, and, as I heard from others: 'Being a policeman is always meeting people at their worst.' This was true. If there was an AF officer 'dog-pile' then SP officers was at the bottom. If you didn't wear 'wings' (pilot, navigator, flight nurse, crew member, loadmaster, etc.) then you weren't 'king shit,' you just got treated like it.

But the 365th SPS was totally different, special, and even unique. Its organizational staffing structure was the diametrically opposed to every other SP unit in the USAF. They had SGTs and SSGTs doing the work of AMNs and A1Cs, TSGTs doing the work of SGTs, MSGTs doing the work of SSGTs and TSGTs and so on. The 365th SPS was overloaded, over staffed and top-heavy in all sections. Some of the sections had two MSGTs when they were authorized only one SSGT or TSGT. The armory had one SMSGT and six MSGTs when they only were authorized two MSGTs. None of this made sense. NCOs of every stripe on base extended their tours repeatedly or returned, some for years - always right back to *U-Tapao*. Some of the veterans were probably well-connected with the assignments people, as many had been constantly in-and-out since *U-T* opened in 1966.

Jake Davis was many things as an officer in my book. (I never found out his real first name, everyone called him 'Jake.' I seriously doubted anyone else on base knew except CBPO, who held his personnel file. Hell, maybe that was his real name.)

I was told by the other SP officers that Jake was the only one of three people on base (the other two were both SSGTs and married to their Thai wives for almost a decade) who spoke any Thai past a few basic words like *'Sawasdee'* and *'Kop khun mach kup.'* (I was slowly picking up a few basic, easy-to-remember Thai words now.) Not only did Jake speak fluent Thai (the only US officer in Thailand, or so it was explained), he also knew every single Thai swear word.

Informally, I started picking up odd, stray pieces of information on Jake from the other SP officers. I had no way to check any of this without asking Jake directly (I wasn't about to ask him out of embarrassment). But I had no way to disprove any of it either. In any event I also felt it was none of my business to pry into his personal life.

Supposedly Jake was from some small farming 'burg in OK; graduated and commissioned from Auburn University AFROTC. Jake's

Father was said to be a full-bird COL in something (Intelligence was the only guess anyone had) and was said to be the Senior Air Attaché at the US Embassy-Bangkok for a number of years back in the early-to-mid-1960s. The story was Jake attended the final two years of grade school and graduated from an international high school both in Bangkok. There he learned to speak Thai fluently and hate Thais (and Thailand) intensely at the same time. No one knew why. The other officers were in complete agreement that if you opened up Jake's head, you'd find a small, single-engine plane inside. Apparently, he loved to eat, sleep, breath, live, drink and screw with flying on his mind in every way, shape, form, or color. It was all he'd think about, or so they said.

But if Jake was that one thing, he was a 'flying fanatic.' The other was he was driven to the point of total obsession in catching the Thai *gigolos* who were incessantly and methodically *ka-moying* everything inside the base and secretly spiriting it all away.

-

**CORNER OF 'A' AVENUE AND 9<sup>TH</sup> STREET, PARKING LOT, OUTSIDE CSC, 365<sup>th</sup> SPS, *U-TAPAO* RTNAB, *CHONBURI/RAYONG* PROVINCES, THAILAND, 1355, 09 JUNE 1975.**

The day was unlike any I had seen yet. The whole sky was completely overcast with high, elongated, rolling and hammered-lead/slate-gray clouds. It was cooler and slightly less humid. No sun today I thought.

After Guard Mount broke, Jake said:

"Let's go see something historic."

We climbed in the jeep and drove a short distance through ECP #1 to the flight line. We parked next to the control tower over past the 365<sup>th</sup> CSG HQs building. We could just as easily have walked. It was just several stone throws away from CSC. I noticed small knots of people were also gathered all along the flight line.

The aircraft were already lined-up on the other side of the runway and ready to taxi for take-off, BUFFs, all of them. This was it! The final departure. The B-52s were going home. At 1400 sharp they started rolling. One-by-one they maneuvered into position at the far north end of the runway. The first pilot pushed the throttles forward. The four-dual, nacelle engines quickly screamed with take-off power. The great metal bird started its take-off roll, gained momentum and lifted-off. We watched them depart until only one was left. But when the last B-52 lifted off, it turned into the pattern instead of going straight off over the Gulf of Thailand and eastwards. The BUFF came in low, paralleling the flight line, flying under the Control Tower one last time. Then it faded into the southern horizon. I thought to myself now the Vietnam Air War was finally over. We got into our jeep and went back on patrol.

Jake started talking about when he arrived in August 1974.

"I'd originally wanted to go over to C.C.K.," he explained. "Try some of that Chinese *nookie*. When they handed me orders to *U-T* I went out kicking and screaming. Thailand was the LAST place I wanted to get assigned to. But I couldn't get out of it."

Jake then changed gears.

"Camp *Samae San* is the US Army's deep-water port and transportation center just down the road, maybe ten kilos west, closer to the big RTN Base at *Sattahip* and a couple of kilos east of it. *Samae San's* where the *S.S. Mayaguez* sailed from, loaded with bombs from the bomb dump here. It got intercepted by the Khmer Rouge off of Cambodia and the crew held hostage. It was right before you got here. One CH-53 full of SPs from *NKP* was headed here to support the military rescue operation. It crashed like mid-way killing everyone. Rumor was it got shot down. I think the 'official' version was 'mechanical failure.' But nobody on base bought that. Who-the-hell knows?"

"For local R&R there's *Pattaya* Beach, about 30 minutes from here. Not a lot up there. It's a popular place to get away without going too far. There're some bungalows you can rent pretty cheap, nice beach, a big hotel or two and a number of cheap smaller places to bunk. It's got beer bars, friendlier hookers, a few decent restaurants, and souvenir shops. It was more popular during 'Nam as an R&R place for the troops, but things died since the 'Big War' shut down."

"I'll remember that."

"There's a small market west of here on the main drag called Kilo *Sip*. Some bars, a little shopping, not much, just a little place between *Sattahip* and *Ban Chang*, junior enlisted types live out there because it's cheap."

"*Ban Chang* is a small town just east of here. Lots of people rent houses, apartments, or bungalows, or they just move in with their *tee-locks* or girlfriends and cover the rent and utilities. Some bars, restaurants, a bank - nothing to write home about."

Jake grew serious.

"The ONE AND ONLY thing I want out of Thailand is a set of 'Thai Security Guard Wings'."

"What's that Jake?"

"'TSG Wings' are a decoration only given to the AF people who work with the TSGs. They're issued through the Royal Thai Supreme Command Headquarters. That means only SPs get awarded them, but not all SPs rate. If they've presented them to anyone else, I've never heard about it, but it's possible. They've given them out from way back, but they stopped doing it when I got here. No one knows when they'll start awarding them again."

"Can't you make some discrete inquiries?"

"I've tried. No answers. Typical 'Thai' response: *My loo see* - 'I don't know'."

"What're they exactly?"

"They're really impressive," Jake continued earnestly. "The TSG 'Wings' are composed of three parts. One is the center, the *Chakra*. It's a circular, sharp-edged, Frisbee-looking, center-holed weapon used by the Hindu God Rama, which represents the Thai Army. Then an anchor through the middle of it, which represents the RTN. Then a wing on both sides, which stands for the Thai Air Force. The First Class of the award has a star surrounded by a wreath above the *Chakra*. That's reserved for officers. The Second Class is just a star, no wreath - that's reserved for senior NCOs. Third Class is no star, no wreath, that's reserved for junior NCOs and Airmen. It's possible for someone who rates a lower class to be given a higher class for exceptionally service, but that's rarely done."

"The whole thing is done-up in heavy gold-colored, twisted filigree wire and some other colors. It's almost the width of your palm, about 3 ½ inches. You wear it above your name tag. I've seen some SPs wear them through the years. Impressive as hell. But you must get 'official' permission from DOD through AFMPC to permanently retain the decoration. You can go the ceremony for a 'token acceptance.' But you can't legally retain it until you get written authorization from higher-up."

"I'd love to get a set myself. Maybe things will change in the future."

"Maybe. Who knows?"

"What do you know about SP History?"

"To be honest Jake, not much."

"You knew SP was formed after the AF spilt from the Army back in 1947. Back then we were the 'Air Police.' But APs got changed to SPs in 1966. In fact, some of the older officers and NCOs still refer to us as 'APs' or 'Sky Cops'."

"I heard both terms back at Maxwell."

Jake continued.

"Security and LE were split in 1971. SP just went to the 'Shift Supervisor' concept. One officer is on duty for every eight-hour shift. He's responsible for everything that goes on the base: Security and LE. There are NCOIC Assistant Shift Supervisors for each section. But everything's on his shoulders."

"Got it."

"We don't do much with the RTN. They have their own separate entry gate closer to the flight line that lets out on the main highway called the 'Thai Navy Gate.' We have one SP on duty mainly for show. No Americans can come through there, just RTN vehicles. But the RTN uses the

Main Gate since they have their own guards there too. There was another gate out to the main highway just past the end of the north runway on perimeter road at one time. But so many stolen vehicles were flying out of there they just shut it down permanently. That was right before I arrived. The little two-man guard shack is still out there. They have triple-stacked concertina wire and steel crossed-beam barriers where the gate entrance used to be to block it off. It used to have just single concertina wire across the entrance, until someone crashed a deuce-and-a-half through there carrying the concertina along with it. They'd bring in long truck convoys loaded with bombs from the deep-water port at Camp *Samae San.* There's one other entrance called the 'Back Gate' that leads directly over to *Samae San.* I'll take you over later."

"OK."

"I'll brief you on the Thai Security Guards. The TSG Swing Shift Supervisor is OK. But TSGs are lazy-ass, useless, civilian contract guards in O.D. military-style uniforms. They bunk-out as soon as they get to their posts. Always make a lot of noise when you pull up on a TSG post check and keep at it as you start walking toward their position or tower. You don't want them waking up suddenly and think you're a C.T., or somebody sneaking up on them. They'll probably blow your sorry ass away by mistake."

"Great, I needed a new headache."

Jake changed gears.

"I'm sure you noticed the shift patch on one shoulder, the 365th SPS is on the other. Each shift has its own separate patch, plus K-9, LE, 'Shadow Patrol', Customs, 'Tiger' Flight, SP Investigations and a number of other sections all have their own. All locally designed and made. Plus, they're getting ready to authorize MAJCOM pins for wear on the new dark blue berets for SP use, AF-wide. They expect the 'official' authorization to be announced any month, but some of the local shops are already making 'beer-can' PACAF crests for wear. I'll try and remember to get you a set. We're either all wearing 'Boonie' hats or ball caps now, but I expect a lot of the troops to shift over to the new berets soon as they hit the street."

"What else? Almost forgot! Royal Thai Marines!"

"What do they do?" I asked.

"The RTMC always gets called-in for security duties when the TSGs go out on strike, like they did twice last year - always for more money, which they always get. It'll probably happen again this year. Throws a big money-wrench into everything. The RTN always gets involved and eventually straightens it out by giving them raises. For what, I don't know. The TSGs don't do jack anyway. Since the RTMC are part of the RTN they have their own separate compound down behind the RTN O-Club, big tents, and cots. I love these guys! They take no BS from anyone, ever. They pattern themselves right after the USMC, even right down to using the same globe, anchor, but a *Garuda* is substituted for the eagle on their emblem, real big bad-asses. The fence *ka-moys* always disappear when they see the RTMCs on duty. They know they'll shoot-to-kill if they see them stealing, unless the *gigolos* are unbelievably stupid enough to try that shit, like they did once last year."

Jake paused for a moment to think, and then added: "Thais will always tell you exactly what they think you want to hear," Jake explained. "And never what you need to know. Everything is a 'yes', no matter what you ask them. Thais do have a word for 'no,' but they rarely use it, and never with *farang*s. So, you have to be careful not only what you ask them, but how you ask them. Any question that requires a 'yes-or-no' answer will always get answered with a 'yes'."

"Why's that?"

"They'll 'lose face.' If you ask any Thai a question, they'll assume you think they're smart enough to know the answer. So, they'll always GIVE you AN answer, it doesn't necessarily have to be the RIGHT answer. If they told you: 'I don't know,' it's a big loss of 'face.' They'll think you think they're stupid. No Thai wants that. Plus, no Thai will ever tell you they don't know something, whether they know it or not. And they also think you should be smart enough to figure out they wouldn't have known the right answer in the first place."

"Sounds crazy, Jake."

"Welcome to Thailand!"

-

**BETWEEN 'C' AND 'D' AVENUES, 8TH STREET, CASHIER'S CAGE, USAF O-CLUB, *U-TAPAO* RTNAB, *CHONBURI/RAYONG* PROVINCES, THAILAND, 11:35, 10 JUNE 1975.**

Prior to lunch chow-down I wanted to get a 'ration card.' I never drank anything except beer, then only occasionally. I serious doubted I'd ever use it. I just wanted to have it just to say I had it. I inquired at the cashier's window. The high cheek-boned, glamorous, generously-stacked, exotic-looking, long-haired, model-thin cashier inside batted her extra-long, glued-on, thick eyelashes at me and said I had to go to the O-Club Manager's Office around the back. She was another Miss Universe Pageant fugitive. Once there, with few formalities past looking at my ID card, completing an application form and a statement about how I could or could not dispose of the alcohol ration should I chose not to drink it, but make it a gift or donation, I received a wallet-sized, printed khaki card with my name and information type on the other side. It had the twelve months printed on it and numbers of items procured each month. The ration card was lettered: L-Liquor, T-Tobacco, W-Wine, B-Beer, and S-Spirits. I put it next to my AL driver's license in my wallet and went to chow.

I stepped past the entrance to the main dining room. The hard-core lunch crowd hadn't arrived yet since it was still a little early. The hostess at the door greeted me with a *wai*, a "*Sawasdee, ka!*" and a big smile. I noticed she wasn't dressed like the other waitresses. She had on a *moiré* emerald-green, horizontally banded skirt of different bright colors, the various-sized gold, red, dark blue and black stripes that were on the bottom. She had a matching emerald, green jacket with elbow-length sleeves and a 'v' notch in her front collar.

She was standing behind the cash register and smiled. It was on a waist-high, white cloth covered table, with paid bills on a spike to one side.

She appeared slightly older than the other waitresses. Tall for a Thai, maybe 5'8", she had the usual long black, shiny hair falling straight down her back. I could see at first look she was unusually intelligent, well put together in the right places, and healthy. Her hawk-like, sharp eyes were taking everything in a perceptive manner. The only thing that detracted from her being very comely was some fairly thick pancake make-up on her round face, like she had a teenager bout of severe acne that left scarring that she was trying to cover. She had a plastic pin on her blouse that proclaimed "#1."

I nodded at her, smiled back, and replied: "*Sawasdee, kup.*" I walked to a table near the window and had Red Snapper steamed in lime juice and steamed fragrant white rice with Thai iced tea - a perfect meal. A young, shapely waitress serving me. She deliberately bent over several times displaying her impressive cleavage. I left a large tip.

\-

**CORNER OF 'A' AVENUE AND 9TH STREET, SHIFT SUPERVISOR'S OFFICE, CSC, 365th SPS, *U-TAPAO* RTNAB, *CHONBURI/RAYONG* PROVINCES, THAILAND, 1945, 10 JUNE 1975.**

Jake and I sat in the on-duty Shift Supervisors office. The ambiance wouldn't have been out of place in an old, battered, big city police interrogation room. One battered seen-the-'Big-War' metal desk and three simple, gray-metal, folding chairs with a goose-neck desk lamp completed the fancy room decor. The cinder block walls had been painted white maybe ten years ago, but now had an off-white grayish tint. Some, but not all, of the white, acoustic wall tiles remained attached. The ones that did had large gouges and black marks on them. One cork bulletin board in the passageway was riddled with staples and pushpins with a few ragged notices and official AF letters and bulletins all long out of date. Only one printed handbill-like notice on rough, brown-colored paper was still current: 'CRIME STOP: CALL 555 TO REPORT CRIME OR ANYTHING SUSPICIOUS - 365th

SPS LE DESK'. There was no chance 'Better Homes and Gardens' would list CSC in their Top #10 this year.

Jake continued his briefing from last night.

"When you go to the bank and get quarters make sure you bounce them on the countertop before you leave. If they have a metallic ring, they're genuine. If they thud, they're counterfeit. Plus, there're plenty of USD$20.00 'funny money' bills floating around everywhere. Look carefully at your twenties when you get them. A few bills are pretty slick fakes. But most of them can be easily spotted since they're poorly done. Like the time some idiotic counterfeiters started floating bogus bills around without serial numbers on them. I think they actually all got caught and thrown into jail."

"OK, got it! Watch for bogus twenties and quarters."

I thought to myself I'd like to see an actual counterfeit bill just to say I saw one.

"The base is divided into four quadrants or Sectors: Alpha, Bravo, Charlie, and Delta. Alpha is most of the cantonment area, or northwest part of the base, Bravo's northeast, Charlie's southeast, and Delta's southwest. North-South dividing line is the center of the runway. East-West line runs right through the Control Tower. The fighting positions, bunkers and watch towers are all numbered according to sector. For example, the 81mm mortar pit in Bravo Sector is called B-6 and so on. There are over a hundred numbered positions scattered all over the base. CSC has all of them all on their status board. You'll learn them as you go along."

"There's a small K-9 section left, only some dogs and six 'puppy pushers' still around. The MSGT in charge is back for his second tour-of-duty from what I was told. He's the Kennel Master and NCOIC. The section used to be a lot larger years back. The handlers all live in their own hooches; the kennels are out there too. I never go over to K-9. No reason. They're in their own little world. They patrol the beach area where we don't have any watch towers, so we don't get involved with them. Exact same thing with SP Customs over at the APOE, they're a self-contained unit. We don't mess with them unless there's a reason for it and there hasn't been one yet. We have a 'Town Patrol.' Two mid-grade NCOs in a jeep on patrol outside the base, operating between *Sattahip* and 'Newland.' They're supposed to check into the clubs, watering holes, beer bars, and 'dives' to 'assist' any GI in trouble or makes sure no trouble gets started. Everyone loves 'Town Patrol' duty."

"I can see why," I replied. "You get to 'screw off' outside the base."

"Lots of shit has happened around here even before my time. The old timers still talk about when a B-52 crashed and exploded just north of the runway back in December 1972 after getting totally shot-to-shit over North Vietnam. Everyone 'bought the farm' except two crew members."

"Bad day at Black Rock," I replied. "Tough break."

Jake nodded; then changed the subject.

"About six-seven years ago there was a convoy load of ammo coming in here from *Klong Toey, Bangkok's* main port. A dozen semi-trailers filled with millions of M-16, .38 and .50 cal. rounds. Had a whole big shitload of SP, Royal Thai Army and Thai National Police escorts. They were taking the road down along the coast, just south of *Bangkok*, through *Bangkhae,* then suddenly! BANG! The whole God-damn load just evaporated into thin air. Like some weird space aliens just beamed them up to their UFO. No one ever heard or saw them, or the vehicles, again. Either the damn Thai 'mafia' 'bush-wacked' their sorry asses en route, ripped the load off, and then buried the bodies deep in some swamp. Or they all collectively decided to cash out, take the money, fly to Tahiti, and hide. My vote is for 'cash out'."

"Sounds like a hell of a story, if true."

"I wish!" Jake changed the subject again.

"We've got Motorola radios."

He brought out his black, hand-held, portable radio the size of a brick from the canvas-strapped green radio holder on his belt.

"Chargers are on the table behind the LE Desk SGT and in the Armory. There're four channels, but we only use two. One is the primary Security and LE uses. Two is the alternate in case we have a problem with one. Rule Number One is stay off the net unless you have something important to pass, then pass it and get off fast. We use the telephones in CSC and LE for long conversations."

"Channel three is for 'Shadow Patrol.' I'll get to them in a minute. We never use that. It's exclusively for their use. Talking on channel four will get you both sent to Leavenworth and buried in a grave marked 'unknown' in Arlington. To be used 'under instant penalty of death' is how it was briefed to me. Don't even think about it."

"Doesn't look like I'll be using three or four any time soon."

"Damn straight. The real problem is we often get jammed on one and two. Sometimes for 15 to 30 minutes at night, nothing but complete static. No one can call anyone. Sometimes it was up to 45 minutes and a few times at least an hour. Just comes and goes. Really weird. No one can explain it. Radios are fine, I had them looked at. It makes no sense."

"Jake, I don't know. Anything technical is a mystery to me. PFM. Can't help you there. Sunspots? Interference from other radios on the same freq? Excess electrical discharges from overhead power lines?"

He just shook his head about it in frustration then continued.

"Because of all the stealing going on we have 'Shadow Patrol.' They're another self-contained squad operating on both Swings and Mids. Just like SP Investigations, they're autonomous and run right out of the back office. We have no say-so or control over what they do, where they go, how they do their business, or who gets picked for the assignment. 'Shadow Patrol' is supposed to be hiding out in the 'shadows,' or where-ever-the-hell-they-are, always trying to catch these damn *gigolos*. But to date they've had no success. Or if they did, I never have heard anything. Maybe its classified way above my sorry-ass paygrade!"

"It looks like we really have our hands full with the Thais, Jake."

Jake shook his head sadly and added: "These bastards are slicker than axle-greased eel-snot. How they get in and out of some of these places without ever getting caught is beyond me. The Thais must be fucking '*Ninja Masters*'!"

"I don't know Jake, sounds tough to stop."

"But it's killing me!" Jake continued, completely frustrated. "We've got LE roving patrols, guards at the gate, troops at the ECPs, outer checkpoints manned-up, Security patrols, 'Shadow Patrol,' SP Investigations, K-9s, and a big OSI Det. What-the-hell is everyone doing? It seems the only one even trying to stop this BS out here is me!"

-

**BETWEEN 'B' AND 'C' AVENUES, 13TH STREET, CUSTOMER SERVICE COUNTER, CBPO, *U-TAPAO* RTNAB, *CHONBURI/RAYONG* PROVINCES, THAILAND, 1000, 11 JUNE 1975.**

Unless you 'royally-screwed-the-proverbial-pooch,' had the 'kiss-of-death' planted on you, or 'bought the farm,' then promotion to 1LT is automatic two years from the date of entrance onto active duty. Taking my promotion paperwork over to Dentonville, he administered my oath of office before I went on-duty. I counter-signed the forms and dropped them back to CBPO.

I received a pleasant surprise when I walked up to the Customer Service Counter. Behind it was female SGT I had served with for maybe 18 months back at Maxwell AFB. She had managed the SPS administrative duties.

We reminisced back when the CO had sponsored a Squadron Chess Tournament: USD$5.00 buy-in, double-elimination and winner-take-all. There were 16 participants, including me. As she was the most junior person in the Tourney, she was assigned to be the 'Prize Award Keeper.' The tournament probably lasted six weeks due to some people working shifts. However, she swept the field by kicking everyone's little 'butt-skis' hard, including the squadron's acknowledged resident 'Chess Grandmaster'. She was pert, highly intelligent, spunky, sandy-haired and freckle-faced, plus had a cute, bright, perky smile that she gave me once again. I said it was great to see you. She said thanks, great to see you too, and she'd take care of my paperwork.

I now was officially a USAF 1LT, one each.

Since it was my 'promotion day' Jake took mercy on me and let me off an hour early so I could have my own self-run 'promotion party' at the O-Club lounge. Plus, things had been quiet all night and if the proverbial 'balloon-goes-up' on base, Jake could either swing by in the jeep and grab me, or telephone the club and they'd roust me out the door.

I was hot, tired, butt-and-bone sore from long jeep rides and walking around on post checks, plus stinking like an old goat with my uniform totally drenched in sweat - I couldn't have been more soaked than if I'd jumped into the base pool. It'd been like this every night. I always looked forward to stripping off my uniform and jumping into the shower about 0045 after work. I walked into the lounge at 2245. I had the whole place to myself. I bellied-up to the bar since I didn't see any waitresses on the floor. The little bartender, who there the first time I walked in, asked me what I wanted. I ordered a beer. "A *Singha* please, thank you - sorry, *Kop khun mach, kup!*"

The little lady cheerfully smiled, gave me a high-pitched, musical-bell-sounding, 'tee-he-he' laugh and said: "You 1LT Legere now, you promotion today! Congrad-lations *Loi-to, 'ka!*"

How she knew that was beyond me. Maybe she was 'moonlighting' as the CBPO Commander during the day. I thanked her and asked what her name was.

"Cha-lee."

Charlie. Cute. I asked her how long she'd worked on base.

She gave me a big smile, another laugh and said 10 years. About when the base opened, I remembered Jake telling me. She must have seen everything under the sun at least twice in this place.

I suddenly got very tired of warming the bar stool, said I was going to take my beer and sit down. I must have looked like 'death warmed-over.' She was probably happy to get away from my rancid, sweaty odor.

"*Mai pen lai, ka!*" Charlie giggled, smiled, and nodded all at the same time.

I slowly lowered myself into a big comfortable chair, relaxed finally, when one server came over to check on me.

I ordered: "One more *Singha, kop khun mach, kup.*"

She politely smiled back and replied: "*Chi, ka!*"

I saw her when I came in the first time a few days ago. She was a fairly near 'twin-sister' to the other waitress I hadn't been served by yet. All were in the same ballpark; except she was more mature in temperament and had a few more years under her belt than her partner. Slightly better stacked and olive-skinned, she was more emotionally 'detached' than her counterparts. 'Cool' or 'uninvolved' is how I would've tagged her. Otherwise, they were all evenly matched in the 'looks-department.' I decided two beers were enough, left two generous tips, and departed.

"*Kop khun mach, ka!!!*" they both happily replied.

I walked across the street to the BOQ for a shower and some well-earned shuteye. I was asleep as soon as my head hit the pillow.

-

**BRAVO SECTOR, PERIMETER ROAD, *U-TAPAO* RTNAB, *CHONBURI/ RAYONG* PROVINCES, THAILAND, 2200, 14 JUNE 1975.**

Jake continued explaining more about Thai customs and culture. I was always fascinated to learn something more about the country and Thais.

"Thais are always: 'Me first, you last' in everything. People will always rush to be first for something and to hell with you. Like if you were driving up on-ramp to a busy highway, back stateside normally we'd make room for the vehicle to merge into traffic. Not the Thais. No one would cut the person slack to let them into the flow. They'd just have to sit there and wait for an opening. Plus, Thais never say the word 'sorry.' If they make a mistake, like accidently bumping into you, they'll smile. The 'smile' is their apology, the larger the 'smile,' the bigger the 'apology.' Thais are also chronically late. At least one hour at a minimum. The Thai concept of time is very different our view. Where we value our time and being efficient, Thais always say *mai pen lai*, which means 'don't worry about it.' In fact, all Americans hate having their time wasted. But Thais don't care about time. Wasting time and inefficiency is a national sport here, like cheating *farangs* and *ka-moying* stuff. And no Thai trusts another Thai, and for good reason. Even family members don't trust each other. Even if a Thai knew someone for 30 years, they know one day the person will screw them over on something."

"Sounds crazy Jake."

"It is. But this is Thailand. Thais love anything *sanuk* or 'fun.' That could mean anything: eating, drinking, dancing, singing, walking around with friends, fucking - whatever. Thais hate anything they consider 'boring' like sitting in a classroom and studying. The Vietnamese have an old saying: 'When the Thais have nothing to do, they sleep. When the Vietnamese have nothing to do, they read.'"

Jake continued: "Thais are totally hierarchal. There is a strict pecking order with the Royal Family right at the top. The military is just below them, and Buddhist monks are close in status. Thais love to wear uniforms and will put them on any chance they get. It's just another way for them to show their 'status' or 'place' in society."

"Interesting stuff, Jake."

"Last thought. Morality, religion, and sex are intertwined in the West; they can't be separated. In Thailand they're separate concepts, actually they've little to do with each other."

"Real '*Zen*' stuff, Jake."

"Thais just think screwing is a 'normal' human function, like eating, sleeping, and breathing."

"I'm sure I'll remember that Jake."

-

**BETWEEN 'C' AND 'D' AVENUES, 8<sup>TH</sup> STREET, SNACK BAR, USAF O-CLUB, *U-TAPAO* RTNAB, *CHONBURI/RAYONG* PROVINCES, THAILAND. 1230, 15 JUNE 1975.**

I found out only the day before that the main dining room was not the only place to get lunch at the O-Club. Jake said there was a Snack Bar around the back, so I decided to forgo the full sit-down lunch I'd been having before going on shift for a burger and fries. I walked from the BOQ around to the back of the O-Club. I'd an hour to kill before being picked-up. Inside was a stunningly attractive, young Thai girl, or a very petite version of one. (Maybe mid-teens?) I couldn't guess a Thai women's age within 10 years now (I was always under-guessing). She couldn't have been more than 4'8"; long, luxurious, straight, waist-level, black hair, and maybe 80 pounds dripping wet. She was absolutely the most exquisite thing I'd ever seen in my life. She was stunningly perfect - face (slightly squarer than round), figure, mannerisms, an exquisite, miniature Miss Universe-Thailand winner. I felt my heart sink at the visage. She was listening to a disco song on a portable radio, fluidly bouncing from side-to-side and singing right along with the 'Silver Convention.'

"GET UP AND BOOGIE!! GET UP AND BOOGIE!! GET UP AND BOOGIE!! BOOOOOOOGGGGIIIIEEEE!"

Her laughter tumbled out in high-toned, cascading, tinkling peals. Her whole body shook. Her voice reminded me of musical chimes. I was completely harpooned. Her name tag said *Supattra*. I later found out her 'long' nickname was *Nong Nit-noy*, but everyone just simply called her *Nit-noy*. I knew I would have lunch there every day.

-

**ON THE PATIO AT MADAME T'S RESTAURANT AND MASSAGE PARLOR, SIDE *SOI*, JUST WEST OF *U-TAPAO* RTNAB, *CHONBURI* PROVINCE, THAILAND, 1900, 18 JUNE 1975.**

The Swing Shift party had been running since 1500. Everyone attending pitched in some cash for food and booze. Madame T's supplied the Thai food and local beer. Stateside beer and harder stuff were obtained with ration cards at the Class VI store on base. The mess hall supplied the American chow. Jack Daniel's was the favorite hard libation. The music was all classic C&W, Rock, and Hard Rock. Anti-war songs predominated on the playlist and sorrowful ballads about leaving for somewhere else were a close second. Jake and I sat far enough away to hold a fairly normal conversation without shouting at the top of our lungs over the music. Madame T's was within an easy stone toss past the west side of the base's cyclone fence. You could see many of the base building tops from where we were sitting. But we had to leave the base, turn left, and go down the main highway a bit, turn left again, and go down a short side *Soi* to get there.

We sat apart from the troops since we were the only officers in attendance. Jake took a day of leave so we could have the same day off. As CAPT Dentonville had chopped his chit (Jake was notorious about not taking leave), he was good to go. We found we had some things to talk about, mostly of mutual interest and, of course, work. I was slowly nursing another *Singha* beer and feeling no pain. Jake sipped a soft drink. Since he was driving us back to base in the jeep, he wanted to stay completely sober.

"No one dates nurses here," Jake said. "They all got their minds totally blown over the complete lack of GI male interest. Back stateside they think their shit doesn't stink. They always get the pick-of-the-litter for guys to date. Here almost all of them are dating RTN officers on the side if they want to get any action. *Ba!*"

"Sounds like it."

Jake talked about his time at F.E. Warren, doing Security out in the missile fields, his background, life's aspirations; mundane stuff - nothing to write home about. I talked about my time at Maxwell, family, similar subjects - a fairly routine conversation. We both agreed we probably wouldn't be making SP or the AF a career.

"The US military: Where the trivial is important and the important is trivial," Jake wise-cracked. I smiled at Jake's witticism.

"I wonder if you can get the same credit for taking SOS by correspondence, as opposed to in-residence," I mused. I must have asked that same question of 100 different people to date without any real answer.

"No clue," replied Jack.

The conversation lulled.

"Let me give you a 'head's-up' about Guillory," Jake suddenly said in a serious tone of voice.

"About what?"

"Bastard's ambitious to a fault. Guillory would run his grandmother over to get ahead. He'd have been perfect in the Nixon White House doing 'Dirty Tricks for Tricky Dick' as long as he got a pat on the head and a bone tossed his way. He's always got his head right up the ass of the people in SP HQs kissing them big time. Always trying to get early promoted to four-stars. But I think he fell on his face a few days ago."

"How's that Jake?"

"He recommended putting some of the LE troops on bicycles, a base 'Bicycle Patrol!' Got himself laughed out of Dentonville's office."

"I knew he was ambitious when I first met him last year in grad school," I said. "That's no surprise. He was direct about it."

"Yah but watch your butt! I've seen him backstabbing the other officers, including his 'best buddy' Crowley, every chance he gets. Fortunately, Shellenbarger and Dentonville totally ignore it, or don't give a shit. So, he just makes himself look bad. Be careful with this prick, OK? Guy's a total asshole."

"Thanks for the warning, Jake."

Jake grimaced and nodded he had properly passed me a warning in time to protect myself.

I changed the topic.

"Tell me about Madame T."

"According to 'local lore' Madame T showed up when the base was being built back in 1965. She took one look, ran right back to *Bangkok,* 'hired' four *poo-ying* hookers and brought them straight back down the same day. She set up a little 'business' for herself right outside the main gate and it grew like weeds in deep cow shit ever since. Now she runs 50 girls in her 'massage parlor' and caters a lot of parties just like this one. Supposed she had four 'daughters' and got all of them married off to full-chicken COLs over the years. Who knows? They're her 'insurance policy' for when *U-T* finally shuts down permanently. Supposedly she's already got a US Immigrant visa in her Thai passport, a 'Green Card' in her handbag and fat, juicy bank accounts all over the world. Biggest whorehouse in the whole area, does good business. Only the best LBFMs get hired."

I could see Madame T's 'business' was a fairly impressive spread. As Jake described it the place was a large (well-built by local standards I imagined) two-story building with multiple, separate rooms with spa-or sauna-like bathtubs, on each floor. I'm sure already for 'action.' This evening the girls all lounged outside on chairs at round metal tables under center umbrellas, or on the steps into the parlor, waiting for customers to have some *sanuk* or *sabai dee mach*, but away from our party. The girls ranged from 'plain Jane' to 'well above average' in looks. Skin tones ran the full spectrum from white porcelain to dark mocha. A few of the shorter girls might have been called chunky, but the majority was slender or lithe. I'd have guessed their ages ran the gamut from late-teens to maybe early-thirties (with Thai *poo-yings* it was impossible to say). All of them looked as supple as circus acrobats, but none of them were outwardly cheerful today. Maybe they were simply bored from idly sitting and waiting for customers to appear.

The *poo-yings* wore high-cut women's gym shorts, simple t-shirts, beach slip-ons or shower sandals, no make-up or finery - all were ready to strip-for-action, 'wham-bam-thank-you-ma'am.' But they didn't mix with our party. It was going to be straight-up business deals on their part. If you wanted to 'butterfly,' you wandered over, made your selection, and then paid for it afterwards (with a tip). The girls held up their end of the bargain in grand style from all reports.

However, Madam T herself joined in our festivities, gladly greeting everyone with a broad smile, sincere look, and a warm handshake. Why not? We were aiding the expansion of her bank accounts somewhere. Madam T was a well-endowed, medium-sized, solidly built, but matronly, older woman. Very regally dressed in the latest 'chic' style (for her age), she was also perfectly coiffed and manicured. Dripping gold chains and expensive jewelry, Madam T looked exactly like a Thai 'cat-house' madam is supposed to look.

By 2030 I was hungry, starving, in fact, and had a very good 'buzz on' after a fair number of ice-cold beers.

"Try some Thai food. It's delicious," Jake said.

I staggered over to the long tables (feeling no pain). They were heaped with a large variety of Thai food I could only guess at what some of it was. Another set of long set of tables next to it held American picnic fare: burgers, hot dogs, chicken, potato salad, boiled ears of corn, potato chips, etc. I started selecting a bit of everything off the Thai table just to say I tried it and tossed it on my plate.

"Try putting some *pickenoos* on it," one party goer standing next to me said. "Thais love their food very spicy."

"Where's the *pickenoos* sauce?" I asked.

"See the small ceramic dish right in front of you with the tiny green-and-red sliced peppers in the dark sauce, that's it. Use the tiny spoon. Stuff is 'nuclear-waste' hot. *Pet mach-mach!* Be careful if you're not used to it."

"Thanks."

I grabbed about a dozen tiny spoonful's of peppers and sauce and generously sprinkled them all over the mound of food on my plate. I walked back where I was sitting with Jake. My taste buds burned after shoveling it all down, but I was too drunk to pay any attention to it. I think my tongue turned numb too.

-

**BETWEEN 'C' AND 'D' AVENUES, 8TH STREET, BOQ #1, ROOM #6, *U-TAPAO* RTNAB, *CHONBURI/RAYONG* PROVINCES, THAILAND, 0315, 19 JUNE 1975.**

The first excruciating stomach cramp woke me up with an internal mule-kick to my intestines. Even though I had been very intoxicated, the cramp brought me to near full sobriety and fully upright in bed. My innards were boiling and queasy. I ripped the sheet and blanket off, jumped out, grabbed a towel around my waist, slipped into my shower sandals and headed out the door. The second very painful stomach cramp told me half-way down that the turbulent intestinal liquids inside were going to violently explode outwards if I didn't get a moving faster. I raced down the outside passageway, ripped open the screen *hong nam* door, shot into the toilet stall and sat just as my anal cavity exploded with massive stream of watery diarrhea. I knew my asshole had to be aflame. Intestinal cramps repeatedly hammered my inside as I sat there holding my intestines in with both hands. I doubled up in great pain, sweating, panting, and moaning in agony. When I felt I'd completely blown everything in my intestines out, I got up and slowly walked back to my room, clutching my poor intestines. Five minutes later, same drill, over a dozen times, all night, until 0730 when I absolutely had nothing left inside to donate from my body. It was 'The Case of the Royal Flaming A-hole.'

Spicy Thai food. *Pickenoos*. Never again.

-

## CENTRAL MARKET, DOWNTOWN *SATTAHIP*, *CHONBURI* PROVINCE, THAILAND, 1030, 21 JUNE 1975.

Guillory and I rode his jeep quickly headed westwards towards *Sattahip*. I'm fairly sure we didn't break the sound barrier this trip, but not for lack of trying. It was another hot, bright, partly cloudy, and oppressively humid, carbon-copy day. Just like most of the last two weeks had been. Today there were individual rainstorms all around on the horizon as big thunderheads boiled high up. It was my first trip off base. Guillory wore cammos. I was in black chinos, tatty short-sleeve Kansas State sweatshirt, worn jogging shoes, and sweat-stained ball cap. (I know. A perfect example of a non-sartorial, unrefined, total 'slob-ola.' I'd nothing else to wear.) I realized the Thais drove on the left like the British as soon as we exited the base.

The traffic on the main highway was lightly moderate in both directions. Gaudily decorated, colorfully painted, oversized busses sounded their eardrum-shattering air-horns to warn slower vehicles they were passing them that made a battleship's steam-powered whistle sound like a child's squeeze toy. I'm sure the Thais all drove at moderate speeds (for Thailand). Or exactly the same speed you'd drive from somewhere if you heard your house was on fire. Any vehicle not travelling at least the speed-of-light was passed. However, it appeared no Thai would be caught dead simply passing another vehicle on a clear, long, straight stretch of roadway with no on-coming traffic. They all waited to pass either on a blind curve, right below the crest of a hill, or in right front of any on-coming vehicles.

The Thais simply pulled out into the opposite lane, accelerated, passed the vehicle in question, and then swerved back into their lane with perhaps two millimeters to spare between all three vehicle bumpers: theirs, the vehicle being passed, and the on-coming vehicle. And it seemed they all wanted to set the world's record for passing the largest number of vehicles in succession. Every vehicle that was over-taking another precisely timed the speed and exactly measured the distance, in an exquisitely directed choreography, as accurate as big-top circus trapeze artists work without a net. It also seemed every Thai, once sitting behind the wheel, decided to see how close they could come to committing suicide without actually completing the act. I was positive all of Thailand's funeral parlor directors, embalmers, florists, and ambulance drivers were doing a roaring, land-office business, and had long ago become millionaires.

Guillory started his narrative.

The landscape rapidly sped by us as a collage of jungle stretches, scattered small wooden homes, various businesses, open spaces, operating farms, and empty fields. Many homes were surrounded by crudely made, unpainted cinder block walls with various-sized jagged pieces of broken glass embedded in concrete-covered tops. However, much of the land appeared unused or uncultivated. There was discarded dry trash, wet garbage, small plastic bags, empty cardboard boxes, fruit rinds, and assorted litter lining along both sides of the roadway.

"These people are all fucking slobs," he continued, reading my mind. "Anything they don't need they toss out their vehicle windows. But it's funny. They never throw anything away otherwise, or anything of value, which means whatever they can make money from. Junk we'd have long gotten rid of they just hang on to."

Eventually we turned left, passed a large reservoir, and entered the small 'burg called *Sattahip* by the Gulf of Thailand. After negotiating some heavy street traffic on side streets into the heart of what seemed to be downtown, we parked down the block from what he explained was the *Sattahip* Central Market - the center of action. There was a wide variety of retail shops, with trinket and food vendors on the sidewalk with wheeled carts plus more food and trinket vendors with mobile carts or display trays on shoulder straps strolling on foot everywhere. It all looked like a noisy, exotic circus.

"Let's take a walk around the area, sport," Guillory said.

The streets were crowded with vehicles, the sidewalks were jammed with people; a few motorcycles and bicycles also were on the sidewalks. People blandly ignored them. We started walking up the hill slope to the next intersection and turned right. Guillory passed several Sikh tailors along the way with fully dressed male and female manikins inside the windows. The dark-skinned, turbaned, and bearded owners were standing outside their establishments. They highly encouraged us to quickly visit and take a look-see.

"'Arun's Tailors' is the best," he said.

We walked past several jewelry shops, a shoe sales and repair shop called 'Mr. Florida' (get all your shoes hand-made right there, Guillory added); then by more beauty salons and a wide assortment of other shops and businesses. All in unremarkable one and two-story wooden and masonry buildings. The small town seemed crowded with shoppers of all ages, with plenty of khaki-uniformed RTN personnel of all ranks. But the majority were obviously young-looking Seamen Recruits with their lack of stripes and ribbons. We strolled for a while.

Dark clouds were hurriedly rolling in now, and the bright sunshine was quickly being eclipsed by semi-darkness as the cloud ceiling suddenly lowered and started boiling, the wind suddenly gusting. We could hear the rain moving in our direction fast as it quickly thundered in. We ducked under an awning that just as the heavens let loose that second with a burst of torrential downpours that hammered on everything by 'Niagara Falls' load.

"*Fun-toke mach-mach*," Guillory commented.

The wind continued to blow strongly, sweeping the rain along. Within a few minutes, the streets started to flood as the storm drain backed up. We watched the intense downpour as stray people without umbrellas ran across our line of sight, all darting for cover. Then, as suddenly as it began, it was over. The sun poked out through the clouds, which were dissipating rapidly, with the water starting to steam off the pavement as soon as the sunlight hit it. The episode hadn't taken more than 10 minutes. The sun was streaming through the clouds, and the streets were quickly draining off the floodwaters, although I could see at least six other intense, individual rainstorms scattered across the full horizon out in the Gulf of Thailand.

The Central *Sattahip* Market was a large structure, open inside like a huge barn. It was at least three-stories high, covered a small city block, and was slotted with vents and windows on the second and third-story walls. We squeezed in between two food vendor carts on the street. Pushing past a large crowd of people coming in and out of a jammed-with-goods side entrance we ducked inside. The size of a small city block, the cavernous place was strewn far overhead with cobwebs, dust, dirt, and bird poop, unused, abandoned wires, cables, and ropes of unknown origin. It was a Saturday. The whole inside area was crowded with all manner of Thais moving everywhere noisily shopping. The singsong, Thai 'bird-chirping' conversations were almost deafening. The smell hit me with full force as did the tumultuous clamor, making me wrinkle my nose and wince.

We started a slow walking tour. There were open butcher counters with plucked chickens and ducks with various beef and pig cuts on open display, all covered with flies. One stall had pig head 'masks' that were eyelessly staring out from inside glass display cases. Slightly slanted, old dark wood, inclined shelves displayed heavily moistened fresh vegetables and fruits, most of which I had never seen before. Live fish, eels, crabs, shrimp, and other strange aquatic life sloshed around inside plastic washing tubs, some covered with black fish net-like coverings to keep them from flopping out. Various household goods, trinkets, kitchen plastic ware, thatched brooms, Buddha pendants in glass display cases, ceramic ware, cutting utensils of every sort, endless things for sale.

There were also live baby ducks and chicks in large cardboard boxes, plus small birds in bamboo cages sitting on the concrete floor. It was wet and slippery with water, animal blood, slimy fish guts and discarded animal parts, stray, discarded bits of unwanted fruit and vegetable peelings, spilled cooking oil and other unidentified liquids. The air was filled with more flies, smoke, noise and constant cacophony of Thai's lilting, melodious, bird-like chatter. The entire tableau was pure bedlam. But one thing was omnipresent, thick and over-powering.

"What's that smell?" I finally asked.

"What smell?"

-

**CORNER OF 'C' AVENUE AND 3ᴿᴰ STREET, BAR LOUNGE, RTN O-CLUB, *U-TAPAO* RTNAB, *CHONBURI/RAYONG* PROVINCE, THAILAND. 1700, 30 JUNE 1975.**

Jake decided to take me out to lunch at the RTN O-Club. Normally one of us would stay behind in CSC and 'mind-the-store' while the other went. Then we'd switch. But Jake said he had an 'ulterior' motive today. He wanted to keep his 'lines-of-communications' open with *Khun Rungnapa*, or *Khun Bee* (as she was nick-named). Jake had heard through the Thai 'grapevine' that her light-bird COL tanker ('fast burner) squadron commander 'boyfriend' was getting ready to PCS out tomorrow and wanted to be the first-in-line to pick her up on the short hop. The problem, as Jake intimated, was *Khun Bee* almost never 'dated' anyone ranked lower than a full-bird COL, and rarely went out with LTCs, unless they were: a) on the B-T-Z promotion list, and b) 'fast-burners' known to be groomed for stars. She was very picky about who she was a 'Royal Consort' to.

At first glance, *Khun Bee* was most definitely, powerfully attractive - a real eye-catcher. Maybe she couldn't have run long-distance with the girls in the AF O-Club lounge, but no one would kick her out of bed for eating crackers either. She was impressively dressed in what must be a very traditional, very expensive-looking, old-gold colored, heavy-thread Thai silk dress that left one shoulder and both arms bare. It had lots of colorful embroidered beads, tiny glass mirrors and ornate bangles sewn into the garb. Her long black hair was done up high on her head in an elaborate pile with some exotic flowers attached or holding it together - orchids and Frangipani, I think. She was a completely delectable, very desirable sight. With matching expensive, heavy, pure-gold jewelry on her wrists, fingers and neck and perfectly applied make-up, you couldn't help but stop and stare at her captivating loveliness - a perfect package of beauty. Her job was the 'Maitre'd' at the entrance lectern greeting the customers and escorting them into the main dining room.

What impressively set her apart from all other Thai *poo-yings*, or every other *farang poo-ying* I'd ever met, was she could magically make you feel the second she met you that you were simply the most important, desirable person in her life. She oozed sincerity and the happiness out of every pore to see you - like you were a powerful magnet, and she were iron filings. I'd never seen that before. But I was smitten, probably along with every other male that ever-laid eyes on her.

"*Loi-to* Davis!" she brightly smiled, *wai*-ed, and bowed her head solemnly at him. "So nice to see you again!" Her English accent and pronunciation were nearly flawless, just mixing up her 'L's' with 'R's' occasionally like almost all Thais did. "And you brought your flen' *Loi-to* Legere, how nice!" She turned to me and said: "*Sawasdee, ka!*" and gave me her special smile as a 'fren' of Jake's and *wai*-ed as well. I could instantly see Jake's attraction.

We walked into the bar lounge to get a quick sandwich (they also served food). Jake outlined his plan of attack. We would tag-team *Khun Bee* to *kin khao* if I could get someone else to go along. Jake explained if any Thai *poo-ying* seen with any *farang poo-chai,* except in the most professional or business setting, then she was automatically and forever labeled a 'prostitute.' It didn't matter if she was a 100-year-old virginal, crippled, great-great-grandmother-spinster-in-a-wheelchair: 'Hooker!' was the only thing Thais thought. However, if the lady had a female 'chaperone' then they were perfectly fine. And the more 'chaperones,' the better. No one would think less of the lady. Her reputation would be as safe as the gold bars in Fort Knox. I told Jake I had someone in mind.

\-

**CORNER OF 'C' AVENUE AND 3ᴿᴰ STREET, MAIN DINING ROOM, RTN O-CLUB, *U-TAPAO* RTNAB, *CHONBURI/RAYONG* PROVINCE, THAILAND, 2000, 02 JULY 1975.**

Jake and I took *Khun Bee* and her newest, closest 'fren' *Nit-Noy* out to *kin khao*. Jake burned another leave day so he could help me escort the two young *poo-yings* out. *Nit-noy* had referred to *Khun Bee* as her 'sister' even though they were not actually related. She explained that close female 'friends,' even actual cousins, were always referred to that way. 'Very Thai' I thought.

*Khun Bee* was now 'available,' since his LTC 'boyfriend' was 'history,' so she was considered 'fair game.' Jake didn't want to get accused of 'poaching' while she was going out with her boyfriend; an unwritten 'social rule' between the officers on base. Since *Khun Bee* was no longer 'off-limits' he jumped, quickly taking advantage of this new situation (or opening on her 'social schedule'). We set up the 'date' as Jake had planned.

He explained the RTN, and AF O-Clubs had a long-standing, reciprocal agreement. Members of one club could go to the other and be accorded the same rights and courtesies. Jake said occasionally small numbers of AF officers went to the RTN O-Club. A rare few individuals went often. But he added no one had ever seen a RTN or RTMC officer haunt the AF O-Club. He had no idea why.

If the AF O-Club was minimalist (some might have even said 'Spartan') in its functionality and simplicity, then the RTN O-Club was plushy upholstered. The interior was furnished in dark teak wood; expensive Thai paintings adorned the walls. Ornate brass work was artfully deployed, and the lighting was carefully subdued. Top-quality, heavy raw Thai silk curtains were strategically situated to dampen the sound of clinking glasses and cutlery on plates.

The swank eatery would not have been out of place in a small European city where rich businesspeople did financial deals *tete-a-tete* during the day and brought their expensive mistresses to at night. The main dining room servers probably couldn't have run a team of the last five Miss Universe winners off the basketball court, but they could have gone head-to-head with them on any hardwood floor. The final score would be close.

The *poo-yings*, like all Thais, were one hour late. Jake and I had sat there talking about shift and squadron business while we nibbled on dinner rolls and ate ice cold vegetable sticks, fighting off hunger pangs while holding our displeasure in at having to wait. Jake checked his watch frequently.

Finally, they both strolled in together, stunningly dressed. *Khun Bee* was very eye-catchingly attired in a 'chic' pure white, sleeveless, knee-length, very finely woven Thai silk party dress; expensive matching high heels, with a fair amount of gold neck chains, other gold matching jewelry and the latest matching hand-bag. Jake told me it was said *Khun Bee* had the best set of legs in Thailand. She got my enthusiastic vote now having seen some of them (from her knees down) on public display and the implied shape of the rest under her skirt.

"*Sue-way mach-mach!*" Jake exclaimed. I couldn't disagree. Jake and I were in white short-sleeve shirts, dark dress slacks, black loafers, and conservative ties. We looked like Mormon Missionaries converting lost souls in deepest, darkest Africa.

*Nit-noy* was decorously garbed in a bright peach-colored, short-sleeve, hemmed at the knees, demure-looking, very expensive raw Thai silk dress; with matching pumps and a small handbag, plus one thin solid gold neck chain thus completing her ensemble.

The *poo-yings* didn't apologize for being tardy, naturally. They just smiled brightly, walked over, stood, and waited while we pulled the chairs out for them to sit. Both turned every male head in the room.

Jake was more-than-slightly exasperated at *Khun Bee*.

"*Bee*, we've been sitting here for an HOUR!"

Maybe Jake let his irritation show more than he expected. The one thing Jake hated more than anything was someone being late, including him. But Jake knew what to expect on this 'date' with Thais. I was surprised he let himself become so upset.

*Khun Bee* sweetly replied:

"You die *young-kit* in Thailand!"

Jake was not mollified by her flippant comment. He persisted.

"*Bee*, I told you to be one hour EARLY for dinner so you could be ON TIME!"

*Khun Bee* smiled coquettishly and tossed off her reply:

"You die *young-kit* in *U-Tapao!*"

Jake wasn't going to let this loss of 'face' go without an apology.

"*Bee*, I'm NOT *sabai* at all! I'm *mo-ho mach-mach!*"

All he got was another big smile. She was having tons of fun at Jake's expense, and she knew it. She was unflappable.

"You die *young-kit* in America!"

I had the full buffalo steak dinner (well-done for me, thanks.) and several sides. Jake wanted *Gang Mussamun*, *Bee* picked *Pla Talay* in lemon grass and lime sauce and *Nit-Noy* ordered *Pad Prik King*. Jake and I had Thai iced tea (with milk), *Bee* had *Nam See Dang* (a Strawberry Fanta appeared) and *Nit-Noy* had *Nam Yen* (a glass of water with ice cubes appeared).

The conversation was all one-sided. Jake regaled the girls with his fluent Thai. I sat there with total incomprehension. The girls split their sides while falling out of their chairs laughing (Jake explained what he said after dinner) with his humorous stories, silly jokes, goofy puns, and endless bawdy Thai 'Double Entendres': subtle word and tonal substitutions where Thais can make the slightest tone changes to perfectly innocent words become very dirty swear words, crude sex acts, or intimate body parts. The girls thought the whole performance was hilarious. I could see Jake could have headlined any Bangkok nightclub.

The buffalo steak took forever to cut into small pieces and forever-and-day to chew. I had to swallow whole chunks of it finally in defeat. Or I would have been there all night trying. The meat was tougher than old shoe leather. Jake and I split the bill and left a generous tip (not wanting to be called *Cheap Cha-lees*). We waved the girls off the base and into a taxi outside the Main Gate.

"You die *young-kit* in *Sattahip!*" was *Khun Bee's* departing shot at Jake.

I finally had to ask.

"Jake, what's a *young-kit?*

"It's this microscopic frog in Thailand, maybe even the smallest one. You can barely see it because it's so tiny. What she means is she could kill me just as easily as stepping on this tiny frog. An old Thai warning. It's just *Bee's* way of being a total wise ass."

Jake never did get his apology. Nor did he get anything else. By the end of the following day, we heard *Khun Bee* had selected the COL running the Base Dental Clinic to be 'Royal Consort' to. Jake was not in a happy mood for several days. I would almost say he was *mai-sabai*.

## CORNER OF 'A' AVENUE AND 9ᵀᴴ STREET, PARKING LOT, OUTSIDE CSC, 365th SPS, *U-TAPAO* RTNAB, *CHONBURI/RAYONG* PROVINCES, THAILAND, 1555, 03 JULY 1975.

With the departure of the B-52 squadrons from *U-Tapao* (now that the 'Big War' was over), then it was just a matter of time before the remaining up-country ABs started shedding their inventory of aircraft. Every day some of the larger aircraft (KC-135s, etc.) would land here and then depart on their journey hopscotching back across the Pacific to the 'Land of the Big PX'. The smaller aircraft and helicopters (OV-10s, etc.) would be brought here, dismantled, wrapped in protective materials, crated, and then trucked over to Camp *Samae San* for seaborne shipment stateside.

Jake and I were talking inside CSC when a telephone call came in. An in-bound OV-10 'Bronco' was reported to have had landing gear troubles (failure of the landing gear to extend), so the pilot declared an emergency: estimated arrival 15 minutes.

Since there wasn't a single damn thing either Jake or I could do about the situation (and with nothing better to do) we decided to go over to the flight line and do our very best to gawk. We mounted up and inside of a minute were parked next to the 365th CSG HQs building, next to the Control Tower. A base fire department pumper truck was already laying down a thick bed of foam in the middle of the runway. We could see along the whole length of the flight line there were all the fire department's hose, water tanker, and crash-rescue vehicles; the Base Safety Officer had a ticket to the festivities; the Disaster Preparedness Officer was counted among the faithful; all the hospital's ambulances had arrived for the show; the base's flight line crash-and-rescue vehicles were in attendance; the HH-53 'Pedro' was in the air hovering off to the side and at least every single full-bird COL on base was out there as a spectator. In fact, we couldn't have even gotten out on the flight line if we'd wanted to, since all the COLs had their vehicles densely packed in. Didn't even know the base had so many O-6s.

The OV-10 appeared overhead 10 minutes later. The pilot made several low passes over the length of the runway before disappearing over the Gulf of Thailand at the end of the runway each time. Jake explained the pilot was burning off the last of his fuel and gave the Control Tower a chance to visually check for any exterior damage. Finally, he came in to land with his nose slightly more elevated than what I thought was normal. He ever-so-gently lowered his tail down into the foam bed, then the nose - the plane smoothly slid along the foam. The pilot kept his wings level. The aircraft gradually came to a final stop half-way down the runaway with one wing tipping lower than the other. All the vehicles (including every COL) raced out to the plane as the pilots emerged. It had been a picture-perfect emergency landing.

We climbed into our jeep and went back to work. Later, we turned the conversation back to things Thai.

"Jake, I've seen a lot of these small white 'Thai temples' on pillars in people's yards off base all over. Maybe standing about eye-ball high, they seem to have flowers, little human figures, colored light bulbs, candles and incense stick burning on them. What're they for?"

"Spirit houses," Jake explained. "They all look like miniature Thai *wats* or temples. Almost all Thais are Buddhists, but before Buddhism arrived, all Thais were 'animists' from several millennia before. Still are. Thais strongly believe that every animate and inanimate object has a 'spirit' or 'ghost.' Thais say *pee*. People who lived before still live now, but as *pees*. These *pees* need a place to stay, so Thais have these 'spirit houses' outside their homes for them. They're placed so the shadow of the house never falls on it. Some *pees* are thought to be malevolent, so Thais placate them with offerings of food, small coins, bottles of soda pop, glasses of water, prayers, flowers, incense sticks and small plastic or ceramic figurines of elephants, classical dancers, and other things. The most popular Thai movies are horror shows. Where some *poo-ying* who got killed accidently, died in childbirth, or murdered comes back to haunt the living as a *pee,* lots of blood, guts, gore, and more killings. Thais just eat this stuff up whole! *Ba!*"

I was never big on horror movies.

"Let's slide this rig over to Camp Swampy, show you around."

I later found out that the actual name wasn't 'Camp Swampy,' but 'Whiteside.' If anything had changed since the last time I didn't notice. According to Jake, every week (like clockwork) a dedicated 'Freedom Bird' would come in, pick up more refugees and depart.

There still wasn't much to see. The large tents still sat on salt granular-sized, almost powdery, dazzling white beach sand. The encampment still covered quite a few acres. Small clusters of Vietnamese men, women and children still walked aimless around the compound, or sat on the edges of the tent bases talking to each other, just as they had before. We went over to the 'command tent' near the entrance where a few Green Berets in cammos and a US civilian were lounging and BS-ing. Everyone looked like they were bored to death. We chatted for 30 minutes about nothing in particular and listened to the US civilian loudly, and endlessly, complain that if he'd been a little closer to a powerful Senator's admin assistant, he'd be sitting at a cushy embassy job in Paris doing nothing, and not in some 'hell-hole' job in Thailand doing nothing. He didn't get my sympathy vote. Maybe he didn't like Thai food. But the JCRC Green Berets were unanimous in considering this assignment heaven.

-

**BEACH, GULF OF THAILAND, *U-TAPAO* RTNAB, *CHONBURI/RAYONG* PROVINCES, THAILAND, 1500, 04 JULY 1975.**

I skipped my usual lunch at the O-Club and held my appetite as it was 'Independence Day' today. The base was sponsoring a cook-out/picnic for everyone down on the beach. Jake had arranged for either a rotation of posts, so everyone could be relieved to go down to the beach and grab chow or had plenty of chow shipped out to the men on the posts if they couldn't be relieved in time.

I didn't stay too long, even though it was a picture-postcard perfect day to be beachside. And Jake was waiting for me to come back. MSGT Veeres also gave me a list of chow to bring back.

I met the ranking Base Chaplain and his special guest today, an American Roman Catholic priest, who was running a large orphanage filled with abandoned or unwanted half-Thai/half-American children over near *Sattahip*. I made a fair-sized cash donation to the Father. He said he'd say his prayers for me. With that I departed back to collaborate with chow for the troops on covered paper plates.

After we finished, Jake drove me over to the POL storage area south of the cantonment area, well away from the base proper. There was an ECP with two SP guards. This was the only ECP without RTN or TSG personnel assigned to it. I wasn't sure why. Jake showed me the large flock of white geese moving in a group just frittering around not too far from where we were standing. The large white birds were hunting and pecking the ground for a nice bug lunch.

"The ancient Roman Army used flocks of geese as sentries like we use K-9s now," Jake explained. "They're better than guard dogs. Go ahead and try to get past them."

I started walking slowly towards the closest flock. Immediately all the geese became very agitated and started loudly honking and flapping their long wings in protest at my movement. I stopped. The geese went calm. I very slowly started to take baby steps towards them again. Same results. I could see no one could get within eyeshot of them without being discovered.

I was equally impressed with the geese's efficiency and the history lesson.

-

**INSIDE ARUN'S TAILOR SHOP, DOWNTOWN *SATTAHIP*, *CHONBURI* PROVINCE, THAILAND, 1045, 09 JULY 1975.**

*Nit-Noy* demanded I escort her to *Sattahip* to do shopping for clothes and shoes for me. Her 'actual' twin sister, nick-named *'Jom-Jim'* (or, as the Americans had further nick-named her 'Jimmy') would function as her 'chaperone.' (I assumed her friend *Noy* had to work at the O-Club.)  I couldn't tell the sisters apart. They were 'mirror images' of each other right down to their high-pitched, musical-chiming, continual, delightful laughter at all things. I could see they very close. *Jom-Jim,* ("Call me 'Jimmy'!" she demanded in a sharp, piqued tone of voice and stared at me for a moment in mock-seriousness, before she broke into laughter again shaking her whole frame) was leaving with her American TSGT stepfather for the 'Land of the Big BX' shortly, as he was being re-assigned to another AFB (somewhere Northern-Tier). Their real mother and two younger sisters would go along in tow. *Nit-Noy* wanted to remain behind for some unexplained reason. So, she was officially 'parked' with her maternal aunt and maternal grandmother, both lived in *Sattahip.* I detected some faint, troubling 'vibrations' between the twin sisters over *Nit-Noy's* decision to stay, but I didn't inquire.

This 'shopping' trip downtown was sparked when I walked into the O-Club Snack Bar on my day off last week dressed in my usual civilian attire - basic 'hobo tramp' according to her. She was in total shock, mortified, at seeing me so poorly dressed and would lose endless 'face' if I continued to walk around so attired while it was known I was in her company. This sartorial disaster had to be fixed at once.

I met them outside the Pass & ID Pedestrian Gate. We took a *Baht* bus to downtown *Sattahip.* First stop was 'Arun's Tailor Shop'. His tailor shop had been in *Sattahip* the longest, even before *U-Tapao* opened. First attiring RTN Officers in mufti, then many AF officers were added to his clientele. Both sides of the shop were lined with long bolts of fabric for shirts, dresses and suits:  various weights of silks, tweeds, cottons, wools, blended fabrics, pinstripes, pencil-stripes, plain colors, the 'whole nine yards.' Long mirrors were affixed to the back wall. Mounds of fashionable European clothing catalogs were stacked on the side tables next to the comfortable easy chairs. Arun invited us to look at what style of clothes we wanted and just point. He said his people could perfectly reproduce anything we wished from any catalog.

*Nit-Noy* and Jimmy collaborated on the fabric and style selections, while I played 'manikin dummy' for the exercise. They picked two different types of dark blue English-blended silk-and-wool, single breasted and pinstriped numbers with vests (I'd look like an English earl); one white, raw silk, single-breasted outfit (I'd look like a French priest in French Equatorial Africa) and two different dark gray silk double-breasted, French-cut pencil-striped suits (I'd look like the president of an exclusive Swiss bank). Throw in a dozen various pastels silk and cotton shirts, some flashy fine Thai silk ties, six 'safari suits' in khaki, charcoal gray, white, olive green, dark red wine and black and we were done. Everything would be ready for first fitting tomorrow morning if I wanted them that quickly. Second fitting in two days, if needed, but was recommended. Half payment now, half payment on final delivery. The total came to 'cheap.'

Inside the glass-topped counters were dozens of business cards from the assorted AF clientele who had given their orders and money to Arun's over the past decade. One noteworthy, but silly, comedic business card (there were several variants of the same card) had the officer's name, rank and unit that read:

'Fighter by choice. Lover by profession. Virgins seduced. Small wars started. Big wars ended. Battles fought. Bombs dropped. Rockets fired. Countries liberated. Planes flown. Communist regimes overthrown. Police actions our specialty.' I loved goofy military humor.

We walked past a few shops and crossed over to Mr. Florida's Shoe and Repair Shop on the corner. Mr. 'Florida' had hundreds of examples of shoes he had hand-crafted through the years on display on glass shelves in his large shop. He had large glass windows that faced both streets, so you could openly see his entire inventory. Like Mr. Arun, the girls explained to me, Mr. Florida was a long-time resident of *Sattahip*.

"Stand here, *kup*," Mr. Florida asked me as he laid a piece of butcher paper on the floor. I did. Then he drew a No. 2 pencil from behind his ear and carefully outlined both my feet. Jimmy and *Nit-Noy* selected three styles of fancy footwear. One a stylish black loafer for formal evening wear; an ornate brown wing-tip pair; then a par of chic black lace-ups, also for a semi-formal Sunday garden party. Plus, one set of khaki-colored, lace-up boon dockers. Half down now, half on final delivery. Again 'cheap.'

I looked down at his glass-topped counters. It also held the same type of business cards as Arun's. But there was also a not-very-good imitation, counterfeit USD$20.00 bill without serial numbers stuck underneath. I inquired to its historical provenance. Mr. Florida explained some Thai had actually tried using several on him for payment. When he inspected them closely and complained, the *gigolo* ran off leaving them behind. He kept one on display as a souvenir.

"I'd love to get one someday," I remarked.

Mr. Florida went into the back of his shop; came out with one of the counterfeit twenties and handed it to me. I was so happy that I paid him with an authentic USD$20.00 for it.

-

**BETWEEN 'C' AND 'D' AVENUES, 8TH STREET, OUTSIDE OF BOQ #1, ROOM #6, *U-TAPAO* RTNAB, *CHONBURI/RAYONG* PROVINCES, THAILAND, 2130, 09 JULY 1975.**

I decided to write some long-overdue letters to family and friends after my return from *Sattahip*. The day had been typical rainy season weather: partly cloudy with alternating periods of quickly forming, intense thundershowers letting loose for about 20 minutes, then clearing into bright sunshine. And rapidly accumulating rainclouds started the cycle all over again. But the very second I got back under the BOQ overhang from an early dinner at the O-Club the long-accumulating, menacing-looking, heavy black cloud ceiling abruptly lowered, completely shutting off the quickly fading sunset light. It became very dark. (I had sprinted hard to beat the impending downpour.) The wind gusted strongly then suddenly an intense tropical deluge commenced. It started pouring walls of water. I decided to stay in the room and get back into some long-delayed, barely started Len Deighton and Tony Hillerman novels.

I finally took a break and decided on a mid-evening shower. I whipped a towel around my waist, grabbed my toilet kit, slipped into shower sandals, and walked outside onto the walkway. It was very cool outside, actually this side of chilly. I walked down to the end of the BOQ to peek around the corner and see how bad the flooding was. It had kept up for three hours straight. The deep drainage canals were long past satiation, with the water level continuing to rise. The flood was already lapping over the whole roadway by almost a foot and there were no signs of letting up.

If this kept on it was going to make the Great Deluge of Noah's Ark fame look like a brief, passing mid-western sun shower. The incessant hard-driven downpour ricocheted off of the grass outside to knee-level. Thunder cracks and echoes were almost continuous and nearly deafening, with strong gusts of winds adding to the background decibels. Lightning flashes could occasionally be seen. I turned and walked about halfway down the passageway to the showers. A tiny green-red-purple splotched frog, the size of half my little fingernail, sat right in the middle, blocking my path.

I bent over, stared at it and said: "Move frog."

It sat there and ignored me, of course.

I bent over again and repeated: "MOVE FROG!"

It just sat there, continuing to puff its little gills, serenely enjoying the rainfall and the cool evening.

I tried a third time.

Nothing. Either I didn't exist to the tiny frog, or it was simply ignoring me. I walked around it and went for my shower. "Stupid frog!" I muttered.

The next afternoon at lunch I told *Nit-Noy* about the stupid little frog. She instantly became *mo-ho mach-mach* with me.

"Is *Ung-ang!*" she petulantly exclaimed. (Almost yelling at me - a first, raising her voice loudly.) "No 'flog' anyway! Thai *Ung-angs* no stu-pid, only *farangs* very stu-pid! *Ung-angs* no unner-stan' English, they Thai!

You talk to them in Thai, they unner-stan' you!" "Stu-pid *farangs!!*" she added with final emphasis.

Then *Nit-Noy* explained what I had to say to the *Ung-ang* the next time we met. Two nights later after I finished work it was exactly the same situation. I was on my way for a shower when the same frog - sorry, *Ung-ang,* or his twin brother, was sitting in the same place. I bent over and said:

"*By-lay-o!*"

The *Ung-ang* hopped off into the trimmed grass.

\-

## MR. FLORIDA'S SHOE AND REPAIR SHOP, DOWNTOWN *SATTAHIP, CHONBURI* PROVINCE, THAILAND, 1045, 16 JULY 1975.

*Nit-Noy, Noy* and I were out the door early even though it was my day off again. I tried on all the clothes and shirts, now with pins and rough, loose stitches holding the material together. Mr. Arun made a few minor fitting adjustments, using different colored chalk marks on most of the clothes. He said they would be ready for second fitting any time after tomorrow morning. They all made me feel like a million dollars when I eyed myself in the mirror. Growing up back in Danbury, CT, every piece of clothing I ever owned were 'hand-me-downs,' even through college. I felt funny, like I was a new person inside. Maybe they're right: 'Clothes make the man.'

Mr. Florida's shoes were all very easy to slip into. Actually, a bit too easy. They loosely hung on my feet but were still quite comfortable. I explained to both girls that in the US shoes came 'tight-fitted,' but after a few days wear the seams, or stitching, gave somewhat, so the shoes fit comfortably. But you had to go through some discomfort to have them fit properly. The girls waved that explanation away for some unknown reason.

Suddenly *Nit-Noy* grabbed each shoe in turn and bit them lightly on the back opening. I stared in amazement.

"Why did you do that?" I asked her.

Her explanation was simplicity itself.

"I bite them before they bite you!"

Well, that was true. I learned another old Thai tradition.

I asked the girls if there was a military patch shop in town. They were for an old friend who collected Thai-based AF bomber, tanker and fighter unit patches. I promised if I ever got over here, I'd see what I could find. The girls said in unison: *"Samporn Pradit's!"*

*'Samporn Pradit's'* turned out to be in an old, small, wooden shop house not far away. It had RTN uniforms and USAF patches and insignia on open display. But there were also silly/funny souvenir patches and insignia for sale. They had many examples of AF unit patches, many from units previously stationed at *U-Tapao* and then re-numbered, transferred or inactivated, like I knew the 8524th SW was re-numbered the 703rd SW. There were patches for former major AF operations in Southeast Asia: 'Arc Light,' 'Frequent Wind,' 'Eagle Pull,' 'Linebacker I and II' and others. They had sewn-on name patches in blue and white, O.D. and cammo; sew-on 'USAF' patches for uniform shirts in the same colors; embroidered enlisted stripes for Class 'A's,' O.D. and camo uniforms, plus every different type of 'special quals,' 'authorized,' and 'semi-authorized' sew-on from 'SAC Master Mechanic,' through 'B-52-100 Missions' and 'Command Pilot wings,' to 'SP badges' and cloth sew-on officer's ranks from 2LT to LTGEN in blue and white, O.D. and cammo patterns.

But the comedy or souvenir patches were the ones I enjoyed looking at most: '*U-Tapao* RTNB-103rd FMS: '69-'71: Make Love, Not War'; '100 Missions in a *Baht* bus'; Snoopy as the Red Baron flying his dog house while giving 'Jane Fonda' the finger (another one had Snoopy flipping-the-bird at 'Jane Fonda' AND 'Tom Hayden'); AF SGT stripes with each alternating stripe in red-white-and-blue; 'OFFICIAL SEA WAR GAMES PARTICIPANT: 1972-73'; a marijuana plant over the peace symbol; a large patch showing SGT Barry Sadler 'singing': '100 Tons They'll Load Today, To Save The Ass Of A Green Beret' (to the implied tune of his 'The Ballad of the Green Beret'); 'Bury Me Face Down So The World Can Kiss My Ass

When I'm Dead!'; 'Draft Beer/Not Students'; 'When The Power of Love Overcomes The Love of Power, Vietnam Will Know Peace,' with many of them irreverent, risqué, hilarious, rude, crude, lewd, and very anti-war. I had already seen them on many of the bags, windbreakers, backpacks, shirts, hats and anywhere else you could sew a patch onto worn by many people around the base.

\-

## HEADING EAST ON NATIONAL HIGHWAY #3, 'NEWLAND' /'FREELAND' AREA, *RAYONG* PROVINCE, THAILAND, 1900, 16 JULY 1975.

It was early evening, and the last of the sun's rays were quickly fading. Dentonville, Guillory and I flagged down a passing *Baht* bus at the roadside's edge, in front of the Pass & ID Parking Lot and climbed in. It was my first night 'off base.' So, I was both pumped with excitement and anticipation to see what was out there. I had to bend down in the long, plastic-covered, padded bench seat in the back to look out at the rapidly passing landscape.

We sped east along the main highway, occasionally picking up and dropping off passengers. The roadway paralleled the base fence for some kilos as the land slightly, but steadily, rose as we travelled eastwards, then the road started sloping downwards as we passed Buddha Mountain and the *wat* below it. The outskirts of a small town started to appear.

"*Ban Chang,*" shouted Dentonville over the vehicle noise. "A lot of people from the base have hooches, bungalows, or houses here. Some people like living off-base, even if they've got a room in the BEQ or BOQ."

I nodded.

'Newland' and 'Freeland' were supposedly built by RED HORSE several years ago after they cleaned up the area right in front of the Main Gate," added Guillory.

Past the gaily lit little town, the landscape turned jungle again, with a few scattered houses and small roadside shops. Maybe 20 minutes later Dentonville pushed an electrical switch in the center of the inside roof. You could hear a sharp electrical buzz from inside the driver's cab. The *Baht* bus quickly slowed down and stopped along the side of the road. We exited one by one. Dentonville walked back to the front cab and handed the driver some coins through the open window.

He turned, smiled, and said: 'Welcome to Newland!'

We crossed the highway and walked beneath an impressive, white-painted concrete lintel over a side road, with Thai-like stylized lions statues placed on top of the two pillars holding it aloft. It had the appearance of belonging to a temple complex entrance than to a long row of beer bars, dives, and discos. There was a sign being held up by the pillars over the roadway, also in white, that proclaimed: 'WELCOME TO NEWLAND' written in English. I assumed the lettering in Thai to the left on the pillar was a translation of the same thing. Dentonville explained 'Freeland' was on the other side of the highway close by.

As we walked over to what appeared to be the largest disco there, I noticed there were other similar, but smaller, 'clubs' along both sides of the road. A large white 'Playboy' logo was painted on the side of the building we were heading into. It was very close to where we had alighted. Next door was a smaller, black octagonal-shaped building, obviously another noisy, lively 'watering hole.' James Brown was screaming out a song at the top of his lungs from inside the wide-open double doors. The assorted *poo-yings* that were lounging outside who ranged from medium chocolate to very dark-skin had assorted body sizes and heights, with most of them sporting very large (some outrageously out-sized), teased-out, frizzy Afros.

"A popular club for Black airmen, Sport," said Guillory.

We sauntered inside the 'Playboy Club.' The place was as cavernous as a large high school gym. The D.J. had 'We Gotta Get out of This Place' by Eric Burton and the Animals rocking the building.

Dentonville turned and shouted into my ear.

"Supposedly the most popular request at the NCO Club."

I nodded.

We looked through the darkness for a table with enough empty seats for six people. In the middle of the place there was a wooden dance floor lighted from above with spotlights. Maybe 30 girls were on the floor either dancing in pairs or by themselves. There must have been at least 100 more *poo-yings* sitting idly by with bored-to-tears looks on their faces. There were many different types, but almost all of them wore simple party dresses. All were made-up, well-coifed and appeared well-scrubbed. Since it was still fairly early, we were only GIs in the place. We ordered *Singhas* all around and started nursing them slowly.

A well-dressed older woman, with a bright smile and easy manner, walked over and spoke to Dentonville over the throbbing music.

"Wat' you like, *ka?* All per'tee lay-dee' do every-ting'!"

"*Kup khun mai, kup,*" Dentonville replied. "We'll just look for right now."

The Club's 'Mama-san' came back to periodically check with us if we wanted to make a 'selection' out of her 'stable' for tonight's 'temporary companionship.'

Dentonville just told her: "*Mai pen lai, kup.*"

We'd wait to see how things turned out.

Occasionally some of the girls breezed over, perhaps out of curiosity, interest, or sheer boredom, and spoke to Dentonville:

"You buy me one air-conditioned helicopter or one free drink?"

"I lub' you *mach-mach* no-sheet on payday!"

"No money, no honey, no horny!"

"You fren' 'cherry boy'? You fren' 'birthday boy'?"

"You like 'butter-fry' *mach-mach?*"

"We do short-time 'boom-boom' my bungalow?"

"You need 'num-bah' one *tee-lock* too-nigh'?"

"You want per-nent goo' fren'?"

"You no like 'lay-dee'? You like young boy? You like *ka-toey?*"

We sat, drank, and watched the girls dancing and singing along with the songs.

"Yel-low lee-ber, yel-low lee-ber, ees' een' my mind an' een' my eye'. . ."

"We ga' ta' git' out ta' thees' place eef' eet's tha' las' ting' we ev'ah do. . .."

"Do a lee-tul' dance, make a lee-tul' luv,' geet' dow' to-night. . .."

It finally turned late. I ultimately decided to pass on all the wonderful offers of 'temporary companionship.' 'T.S.O.P.' by MFSB thumped away as our departure song.

I was basically 'seeing' *Nit-Noy*. I didn't want to screw up that 'budding' relationship. Dentonville made his 'selection' (she couldn't have been much over 15 (seriously); pure robbing-the-cradle-jailbait). He shot out the double doorway with his 'selection-for-the-evening.' That left Guillory and me to ride the *Baht* bus back to the base, feeling no pain.

"My wife's coming in next week, she's a nurse getting assigned to the base hospital," he explained. "Don't want to bring a little 'surprise' home this late in the game. She'd totally kill me, sport." I thought back to his previous comment once: "Everyone here has a girlfriend, and the chaplains were strongly thinking about it."

I said I understood. *Nit-Noy* would kill me too; if she found out I had taken one of the *poo-yings* somewhere for a 'short-time.' I had been told too many times there were no secrets in Thailand.

-

**CORNER OF 'C' AVENUE AND 3RD STREET, OPERATIONS OFFICER'S OFFICE, 365th SPS HQ UNIT, *U-TAPAO* RTNAB, *CHONBURI/RAYONG* PROVINCES, THAILAND, 1500, 17 JULY 1975.**

I was sitting in front of CAPT Dentonville. His desk and office were cleared of all personal items, but the mountainous piles of paperwork, files, reports, evaluations, written safety warnings, magazines, badly-needed-to-be-updated-last-year AFRs and AFMs plus the rest of it seemed untouched (except for accumulating more dust and cobwebs) since the first time I walked in there six weeks ago. Dentonville was airlifting out in two more days on the 'Freedom Bird' for his new assignment as Ops Officer at Lackland AFB. A huge base, lots of high 'vis,' tons of important people passing through there - a great assignment. I imagined he'd make MAJ off of it for sure. He was happy. I was happy for him.

"Here's your LOE, 1LT Legere. You won't be up for your OER until the end of February, so this will hold you over in the interim. Let me know if you have any problems with it. Sign it after you read it."

I read it. Dentonville had given me a very good LOE. In fact, outstanding. Short, sweet, to-the-point, well-written, and full of praise. I signed it and thanked him.

"Thank yourself. You did all the hard work, and you did a damn good job in a short amount of time. How're things going with the turn-over from Jake?"

To my knowledge Dentonville had never visited Swing Shift, never went into CSC, never checked the LE desk and never went out on a post check. In fact, I was hard pressed to see what he'd done while he was there. In Jake's mind, Dentonville was as useless as a fifth wheel on a car, or as useful as a rubber crutch in a swamp. Maybe Dentonville had some hidden or secret talent no one knew about (or saw) out on the shifts. But I was sure he'd draw either an MSM or a BSM (without the 'V') for an end-of-tour award, unless he really screwed-up - then he'd just rate an AFCM for just showing up at his desk.

"Great - Jake's been showing me all the ropes CAPT. I've learned more from him in one month than a year anywhere."

"Good! Jake and I don't see eye-to-eye on lots of stuff, but I never said he wasn't a good officer or Shift Supervisor. He and I just do business differently. Finally, I'm down to one day and a bag-drag; one day and a wake-up! I'm so damn 'short,' I'm 'next!' This whole place gave me a big headache, but I'm going out the door knowing I screwed almost every *poo-ying* working over in the O-Club - all but three of them."

I had heard Dentonville was a 'major-league pussy-hound' from more than a few officers. But this place was like being a kid in a huge candy story with a million dollars. So many women, so little time. For a lot of guys, I could guarantee it was a race to see if they'd either get completely exhausted or completely exhaust their whole paycheck first by the end of every month. I wondered which three *poo-yings* at the O-Club he didn't 'butterfly' with. It was none of my business.

"OK, 1LT Legere, good luck, and if I don't see you again, you enjoy your time on base. Maybe you can break my record at the O-Club!"

I passed along my best wishes for a safe flight back home and on his new assignment. Then I stood up, saluted, and departed.

-

**AVENUE 'C' AND 1ST STREET, OFFICE OF THE COMMANDER-SECURITY, PASS & ID BUILDING, MAIN GATE, RTN AIR WING, *U-TAPAO* RTNAB, *CHONBURI/RAYONG* PROVINCES, THAILAND, 1510, 20 JULY 1975.**

As I promised Jake, I took the jeep every week for a spin and went down to see the Thai Head of Base Security in his office to pay him a 'courtesy call.' He was always happy to see me. We chatted about inconsequential personal stuff, base events in general, Thailand, and the security situation on base in particular. Without giving anything away, I learned a lot from him, more than I expected. But I'm sure we didn't tell each other anything major (or dramatic) that we didn't already know beforehand about the base. I always asked him if I could do anything for him, like a gift of any bottle of whiskey he cared for out of the Class VI store or a tape cassette recorder out of the BX. He always graciously refused any offer of 'presents.' I strongly suspected he had a whole huge warehouse full of expensive, imported bottles of Scotch whiskey stashed somewhere and was probably a wholesale dealer in electronic recording and playing devices on the side.

"Maybe I can do a favor for you, 1LT Legere," he said.

"OK, sir" I replied. "I'm always happy to owe you a favor in return."

He heartedly laughed at that one and said:

"I know you have two 'special friends' now both working on base. Perhaps I can arrange some passes for them to enter and exit without the usual formalities through Pass & ID."

Anyone who entered the base was subject to search of all their possessions, and (if there was something amiss) their person. Lines tended to be long, especially in the mornings, and the exchange badge system also tended to take some time at the window, depending on how quickly (or efficiently) the people did their jobs (Quickly?: No; Efficiently?: Yes. The Pass & ID people were very precise and methodical in their badge security, issue, and retrievals from all reports). Any complication, no matter how slight and the person was/were simply denied access. As the counter staff didn't have time to straighten out these 'complications' right then and there, the person in question had to wait until they got less busy to look into the problem.

However, I'd heard (through the SP 'grapevine') that the RTN Security Office rarely issued what were, in effect, highly coveted (very exclusive) 'VIP Badges.' These badges (or passes) immediately granted the holder access to the base and exempted them from any inspection of belongings and persons. If the recipient was a *poo-ying* then this VIP badge was called a *Tee-Lock* Pass. Not even the several SAC Wing Commanders, the AF Base Commander, the CSG Commander, and every other permanently assigned and tenant squadron and organizational commander on the base (and their girlfriends) could muster one single 'VIP' (or *Tee-Lock*) Pass among themselves.

"That's very kind of you to offer. I would greatly appreciate that very much. Thank you. I owe you two big favors now."

He laughed loudly at my offer of some 'future' favors to be returned and said: "Just have your 'friends' come down to personally see me at any time tomorrow. I'll see they're taken care of." He smiled.

"*Kop khun mach, kup*, CDR," I replied. "Ah, I do have one more favor to ask of you, if it can be done, sir. I don't know."

"Please go ahead and ask, 1LT Legere. If it can be done, I will do it for you."

"Is it possible the RTN or Royal Thai government can start awarding the TSG 'Wings' again?"

-

## ROYAL JEWELRY SHOP, DOWNTOWN *SATTAHIP*, *CHONBURI* PROVINCE, THAILAND, 1400, 23 JULY 1975.

*Nit-Noy* and *Noy* accompanied me (or should I say I accompanied them) to *Sattahip* on our days off. The ladies were very accommodating in switching their off days for me. The AF O-Club was nowhere near as busy, as opposed to when the 'Big War' was going on around-the-clock every day of the week. As the base was relatively quiet these days, that change of days off was easy to arrange. So, every free day usually found us all down in *Sattahip*. We were doing mainly clothes buying for me (and them, as a thanks) and other minor shopping, like post cards and nick-knacks to send home. Lunch was always on me.

I'd promised family I'd get them jewelry while I was here. I'd heard enough stories about the great deals to be had when I was back at Maxwell. So, this trip would be slightly different in we were buying some things for others and not just clothes or shoes for myself. *Nit-Noy* and *Noy* suggested the Royal Jewelry Store was the first place to stop and shop.

We strolled through the door. The owner was very happy to see both girls again (they all hugged like long lost 'sisters') and to meet me. At first glance she was a refined, demure, elegantly dressed, highly intelligent, smaller, older woman who spoke fluent English. I got the impression she was well-travelled, had lived overseas a while and was quite cultured from her mannerisms and demeanor. She was most gracious in her explanations of what jewelry and other items in her shop that were available.

The owner also showed me many jewelry catalogs of other items she could re-produce should I desire something not in her shop. However, most surprising was she didn't use any 'sell' in her technique. She never pushed (like many other merchants down in *Sattahip*) to buy something. I looked through the multiple glass-topped display cases at a dazzling array of every different type of gem and piece of jewelry placed in either individual felt-covered boxes or mounted on felt trays. The owner was very proud of her collection and her reputation for quality service and quality goods (as later explained to me by the girls). She said that all the other shops would not let you exchange any goods once carried out the door. But she would guarantee any piece of jewelry in her shop with a full cash refund at any time, now or in the future, no questions asked. I found that gratifying, reassuring, and unique. However, I knew *Nit-Noy* and *Noy* would have never brought me into any establishment they didn't trust themselves.

The owner took her time in explaining the different gemstones as she brought out examples of finished pieces. blue and black 'star' sapphires (explaining how to look for what a high-quality, very precisely six-pointed 'star' in the middle of the gem looks like and then compared it to less expensive, slightly more blurry, inferior examples). Then different colored sapphires, Tiger's eyes, emeralds, rubies and diamonds plus the semi-precious stones such as amethysts, turquoises, topazes, garnets and opals. She explained about all the colors that Jade has (green was the most popular, red was second, white, black, and brown rarely sold). She mentioned the Chinese, as did some Thais, considered green Jade very lucky. There were white gold, yellow gold and platinum settings all available. She explained Thais never wore anything less than pure (24k) gold, or gold slightly strengthened by a nickel or a nickel-alloy, in effect 23k gold. They considered anything less to be 'unlucky,' or gold sold to 'tourists,' like 14k or 18k. She said all the Thais would turn their noses up at it.

I was dazzled at the selection. I told the owner I wasn't able to buy anything today, but I promised I would soon return (after payday). She smiled graciously, even though I had taken up so much of her time.

-

**BETWEEN 'C' AND 'D' AVENUES, 8TH STREET, PARKING LOT, OUTSIDE BOQ #1, *U-TAPAO* RTNAB, *CHONBURI/ RAYONG* PROVINCES, THAILAND, 1245, 24 JULY 1975.**

1LT 'Tom' Crowley picked-up me in the BOQ parking lot to drive me to work.

"Favor to ask you," he asked as soon as I got settled into the jeep.

"Shoot."

"My wife's flying into Thailand next week. But I don't want to stick her in the Swan Lake Hotel and blow bucks on a room for two weeks. And I don't want to take a taxi to *Pattaya* Beach roundtrip every day."

I knew dependents (meaning wives and/or families) were not authorized for 'command-sponsored,' or PCS, moves to accompany their husbands here, especially into what was still technically considered a 'war zone' even though South Vietnam, Laos and Cambodia had already fallen to the Communists. Also there was no base housing for them anyway. Everyone was considered a 'Geographic Bachelor.' Most wives flew into *Bangkok*, but they came at their own expense and their husbands took leave to meet them. The rest of the wives either went to *Pattaya* Beach, or their husbands met them in places like Hawaii, Hong Kong, the Philippines, or Japan.

"What do you want me to do?"

"I'd like to swap rooms with you for two weeks while my wife's here. Then I can stay with her every night. I got a roommate - he's a great guy, very quiet - but you don't. After she flies back stateside, we'll swap rooms again, OK?"

I knew some of the officers in the BOQs were stacked two to a room. The other officer was bunked in a wooden walk-up 'loft' above. I'd been lucky to get a single room.

"Sure, I don't care. When?"

"Thanks a lot! That's great! Next Friday? If it's OK with you."

"Sure. I'll pull my stuff out by next Thursday morning."

-

**CORNER OF 'A' AVENUE AND 9TH STREET, SHIFT SUPERVISOR'S OFFICE, CSC, 365th SPS, *U-TAPAO* RTNAB, *CHONBURI/RAYONG* PROVINCES, THAILAND, 1400, 25 JULY 1975.**

Guillory also asked me for a big favor.

"Sport, I need a big favor. I get relieved at 1400, but my wife at the hospital doesn't get off until 1700. It's difficult for her to catch a ride home. Can you swing by, get her and drop her off at the trailer?"

"Sure thing, CAPT. Happy to do it."

"Thanks, sport. That'd be great!"

So, it became a regular daily occurrence for me to collect CAPT/Mrs. Guillory from the Hospital Emergency Room entrance at 1700 sharp, five days/week. Guillory had another officer handle pick-up-and-delivery on day six (my day off) and the seventh day she was off duty.

-

**CORNER OF 'C' AVENUE AND 3RD STREET, OPERATIONS OFFICER'S OFFICE, 365TH SPS HQs UNIT, *U-TAPAO* RTNAB, *CHONBURI/RAYONG* PROVINCES, THAILAND, 1530, 25 JULY 75.**

Jake and I were sitting in the Ops Officer's office. CAPT A. Van den Dardener, Dentonville's replacement, was set up and ready for business. He arrived a week after Dentonville's departure for Lackland, so there was no 'formal' turn-over. At first impression, Van den Dardener exuded competence, self-confidence, some fair intelligence and a self-assurance that bordered on arrogance. He was a shade taller than small, not out-of-shape and looked like he was making his mind up whether to take you into his little

114

'personal' tight circle of friends ('personal posse' or 'ass-kissing sycophants'), or permanently exclude you from membership. Usually when it comes down to those types of decisions I never get included. I'd say he was a senior CAPT like Dentonville, probably up for B-T-Z MAJ in the next go-around, if he wasn't already in the Primary Zone for selection now.

I could have taken bets in some quarters on Dentonville being nominated for one of the worst Ops Officers in the business. But at least we HAD an Ops Officer, no matter how ineffective or figurehead-like. That counted for something. At least some things were getting done administratively and operationally as the organization lurched forward in fits and starts under his reign. There was not a way to avoid forward movement. But with Dentonville's departure the whole SPS operations organization immediately ground to a screeching halt, and with it, critical shift operational support. Nothing was getting done, total chaos abounded that no one, no matter how much assumed 'authority' or 'experience' they could muster on their own, could untangle or solve. So, Van der Dardener's arrival was welcome, and well-anticipated, even if he turned out to be nothing more than a replacement figurehead.

Jake gave Van den Dardener a detailed briefing on Swings, the SPS in general, the current overall base security situation, the TSG problems, relations with RTN Security and the on-going, chronic thievery. I didn't say anything. Van den Dardener took it all in without commentary.

"I broke-up a large SP theft ring when I was in Guam," he started in, smiling at the recollection. "They were stealing everything and moving it out the gate at night. The whole damn squadron was in on it. Finally busted them all. I noticed they were all wearing expensive hand-made Bostonian shoes when they were off-duty. The footwear was way, way past the budgets of the AMNs and A1Cs."

Jake and I didn't comment, we only nodded. But we both knew no one in the SPS had any pricy 'Bostonian wing-tips' collecting dust in their closets, under their bunks, or anywhere else. We had a tight group of people on Swings. And we also kept close tabs on what was happening with them and all the events on base. I knew the other two shifts were the same. So that scenario was out.

However, who-the-hell-knew what the Thais had stuffed in their off-base closets? We could only guess. But we'd a pretty damn good idea whatever was in there was all marked 'USAF' and 'US government' property. Jake's and my 'war' with the Thai *gigolos* would go on. We would not quit. It was only a matter of time to see if Van den Dardener would climb on-board to help us or not.

"OK," Van den Dardener finally said. "Thanks for the briefing. That's all."

We stood up, saluted, walked out and went back on roving patrol again.

-

## CORNER OF 'C' AVENUE AND 3RD STREET, OPERATIONS OFFICER'S OFFICE, 365TH SPS HQs UNIT, *U-TAPAO* RTNAB, *CHONBURI/RAYONG* PROVINCES, THAILAND, 1500, 26 JULY 75.

I wasn't supposed to 'formally' relieve Jake of Swing Shift until one week prior to his PCS-ing out so he could pack his stuff and take care of business to clear the base. Although I'd already been running Swings 'de facto' for at least two weeks prior, with Jake looking over my shoulder and really doing nothing, I felt I could handle the load. I told him I'd cover for him for his last two weeks. If I had any problems, I'd contact him for help. But I knew I had everything covered after a great turn-over and the intensive training Jake had given me.

I also knew Jake wanted to kick-up-his-heels, go out and have some fun out in town. I'm sure he had (long-ago) packed. He was just waiting for the 'Freedom Bird' to wing him back to the 'Land of the Big BX' and his new assignment. Jake couldn't wait to leave. So, I said tonight was his last day on shift.

I doubted anyone would come looking for him. And if they did, I'd simply say it was his 'day off.' The back office never paid any attention to us before. And I didn't see them suddenly getting interested at this late date. With Dentonville already a fond memory, plus Shellenbarger rarely doing post checks, I knew we'd be OK in Jake having an extra, well-deserved, week off.

Jake just said: "Fourteen days and a wake-up."

Later that afternoon a troubling problem arose. I'd always taken the time to listen to the troops and their complaints or problems, so had Jake. He was well-attuned to problems they might have and did his best to fix them quickly, hence Jake's continued popularity. But this problem had seemingly flown under the 'radar scope' of both of us and MSGT Veeres.

The Black troops detailed post assignment 'favoritism.' In that certain posts, like the more 'exciting' riding patrols, almost always went to 'Whites.' And the more 'boring' static posts, like ECPs, bunkers, towers and checkpoints, almost always went to 'Blacks' and some 'Hispanics.' I'd never even paid any attention to post assignments or rotations, nor had Jake or Veeres to my knowledge. We all naturally assumed the SGT in charge of all the post assignments had been totally impartial. Apparently, he hadn't. And he was also 'White.'

I continued my discreet inquiries about the post assignments and rotations on the Shift. Everyone confirmed the 'favoritism.' But they also told me they didn't want to trouble Jake about it either. They felt he had enough on his plate already in fighting for their benefit and didn't want to cause any more internal problems for him, not that we had many. Maybe that was why Jake didn't put his foot down more on the *DAP* delay problem in the weapons issue line. But the post rotation problem was causing some low, smoldering resentment among the Black and Hispanic troops. That issue needed to be immediately addressed.

The man in question was a SGT. He also handled the entire Shift's administrative paperwork too. I asked him about the shift's post rotations and assignments and how they were made. Then I explained the concerns of the troops.

"They could have asked me!" he exclaimed. "Anyone could come to me for a 'special assignment' like a riding post. The Blacks just didn't, the White guys did!" I exhaled in slight exasperation, holding in my temper.

An easy problem to fix. We had no other major or pressing problems afterwards, or so I was told.

-

**TEMPLE GROUNDS, *SATTAHIP* MAIN BUDDHIST *WAT* COMPLEX, DOWNTOWN *SATTAHIP*, *CHONBURI* PROVINCE, THAILAND, 0900, 30 JULY 1975.**

*Nit-Noy* and I talked, as we did every day at the Snack Bar. Then on the one day we both had off, we took a *Baht* bus somewhere, usually to downtown *Sattahip*. Normally *Noy* had been accompanying us as the 'chaperone.' But today she couldn't. So we rode the *Baht* bus by ourselves.

We mostly talked about her and her family, her life, her dreams, her past, the present - anything, but never her future. I never felt there was much of anything of interest to talk about myself. So I never really brought anything up on my end, a few biographical facts. There was nothing much to tell her honestly. But *Nit-Noy* was a little 'magpie.' Endlessly talking about everything under the sun, a constant stream of chatter and stories; always with a sweet laugh at the end of every other sentence. Her whole body jiggled from the high sing-song peals of giggling. We didn't have a lot of time today, as she said she had other things to do in the afternoon. So, we made the best of what time we had.

I was hopelessly hooked. I knew it. I just hoped she knew it too. I was also just as happy to listen as she was to talk.

Today *Nit-Noy* talked about how very successful her twin sister, Jimmy, was. She once served as the principal dancer in the Royal Thai Classical Dance Troupe at the National Theater in Bangkok not far from the Grand Palace. She told me that Jimmy was a graduate of the Royal Thai Dramatic Arts College and number one in her class. A stand-out student from the first day she stepped onto campus. She said Jimmy danced individually; in smaller groups of four, eight and twelve, and with the whole troupe with 'command performances' for everyone from his Majesty, the King, the whole Royal Family; all the current and former Prime Ministers, plus other important government and ministerial officials; all the Royal Thai Army, Navy and Air Force commanders; foreign diplomats and other noteworthy, important foreign visitors to the Kingdom; ambassadors and minister plenipotentiaries down to regular paying audiences.

*Nit-Noy* explained Jimmy started dancing in front of the TV along with the dancers she saw at the ripe old age of four and never stopped. She said that Jimmy had trained *Nit-Noy* and her other two sisters to do a number of simple dance numbers to perform at exclusive 'private parties,' usually sponsored by powerful, influential (meaning rich) businessmen and other national leaders. These were always held in restaurants or other large venues. It also included dancing at birthday and engagement parties, graduations, and weddings, plus they always performed on important national and religious holidays. These venues were good sources of extra income for the family. *Nit-Noy* said that she and her sisters had to master all 108 hand and arm gestures precisely (these expressed different ideas and words) to be able to classically dance. She explained it had taken many months of intensive hard work and endless practice to perfectly master the high art form. Classical dancing was the essence of Thai culture. She also said it was a great honor to be able to perform.

*Nit-Noy* expressed no future 'ambitions' about anything. She explained she and her two youngest sisters all finished high school and had college classes in *Bangkok.* But they ended their studies when their mother got re-married to her USAF stepfather. Her mother owned and operated the most popular beauty salon in *Sattahip* until recently. So, she and her mother were totally 'hard-wired in' to the RTN, Army and AF bases (*Sattahip, Samae San or U-Tapao*) 'gossip' cross-cutting all ways, since her place was frequently attended by all the important 'ladies' and appointments were booked weeks in advance. Another beauty salon in *Ban Chang,* was the second most popular venue.

*Nit-Noy* said her family had frowned upon her working in the O-Club Snack Bar, but they didn't (and probably couldn't) stop her. (I soon found out that no one could once she had made her mind up about something. She dug in her cute little heels and refused to be budged until she got her way in the end.)

*Nit-Noy* had a very strong will when she chose to exercise it (which was frequently). She explained anyone taking a job on base was considered 'low-class' by most Thais. But she didn't care. She was going to do whatever she liked. It apparently beat hanging around her aunt's house all day, or hanging around in *Sattahip,* doing nothing and being bored. She said she didn't want to go with her family to the US, or at least not yet. She didn't say why. I didn't press the issue.

I got the general impression that Jimmy was the 'favorite' in the family over her three sisters, her being the 'picture perfect' example of a dutiful 'eldest' daughter. According to *Nit-Noy,* Jimmy never made any mistakes or goof-ups. But *Nit-Noy* implied she had and didn't care who knew about it, or how they reacted to it, including her whole family.

Up to now *Nit-Noy* had also given me the impression she was the 'wild one' in the family: uncontrollable, strong-willed, and independently minded, with a devil-may-care attitude, petulant (when necessary) just to get her own way. She was probably the mirror opposite of, or counterpoint to, her twin sister, all things considered.

She led me to the *wat* across the sandy courtyard from the bench (under a large shady tree) we'd been sitting on and talking. She said the day was *lawn mach-mach!* The complex was flooded with bright sunlight. It was so hot even the Thais were sweating. We removed our shoes and left them at the *wat* entrance. Walking up the short flight of wooden steps I could see the large brass statue of Buddha (polished to the consistency of bright gold) sitting cross-legged and serenely contemplating bliss into eternity. We entered the quietness and coolness of the well-shaded interior.

*Nit-Noy* bought us two packets of items that included three maroon-colored incense sticks, one small, thin yellow candle, three small squares of rough paper that held smaller squares of gold foil and one orchid, all wrapped tightly together with a red rubber band.

She had me light my candle in a brass oil lamp and place it in a long brass candle holder with 30 similar candles; a few were still lit, but most were extinguished or had melted. The holder was in front of the Buddha statue. Then she lit and placed hers. Next, she placed her flower in a pot. I did the same thing. She lit the sticks of incense from one candle, and then sat on the wooden floor with her feet pointed behind her. Holding the incense sticks in her palms joined for prayer, she closed her eyes, bowed her head and wordless mouthed something. I followed her every move. Then she arose and placed each small square of gold foil on the head and shoulders of another small Buddha statue on the side there for that purpose.

*Nit-Noy* reached down for a cup on the floor near her. It was formed from large bamboo pole. The cup was painted dark red, with perhaps 30 black 'chop-sticks' inside with a Thai number painted in white on each flattened end. She held the cup up to her forehead, mouthing more silent prayers, then gently shook it back and forth at chest level. Eventually one of the chopsticks slowly moved up higher and fell out. She looked at the number, went to a side display rack of 30 rough brown-paper sheets and selected one.

"My fortune," she said.

"Good or bad?" I asked. She read the print printing and smiled.

"So-so!" she merrily laughed.

I did the same thing. I handed her my chopstick. She went to the board for my number and retrieved it. I asked her what my fortune was.

She looked and said: "So-so!"

We both laughed. She said both foretold we would both have very good luck in the future. I only wished it were so. I asked her what she prayed for. She said: "Happiness." Although she didn't ask me what I had prayed for, I was ready to say: "Your happiness." Then we said our good-byes. I took a *Baht* bus back to *U-Tapao*.

-

**BETWEEN 'E' AND 'F' AVENUES, 11<sup>TH</sup> STREET, OUTSIDE THE USO, *U-TAPAO* RTNAB, *CHONBURI/RAYONG* PROVINCES, THAILAND, 1615, 30 JULY 1975.**

I was walking back from the USO after getting some soft ice cream, when I met an older, not unattractive, fairly shapely Thai lady coming from the other direction. I could see she was just as perky, lively, and outgoing as she was happy to see me. I could also see as we got closer that her 'odometer' had turned over more than a few times, but she still had a lot of good 'tread life' left on her. I politely nodded to her as we closed the distance.

"*Sawasdee, ka! Khun sabai dee?* You *Loi-to* Legere, you be *Loi-to* Davis replacement!" she merrily sing-song chirped in fairly good English, with a big, animated smile tossed in.

"*Chi, kup.* He'll be leaving in about ten more days."

I had long stopped asking myself how the Thais knew more about me and my business than I did.

"You tell him 'B-52' miss him a lot *ching-ching!* I love him only. He *yai-yai* 'su-pah' big size like 'Supah-man' make me happy only. He 'num-bah' one. You say he come see me again one mo' time, so'k?"

"I promise to pass the message to Jake, Miss, ah . . . .. 'B-52'?"

"*Kop khun mach, ka! Choke dee!*"

"*Kop khun mach, kup,*" I replied.


-


**BETWEEN 'C' AND 'D' AVENUES, 8<sup>TH</sup> STREET, BOQ #1, ROOM #6, *U-TAPAO* RTNAB, *CHONBURI/RAYONG* PROVINCES, THAILAND, 1145, 30 JULY 1975.**

I had collected all my personal gear and moved over to Tom Crowley's room the day before. His roommate was already occupying the upper 'loft' bunk. I asked him if he wanted the lower, but he said no. He was happy where he was and didn't want to switch just for the two weeks I'd be in the room. Since he worked Days and I worked Swings, we wouldn't actually see each other. I had done everything, including giving my key to Crowley. Everything except tell *Khun Oy* I was switching rooms.

The next day *Khun Oy* knocked first, then unlocked and opened the door to my 'old' room mid-morning. Suddenly awakened, a svelte, small, very attractive, young blond woman was holding the gray woolen blanket and sheet up to her chin and stared back at *Khun Oy*: Crowley' wife.

*Khun Oy* said: "Solly, solly!! *Kor-toedt, ka!!*" and started to close the door.

"NO, NO! IT'S OK! I have to get up anyway!"

Mrs. Crowley jumped out of bed in her frilly night gown and moved towards the door to reassure *Khun Oy* that everything was OK. This went on every day for two weeks. *Khun Oy* and Mrs. Crowley ("Call me Sandy, please.") became fast friends, since *Khun Oy* had no one to talk to during the day while she cleaned BOQ rooms and Sandy had nothing else to do until her husband got off shift early in the afternoon. So they went around together all morning while *Khun Oy* worked to clean rooms, chatted and became close.

*Khun Oy* saw me when I moved back to my room two weeks later. I noticed she was smiling very broadly this morning.

"*Loi-to! Dee mach-mach!* You 'num-bah' one! You WIFE come from USA see you!"

"Hi, *Khun Oy*. No, it's not my wife, it my friend's."

"*Loi-to! Dee mach-mach!* You 'num-bah' one! You FREN' come from USA see you!"

"No, *Khun Oy*. It's my friend's WIFE."

"*Loi-to! Dee mach-mach!* You 'num-bah' one! You FREN' WIFE come from USA see you!"

"No, no, *Khun Oy!* It isn't my friend's wife! Its. . . ."

I was just getting myself in deeper. It was quickly getting equally hilarious and confusing. I gave up.

*"Mai pen lai, Khun Oy,"* was the last thing I could say, shaking my head.

\-

## BETWEEN 'C' AND 'D' AVENUES, 8<sup>TH</sup> STREET, MAIN DINING ROOM, USAF O-CLUB, *U-TAPAO* RTNAB, *CHONBURI/ RAYONG* PROVINCES, THAILAND, 1645, 01 AUGUST 1975.

If I talked with *Nit-Noy* in the O-Club Snack Bar every lunchtime, then I was talking to her 'fren,' *Khun Noy*, in the O-Club main dining room every dinnertime. Because I was busy, I wanted to get in and out of the main dining room relatively fast. That way I could get back and relieve Jake so he could chow down. I went in to eat as early as possible. Since the main dining room was usually empty when I went in every day, I got the chance to speak to *Noy* for a few minutes after I finished dinner. As this had been going on for the past two months, we became friendly.

*Khun Noy* explained she was the very first Thai employee hired on base back in January 1966. She and two acquaintances had simply walked onto the still-being-constructed base on one fine, sunny day. *Khun Noy* then demanded to see the Base Commander. When he appeared, she asked the COL for a job for herself and her two friends (speaking to him in excellent English, her friends' English was minimal). The Base CO, completely taken back at this young *poo-ying's* boldness, quickly hired one of the girls to work in the newly built Base Chaplain's office. *Khun May* went to work in the still-being-constructed mess hall. The other went to work at the O-Club as their first employee. Hence the '#1' Badge she very proudly wore since.

*Noy* said being a waitress in the main dining room was very hard (but lucrative) work during the height of the 'Big War.' She explained they all worked double, overlapping shifts almost every day (and evening) of the year. She knocked down almost USD$400/night in tips for years on end. (Her first NAF-paid salary in 1966 was *Baht* 2.29/hour, the equivalent of almost nine cents US) *Noy* said the O-Club never closed.

*Noy* mentioned the big-spending aircrew officers might never know when they'd have a steak dinner in the O-Club again (or grab a drink in the bar lounge), so they tipped lavishly. And if they survived the harrowing, every damn sortie, sky-filled, multiple SAM-launched, MIG-entangled, and intense AA-fire over Hanoi or Haiphong, they'd tip lavishly in celebration and relief.

*Noy* also explained she gave almost all her money to her parents, plus four brothers, five sisters, all their spouses and her innumerable nieces and nephews (for school) and other assorted relatives in financial support (none of them were really working, except her poor father who was an honest Thai Police SGT in *Thon Buri)*. She said she had owned a large house out-right near *Ban Chang* at one time; closets filled with hundreds of fine silk and other fancy dresses; mountains of expensive shoes; gold and jewelry by the fistful, hand-made expensive furniture, and other ostentatious things. But now with the base operations rapidly closing down (I could see the main dining room traffic was quickly dropping), she had cut back on her lavish spending too late. She explained she was 'pinching-pennies' (or *satang*) these days. Almost all of her gold and jewelry was now gone (and along with the paid-for-in-cash house) to pay for current expenses. Unable to support her extended family, *Noy* said they quickly cut off all contact and forgot her. She did have one remaining, loyal, younger sister named *Khun Yee* still at home to assist her.

Jake filled me in later on more of *Khun Noy's* background. He said *Noy* was corrosively 'acid-tongued;' totally-direct-in-your-eyeball-to-the-point plus completely, utterly, and scathingly sarcastic, when needed. She administered profanity-filled tongue-lashings (in Thai and nearly fluent English) when irritated or provoked. As she was also not-taking-absolutely-any-boo-shit-from-anyone-from 2LT-to-GEN, she quickly became the 'favorite' or 'very special girlfriend' of every Base Commander, Wing Commander, Air Division Commander, numbered AF Commander, and higher-ranking general that walked into the O-Club for chow. And she came to know all of them and their families. Plus, they all got to know her, especially as they cycled back through *U-T* on assignments (PSC or TDY) through the years and rising through the ranks. She held no officer, no matter how senior, in awe or respect. As long as you were friendly to her, she was friendly to you. Jake said he had heard several AF Chiefs-of-Staff went right to the O-Club for lunch upon their arrival at *U-T* and gave *Noy* a big hug (as soon as they saw her), declaring "Here's my girlfriend!" before doing anything else. She simply told them what she thought, and they loved it. However, there was no 'off-switch' to her mouth, so when she got started into screechingly ripping someone's head off of their shoulders, there was no stopping her. The other Thais on base feared little, but they feared her. Or at least they respected her 'position' of influence.

Jake said if the base had an 'unofficial' historian then *Noy* was definitely it. She knew everything about everyone from way back when the base first opened. She knew where every skeleton was hung, knew where every girlfriend, stateside major wife, Thai minor wife, *tee-lock*, *mia-noy* and 'butterfly' *poo-ying* were situated, plus where all the secrets (or bodies, as it were) were buried. No Thai liked that. And no one would cross her, as she commanded respect. So, the Thais gave her a wide berth just to be on the safe side.

*Noy* explained she once had the one great love of her life: the impossibly handsome, 'Adonis'-twin, major movie star-looking, *lub-loy mach-mach*, MAJ. Marriage was in the cards in the near future (as soon as he divorced his American wife); they were seriously 'engaged.' Or until he went on another TDY again over to Guam, where his new Filipino 'sweetie' (in the BOQ room they were staying in) planted her bright red, sweaty, frilly-skivvy shorts (as in a 'message' saying: 'He's mine now, bye-bye, tootsie!') right in the dummy's baggage which *Noy* opened on his return to get his dirty laundry out to wash it.

That ended that romance.

However, the dupe (virtually on-his-knees now) begged her to return, but she wouldn't even speak one word (or to all the high-ranking emissaries he sent to speak to *Noy* on his behalf). The split was irrevocable. *Noy* had said 'goodbye' in her mind and through her non-responses to his fervent entreaties. The forlorn MAJ finally rotated back stateside and was forgotten about. She never dated again.

-

## BETWEEN 'B' AND 'C' AVENUES, 6<sup>TH</sup> STREET, BASE SWIMMING POOL, *U-TAPAO* RTNAB, *CHONBURI/RAYONG* PROVINCES, THAILAND, 1700, 04 AUGUST 1975.

Jake's 'going away' party was going to be special. It was being held at the base pool and started mid-afternoon. If the Thais ever secretly hated Jake for his language fluency; his constantly hidden, acidic distain of all things Thai; his in-depth knowledge of all the whole country and the people - warts and all, then his men on Swings admired him. Or at least they respected him. He was always supporting them against the endless back-office politics and stupidity; doing his very level best to see whatever the troops needed they got and trying to reduce SPS or AF BS down to minimal levels, often without much success. I came to understand the men gave him their highest possible accolade - 'a good officer.'

It would be a really memorable wingding in any event. Jake arranged everything himself, the food, and liquid refreshments, mainly *Singhas* and Buds. The mess hall provided the American 'picnic spread' chow. The music was provided via cassette tape with outsized speakers blasting out eardrum pounding alternating heavy metal, C&W, rock, acid rock, olden Goldies, and hard rock songs; music for most tastes. As Jake hated disco music none was played. Although it was his informal 'send-off' party from Thailand, he paid for everything out of his own pocket. Everyone who had them available brought their *tee-locks* or girlfriends along with them.

I was on-duty that night. So, while I couldn't partake in the free-flowing spirits, I could make it one of my 'post checks.' I showed up two hours into it. The place was in hard-jamming, max-throttle, emergency-power and full-swing. I didn't stay long. It was Jake's party and suspected

I'd be the only officer there except for him. I knew the enlisted men wouldn't like any officer present at this (or any other) party, so I kept my 'post check' deliberately short.

Plus I liked to be constantly roving, making random stops and post checks, just as Jake had indoctrinated me. The patio area around the pool was crowded with off-duty enlisted men from the shift and a few other people that I guessed Jake either knew or was friendly with. *Poo-yings* equaled the numbers of GIs. Everyone had a plate of chow in one hand, a beer in the other, or both. All were having a very good time. Jake, probably half-plastered by now (but holding it in remarkably well), walked over to me and shouted above Credence Clearwater Revival blasting out 'Proud Mary' in the 'only-five-centimeters-from-a-B-52-engine-intake-so-you'll-have-serious-hearing-loss-across-all-decibel-ranges-when-you-retire' mode.

"FIVE DAYS AND A BAG-DRAG!! I CAN'T BELIEVE IT!!" Jake shouted at me.

"CONGRATULATIONS JAKE!! AND YOU MADE IT ALL IN ONE PIECE!!" I yelled back.

"WE'RE MISSING SOMETHING HERE!!" Jake screamed into my ear.

"WHAT JAKE?!!" I blasted back.

"MORE *POO-YINGS!!*"

"JAKE, WHERE ARE WE GOING TO GET MORE *POO-YINGS* FOR YOUR PARTY?!!"

"I'M NOT!! <u>YOU</u> ARE!! DRIVE DOWN TO THE MAIN GATE. THERE'RE ALWAYS SOME *POO-YING* 'BUTTERFLIES' HANGING AROUND OUTSIDE PASS & ID IN THE PARKING LOT. THEY'RE ALONG THE FENCE LINE ALWAYS LOOKING TO SNAG SOME GI *POO-CHAI* FOR A 'SHORT TIME'!"

I nodded, got into my jeep, and drove down. The SP guard at the walk-through Pass & ID entrance gate stared at me as I passed and walked outside to the parking lot.

"1LT Davis needs some extra 'company' at his party," I explained to SGT on the gate.

The SGT just chuckled and said:

"I wish I were at the party, 1LT L."

I nodded and replied: "It has all the makings of a classic there."

I walked over and nodded at three *poo-yings* closest to me standing along the chain-link fence that separated the Pass & ID parking lot from the roadway out of the Main Gate entrance. I asked them if they'd all like to go to a party at the base pool. All three were young, slender, had various shades of tawny skin, long black-hair, cheerful smiles and made-up nicely. With simple, bright, single-colored, short-sleeve party dresses and matching low-heel slip-ons these *poo-yings* would do perfectly for this shindig. They eagerly responded to my invitation with big smiles, eager laughter, and animated nods. The three following me to the jeep after I signed them onto the base as their 'sponsor.' They happily jabbered away to each other in loud, singsong, bird-chattering Thai.

I made five more trips with three 'ladies' each, clearing the parking lot of *poo-yings*. I decided that was all I could do for my contribution to livening up the party. Each time I dropped my 'taxi load' off I heard the party blasting away at maximum decibels, if not getting even noisier. That meant people were really getting drunker, or happier, or both - a good sign. This would be a memorable bash that would be discussed for years to come whether the people telling the story were there or not: a classic smash-in-the-making.

After I dropped the last batch of young, nubile, happy-to-go-to-a-party *poo-yings* off at the pool entrance I decided to make my rounds for a few hours. The sun had long set when I decided on one last check of the festivities. It had toned down only slightly. But this had all the signs of lasting well past midnight. I really expected no problems, simply out of the men's respect for Jake and his departure in another six days. No one wanted to show him any disrespect by being extremely stupid; like punching someone's lights out, throwing empty beer bottles around, drowning in the pool's deep end, or drunkenly smashing into the pool house windows.

One forlorn-looking young, short-statured, sandy-haired airman was walking towards me, muttering all to himself, more in shock than in inebriation. He had a stunned look on his face, as if he'd been smacked on the back of the head with a '2x4'. He even looked physical ill.

"My fiancé, my fiancé," he kept muttering to himself as he came up to me. He gave me a 'thousand-yard' stare.

"What about your fiancé?" I asked him.

"Over there." He pointed over to one of the first young *poo-yings* I had brought to the party. She was talking animatedly to another drunken SP SGT who I recognized from the shift. She suddenly grabbed his arm; her whole body shaking from laughter at what he said to her.

"Oh. . . .her? She was one of the first *poo-yings* I brought to the party. She was waiting for someone outside the Main Gate."

"My fiancé, my fiancé," he kept repeating, more to himself than anyone, and staggered off in a catatonic stupor.

I felt sorry for the poor guy.

Jake walked over, slightly drunker, and looser than I had ever seen him before.

"GREAT PARTY JAKE!!"

"YAH, IT TURNED OUT WELL!!"

It apparently had. The attendance hadn't dropped any from what I could see. There might have even been more people there. The music abruptly stopped as the song finished. They changed cassette tapes.

"I got a message for you before I forget. A lady named 'B-52' saw me last week and said she missed you a lot. In fact, she said she loved you and you were the only guy to make her happy. She told me you were 'Superman.' And she wanted you to come over and see her one last time. What-the-hell kind of a nickname is 'B-52'? What'd she do, 'pull-a-train' on a whole damn BUFF crew one time?"

Jake laughed at the request and the memory.

"The base hospital has a book of photographs of girls who've contracted VD out in town. If any GI walks in and gets treated for the clap they show them the picture book to try and identify the girl who gave them a dose so she can get treated too. All Thais use a nickname and some of these *poo-ying* nicknames are the same: *Noy, Oy, Nok, Nid, Nit*. Who knows what their real names are?"

"Each photograph has a letter and number beneath it, so if they've been treated for VD at least once, they're in there. It had 300 photographs last time I knew: A-1, A-2 to A-100, then B-1, B-2 to B-100, C-1 and so on. She's 'B-52' in the book; the oldest working, happiest and most *ba-ba ba-bor* hooker in Thailand."

"Well Jake, said told me you really made her happy. All she could talk about was you."

I couldn't tell from the cross-directional lighting if Jake blushed or not.

-

## ROYAL JEWELRY SHOP, DOWNTOWN *SATTAHIP, CHONBURI* PROVINCE, THAILAND, 1900, 06 AUGUST 1975.

I waited outside the jewelry shop while *Nit-Noy* and *Noy* were inside still shopping. I had finally gotten some beautiful jewelry for my relatives back home and shipped it all off via registered mail. Now I let the ladies have fun on my tab (finally got a payday under my belt) as a reward for all their help. I left them all happily jabbering away and content to examine everything in her shop before making their final selections. The day's heat had finally started to dissipate with an onshore breeze now helping cool things off a bit. The golden sunset over the Gulf of Thailand was a brilliantly colored palette (but now quickly fading) light show, as happens so close to the equator. As dusk settled, I passed the time just watching the passing shoppers, partiers, families, and couples as they strolled past the shop front.

Then from around the corner came two stunningly, achingly beautiful *poo-yings*. I stared with my mouth agape. Both had straight, shining black hair all the way down to their butts, were tall, light golden-skinned, and shapes like statuesque, voluptuous hourglasses. They didn't make any attempts to be demure about it. The one on the left was in a slinky, tightly fitted (that left little to the imagination) bright cherry-red night party dress with very low-cut cleavage, her twin Mount Everest-like, impressive mammary glands firmly bulged out prominently on all sides. The humongous pair strained the dress top hard (all without a bra for support). Her outfit had long slits up both sides, while showing her long legs off (from her ankles to her upper thighs) to good advantage. She matched the dress with an exact same-colored small, chain-handle handbag and high-heeled shoes with a red rose placed above her left ear. The one on the right dressed precisely the same, except everything in her ensemble was white. They might have been twins. My mouth remained dropped at the sight. I'd never seen anyone (or anything) before that matched them. Both were spectacularly, drop-dead, gorgeous. I continued to stare dumbly. As they came abreast of me both glanced in my direction and smiled at my dropped jaw and stupefied expression. I must've looked like a landed large-mouth bass on some lakefront dock in AL.

Then I sensed someone beside me. *Nit-Noy*. Oh, shit! I was really in for it now. She was going to start royally (and loudly) busting my chops about staring at these wild-ass *poo-yings*. I KNEW I 'wasn't supposed to be looking at any other *poo-ying* (or *poo-yings*) when I was in her company': a major-league *faux pas* on my part. I waited for the inevitable, jealous, explosion of loud words and harsh invectives. I was going to get a complete earful blast of Thai profanities that wouldn't end. She glanced at them once and simply said: "*Ka-toeys*."

-

**CORNER OF 'A' AVENUE AND 9<sup>TH</sup> STREET, SHIFT SUPERVISOR'S OFFICE, CSC, 365<sup>th</sup> SPS, *U-TAPAO* RTNAB, *CHONBURI/RAYONG* PROVINCES, THAILAND, 1400, 07 AUGUST 1975.**

I sat in the Shift Supervisor's Office with the MSGT Veeres and MSGT Wozniak after post-out. I briefed them on the earlier morning arrival of BGEN (MAJGEN selectee) Larkin and a small inspection staff, as was explained to me by Guillory. I reminded them BGEN Larkin would be here on an inspection tour for the next three days. This was no surprise, as the swing around the PACAF bases had been announced at least six weeks prior. This included Alaska, Hawaii, Japan, Taiwan, the Philippines, and Guam. Thailand was the last country on the 'Grand Scenic Tour' and *U-Tapao* was the last stop in Thailand.

"Do you want us to do anything differently, 1LT?" MSGT Veeres inquired.

"Nothing, do exactly what you'd normally do. Just expect the BGEN and his staff to pop-up unexpectedly at anytime, anywhere to see everything. Just like me."

Both either grinned or grimaced, I couldn't tell.

"Do you want us to give you a shout on the radio if he does show, sir?" asked MSGT Wozniak.

"No, MSGT Wozniak, only if he specifically asks to see me, or if there's a problem or question you can't deal with. I know you both have a wealth of experience and knowledge in the field, and you've seen these types of inspections many times in the past. You handle it. I trust your judgment. Call me if you need me. Otherwise, I'll be doing what I normally do. Any questions or comments, guys?"

There were none. We all got up and went out on patrol. Neither the BGEN or any staff members paid us a visit that evening, or the next.

-

**CORNER OF 'A' AVENUE AND 9<sup>TH</sup> STREET, PARKING LOT, OUTSIDE CSC, 365<sup>TH</sup> SPS, *U-TAPAO* RTNAB, *CHONBURI/ RAYONG* PROVINCES, THAILAND, 2155, 09 AUGUST 1975.**

Guard Mount had just broken and Mids was scrambling everywhere to get to post-out. There was a rugby scrum of Americans and Thais moving in the poorly lighted parking lot to get into their vehicles and move out. The on-coming Shift Supervisor for Mids was still inside of CSC. I was standing in the middle of lot when the M-113 QRF pulled up right beside me and stopped. Men were scrambling to get in and out of the back. I was watching to see we didn't have an accident on post-out with so many men and vehicles in motion. Two figures off from the side came up to me out of the darkness. One spoke.

"Excuse me, son. You the off-coming shift supervisor?"

I turned and noticed one-star on each cammo uniform lapel: BGEN Larkin was standing there with his aide. The aide and I briefly exchanged 'we've-seen-each-other-before-somewhere' nods but didn't speak. I came to attention and saluted.

"No, sir. We're still on until 2400; Mids overlaps us from 2200."

The general returned the salute. He glanced at my name tag.

"1LT Legere, does this M-113 have a fire-extinguisher?"

"I don't know sir, I'll check."

I poked my head inside the back entrance and asked the on-coming Mids troops, now getting ready to move off on their roving patrol, to look for one. The men started methodically searching.

Someone in the M-113 said: "Negative, sir!"

I turned around and said: "No, BGEN Larkin, it doesn't have one."

"Well, 1LT Legere, this vehicle isn't going anywhere until it does have one."

"Yes, sir!"

I stuck my head back into the M-113.

"OK people!" I shouted, "This vehicle is now dead-lined until we find a good working fire-extinguisher. It's not going anywhere. Let's everybody get moving and go find one!"

Everyone scrambled out of the vehicle fast and scattered.

"We'll get one, sir."

"Good, 1LT Legere!"

He looked around the scene, still a chaotic shuffle of men heading in almost every direction.

"Let me tell you a 'war' story, son. Back when I was in Vietnam there was another M-113. They didn't have a fire-extinguisher inside either, just like this vehicle. But they did have a small fire get started. They could have gotten it out fast enough if they had one, but they didn't. It destroyed the entire vehicle. Luckily for them everyone got out alive."

"Yes, sir! I'll remember that."

After we saluted each other, BGEN Larkin smiled, turned and strode off into the darkness with his aide in tow.

\-

## CORNER OF 'A' AVENUE AND 6<sup>TH</sup> STREET, WING COMMANDER'S BRIEFING ROOM, 703<sup>rd</sup> SW HQs BUILDING, *U-TAPAO* RTNAB, *CHONBURI/RAYONG* PROVINCES, THAILAND, 0900, 10 AUGUST 1975.

All the officers, back-office, and duty section senior NCOs, plus each of the LE and Security Shift and Assistant Shift NCOs (even those on-duty) were sitting in the 703<sup>RD</sup> Wing Commander's Briefing Room and waiting in various states of anxiety, dread and anticipation. Every seat was filled, and the most junior NCOs were standing along both sides. BGEN Larkin had completed his short, but vigorous, three-day inspection tour of the 365<sup>th</sup> SPS. We were going to find out the results verbally.

BGEN Larkin had been appointed as the Chief of Security Police in March, the first time a general officer was in command of the career field. All former SP commanders had been full-bird COLs. That BGEN Larkin was a command rated-pilot and never had an SP tour of duty before did not faze anyone in the career field at *U-Tapao*. All the old-timers felt that the career-field was always slighted by not having enough 'clout' (i.e., a mere full-bird COL) at HQs, USAF in DC. Full-chicken COLs went out for the coffee at the Pentagon (MAJs were hat-racks). This would redress an injustice, or at least an imbalance of influence. With a one-star in command the SPs had some muscle, and hopefully would get some respect, in the USAF 'Head Shed.'

There was no question of BGEN Larkin's impressive background and experience. A bio released prior to his arrival listed extensive 'in-the-front-line-trenches' war-time experience in WWII, Korea and Vietnam, with an impressive assortment of combat and service decorations and a wide variety of different command assignments, a Master's degree from George Washington University and an AWC graduate.

The BGEN Larkin entered the conference room.

Everyone came to attention.

"Gentlemen, please be seated."

He had the strong reputation for coming straight to the point. (He did.) And pulling no punches. (He didn't.)

"Gentlemen," the general seriously intoned. "This is the worst Security Police Squadron in Thailand, and one of the worst in the AF. I don't understand how, with as much senior officer and enlisted experience here, these chronic problems you have persist. There is no leadership. Morale is poor. Records keeping and administrative files are sloppy. The Armory is a disaster. The base fighting positions, bunkers and observation towers all are badly in need of repair. I could go on for an hour with this, but I will not. I could understand this situation better if there was a lack of rank, manpower, or experience. But this is the most top-heavy, over-manned unit I have ever seen in my entire 33 years of AF service. This SPS should be one of the best we have, but it is not. This situation is absolutely inexcusable, bordering on criminally negligent."

BGEN Larkin paused to let those comments sink in.

"Now, I am not talking about those who just arrived. . . ."

I was looking downward at the time, carefully pondering what was being said. One of my troops later told me BGEN Larkin was looking straight at me when he spoke.

". . . .I am talking about those who have the rank, the experience and the ability to quickly straighten this organization out. And I want it done immediately. Any questions?"

No one said anything. We were done.

"Dismissed!"

Everyone rose to attention as BGEN Larkin stood up and departed with his Aide.

By the end of the day everyone had heard MAJ Shellenbarger had been summarily relieved of duty.

-

## CORNER OF 'A' AVENUE AND 9TH STREET, PARKING LOT, OUTSIDE CSC, 365TH SPS, *U-TAPAO* RTNAB, *CHONBURI/RAYONG* PROVINCES, THAILAND, 1400, 10 AUGUST 1975.

After Guard Mount broke I leaned against the sand bags surrounding the emergency generator and reflected on yesterday's events.

I didn't see Jake off at the APOE this morning. He departed on the 'Freedom Bird' at first light. We'd already said our final good-byes the day before at lunch. I wished him well, a safe flight home, and good luck on his new assignment.

"Just a wake-up!" Jake loudly exhaled, half not believing the day had finally arrived for him to depart for good. I'd no doubt Thailand would never see Jake again - or at least not in my lifetime.

Jake relaxed at our last time together in the O-Club lounge. Jake had a beer; I had a cola. I went to the cashier's cage to change some US dollars into Thai *Baht* and came away with some large purple 500 *Baht* bills. Must be a new issue I thought, as the largest Thai *Baht* note in circulation then was a red 100 *Baht*. Jake said he was all packed and ready for his ride over to the APOE tomorrow.

"FINALLY!! A 'ONE-GOD-DAMNED-WAKE-UP'!! NEXT!!" Jake was exuberant. And I was happy for him. We reminisced a bit. Then I presented him with a heart-felt handshake and then departed for work. Later that evening I heard MAJ Shellenbarger was also a passenger on the same flight.

I don't know what I felt when I left Jake in the O-Club bar lounge; like a permanent loss, or an important piece of my life was over. Very strange. Like a family member had departed, or a noteworthy milestone in my life had passed. I was going to miss Jake and his company very much. I'd learned more about more things in the last three months from him than I'd ever learned from 10 other people put together over the same time. I loaded myself into the jeep and went back out on patrol. Just as Jake had taught me.

The day after Jake and the old CO departed, two shift officers also headed for home on their 'Freedom Bird'. And their replacements arrived on the same flight, one was named 1LT "Joe" Vogelesgang, now assigned to Swing Shift.

-

**CORNER OF 'A' AVENUE AND 9TH STREET, SHIFT SUPERVISOR'S OFFICE, CSC, 365TH SPS, *U-TAPAO* RTNAB, *CHONBURI/RAYONG* PROVINCES, THAILAND, 1355, 19 AUGUST 1975.**

There had been a large on-going flap from this morning on Days, according to what I was briefed from Guillory at shift turn-over. DPDO personnel had shown up first thing this morning (at 0800) only to quickly discover the big salvage yard had been 'raided' big-time and undoubtedly sometime during the hours of darkness. Since everything was there at close of business the previous day (all according to them) that narrowed down the list of the usual suspects fairly quickly. They reported the yard had been fairly well-stripped of scrap copper wire - some of it collected in large wooden spools on pallets and in cardboard boxes; various broken, but still fairly serviceable, appliances; pretty much all the inoperable a/c units and unserviceable spare parts and anything crafted out of stainless steel. Apparently, a lot of stuff in the yard was now MIA. There were no visible signs of forced entry. No other clues were available, past the stuff was obviously missing. This wasn't the first time this had happened. Continual reports of minor 'inventory leakages,' 'minor, petty thefts,' and small 'scrap/re-salvageable turn-in' disappearances out of the DPDO Yard had been sent into the SPS LE Desk going back well before the time I arrived, all briefed by Jake beforehand. He said no progress had ever been made on any investigation into the thefts.

I read between the lines in what I was being told now. Mainly that there was a lot of finger-pointing this morning between DPDO and the SPS back-office, some of it heated. Guillory told me the Mids Shift Supervisor denied anything happened on his shift. Since Days was apparently innocent - not having been on-duty at the time of the disappearances. That left only Swings as the remaining responsible party for the incident having occurred.

At 1505, I got a call from CSC on the radio to meet the Ops Officer's jeep over by the 703rd FMS at the corner of 'B' Avenue and 10th Street. I parked my jeep near his, dismounted, walked over, and saluted.

Van den Dardener came out slashing away, right to the point.

"Your people were stealing everything out of the DPDO Yard last night, 1LT Legere."

I immediately got red-hot under the collar and tried to slam-the-brakes on my vertically rocketing emotions. There was one thing I hated worse than anything in my life: a false accusation. I immediately defended my (and my shifts') honor.

"NO, SIR! I move my people around constantly and keep them mobile! I'm always on roving patrol, as they are. I don't let anyone sit around. And I check up on them all the time. I went by the DPDO Yard several times last night at odd hours; and was in the same general area pretty much all night. I didn't see a thing, sir. It wasn't my people, CAPT!"

Van den Dardener remained unswayed.

"Your people did it, 1LT Legere. We'll just wait for the proof to come out. It always does, no matter how long it takes. Your people are guilty. And I also don't like you seeing *Noy* in the O-Club."

What that he drove off. This was not good, not good at all.

First, my people were innocent. I was convinced of that. And I totally despised false accusations. Second. I was 'seeing' *Nit-Noy* in the Snack Bar, not *Noy* in the Main Dining Room. *Khun Noy* was just a friend. We chatted when I went in there and we went out shopping sometimes. And third, what concern was it of his who-the-hell I saw? Actually, I answered that question myself: It was none of his damn business! I started to lose the rest of my temper, something I never tried to let myself do.

And what was this place becoming, a damned monastery? Plus, *Nit-Noy* and I weren't even 'butter-flying'! Everyone else on base was screwing their brains out at every chance. Now he was giving me total grief for my 'friendships!?' This was 100%, pure, unadulterated, complete, total BS. What right did the AF have to get into my personal life anyway? I wasn't doing anything wrong. Van den Dardener was a total jerk! I was royally pissed, a personal state-of-mind I had always tried to avoid. I fumed for the rest of the shift.

\-

**CORNER OF 'C' AVENUE AND 3RD STREET, COMMANDING OFFICER'S CONFERENCE ROOM, 365TH SPS HQs UNIT, *U-TAPAO* RTNAB, *CHONBURI/RAYONG*, THAILAND, 1600, 24 AUGUST 1975.**

Shellenbarger's replacement, LTC Hubert O. Sprayberry, finally arrived. This was the first time all the officers were getting to meet him. Like Shellenbarger, Sprayberry was a recycle out of the Northern-Tier Minuteman Missile Field. This meant he had a 'pocket rocket.' This was his first assignment as an SPS Commander. With so many mid-and-senior 'been-in-the-SP-career-field-since-day-one' squadron commanders getting fired left-and-right for slights, real or imagined, by base commanders on an AF-wide basis, there was always a critical shortage of SPS commanders. The USAF, in its infinite wisdom, 'career-broadened' pilot, navigator and 'missile-leteer' MAJs, LTCs and COLs, who were not going any higher in the organization for various reasons (that usually meant either 'non-performers' or with no 'political' connections), slapped SP badges on them and turned them into SPS commanders. Many of them didn't know their butt from a hole in the ground. With a few of them, usually too-sharp-for-their-own-good, or politically-out-of-favor-to-the-Big-Head-Shed full-bull COLs and LTCs, it was just the pyramid got too constricted as they moved closer to the top, so naturally some of the good ones were squeezed out on the declining, available promotion slots, but few. I was lucky at Maxwell. Both COs I drew as bosses were career SP officers and very, very good at what they did. They were totally professional, seriously minded officers. Maybe I was spoiled. But I'd heard too many horror stories about incompetent SPS COs on other bases.

Sprayberry was shaped like an undersized, human bowling-ball. He had closely cropped-to-the-skull gray and white stubble that monocle-wearing, Nazi *SS*-Slave Labor Camp Commanders, and steel-tooth, scar-faced, KGB COLs liked to sport. With pince-nez glasses, a penguin waddling-like walk and a high-Missouri 'twang' that grated on you like fingernails-across-a-blackboard, he was a very sorry sight to behold. He also had a fussy, prissy, 'always-irritated-what-or-why-are-you-bothering-me-for-now?' old grandmotherly attitude toward everything and everyone. He said nothing in the meeting except he was from Malmstrom in Missiles. If he was happy to be here, he gave no inkling of it. He looked like he had just swallowed a handful of *Ung-angs* by accident. I had a very bad feeling in the pit of my stomach after the meeting. The troops immediately nicknamed him 'Spraybelly.'

-

**CORNER OF 'A' AVENUE AND 9ᵀᴴ STREET, SHIFT SUPERVISOR'S OFFICE, CSC, 365ᵀᴴ SPS, *U-TAPAO* RTNAB, *CHONBURI/RAYONG* PROVINCES, THAILAND, 1345, 25 AUGUST 1975.**

Today was one of those very interesting days at work you write home about. Promptly at 0545 the TSGs went out on strike - again. Since they didn't do much anyway, no one in the SPS was too sad about the occurrence. In fact, no one noticed anything amiss until no one showed up for TSG Guard Mount on Days. So, Guillory assumed the TSGs were out on strike again since he was also not duly informed by anyone. The TSGs coming off of Mids turned in their weapons and ammo then quickly disappeared. Once this was known, the word went promptly up both the RTN and AF chains-of-command. Negotiations were inaugurated at 0800 between the RTN Security Commander, who had the overall responsibility for them, and the TSG 'ringleaders' over another pay increase. The RTMCs were duly summoned as replacements and quickly filled the void in the base's perimeter security.

At 0415, bright (or actually dark) and early the next morning, one *poo-ying gigolo* was attempting to steal some of the perimeter fence, along with a small team of *poo-chai gigolos*. They did this by starting to snip the twisted wires holding the cyclone fence to the concrete posts right behind the RTMC encampment: a big mistake. The RTMC Guard, a young Petty Officer Third Class, sitting alert inside his fighting position (on hearing the noises and knowing what was happening), and under strict orders to shoot anyone attempting to gain entrance onto the base by cutting the perimeter fence, promptly opened fire with his M-16 on full-automatic at the shadowy figures. He killed the *poo-ying gigolo* outright and wounding at least one of her companions. The others quickly ran (or limped) off. After sunrise, there was some blood trails discovered on the grass that led towards the main highway. But no one was able to determine how many people there had been, how many were wounded, or how badly. The RTMC Detachment Commander immediately praised the RTMC Petty Officer Third Class for doing his duty in defending the base and ordered the body of the *poo-ying gigolo* to be left there for 24 hours (very unusual, according to CDR Sawasdiyothin when we spoke later) as an 'example' to the other *gigolos*. The word about the incident spread at the 'speed-of-light' (or the 'speed-of-

Thais-talking': same speed) far and wide. There were no more attempts at fence *ka-moying*.

Two full months later all TSGs returned to work with new pay raises. The RTMCs went back to their tented compound. The fence *gigolos* were back in operation that evening, trying to make-up for lost time.

-

## CORNER OF 'C' AVENUE AND 3RD STREET, COMMANDER'S CONFERENCE ROOM, 365TH SPS HQs UNIT, *U-TAPAO* RTNAB, *CHONBURI/RAYONG*, THAILAND, 1600, 28 AUGUST 1975.

All officers, on duty or not, were assembled in the SPS Commander's Conference Room. Although we had all met Sprayberry when he first came a few days ago, our meeting with him was nothing more than a mere handshake and exchange of names. He didn't ask me (or anyone else to my knowledge) any questions about the shift. But I heard through the SP 'grapevine' Sprayberry was spending max facetime with Guillory behind closed doors, but no time with Van den Dardener. That was very strange.

"OK," 'Spraybelly' said to quiet everyone when he walked into the room. We came to attention. "I'll be brief," he intoned with his high nasal, grating twang. "CAPT Van den Dardener is being re-assigned today to Camp *Samae San* as the 'Liaison Officer' to the 482nd MP Company. I'd like to pass along my congratulations to him on this new, important assignment."

CAPT Van den Dardener beamed at everyone like he had just won the Blue Ribbon at the Iowa State Fair Hog Calling Contest.

This made absolutely no sense. There was no 'authorized billet' for an SP 'Liaison Officer' over at *Samae San*. It was a totally invented, useless, BS job. And everyone in the room knew it, except for Van den Dardener and 'Spraybelly' from their wide grins. If anything, we needed an Ops Officer now more than ever. Van den Dardener had been very slowly getting a handle on SPS Ops. We were starting to see faint glimmers of organization back there. He'd been a small step in the right direction, like turning a

143

battleship around in mid-ocean while going head-on into heavy seas at three-knots, barely making headway. Now that was gone. And there was no announced replacement. That meant chaos again. The whole thing was surreal, like a bad acid trip.

With no more announcements everyone stood in line to shake Van den Dardener's hand and wish him well on his new assignment.

"1LT Legere. I want to talk to you for a minute," Sprayberry harshly twanged at me.

I followed as he walked away from the others, now out of earshot. He was blunt.

"I don't want to see you in the back office at all, unless you are SPECIFICALLY REQUESTED by myself personally, or one of the members of my staff at my direction, to come. Do you understand that? SPECIFICALLY REQUESTED! I don't want to repeat this direct order to you twice. I don't want to see you in here! Understand?"

"Yes, sir!" I replied, completely bewildered.

With that he turned on his heels and went to speak to Guillory standing close by.

Two days later (the day before Van den Dardener was scheduled to rotate over to Camp *Samae San*) I was called into his office. I received my LOE, as all of the other officers did, each one in turn from Van den Dardener. It was bad - very bad. I had a sour acid taste in my mouth all day.

\-

## CENTRAL MARKET, DOWNTOWN *SATTAHIP*, *CHONBURI* PROVINCE, THAILAND, 1030, 27 AUGUST 1975.

I decided to take 'Joe' Vogelesgang, my new shift mate, down to *Sattahip* for a quick look-see around, being it was my day off. He had been bugging me about it ever since he first arrived. So, I figured I'd show mercy and take him on the 'Grand Sight-seeing Tour.' I borrowed one of the spare jeeps. We drove slightly slower than the break-the-sound-barrier-speed

Guillory had attempted back in June. He made the same comments I did about the Thais throwing trash out their vehicle windows, but nothing else seemed to faze him. He said he came in from Minot off Missile Security and little else. I started giving him the same type of initial overall briefing that Jake had given me about Thais and Thailand. So, he was having a lot thrown at him very quickly, all without his commentary. But I suddenly wondered if he had any interest at all (or if he was even paying any attention to what I was saying), by his nonchalant manner and completely disinterested attitude. I just cut the briefing off after a few minutes.

Vogelesgang was reserved, mildly friendly, taciturn, somewhat laconic and slightly over six foot tall. So, I had another speaker with an unplaceable, slow, Midwestern 'twang.' He was unusual in that he had more of a 'Pear'-shaped body than anything else I could describe, bigger bottom than top. I'd seen some women so described, but never a man - strange.

We did the standard walking tour of the town. I pointed out various jewelry, clothes, and souvenir shops, plus Mr. Florida's establishment, the *wat* compound, the seawall and all the rest, including a seafood lunch along the waterfront.

As we walked into the Central Market building, he suddenly cringed and said:

"What's that smell?"

"What smell?"

-

**CORNER OF 'F' AVENUE AND 12TH STREET, BEQ, 703rd FMS, *U-TAPAO* RTNAB, *CHONBURI/RAYONG* PROVINCES, THAILAND, 1700, 05 SEPTEMBER 1975.**

Guillory and I walked towards the closest BEQ after parking in the huge asphalt lot perhaps 50 meters away. The over half-dozen, white, three-story, long, BEQs were situated not far from the USO and Buffalo Village. He announced that K-9 was no longer taking drug-detection dog teams into the BEQs. Guillory explained he dogs would 'alert' to the marijuana smoke at the same distance we were at now.

"Waste of time, sport," Guillory drolly commented.

As we walked closer, the acrid-sweet, distinctive aroma of marijuana smoke started to envelope us like a light fog. By the time we reached the open bay concrete stairwell at closest end of the FMS barracks the smell was over-powering. I could see the air down the ground floor hallway inside the barracks was well-fogged with dope smoke.

"We don't even search rooms anymore. Nothing will be in there anyway. If they keep their 'stash' it will be in 'common use' areas."

Any contraband seized in a search: drugs, weapons, porn, whatever - could not be used as evidence in a trial against anyone, if it were found in a 'common use' area; i.e., in an area anyone could have had ready access to. We walked up one flight to the spacious area or landing at the end of the hallway that served as a break room/lounge for the floor. There were some used couches, old but serviceable padded chairs, some battered coffee and end tables, a TV, scattered magazines and dog-eared paperback books in an old wooden bookshelf and half a dozen standard-issued gray storage lockers against one wall. No one was around.

"We'll do a search anyway, sport."

Guillory started slowly and deliberately looking through everything in the room, but I could see he was just going through the motions. Either he had done this drill 100 times before and was jaded by the exercise, or didn't care through apathy what happened, knowing his effort wasn't going to change a single thing.

He reached behind one of the gray metal lockers that held cleaning supplies. It was set slightly away from the cinderblock wall. His hand came out holding a sandwich-sized plastic bag of marijuana leaves and seeds.

"What a surprise!" he said in an unsurprised, knowing, and sarcastic-toned voice, or as much as he could muster.

Guillory walked over to one of the couches and flopped down. He got an SP Evidence Custody Form out of his US Army green canvas zippered field map folder he used to carry around all his paperwork and forms, and then set it on the seen-the-war wooden coffee table. It was burned all around by ignored, previously lighted, cigarette butts.

"We have to 'Chain-of-Custody' this contraband now. I'll do an incident report later, sport," smiling triumphantly as he said it. Guillory started filling the form in.

Even though Guillory was 'off-duty' today, he was still in uniform and out there 'working.' I later figured out this whole useless 'Chinese Fire Drill' was to simply impress the back-office types to see the ubiquitous 'CAPT Guillory' was 'on the ball' and efficiently hunting down rampant enlisted drug users and depleting all the big drug dealers' stashes, when they saw the Incident Report and Chain-of-Custody Forms of the confiscation of contraband cross their desks. He was always going for the 'Gold Star' in a fanatic effort to make deep selection to MAJ. Maybe he'd trade the one shiny 'Gold Star' for a pair of 'silver stars' in the future. I had little doubt.

I walked into LE and asked the Desk SGT, SGT Balough, where MSGT Wozniak was. Balough said was still out his rounds but would be back in about 20 minutes. I said I'd just hang around and wait. I usually spent almost all of my time with the Security. LE basically took care of itself and didn't require lots of handholding. Although the people assigned to Security rotated every day on the duty roster, the LE people were assigned to permanent posts: gates, ECPs, LE Desk or riding patrols. That wasn't in line with written SP Policy. I had spoken to MSGT Wozniak about it a few times after Jake's departure.

"Everyone's extremely happy where they are, sir," he explained. "We got a tight group of people who all work well together. I don't want to cause that teamwork to end or get disrupted, 1LT. We have an extremely smooth-running operation. Hate to break that up, sir."

I thought about that. He was right. Everyone seemed to be very tight. He had a harmonious group of hard-working, dedicated Airmen and NCOs. Every time I checked their posts the troops were formal and professional, a little too nervous when I visited. Maybe they were worried I was going to hit them with some chicken-shit enforcement of the regs like more than a few officers did. But I prided myself on not being that type of officious, ego-driven, over-bearing, brain-damaged, automaton, asshole who thought enlisted men are worthless and only good for getting their sorry butts fired. Some officers constantly rubbed their rank in people's faces for no other reason that they could and get away with it. I always thought that was pure BS, since the only thing in my book that separated officers from the troops was a college degree.

But being nervous was naturally to be expected. Plus, I never had a complaint about them from anyone. I decided to let the situation stay as is, even though the SOP was to rotate everyone every shift except for senior supervisors. I didn't feel exactly right about that, but I didn't want to cause unnecessary animosity on the shift just to be a stickler for the regs. Plus, Jake had left the situation as it was, so he must've had a good reason.

"OK, MSGT Wozniak, just leave everything the way it is."

He seemed quite relieved I had made the right decision.

SGT Balough was behind the counter as the Desk SGT, as always. I had chatted with him a few times in passing before. He was a big character and master mimic. He couldn't even hold water. No secret was safe with him as his mouth was locked into a permanent 'jabber' mode with no known off-switch. That was the first thing I learned about him. He was also a rapid-fire, East Coast-somewhere, sarcastic, staccato chatterbox and leaker of any information (real or imagined) that came into his range which was within 100 kilometers.

"1LT, wuz' happin' out there tonight? Gettin' any?"

SGT Balough was also a big card.

"Nothing much there, SGT Balough. What's going on with you?"

Balough leaned back in his chair behind the desk and put his hands behind the back of his head.

"Same ol' shit, sir," Balough said with a fake Southern Ozarks drawl this time, imitating, or maybe jiving, some of his contemporaries on shift who were from the rural South or West. "New day," he added.

"Still haunting your favorite tables at all the dives of 'Newland' and 'Freeland,' there SGT Balough. I heard they can't keep you out of either."

I hadn't heard that exactly, but if it made Balough happier hearing it, then OK. The second thing I had heard about him: a notorious, major-league, pussy-chaser.

He laughed uproariously. "Damn straight! You bet, sir! I'm their BEST customer!"

I said: "You know SGT Balough. I actually had a weird dream about you last night."

Balough perked straight up in his chair now.

"Really, 1LT!? Whattin' it about if ya'll don't mind muh' askin,' suh?"

He was more 'Rhett Butler' now than 'Lil' Abner.'

"Well, I can't exactly remember. But you and I were out on patrol near the back gate late one night talking, when we saw some *gigolos* breaking into the DPDO Yard and went after them."

"Really, 1LT?! Damn straight?!"

"Then I woke up."

"Too bad, sir!" He was back to an East Coast accent. "Maybe we coulda' have caught some of them *gigolos* here finally."

"That would've been something there, SGT Balough. But keep it to yourself, OK?"

"Sir, I wouldn't tell another livin' soul. Swear to God!!!"

I walked into the NCO Club at 2100 for the first time. I could hear an Acid Rock song loudly blasting even from the parking lot on the side where I left my jeep.

There were a couple of 'heavy-weights' hanging by the cashier's cage, one watching the door and the other scanning the inside the cavernous dance hall, as large as a large college gymnasium. I immediately identified them as 'security' or 'bouncers.' I figured they knew their business from their demeanor, watchfulness, and deliberate moves. Both wore black dress shoes; dark, well-tailored slacks and white Thai open-neck, short-sleeve shirts. One shirt had red ornate Chinese 'dragons-trying-to-catch-the-highly-stylized-ornate-red-fireballs with their wide-opened mouths on both sides.'

The other was in light orange with an intricate pattern around the edges. I could see they were intelligent and experienced at what they did.

The largest one ambled over to me.

"Problems tonight, 1LT?"

"No problems, just routine. I just came in to see what the place looked like. I heard so much about it."

The big man laughed and said "Help yourself. We like to keep things quiet."

I had no doubts they did. I walked over to the entrance to the dance hall. A rear-curtained stage about five feet high and spanned the whole right side. It had curtained wings on both sides off stage. It was set up as if you could put on a play or have a high school prom. There was a wooden dance floor with couples locked together in this slow dance number - the GIs were in civilian clothing and Thai *poo-yings* in various states of attire. Away from the dance floor to the other end of the building were dozens of round tables and metal framed, padded chairs, not out of place in any large hotel convention hall. Nearly every chair was filled, less the dancers on the floor. Short-skirted, young, attractive waitresses, with numbers on their blouses the same as at the O-Club, continually darted to and from bar area with trays of drinks. Other girls in different colored, short-skirted dresses were giving GIs massages. They sat reverse faced in the chairs, resting their chins on the chair's top and grabbing their wrists in front, while the massage ladies worked their arms, backs, and heads with supple fingers plus necks and faces with washcloths.

The D.J. switched to 'War' by Edwin Starr. Another all-time favorite request I figured. I started walking out.

"Seen enough, 1LT?" the big security man said.

"Enough for tonight, thanks."

-

**CORNER OF 'A' AVENUE AND 9TH STREET, SHIFT SUPERVISOR'S OFFICE, CSC, 365th SPS, *U-TAPAO* RTNAB,**

MSGT Veeres stuck his head in the doorway and said: "1LT Legere. We have a problem, sir." That meant I had a problem, since he couldn't solve it at his level. That was rare. MSGT Veeres always solved shift 'problems' before they got up to me.

"What's the problem, MSGT Veeres?" I asked.

"A1C Jones, Richard, not the other Jones. He's in 'love' with some Thai 'butterfly' *poo-ying* he just met out in 'Freeland.' Jones wants to get married right away, or as soon as he can. He's determined to float his marriage chit up through the chain-of-command and then see the Base Chaplain about getting hitched."

MSGT Veeres tried very hard not to roll his eyes.

"All the senior NCOs have talked to him, sir. No good. But we thought if you talked to him that might do something, since you're a lot closer to him in age than we are."

MSGT Veeres had the expression on his face that my talking with A1C Jones wasn't going to make a single bit of difference. I inwardly sighed. This one was going to about as easy as putting in a landscape on a large canvas using a small paintbrush in my mouth.

"OK MSGT Veeres, I'll be happy to talk to A1C Jones. Where's he now?"

"Great, sir! He's out at the aircraft fuel oil pumping station ECP."

"I'll drive out and have a 'fatherly' chat with him, MSGT Veeres. Thanks."

I could see Jones in my mind's eye, or actually his situation, or both; even though I couldn't have picked him out of a line-up. I knew, even before I started the ignition to fire up the jeep, this was going to be a 'lost cause.' I'd heard enough 'horror' stories from the senior NCOs, and Jake, to know how this was all going to play out in the end.

Jones probably just transferred in from stateside to *U-T* this being his second assignment. A strapping Midwestern farm boy, who probably had stray hay stalks still sticking out right behind his ears, my guess was he'd never even kissed a girl (much less held her hand). Then he hit the 'Land of Endless, Cheap, and 'Young Thang' Pussy.' Of course, as soon he got his first day off, his squadron buddies hustled him straight out to 'Freeland' to get his 'ashes hauled.' They told the club Mama-san he was a 'cherry-boy.' So, she fixed him right up with some nubile, skinny, angel-faced, long-haired, young *poo-ying* - who probably had stray rice stalks still sticking out right behind her ears - straight in off the bus from *Isan*, or out of the rice-paddies near *Lop Buri* or *Ayutthaya*, just arrived yesterday. The *poo-ying* took Jones back to her little bungalow room, probably humped the royal shit out of him five or six times, then gave him a couple of 'knobbers' for good measure. All that 'real love' for about 100 *Baht* tops (or USD$5.00). Then she said the magic words: "I lub' you no sheet!" Poor kid was caught hook, line, and sinker:  a goner. Now he'll give her his whole paycheck and she'll support her whole extended family back in the little village off it.

If she's 'good,' they'll get married, go back to the 'Land of the Big BX.'  She'll get in tight with the other on/off base Thai wives, spend all his money gambling or shopping, get bored, then start getting regularly 'banged' by some horny, 'player' NCO (probably not in Security) on the side who's preying on 'lonely' oriental wives in the housing areas (while their clueless hubbies are out working Security in the missile field four days on and three days off). They'll eventually get caught in the sack together when he gets off work early one day - then divorced (unless Jones gets enraged and shoots them both).

If she's 'bad,' she'll get married, have him immediately sign over his SGLI to her, then get one of the local Thai mafia 'hit-men' to blow his dumb-ass away for USD$100.00 (if she can't get it cheaper, which she probably can) in another month or two. Then she'll show up the day after at CBPO to collect on his '100%-named-to-her-and-no-others-as-beneficiary' SGLI payout.

But no matter what she'll turn out to be, she damn sure knows this young A1C is her first-class ticket out of grinding poverty and a life endless drudgery in the rice paddies, beer bars, or sewing shops. She also knows 'butterfly' *poo-yings* have a shelf-life of maybe a decade in the business, tops. By 26 years-old they're considered 'old hags' in the profession, as an always younger, fresh 'crop' of *poo-yings* sprouts up every year looking for a free trip to the 'Land of the Big BX'. But no matter what she is, she isn't stupid. She knew how it all works with Americans, even if she didn't even have a grade school education. What a mess!

I pulled up to the ECP. I sighed to myself and thought: Here we go. A1C Jones came to attention and saluted. I returned it, parked, got out of the jeep, and come over to the gate shack.

"A1C Jones, I heard from MSGT Veeres you're thinking about getting married. That's a big step in life. Congratulations. Want to talk about it?"

"Well, sir. I know you're going to try and talk me out of getting married just like MSGT Veeres and the other older NCOs tried. But darn it sir, I'm really in love! I love my fiancé and she loves me! I know it can work, sir!"

I looked at Jones. He probably wasn't about the five years younger than I imagined his estimated age to be, he just looked like it. He sported short-cut sandy hair, with face freckles on sun-darkened skin. Above average in height, wiry, he'd become a handsome young man when he matured. I could see he was in excellent shape from slinging all those heavy hay bales back on the farm.

"A1C Jones, where you from?"

"Wamego, KS, sir.

"Wamego's a small farming community, right A1C Jones?

"Yes, sir."

"Does your family back there in Wamego know anything about the impending nuptials with, ah. . . .your fiancé?"

"Ah. . . .no, sir."

"Going to tell them soon, A1C Jones?"

"Ah. . . .yes, sir! I was going to get to it very soon."

"Speak any Thai, A1C Jones?"

"Ah. . . .no, sir. Well, just a few words. But I can learn, sir!"

"Your fiancé speaks any English?"

"Ah. . . .a little, sir. But I'm going to start teaching her English. She can learn much faster when she gets to the USA."

"Thinking about having any kids, A1C Jones?

"Ah. . . .we haven't discussed it yet, sir."

"Can you support her, and any kids, back in the USA on your salary? You know you don't rate family housing on any AFB until you make at least E-4. Then that's even IF they have housing for E-4s. Most bases don't and there're long waiting lists for openings that usually start with more senior E-5s. That means you live off-base with your spouse, which can be expensive, depending on where you get stationed. Last time I checked the pay charts A1C don't draw that much money every month."

"Ah. . . .I didn't know about being an E-4 to be eligible for the base housing, or the off-base housing situation back home, sir. I never even thought about where we'd live."

"Do you know if she can drive a car? Unless you live in a large city with public transportation, she'll need to have her own car, insurance, and driver's license to get around while you're working."

"Ah. . . .I don't know, sir. I don't think she can drive anything. I hadn't thought about that, sir. I guess she can learn when she's there, sir."

"And supporting the kids if you decide to have some? Do any future financial planning together: the rent, food, transportation, taxes, diapers, baby's clothes? The usual family expenses you'll get hit with right from Day One?

"Ah. . . .no, sir. We haven't discussed any of that yet either. I hadn't thought about it to be honest, sir."

"Think she'll like Wamego, or KS, there A1C Jones? Ever describe the place to her, if you decide to get out of service after your first hitch? Or decide not to make the AF a career later-on downstream?"

"Ah. . . .no, sir. I haven't even talked to her about where I'm from, or what it's like back home. Or if I'll even make it a career or not."

"Can she cook, A1C Jones? Thai, American, Southern, Kansas, Chinese, anything?"

"Ah. . . .I don't know, sir. I never asked her. We don't spend much time together talking."

It was fairly obvious what they both were doing with their time together. When he was finally off-duty, Jones and her were stripping off their clothes, hopping onto the single mattress on her bungalow floor and bumping their bodies together in the hopes of getting lucky. If the guy weren't totally 'pussy-whipped' by now, he'd soon be. Probably their conversations revolved around: "I lub' you, you lub' me! Gimme' hug, gimme' kees'!" and "I love you soooooo much!"

"Well, A1C Jones. I never interfere with a man's 'personal' business. Who you get married to is your concern. However, I think you and her need to sit down together. I strongly recommend you do it fairly quickly. And you need to bring along a very good interpreter to the meeting. Then discuss every topic in detail with her that I've discussed with you. When you've done that, let me know. When your request to see the Base Chaplain for marriage counseling comes up the chain-of-command through me, I'll favorably endorse it. I can't speak for the CO, or anyone else, on what they'll do on approving your request. So, I wouldn't get my hopes up too high right now. In any event, good luck. Hope it all works out for you both."

"Thank you, sir! Thank you very much! You don't know how much you've helped me, 1LT! I really want this marriage to work! I love her and I know she loves me!"

"OK, talk to you soon there, A1C Jones. Give my best regards to your 'fiancé'."

We saluted and I went back on roving patrol. I wondered how many more similar briefings I'd have to give to other Airmen or junior NCOs before I left *U-Tapao*. Or how many briefings other officers had given in the past. More than a few I'd have guessed.

-

**CORNER OF 'A' AVENUE AND 9TH STREET, SHIFT SUPERVISOR'S OFFICE, CSC, 365th SPS, *U-TAPAO* RTNAB,**

I was in Shift Supervisor's room starting to read Day Shift's CSC and LE's 'desk' blotters. This let me know what had happened in greater detail during the previous eight hours, before they got sent to the back office to be filed-and-forgotten. I was thinking about something else when I heard two off-coming Day Shift SGTs exiting the CSC. They were laughing and talking as they walked down the hallway. One said: "No, it was about a crazy dream one of the Shift Supervisors had about catching some *gigolos* over at the DPDO." My ears immediately perked up. The second SGT laughed and asked him where he heard that from. The first SGT replied in the LE Office just as they walked out the door, cutting-off the rest of the SGT's reply.

Balough. And his big, uncontrollable mouth. I should have known better. It was my fault. I should have never opened my yap. But I couldn't let this sit. Balough had to be taught a lesson. I wasn't going to take any 'official' or 'disciplinary' action, his indiscretion didn't merit either. It was my mistake, not his. But I decided to have just a friendly, fatherly 'chat' and express my disappointment and dismay at his lack of verbal 'self-control.'

I didn't dash right down to the LE Desk in anger. I waited to hit it roughly about the same time I usually checked in after dinner time. Give me some time to cool off and think about how to approach this problem. I also wanted to do this unemotionally, or professionally.

I walked into the LE Desk area. Balough was alone.

"SGT Balough, got a minute?"

"Sure, 1LT Legere."

I motioned with my head to have him move over into the small room right next to the LE Desk. It had a wooden flat, wide, countertop supported by legs along one wall and some chairs where people sat to write out their statements. The walls had cork peg boards with various AF and SP notices and a large, laminated copy of the UCMJ. Balough sat in a chair; I leaned against the countertop.

"SGT Balough, about that dream of mine we discussed last time. . . ." as I started in with an even, very patient, fatherly tone. I didn't even finish my sentence.

If Balough suddenly started jumping out-and-down, flapping his arms like a chicken; began tearing his hair out; commenced to froth-wildly-at-the-mouth; went goggled-eyed-totally-berserk on me, or started making Tarzan-like screams while pounding his chest with his closed fists, he couldn't have surprised me more than what he did next.

He burst into tears.

Whole gushes of tears started pouring down his cheeks. I was abruptly and completely taken aback. He started loudly bawling. I stared at him with incomprehension and amazement.

"Look 1LT Legere, I didn't mean to say anything to anybody! Honest sir! But I just can't keep a secret! I know I'm the biggest blabbermouth in the world! I know it! Everyone knows it! But the back office just doesn't trust me! I know I'll never get in there, sir! No matter what I do they'll never let me get a job back there. I've tried really hard, sir! I have, believe me, sir, I have! But they just keep me here trapped on the LE Desk. I'll never get anywhere with them! They'll never let me in there! I'll never work in the back office!"

Now Balough was heaving with sobs, his shoulders were moving up and down with his breathing heavy. He was red-faced now, wet with crying, then holding his head in his hands and elbows on his knees, tears dripping on the floor now. When he looked up at me again for askance, Balough looked exhausted - a poor retched, wreck of a man. I was completely speechless, stunned. I composed my thoughts then said:

"Ah. . . . .SGT Balough, ah. . . . .look, let's forget about the dream, OK? Forget I ever even mentioned it, alright? It isn't important. Let's let it go, I won't talk about it again. It's totally forgotten. See if you can pull yourself together, OK?" I put my hand on his still shaking shoulder to reassure him. I walked out of there not knowing what to think.

-

**BRAVO SECTOR, AIRCRAFT PARKING APRON, FLIGHT LINE ACROSS FROM 703RD SW HQs BUILDING, *U-TAPAO* RTNAB, *CHONBURI/RAYONG* PROVINCES, THAILAND, 0605, 10 SEPTEMBER 1975.**

One SGT named Randolph was driving the Day Shift post-out deuce-and-a-half. He first went to the RTMC encampment and picked up the usual load-out of young RTMC troops for distribution out in the Bravo Sector towers, bunkers and fighting positions. When he pulled up (being they were RTMC troops), everyone was completely ready with their gear, weapons, and emergency food rations (all standing at attention in formation, of course), and set to load-up for transport to their assigned security posts.

Randolph dropped them off one-by-one. He'd return to pick up the off-coming shift after the on-coming shift had relieved them. Now only one young RTMC Seaman was left. This SGT (never known for his common sense) decided it would be fun to play 'drag-race' along the aircraft parking apron to ECP #1 about halfway down the flight line near the Control Tower. Being it was still early morning and, with no other traffic, aircraft, or supervisors in sight, he quickly accelerated down the parking ramp. Randolph had reached 60 MPH when he went over a low, upside-down pie pan-shaped, fueling port, perhaps raised six inches or so above the pavement. The posted speed limit anywhere on the flight line was '10 MPH'. At that speed, you probably wouldn't even notice going over the fueling port. At 60 MPH, you did.

The deuce-and-a-half wildly see-sawed as the left front and rear wheels went over it. The driver was almost tossed up-and-down hard inside the truck cab. He was OK as he was at least smart enough remember to have his seatbelt buckled. The RTMC Seaman was tossed up-and-down hard too. Unfortunately, he was sitting on the vehicle's far back wooden bench (without a seatbelt available for him to put on). He was abruptly tossed up into the air, arcing forward and came down right in front of the wheels as it ran over his now prostrate body.

Guillory did three correct things. One, he immediately reported the accident up the chain-of-command. They, in turn, informed the RTN Base Commander, who informed the RTMC Detachment Commander. Two, He had the body of the now deceased RTMC Seaman brought over the base hospital Emergency Room via ambulance for further disposition. Three, he had the driver waiting with MSGT Boatwright in 'hot-stand' stand-by in SP HQs also for further disposition.

Then he did one incorrect thing. While Guillory was at the hospital (talking to his wife) the word reached him that one RTMC Seaman was in the hospital looking for the driver. Guillory totally panicked. He automatically 'assumed' the RTMC Seaman was going to do a 'contract hit' on the SGT in retaliation for causing the fatal accident to his follow RTMC buddy. He immediately departed the hospital, quickly went over to SP HQs, pulled Randolph out, and then jammed him into one of the old, now long vacated, portable B-52 crew TDY trailer quarters.

He remained there for four full months; never allowed to leave for any reason. At Guillory's direction, all of his meals were brought to his isolated trailer. This further kept him completely hidden and safe from being killed. But the SP back-office refused to take any action on him, as in either changes being preferred for courts-martial or Article 15; some other disciplinary action being taken; returning him to work, transferring him to another AFB, or processing him for an administrative discharge. Nothing. He became 'The Man in the Iron Mask.' No one in the SPS HQs wanted anything to do with him or about him. They just let Guillory handle it. Guillory, in turn, kept everyone away from Randolph and kept reassuring him that this was the only way to keep him alive from all the countless squads of RTMC 'assassins' that must be out there trying to hunt him down and put a bullet permanently into his sorry-ass brain.

Finally, in total despair, Randolph tearfully pleaded to be allowed out or transferred from Thailand. He was having severe psychological problems now, going nearly insane at being kept in continual 'isolation.' It was worse, he cried, than being in solitary confinement. At least you got one hour a day in the yard for exercise. Plus he was rarely allowed to talk to anyone. Finally Guillory relented. He coordinated with CBPO for him to be transferred to Grand Forks AFB, was taken directly to the 'Freedom Bird' and finally shipped back to the USA.

Few on shift knew any of this, as the people in the back office kept everything a closely held secret. No one cared, of those who did know, to get involved in the total mess was 'messy.' And Guillory refused comment to anyone. Only later did it leak out about what had happened after he departed. I eventually asked *Nit-Noy* why the RTMC Seaman was in the hospital looking to kill the driver for accidently causing the death his fellow RTMC buddy.

She shook her head sadly back-and-forth, got very sad, and then explained:

"Thai no doing any-thing there! No one do the 'contract'! *Sip-loy* 100%!' Gee-low-ree *ba-ba ba-bor, mach-mach!* He be he older brother go to the hospital, he be same-same RTMC. He just wan' to bring he brother body home to family for funeral ceremony. Do the cremation for the happy better next life. Thai Marines no be *mo-ho* at GIs. Thais are all be say *mai pen lai.* Thai peoples no get angry same-same *farangs.* They no want to keel' anyone. He brother be very sad, no angry, he unner-stan.' No one wan-ting keel' any the *farang* GI. Is the accident, just happen. 'Num-bah' ten! Everyone get the 'bad luck'! Marine no got the lucky Buddha. 'Gee-low-ree 100% stu-pid!' He *mai sa-mong mach-mach!*"

-

**BRAVO SECTOR, NORTHERN PARKING RAMP AREA, FLIGHT LINE, *U-TAPAO* RTNAB, *CHONBURI/RAYONG* PROVINCES, THAILAND, 2030, 19 SEPTEMBER 1975.**

I was slowly riding along the northern parking ramp area along the west side of the flight line that evening when I saw small clusters of Thais gathered under the tall, multiple-lamped apron ramp-lights. All had small yellow plastic buckets in hand with some sort of lid on them. Some had various-sized butterfly nets or small-netted fish scoops, and everyone seemed to be chasing large flying insects. I stopped in amazement and watched the show for maybe 10 minutes. Many dozens, perhaps hundreds, of these bugs (looking like large cockroaches) were flying in erratic patterns: loop-the-loop, quick curving swoops, dive-bombing patterns and figure-eight's under all the lights along the flight line. Like moths driven to the flame, none of the insects strayed very far outside the cones of illumination. As soon as one of them decided to take a break on the pavement and crawl around for a bit, the closest Thai rushed over and either snagged the dark brown insect in their net or picked them gently up by hand and deposited them into their plastic buckets. I started the jeep up and went back on patrol, shaking my head at the sight of it.

The next day I described the tableau to *Nit-Noy*. She gave me the full briefing.

"*MANG-DAS!*" she happily screamed and started laughing like I had mentioned I had seen her favorite circus clowns performing.

"What are *mang-das*?"

"*Mang-das* are *yai-yai* water bugs. 'Su-pah' *alloy-mach-mach*! Everyone catch them to sell in market. Three *Baht* for a *poo-chai mang-da* and two *Baht* for a *poo-ying mang-da*. Thais love them to eat a-lot, very good, *dee-mach! Ching-ching! Mang-da* juice very healthy! You will like it no boo-shit!" She uproariously laughed again.

I seriously doubted I'd be adding *mang-das* to my food intake, or as my favorite menu side any time soon. Giant water bugs. Cute.

-

**ON 'A' AVENUE, BETWEEN 9TH AND 10TH STREETS, NEAR THE CONTROL TOWER, *U-TAPAO* RTNAB, *CHONBURI/RAYONG* PROVINCES, THAILAND, 2115, 20 SEPTEMBER 1975.**

I was driving past the Control Tower on 'A' Avenue when the radio crackled: "SHOTS FIRED, BACK GATE!"

I struggled to get the hand-held radio out with my left hand. It wanted to stay tightly in the holder. I finally wrestled it out of the webbed carrier on my belt and responded.

"10-4! IN ROUTE!"

I immediately slammed the accelerator, the tires grabbing the roadway, as I sped off in that direction. My mind spun just as furiously as did the tires. All I could imagine was the worst: someone shot, killed, injured or bleeding! Christ! Who-the-hell knew? I tried to keep calm and fight off my growing apprehension. But I'd know soon enough.

I jammed the jeep to a halt directly behind the Back Gate shack. It was cloudless, a full moon was up, and I could quickly see there was no one lying on the ground. One good sign. Inside the shack were three people:  A SSGT named Kenley, a young RTN Third Class Petty Officer and a younger RTMC Seaman. I surveyed the scene. I could immediately see that he was almost white from shock even in the bright moonlight, as if all the blood had been drained out of him. Kenley was trying hard, but failing, not to shake. I directed my questions to him.

"What happened here, SSGT Kenley?"

It took some moments for him to recognize I was standing in front of him and collect his thoughts. He hesitated for a few seconds and said in a shaky tone of voice:

"The Thais opened the barrier bar and let a deuce-and-a-half through, sir."

"And?"

"I fired some shots to get them to stop, sir. They just kept on going."

Since there obviously was no truck there now, so that attempt to stop it hadn't worked. Just then the RTMC Shift Supervisor, a Petty Officer First Class, roared up and parked behind my jeep. He jumped out and hustled into the guard shack.

"SSGT KENLEY!!" I exclaimed. "GREAT WORK, GOOD JOB! At least you did something to stop the *gigolos*!!"

"NO, SIR!!" He said in a very worried, almost frantic tone of voice now. "I'm really in trouble now, sir!"

"SSGT Kenley!" I said in astonishment, "You aren't going to get into trouble! You did the right thing here! A really great job! You should be commended!"

"NO, SIR!" He repeated, even more urgently, "I'm really in big, big trouble with the back office now, sir!"

I tried my best to console him, reassuring Kenley several times saying he did the right thing, that he should be officially recognized for at least trying. Nothing worked.

Refusing to say anything more about it, he remained completely silent. He was as stiff as a manikin's dummy except for his shallow breathing.

"What happened here, Petty Officer?"

He spoke to the RTN Petty Officer and his RTMC Seaman. They quietly jabbered in sing-song Thai.

"They be say GI lift barrier and let the truck go *by-lay-o!*"

"What?!"

"What they be say. *Ching-ching!*"

"Ask them again."

He did. They talked briefly.

"They say same-same. Truck come to gate, GI lift barrier, let truck go *bi-lay-o* and then shoot with gun."

I knew the Thais were lying. I had no doubt about the scenario, except the Thais were the ones lifting the barrier gate and waving the now stolen deuce-and-a-half onwards off-base, never to see seen again. I looked at them carefully. The two gate guards were composed, calm, serene even. That was strange. I'd have thought they'd be animated or at least agitated at the incident, or to the obvious unspoken, implied accusations. But they acted like nothing had happened. Almost as if they were completely indifferent. Totally *mai pen lai,* or *mai mee ban han* attitudes. I decided to let it go. I knew they would not change their stories or shed any lighter on what happened.

Just then MSGT Wozniak and TSGT Bernardo raced up in their jeep, jammed it to a halt, then both jumped out. I met them outside and went over in detail what the gate guard and the Thais said to me. All three of us walked back into the gate shack. He was still as immobile as a statue and refused to answer questions from anyone, only repeating he was in big, big trouble with the back office.

I looked at Kenley a little harder now, trying to remember anything about him and trying to understand why he felt he was going to be in 'big, big trouble.' He was one of those people who always stayed off the shift's 'radar scope.' He never did anything wrong and never attracted anything attention to himself, so I couldn't peg him to anything previously in my mind. Kenley was a 'cipher' for lack of a better description. Almost six feet tall, he was blond and muscular. I vaguely remembered seeing him once or twice somewhere before.

I finally realized, after staring at him, that he had a shortened leg. His right boot had a sole at least three-four inches higher than the other. I never noticed that before. Either he was a wounded Vietnam War combat vet or injured in some service-connected accident and allowed to remain on active duty. I wasn't sure and it was unimportant now. I'd be involved with the paperwork long after the shift was supposed to change that evening. That would be a good break for the on-coming shift. They couldn't come on to relieve us until all incidents were cleared before their shift took over. So, they'd just relax around the CSC parking lot and wait. I turned everything over to MSGT Wozniak to handle and went back to CSC. It was going to be a long night.

But none of this made any sense at all. All I could think of is the Thais were lying, I was sure of that. But why did he keep saying he was 'in big, big trouble' and then tightly, clam up all of a sudden? I'd ask *Noy* to ask the Thais. She would find something out. There are no secrets in Thailand. Then I'd have my answer.

The next day I saw *Noy* in the O-Club Main Dining Room and told her what happened. She already knew all the general details (of course - this being Thailand), but promised she get hard-wired into the Thai 'grapevine' and see what really happened. Her answer the very next day made as much sense as the whole incident did - which was none.

"It wasn't supposed to happen," she explained.

"That's it?"

"That all they be say, *ka*."

It wasn't supposed to happen. I thought about that for a full minute, turning it over in my mind. I couldn't understand that statement at all. It wasn't logical.

-

**CORNER OF AVENUE 'A' AND 9TH STREET, SHIFT SUPERVISOR'S OFFICE, CSC, 365TH SPS, *U-TAPAO* RTNAB, *CHONBURI/RAYONG* PROVINCES, THAILAND, 1330, 25 SEPTEMBER 1975.**

Guillory informed me that the 'Freedom Bird' brought two new officers. Van den Dardener's replacement, a MAJ Slattermann and a 'newbie' a 2LT Trespalacio slated for Mids. I paid no attention to the news. Maybe it was just me withdrawing into myself as events on the base slowly started to tilt and spin more out of control. I had a strongly growing sense things were not working out. It was like some bad nightmare I couldn't wake up from. All I could do was try to gamely move on with life and do the best job I could, no matter what the future would bring. I just couldn't shake this disheartening premonition of doom.

But my 'rock' of support now was *Nit-Noy*. She was the world to me. If I could at least talk to her, or have her in my life, then no matter what the future would bring we could work everything out. I was depending more and more on her support and encouragement. I fervently all hoped it would all work out in the future.

However, in the passing days I was not to be royally summoned to meet with the new Ops Officer to discuss Swing Shift, base security, or SPS business. Neither did he make any visit to the Shift, nor conduct any post checks. I spotted Slattermann once in the BX: tall, hulking, moronic and blank-faced. But I heard all the other officers talking about their invitations for individual meetings with Slattermann in his office. My sense of isolation deepened. I started to do something I thought I'd never do in my life - not to care.

-

**CORNER OF AVENUE 'A' AND 9TH STREET, SHIFT SUPERVISOR'S OFFICE, CSC, 365TH SPS, *U-TAPAO* RTNAB, *CHONBURI/RAYONG* PROVINCES, THAILAND, 1330, 30 SEPTEMBER 1975.**

Guillory announced the 703rd SW would be inactivated this date. So, SAC was slowly out-of-business and going home. There were signs everywhere now that the AF was packing up and slowly starting the long withdrawal for home. There was no reason to remain. With the Vietnam War over, Thailand (in contrast to some decades-long, firmly held political and military theories or tenets, now all completely disproven) had not fallen as a 'domino' to a world-wide coordinated Communist aggression. None of these learned 'political theorists' had considered that each country in Southeast Asia had their own unique political, cultural, social, and historical developments. That each country, Laos, Vietnam, Thailand, Burma, and Cambodia, were mutually antagonistic based on centuries-long periods of invasions, conquests, hegemony, and subjugations and the attendant mutual, if not unwaiverable, suspicions. These academic 'political theorists' did not count on Thailand's strong monarchial rule. With the Thai's total devotion and love of King as the central unifying force in the country; the Thai's rabid, stringent anti-Communist beliefs and very deep nationalistic tendencies to have the country (called *Muang Thai* or *Pratet Thai* by the Thais) would unify them against these outside forces.

The Vietnamese government started applying strong pressure to the Thais to have the remaining US forces there immediately withdraw, as the Vietnamese considered the US's continued presence 'provocative.' The Thai government normally would have given a sharper response to the

Vietnamese (another ancient enemy) for interference in Thailand's foreign relations, but the defeat of the US in SVN made the Thais feel vulnerable. The Thais were reminded of the ancient Chinese proverb: 'Distant water does not put out a nearby fire'; i.e., the Americans would be of no help in a fight now with a unified VN. Surrounded on the one side, Laos and Cambodia, now Communist regimes, and Burma (Thailand's most ancient, implacable rival) on the other, the Thais considered making an accommodation based on the new geo-political realities at hand. The new Vietnamese regime, now seen from both sides of the Pacific seen as the strongest military power in Southeast Asia, had defeated two 'Great Western Military Powers' over the past 30 years. It was now only a matter of when (not if) the US would finally withdraw from Thailand.

-

## ROYAL GEMS JEWELRY SHOP, DOWNTOWN *SATTAHIP*, *CHONBURI* PROVINCE, THAILAND, 0945, 08 OCTOBER 1975.

*Nit-Noy* and *Noy* decided to bring me in to their second favorite jewelry shop, Royal Gems, to visit their very best, closest, and dearest friend, just for a look/see. To not have done so, they explained, they'd lose endless 'face.' 'Closest friend' in Thailand could've meant they'd either known her since she was born and they all grew up together, or they'd just met five minutes ago.

The owner was slightly on the mature side (like many fine wines and expensive European cheeses that only gets better with age). She was highly intelligent, expertly coifed and 'war-painted' at local beauty salon. Very classy, demeanor polished, impressively attired (as in eye-catchingly 'chic') and not dripping too much gold jewelry. I would have said back in her 'salad days' (not too many years before) she was either a *Bangkok*-based fugitive-from-a-runway/big fashion magazine model, or the lead Thai Airlines stewardess in First Class on the London-Zurich route serving sweet cocktails with little umbrellas, or Johnny Walker Black's over ice to Royal Thai Army

Generals and Field Marshalls who were bringing their spare change to deposit in their secret Swiss bank accounts in person - or both. Her English (no surprise) was near fluent. She must have cashed in all her chips at some point, come down to *Sattahip*, and jumped into the jewelry business. Everything looked brand-spanking new.

Of course, there were hugs and kisses amongst the ladies. I received a warm, polite, firm handshake and bright smile thrown into the bargain. I looked at the shop's wares and was impressed. She must have either brought down a very good master craftsman or tied in somehow with the local jewelry crafter's sweatshops. I said I would be back after payday. I let the ladies run with their conversation for several hours before we all moved to lunch.

\-

**CORNER OF 'A' AVENUE AND 9TH STREET, SHIFT SUPERVISOR'S OFFICE, CSC, 365th SPS, *U-TAPAO* RTNAB, *CHONBURI/RAYONG* PROVINCES, THAILAND, 1545, 14 OCTOBER 1975.**

"1LT Legere, can we speak to you for a minute?"

"Sure thing, come in there, SSGT Farrita. And who's out there with you? SGT Shanley? You come in too, please."

I bade them both to sit, smiled, folded my hands on the desktop and waited.

"Sir, it's about A1C Quarles and his eval, sir."

"What about A1C Quarles' eval, SSGT Farrita? Is there a problem?"

"Yes, sir, there is."

"You're talking about what I told MSGT Veeres after you told him how you were going to rate A1C Quarles in the up-coming eval period, right SSGT Farrita?"

"Yes, sir."

Someone in the US Navy back a few years ago once told me that sailors who couldn't quite keep their hair cut to the regulation, couldn't quite keep their uniforms in proper order or couldn't quite keep their shoes shined were, in general, called 'dirt-bags.'

Quarles was a 'dirt-bag.'

However, that was not the only problem. Ferrite and Shanley were 'White.' Quarles was 'Black.' Inter-racial relationships were further made more complex as the leadership on Swings was virtually all White; the ranking Black NCO was only a SSGT. However, I saw that racial tensions were not pronounced, or at least not to my eye.

A few of the White and Black troops pushed the edge of Jake's patience with basic grooming standards (like sporting longer hair than the regs permitted), but he cut everyone some slack up to a point. I knew he was seen by everyone as fair and impartial. So that was a good thing. As long as you did your job and didn't cause any major problems, Jake left you alone (and had everyone else leave you alone as well). I did the same.

I had done post checks on Quarles. Apparently, he always volunteered for the most isolated, easiest and least busy post on Swings - the aircraft fuel oil pumping station ECP on the low-rise hill overlooking the flight line and bomb dump in Bravo Sector. A1C Quarles would not have been considered a 'blabber-mouth' by anyone. If he ever said anything past single word, mono-tonal responses, then someone might die of shock. He struck me as a moody, apparently disinterested, self-contained, in-his-own-separate-world, young man. He was also tall, muscular, highly intelligent and from the inner-city somewhere. Maybe, like Thoreau, he just marched to the beat of a different drummer.

But it would soon be time to evaluate Quarles' performance again. And there lay the nub of the problem. Farrita and Shanley wanted to rate him very poorly on his eval. Farrita was Bravo Sector Supervisor and Shanley his Assistant. Each of the four sectors had a Supervisor, usually a senior-ranking SSGT, and an Assistant, a senior SGT up for promotion. They ran herd on all the posts and people assigned there on shift and reported directly to MSGT Veeres, or his Assistant. My problem wasn't that Quarles was a 'dirt-bag.' He most certainly was. However, Farrita and Shanley made several fundamental errors of supervision. That's where the real problem lay, not with Quarles.

"Let's go over A1C Quarles' performance for this rating period, SSGT Farrita."

"Sir, the guy's a real bum, a total pain-in-the-ass!" Farrita exclaimed. "We've told him both at least a thousand times to get a haircut, get his uniform squared-away, get his boots shined, and dozens of other things he needed to take care of. He eventually gets them done, but not as fast as he should. He isn't exactly insolent, but he doesn't do anything quickly when he's told. He moves like he's on drugs. We've had nothing but endless problems with him."

"OK, SSGT Farrita. Then it should be very easy to rate him. You've done numerous verbal counseling's on A1C Quarles. I agree with you. You got that one covered. Now show me the written counseling statements you did on him."

SSGT Farrita was momentarily speechless.

"Ah. . . .no, sir. We didn't do any written counseling statements."

"No written counseling statements there, SSGT Farrita? OK. How about any verbal admonishments? Written admonishments? Letters of reprimand? Article 15s? Courts-martial's? Anything?"

"Um. . . .no, sir. Nothing."

"OK, SSGT Farrita. Now you see my problem and what I told to MSGT Veeres about the little mess we have here. I'm unhappy there's no accompanying paperwork to justify a poor eval on A1C Quarles. If you're going to rate him, the worst you can give him is all 'average' marks all across the board. You have no paperwork to back you up, SSGT Farrita. Sorry."

"BUT SIR! We TOLD him a MILLION times to get his shit-in-one-bag! He never did!"

"I 100% agree with you, SSGT Farrita. I know you did, but you hit the 'operational' word in the little problem we have here: 'Told.' You didn't document your verbal counseling and you didn't do any 'written' counseling statement to back up your verbals. One million verbal's counts as one with me. No, SSGT Farrita, you rate him as 'average.' The next time document you're counseling him with 'written' statements after a verbal warning. Escalate up from there if the verbal counseling doesn't work. You both already knew this was going to happen. And you both know how this system works."

They both were silent.

"Do you have any comments, SGT Shanley? Anything further SSGT Farrita?"

They didn't say anything. As unhappy they were from the looks on their faces, I could also see they both knew I was right. Both of them didn't like it, and I really didn't blame them. However, they had simply been either too lazy, or too slack, to do their work as supervisors. And now they are paying the price for their laziness and poor supervisory skills. I had to be fair to everyone, including Quarles.

"OK, guys, get it done. Have MSGT Veeres chop off on it and I'll endorse it. I'm sorry, SSGT Farrita and SGT Shanley. I empathize with you both. But you both need to document any discrepancies on A1C Quarles the next time this happens as his 'direct' supervisors. Consider it a good 'lesson learned'."

Later I saw A1C Quarles on my Bravo Sector post checks.

"Heard what you did, 1LT Legere. SSGT Farrita and SGT Shanley came by and talked to me. Thought for sure they're going to give me a bad eval again, sir."

"A1C Quarles, this is just as much of a good lesson for you as it is for them. There won't be a next time in their book. You need to get your shit together in one sock now, so I strongly recommend you get it done pronto, or get out of the AF. You're just wasting your time, talents, and efforts here. Either get serious about your career or get a new one. But if you don't, then SSGT Farrita and SGT Shanley will do their very best to speed your way right back to civilian life."

I continued.

"A1C Quarles, I'm going to give you some 'friendly advice' as an 'interested party' in the matter right now rather than as a 'supervisor.' Make a decision on what you're going to do, then do it. You have the capability to be an outstanding Airman or NCO if you wanted. You're very intelligent and sharp from what I can see. But if you don't like the AF's rules and regs then simply get out. Or just keep on going the way you're going now and SSGT Farrita and SGT Shanley will take care of it for you. Very fast. Good luck there, A1C Quarles."

We saluted and I drove on to the next post and the next problem.

-

## ROYAL GEMS JEWELRY SHOP, DOWNTOWN *SATTAHIP, CHONBURI* PROVINCE, THAILAND, 1645, 15 OCTOBER 1975.

I bought *Noy* and *Nit-Noy* a one *Baht* 24k gold chain in jewelry shop as an appreciation gift for all their help on my shopping needs. We walked over to the *wat* to get another 'Buddha' charm for my 'Buddha' chain. Ever since I saw this one SGT outside of CSC with his 12 'Buddhas' on a chain around his neck, I vowed to have the exact same thing. So, each week *Nit-Noy*, or *Noy*, brought me to the local area *wat* complexes to procure a different one each week and added another little 'Buddha' to my chain.

This week *Noy* added a very special one to my growing collection of a half dozen. It was very large, the size of a US half-dollar, polished brass, and in a gold frame setting. She explained it was over 100 years old (I had no clue) and the image was of 'The Father of the Royal Thai Navy'. Supposedly it was very, very lucky, rare, and valuable. Noy said it would fetch 50,000 *Baht* in the 'Buddha' retail market. She said it belonged to her father. I assumed he didn't want to give it to any of his sons, so she inherited the 'Buddha.'

Right outside of the *Sattahip Wat* main gate entrance, just along the white painted masonry wall, was an older, dark brown skinned, sun-worn, wrinkled woman seated on the ground. She was selling birds housed in little

172

dark red wooden birdcages. The woman had at least three dozen. A few held up to three small sparrows each, but most held only one. Both *Noy* and *Nit-Noy* paid the woman some coins, picked up their birdcage and placed it on their forehead, holding it with both palms. They closed their eyes, bent their heads down, and silently mouthed some words. They took the birdcage down to chest level, opened the sliding doorway, and then lightly tapped the bottom until the little birds got the message, they were finally free. Both sparrows quickly fluttered off to the nearest tree. I had never seen anything like it before.

"Is for *choke-dee*, good luck," *Nit-Noy* explained. "You let *nok* go free, then they very *sabai*. You feel *sabai* too."

I couldn't argue with that.

-

**NEAR 'A' AVENUE AND 14<sup>TH</sup> STREET, CHARLIE SECTOR, SOUTH PARKING APRON, FLIGHT LINE, *U-TAPAO* RTNAB, *CHONBURI/RAYONG* PROVINCES, THAILAND, 1500, 21 OCTOBER 1975.**

One week prior it was 'officially' announced by the RTN Base Commander that certain named SP officers, senior NCOs, and junior NCOs on 'official' orders, as promulgated by the Royal Thai Supreme Command Headquarters, Forward, would be presented the 'Royal Thai Supreme Command Headquarters, Forward, Badge' in the grades of First Class, Second Class and Third Class. The Class was awarded depending on the recipient's current rank.

So, some troops (but not all) would have the coveted TSG 'Wings' presented in an appropriate outdoor flight line ceremony, with accompanied citations (written in English). Now I owed CDR *Sawasdiyothin* a third favor.

The appropriate full-scale ceremony was held on the parking apron next to the few remaining SVN AF aircraft, still positioned in rows, all still collecting dust, cobwebs, and rust.

After the Thai and American national anthems were played, the band played some Thai and American marital musical airs. Speeches were made in Thai by a few senior RTN commanders. These were badly translated into English by one of the SSGTs who spoke fairly passable Thai. Then 'Spraybelly' got up in front of the formation and thanked the Thai commanders for the honor in English and this was badly translated into Thai (all explained to me afterwards by CDR *Sawasdiyothin*).

Then, one-by-one, the recipients stepped forward to be handed their TSG 'Wings.' Every one of the 20-odd awardees, including me, was an SP - all the officers, senior back-office NCOs, senior shift supervisor NCOs (Security and LE) and a small smattering of junior NCOs 'who have made noteworthy contributions to the success of the Royal TSG mission' (according to the citation). We were all standing smartly in two rows in front of the assembled formations of RTMC, RTN and other non-recipient AF personnel.

I thought about Jake through the whole ceremony and badly wished he were here. I felt equally bad he couldn't have received his well-deserved TSG 'Wings.' In fact, he'd earned them more than anyone else standing there today, including me. I hoped I could arrange to have him presented a set one day.

-

**CORNER OF 'A' AVENUE AND 9TH STREET, ASSISTANT SHIFT SUPERVISOR'S OFFICE-SECURITY, CSC, 365TH SPS, *U-TAPAO* RTNAB, *CHONBURI/RAYONG* PROVINCES, THAILAND, 1400, 25 OCTOBER 1975.**

I was in the Shift Supervisor's Office talking with MSGT Veeres after post-out when MSGT Boatwright strolled in. I didn't speak much to him mainly because I never had the opportunity. Day Shift was always anxious to clear out after relief by Swings.

MSGT Boatwright was tall, solidly built, completely jolly, very rotund (you might say bulky), but very light on his feet. He had short-cropped, buzz-cut, gray hair, had a continual smile on his face, and always wore metal-rimmed, Owl-like glasses that were supplemented with a deep Oklahoman drawl. He said he still received his small hometown newspaper almost every day by mail and kept up with all the events, personalities, and goings-on back there, even though he had joined the AAF over 30 years ago before the end of WWII. I asked him the first time I saw him (when I noticed him reading it) if his name was ever in the paper. Boatwright smiled and said: "Every day!" He pointed to where his name and address was impressed in ink on the newspaper's front-page corner to show whom it was mailed to. We both laughed. I liked MSGT Boatwright, and he knew it. He was undoubtedly the oldest, most experienced NCO at *U-Tapao*. In fact, it was said that MSGT Boatwright had spent more time waiting in the chow line than most NCOs had in their whole careers.

According to the SP 'grapevine' MSGT Boatwright had been at *U-Tapao* almost continually for the past 10 years, or ever since the base opened - he had more time piled up here than any two NCOs put together, or so it was said. He was the SPS 'corporate knowledge,' having forgotten more than most venerable, old-timer NCOs learn over their careers. MSGT Boatwright loved to play the role of a 'dumb-ass/farm-boy-cracker' for everyone. But beneath his folksy, home-spun, easy-going-manner exterior, he had the sharpest mind of anyone on base. Behind this innocent façade was an expert Mississippi Riverboat gambler who held his cards very, very close to his chest and had a damn good idea what the other players were holding by the reflection in their eyes and the expressions on their faces. I could see he never lost. And nothing got past him.

But the same SP 'grapevine' also attributed (all allegedly) his many, even extensive, financial 'holdings' or 'investments' out in town: land, houses, buildings, tailor shops, night clubs, massage parlors, 'short-time' hotels, laundry facilities, beer bars - the list was endless, all controlled through his Thai 'wife,' or so it was intimated. Who knew? Supposedly he was as rich as King Croesus.

There was only one disagreement we'd had a month ago. One of my SGTs wanted to trade Security shifts with another SGT on Days. It required the approvals of both sets of Shift Supervisors and Security Shift NCOICs. Guillory and I said OK. I never had had any problems with him to date. MSGT Veeres had no objections. MSGT Boatwright not only flat-out said: "NO!!" but "HELL, NO!! NO WAY!!"

"They're drug dealers on their shifts," he sharply replied. "They just want to get in deeper into it. Anyone wants to trade shifts is dealing dope. No way, sir! I don't let these drug traffickers do any more business if I can help it." So, the trade never happened.

"1LT Legere," Boatwright spoke as soon as he saw me. "I want you to watch out and better be careful, sir. Someone is trying to 'back-door' you tonight."

"I don't understand MSGT Boatwright, who's trying to do what to me?"

"'Back-door' you, 1LT. You walk out the 'front door,' someone walks in the 'back door.' just be careful, 1LT Legere. I don't want to see you get 'bush-whacked' by someone. I'm not saying who, but just be very careful, OK, sir? I also don't want you to have a big problem. And watch your back too, 1LT."

"OK, ah, yah. . . . Thanks for the warning there MSGT Boatwright. I'll be careful. I appreciate you giving me a head's up. Thanks again."

I had absolutely no idea what MSGT Boatwright was talking about.

Until I got back to my BOQ room that night. *Nit-Noy* was staying there.

"HEY!! GOD-DAMN!! FINE-LEE!!"

She started right in as soon as she heard my key in the keyhole, with her frantically ripping the inside screen door open.

"*Loi-to* 'Joe' come by to seeing me in tha' room at-like-a-be-about 1900. He 'su-pah' *kee-mao mach-mach!* He say he wan' tal-king to me, but he no wan' talk!! *Mai-dee mach-mach! Alai-wah!?* Thes' boo-shit, he 'su-pah' *go-hoke mach-mach!* I kick hees' stu-pid *toot* right out door, *lay-o, lay-o!!!* God-damn-mutha'-fuck-kees'-my-ass!!! *Chang-yet!!!* I do 'SU-PAH'

BIG contract on he 'damn-ass' 100% for sure! He 'su-pah num-bah' ten!! He die *young-kit* in the Thailand for sure! I be 'su-pah' s*ip-loy mach-mach mo-ho! Sun-teen!!*"

She was still jumping up-and-down some four hours after it happened.

Vogelesgang. Back-door. DAMN! MSGT Boatwright was warning me about Vogelesgang trying to 'back-door' me and nail *Nit-Noy* tonight while he had the day off and I was on duty. That stupid, back-stabbing, scummy, motherless prick, son-of-a-bitch!

-

**CORNER OF 'A' AVENUE AND 9ᵀᴴ STREET, PARKING LOT, OUTSIDE CSC, 365ᵀᴴ SPS, *U-TAPAO* RTNAB, *CHONBURI/RAYONG* PROVINCES, THAILAND, 1900, 31 OCTOBER 1975.**

The several-times-a-day-every-day; very brief, but very intense, downpours; steam-bath-like weather; with temperatures-matching-the-humidity-in-the-high-nineties and constant mix of sunshine, thunderstorm clouds and overcast had been slowly abating over the past few days. It was noticeable in that the temperatures moderated slightly into the low nineties, but the humidity was dropping even faster, perhaps half of what it was. It was actually starting to get pleasant. According to the Thais, the traditional 'cool season' wasn't supposed to start until the end of November. But the fact it was making an early appearance a month ahead of schedule meant only one thing: that a very cold 'cool season' was predicted. I didn't even bring my USAF field jacket with me. I had left it with my youngest brother back in CT. I never thought it would get cold in Thailand.

-

**CORNER OF 'A' AVENUE AND 9ᵀᴴ STREET, SHIFT SUPERVISOR'S OFFICE, CSC, 365ᵀᴴ SPS, *U-TAPAO* RTNAB,**

I walked into the CSC Shift Supervisor's Office after relieving Guillory and Day Shift. SGT Perryman stuck his head in, gave me pointed look and said: "1LT Legere, see the CO." He didn't smile saying it and disappeared.

Then he ducked his head back in and said:

"If a 100 lb. man had 50 lbs. of testicles would that make him half-nuts, sir?"

It was the first time 'Spraybelly' wanted to see me. Except for the first meeting with the other officers when he arrived and the second at Van den Dardener's 'send-off,' 'Spraybelly' hadn't said a single word to me. He never came out of his office, unlike Shellenbarger, who actually made rare, periodic post checks. At least I could at least hand him that. 'Spraybelly' was a total hermit. I got in my jeep and drove over.

After entering I told the CO's new Thai secretary I was here at the direction of the CO. She quickly ushered me into Sprayberry's office.

MAJ Slattermann was standing next to LTC Sprayberry, who was seated. Both were going over some papers on his desk. They both looked up with stern expressions on their faces. I came to attention and saluted.

"1LT Legere," he high-pitched twanged. "The Base Commander has just authorized me to raid Buffalo Village. I will need you and your LE Shift Supervisor to come with me and MAJ Slattermann. I have told no one else about this raid. It will be a total surprise."

"Yes, sir."

I thought maybe this was a 'real' secret in Thailand. That would be a first in Thailand's recorded history, though I might've been wrong.

"1LT Legere, we will convoy to the LE Desk where you will pick-up MSGT Wozniak. He is waiting there now. We will proceed directly to the Main Gate to link up with the RTN Security contingent. We will all convoy to the Buffalo Village gate where the RTN Commander and his people will

178

enter. Since it is their village, they will take what action is appropriate for whatever they find or uncover. Understand all that?"

"Yes, sir!"

He turned to Slattermann and said: "Then MAJ, let's get this show moving!"

'Spraybelly' was acting like he was mounting the D-Day invasion of Europe again with the gravity of how he was expressing himself.

I followed the CO and Ops Officer over to LE, where I picked up MSGT Wozniak. Then we all drove down to the Main Gate where Slattermann went in to get CDR *Sawasdiyothin* and his people. I saw the CDR was his usual exuberant self, like he was being going to a big party or massage parlor. It took a minute for him to muster his LT(JG) Deputy Commander into his gray jeep. A second jeep was filled with RTN Petty Officers carrying side-arms and wearing white helmet liners and armbands.

I thought several things. First, Jake had been after everyone, including the SP COs, as long as he had been here, to raid Buffalo Village. His recommendations were always rejected. Second, I had personally picked up Jake's banner on this crusade. I kept pressing the back office to do the exact same thing. Same results - nothing. I thought it very strange that permission would be suddenly granted. Third, if an operation had anything to do with Thais, then it was no secret. The Thais would know about this caper long before we did. I didn't know how; I just knew they would. There were no secrets in Thailand. I was keeping my expectations and hopes dead low. I didn't know what would happen next. Maybe we'd catch them with their pants down with mountains of stolen IBM electric typewriters, a/c units, aircraft spare parts and who knew what else just waiting to be moved out. But I seriously doubted it. There were just no secrets here. I grew more skeptical every second as we drove along.

The convoy went down 'C' Avenue to 9th Street, behind the AF O-Club, turned right and went down past the 'COL's Country'. Less than a minute later we were parked in a line by the side of the road near the village entrance. The road into it was nothing but a washed-out gravel track down the middle of a wide field of head-high elephant grass. I let my enthusiasm get away with me and went first. Everyone else was walking behind me unusually slow and packed together in one bunch, like they were very afraid of land mines and booby traps. I kept peering back to see if they were still following me. My curiosity was overwhelming since I was going to be the first American inside the 'inner sanctum' of Buffalo Village. I picked up the pace and walked faster. The road, not any wider than a jeep's width, twisted for several dozen meters and abruptly ended at a small clearing. I could see we were very close to the base's perimeter fence. You could also see the tops of the BEQs in the near distance. There were six ramshackle huts, all constructed out of cast-off debris, packing crates, wooden pallet boards, upright bamboo poles and flooring, mainly from tossed-out or discarded base materials.

The whole village was nothing more than a concentrated trash yard. Everywhere was discarded plastic bags, used food containers, base IBM computer print-outs, 'Southern Star' base newspaper pages, old cardboard boxes, litter, plastic trash bags of all sizes, used plastic and glass bottles and dozens of other useless items. It could have qualified as the base garbage dump. A light wind picked up some of the newspaper sheets and plastic bags, sending them airborne. They wafted like lost kites. It was the worst mess I'd ever seen - a complete pigsty. The half dozen men and women and perhaps two dozen scruffy children of varying ages were all attired in horizontal striped sarongs with dirty men's short-sleeve shirts, slip-on shower sandals and no jewelry. There were no *ka-moyed* piles of IBM Selectric typewriters, or mounds of stolen a/c units. It was highly unlikely we'd find anything more than trash.

The 'sheriff's posse' finally arrived. They stood near me, stared at the mess and said nothing. The oldest-looking male (probably the village headman, being gray-haired) walked over to CDR *Sawasdiyothin* and *wai-ed.*' They started an animated conversation in Thai for a few minutes. While they were jabbering away, I wandered around to see the place more closely. Inside the open-air huts were nothing but simple bamboo cots and blankets. There were no animals. If the place collectively had more than USD$20.00 to its name, I'd have been surprised. I walked back to the high elephant grass along the roadway. I noticed a well-worn trace at one point into the thick foliage. I walked over and separated the stalks. I could see a narrow foot-trail once the grass was parted. It led off in the direction of the main highway. After a quick inspection tour, I found twelve more paths leading out of the village, radiating in a rough circle. A few were from the base, but most of the others angled off in different directions to the main highway or west towards Camp *Samae San.* That would explain how the stolen items were transited after they left the base, especially when the perimeter fence line was cut. I brought this to the attention of Sprayberry and Slattermann. Both simply, and sternly, grunted.

Everyone was wrong. Buffalo Village wasn't the staging or storage area as had always been thought, but simply a convenient conduit for anything *ka-moyed* on-base and heading out-bound. It was a safe passageway, or transit point, for the *gigolos* to use without being observed.

CDR *Sawasdiyothin* started a briefing for everyone in English on what the village headman had said. I walked back to the assembled group.

"This man said the villagers see nothing. They hear nothing. He said nobody *ka-moyed* anything from the base. He said nothing here. You can look if you want. They just get all free stuff the *farangs* throwing away, just trash. They very *sabai mach-mach.* The headman said the villagers know nothing about *gigolos.*

We all walked slowly back to our jeeps. The raid had only been a total comedy road show. A complete, utter farce. There are no secrets in Thailand.

-

**CORNER OF 'A' AVENUE AND 9ᵀᴴ STREET, SHIFT SUPERVISOR'S OFFICE, CSC, 365ᵀᴴ SPS, *U-TAPAO* RTNAB, *CHONBURI/RAYONG* PROVINCES, THAILAND, 13:35, 11 NOVEMBER 1975.**

Things were cooling off nicely now. The skies were clear and cloudless, the days pleasant. The temperatures were sharply dropping as waves of cold fronts started coming in from the Himalayas. I could really see the need for my field jacket.

TSGT Bernardo had already PCS-ed when TSGT Bowen arrived. Being the most senior TSGT on Swings, Bowen naturally assumed the Assistant NCOIC for Security slot to MSGT Veeres.

I immediately liked TSGT Bowen for three reasons: One, he looked sharp in his uniform, just as Jake did. In my mind if someone looked sharp, they usually were sharp. Two, he acted in a no non-sense manner, having a professional demeanor toward his duties. Three, the first words out of his mouth were:

"1LT Legere, I'm here to help you catch all these Thai *gigolos.*"

That made him 'aces' with me.

\-

**CORNER OF 'A' AVENUE AND 9TH STREET, SHIFT SUPERVISOR'S OFFICE, CSC, 365TH SPS, *U-TAPAO* RTNAB, *CHONBURI/RAYONG* PROVINCES, THAILAND, 1600, 12 NOVEMBER 1975.**

SGT Perryman stuck his head around the door frame of the Shift Supervisor's office with a grim look on his face.

"1LT Legere, see the CO in his office."

Then he stuck his head back around again.

"Guy wants to join this monastery. The Head Abbot says OK, but you only get to say two words every ten years. Guy says OK. First ten years goes by the guy gets brought in before the Abbott and gets to say his two words: 'Lousy chow' he says. Next ten years goes by the guy gets brought in again and says: 'Hard bunk.' Next ten years goes, same thing: 'Cold showers.' The Abbott says: 'Sorry, we'll have to ask you to leave now.'

182

'Why?' the guy asks. 'You've done nothing but complain ever since you got here.' Sir."

I felt the same way.

After walking into the SPS HQs I told the CO's Secretary that the CO had requested to see me. I was announced and escorted in quickly.

"1LT Legere, I want you and your LE NCOIC to go and place CAPT Anderson under arrest. You will escort him over to the base hospital where you will turn custody of him over to COL Cahill at the hospital Psychiatric Ward. Do you understand me?"

"Yes, sir."

"Do you have any questions?"

"No, sir."

"Then get going."

"Yes, sir!"

I saluted, turned, and left his office.

CAPT Anderson, I thought. Christ. After that first day at lunch when I arrived, I hadn't seen him since. That was back in June, now it's November. My first impression was the guy's lights were on, but no one was home. But place him under arrest? This was not going to be fun.

I mounted up and drove over to LE. I had the Desk SGT call MSGT Wozniak on the radio and had him repair to that location ASAP. He arrived within five minutes. I walked him outside and explained what we had to do. He was speechless past one "OK, sir." I could see from his face this was going to be as distasteful to him as it obviously was to me.

For some strange reason SPS Admin had a separate micro-office building, like a large, separate wooden tool shed, or a small gate shack next to a small-town railway crossing barrier. It was right next to the new base theater and just down the street from the NCO Club on 11th Street. It had enough space to squeeze in two desks and chairs plus several long, two-level, metal cabinets with hinged glass-fronted doors with knobs - the kind you store AFRs and AFMs in numerical order. I knew about the place, but never had any reason to go in. Maybe Anderson had commandeered the place and felt less constricted working there than he did in the claustrophobic, sardine packed wooden SPS hooches. I'd seriously misgivings about the whole situation as we drove. I caught MSGT Wozniak out of the corner of my eye looking just as uncomfortable as I was.

We walked into the tiny building, saluted and I requested if the CAPT wouldn't mind meeting with us outside. Anderson at first appearances seemed to be OK - mentally anyway. I didn't detect anything amiss, other than his senses were on edge, maybe thinking about a 'flight-or-fight' situation. I didn't need to cope with either one. I finally caught that his eyes looked 'dead' for lack of a better term, if eyes can be described as such. No 'light' was coming out. Maybe 'dull' or 'flat' would be a better term. I chose my words carefully when we cleared the building.

"CAPT Anderson," I said as formally as I could: "I have been ordered by the Commanding Officer, LTC Sprayberry, to place you under arrest and escort you to the base hospital. Are you willing to come with us, sir?"

"No, 1LT Legere, I will not."

I didn't expect that. I must've had a real 'deer-in-the-headlights' look. I mindlessly stood there for a few moments, clearly taken aback at his answer. I was silently wondering what the hell I was going to do next.

Anderson spoke again.

'1LT Legere," he gravely intoned. "Let me explain a few things to you. First, you cannot place me 'under arrest.' I may be ordered, by properly-constituted military or legal authority, say in a courts-martial proceeding, to be placed in my quarters, for example, 'under arrest.' But you do not have that authority. Second, you may place me 'under apprehension,' but not 'under arrest'."

Damn! He was right. I had forgotten that subtle distinction in military law. I'd used the term 'Spraybelly' had given me without considering the application. Then again 'Spraybelly' had never been an SP officer. He'd have no idea about either concept.

"OK, CAPT Anderson," I formally said again. "I am now placing you 'under apprehension' at the direct orders of LTC Sprayberry. Will you accompany us, sir?"

"No, 1LT Legere, you cannot place me 'under apprehension' either. The only person who can do that is my Commanding Officer, or any other officer of higher rank, duly appointed or directed to do so, by competent, legally authorized, or higher authority."

Damn! He was right again. No officer who is junior or inferior in rank to another officer can place that (or any) higher-ranking officer under 'arrest' or 'apprehension' even if they had the technical authority to do so, say as an SP performing his official duties. A more senior officer in grade to the officer in question would have to do that. Then 'Spraybelly' would have to come over here and order Anderson's 'apprehension' himself personally if he wanted it to be done.

"Would you excuse us CAPT Anderson for a moment?"

Anderson nodded slowly and sagely.

I walked off with MSGT Wozniak a short distance. We turned and faced.

"1LT Legere, what CAPT Anderson said is completely true. We can't do it. We'll have to get the CO to come over and handle this. I don't like this any more than you do, sir."

"I agree with you MSGT Wozniak. We need to get the CO here." A bad taste had formed in my mouth at how this was going.

I went back to Anderson, saluted, asked him to please excuse us, loaded up and drove off. Anderson maintained a serene, bemused look on his face as we departed the area. We drove to the LE Office first. I used the telephone to call the SPS HQs building for LTC Sprayberry. I was placed on hold. Then the CO's secretary came on and finally gave me answer no one could find him. She said he'd already departed the HQs. I looked at my watch, where the hell could he be? I called him on the radio. No response. I asked her for his address. She checked and said she didn't have it, no one had it. Shit! I said I'll come over there. I called 'Spraybelly' again on the radio, No response.

I got her to go through his desk to find something that had his address on it. Apparently, he hadn't given it to her or anyone. I had to think. Who would have it? Billeting! That's it! They would have assigned him an a 'hooch' in 'COL's Country' due to his important position here, regardless of the SPS CO's rank. I called 'Spraybelly' on the radio twice again. Silence. Damn!

Then it slowly, finally dawned on me. That lousy, low-life, slimy-rattlesnake-for-a-father, lousy-son-of-a-bitch turned his radio off and was hiding in his quarters! Those cowardly, yellow-bellied, no-balls, useless bastard! He didn't want to be contacted or bothered about any of this. He was ducking out on the whole thing. We went over to billeting and got 'Spraybelly's' address. More profanities formed in my mind. Then I went straight to 'COL's Country' with a grim determination and more speed than I usually drove. I did my best to control my indignation, frustration and anger at being sent on a useless mission by a complete fool.

'Spraybelly' could have handled this problem 100 different ways, all of them better, like ordering Anderson by telephone show up at the base hospital and report to COL Cahill in person. Then he could then have had Anderson evaluated and committed, if needed, right there. But no. I was in 'Spraybelly's' little 'comedy act' now as the star buffoon.

I rapped on his outer hooch door forcefully. 'Spraybelly' finally opened it appeared in his shorts, socks, and t-shirt with a blank look on his face that described he knew exactly why we were there but had not been expecting to see us. I explained the conversation I had with Anderson; explained I tried to get him on the radio repeatedly without success, and the reason for our visit to his hooch. 'Spraybelly' didn't say a word. He looked like he'd been 'Jap-slapped' hard in the face with a large mackerel, completely stunned. He went back inside, got dressed in his cammo uniform and walked out, just as wordlessly. We convoyed back to see Anderson, who was still standing outside, waiting for our inevitable return.

'Spraybelly' walked over to him and simply said:

"OK Ken, let's go."

CAPT Anderson gave him a slightly crooked smile, saluted, slowly nodded; and then climbed into the shotgun seat of 'Spraybelly's' jeep. As they moved off to the Psychiatric Ward, I turned to MSGT Wozniak, shook my head back and forth a few times and muttered some things under my breath I wouldn't have wanted my mother to hear. MSGT Wozniak just nodded his head in understanding. We loaded up and went back to the LE Office.

-

**CORNER OF 'A' AVENUE AND 9TH STREET, SHIFT SUPERVISOR'S OFFICE, CSC, 365th SPS, U-*TAPAO* RTNAB, *CHONBURI/RAYONG* PROVINCES, THAILAND, 1355, 17 NOVEMBER 1975.**

It was another interesting day to put pen-to-paper and write home about. The TSG contingent went out on strike again promptly at 0545 for another pay raise. The word was again duly passed up the RTN and AF chains-of-command. At 0800 sharp, CDR *Sawasdiyothin*, pointedly and directly (with smiles, *wais,* and politeness of course - these were Thais, naturally) informed the TSGs ringleaders (much to their total surprise) that all TSGs were summarily fired - effectively immediately. They had just 30 minutes to get their personal belongings and clear off base. All TSG ID cards were confiscated on departure through the Pass & ID gate. The RTMC troops again took up their tower and bunker positions on the perimeter posts. The word again spread quickly through the fastest form of communications known in the history of mankind - the Thai 'grapevine.' No further attempts were made to *ka-moy* any more perimeter fencing.

-

**CORNER OF 'A' AVENUE AND 9TH STREET, SHIFT SUPERVISOR'S OFFICE, CSC, 365TH SPS, *U-TAPAO RTNAB, CHONBURI/RAYONG* PROVINCES, THAILAND, 1500, 19 NOVEMBER 1975.**

SGT Perryman stuck his head around the door frame of the Shift Supervisor's office with a grim look on his face.

"1LT Legere, see the CO in his office."

Then he stuck his head back around again.

"Young Italian girl gets married to this older Italian construction worker. She's worried about what happens on her honeymoon night. So, she talks to her Mother in their kitchen. "Mama-Mama, what do I do?" she says. And the mother says: "Don't worry. Just go upstairs an' be witha' you husband, everything will be all right. I just stay down here an' stir tha' spaghetti sauce." So, she goes upstairs and sees her husband taking off his shirt. She runs downstairs and cries: "Mama-Mama, he gota' hairy chest!" And the mother says: "Don't worry. Just go upstairs an' be with a' you husband, everything will be all right. I just stay down here an' stir tha' spaghetti sauce." So, she goes upstairs again and sees her husband taking off his pants. She runs downstairs and cries: "Mama-mama, he gota' hairy legs!" And the mother says: "Don't worry. Just go upstairs an' be with a' you husband, everything will be all right. I just stay down here an' stir tha' spaghetti sauce." So, she goes upstairs again, and he's taken his shoes and socks off. Now she sees he's lost half his right foot in an accident. She runs downstairs and cries: "Mama-Mama, he gota' a foot an' a half!" So, the mother shouts: "YOU STAY DOWN HERE AN' STIR THA' SPAGHETTI SAUCE AND I'LL GO UPSTAIRS!""

"Sir."

I thought to myself this was getting to be a really bad habit, like inhaling opium smoke, in 'Spraybelly' summoning me to his office for all these off-the-wall *ba* projects.

I walked into the HQs and told the CO's secretary that the CO requested to see me. I was announced and escorted in quickly. I came to the position of attention and saluted. I didn't get a salute in return.

"1LT Legere, I have a task for you," he high-pitched twanged at me, as usual. With about as much warmth as the Lord-High Executioner has for a condemned man at the block.

"I am directing you to escort a BX semi-trailer truck to the port at *Klong Toey* in *Bangkok* first thing tomorrow morning. You will RON in *Bangkok*. There you take custody of another BX semi-trailer loaded with BX goods and escort it down here the following morning. You will be authorized two days of per diem. You will be accompanied by the RTN and the Thai National Police who will provide front and rear security for your convoy, but it is your responsibility to see the first shipment gets up there and the second one gets back safely, no one else's. Do you understand me?"

"Yes, sir!"

"1LT Vogelesgang will assume the rest of your duty today as Shift Supervisor. You will need to get to sleep early. The rendezvous time tomorrow is 0500 at the rear of the BX loading dock. The BX Manager will meet you there. You can sign all the forms, get the routing and convoy composition and any other information from the Thai National Police Commander in charge of convoy security. You roll-out at 0530 sharp. Any questions?"

"No, sir!"

"Then get going."

"Yes, sir!" I saluted, turned, and marched out.

I called Vogelesgang on the radio and told him to meet me in the CSC parking lot ASAP. He was only a few minutes away, arriving just as I turned in my .38, GAU, ammo clips and radio in.

"What's up?"

"Special project," I said. "CO wants me to escort a BX semi to *Bangkok* tomorrow morning at 0-dark-30 and take another one back the following morning. I get to RON in *Bangkok* one night. I have to hit the rack early, so rest of the shift from today is officially yours."

It would be my first trip out of the immediate area and to *Bangkok*.

"No problem."

"I'm going to meet *Nit-Noy* in *Bangkok* if she can get off. Maybe we'll catch some dinner or see a movie afterwards."

The LAST thing I wanted was Vogelesgang trying to 'back-door' me again on *Nit-Noy* while I was up in *Bangkok*. So, I wanted him to know she wouldn't be here just in case the slimy bastard got any bright ideas and tried - again.

"OK - sounds like fun."

"Hope so. See you in three days."

-

**BOOTH BY THE FRONT WINDOW, TAMPA RESTAURANT, FLORIDA HOTEL, 43 *PHAYATHAI* ROAD, *RAJATHEVI* DISTRICT, *BANGKOK*, THAILAND, 1800, 20 NOVEMBER 1975.**

We decided not to go out for dinner elsewhere. Partially because *Nit-Noy* was worried about the extremely remote chance someone might see her in *Bangkok* and say something to her family through the Thai 'grapevine' if they saw her alone with a *farang*, and partially because I was very tired from getting up so early. The convoy ride up to *Bangkok* was uneventful. We were neither abducted by space aliens, nor beamed mysteriously anywhere else in the galaxy. Neither were we stopped by phony roadblocks to hi-jack our cargo, nor kidnapped, killed, and buried in the swamp by the Thai 'mafia.' We also did not collectively agree to sell the contents of the BX container, split the profits, and disappear to Tahiti forever.

I left the jeep at the *Klong Toey* Port in a supposedly 'secure' area (according to the Thai National Police Commander accompanying us, since they were supposedly leaving their vehicles there too, along with the RTN Security escort vehicles. I assumed they'd all be safe from theft) and took a taxi to meet *Nit-Noy*. We had previously agreed to meet in the lobby of the Florida Hotel on *Phayathai* Road (at her suggestion) with no time being set except 'afternoon.'

Dinner was equally uneventful. Our conversation was subdued. We didn't really say much to each other. We had the whole restaurant to ourselves. You'd have thought we could speak freely now as with every other conversation we'd ever had there were always other people within earshot, or close-by us as chaperones, listening in. There was not a time that we were ever alone by ourselves.

But it seemed strangely awkward now for some unfathomable reason. We had talked about everything under the sun to date, speaking to each other virtually every day about every subject, thought and thing imaginable, all except for one huge looming subject:  the future. I didn't know how to broach my future together with *Nit-Noy* if we (or I) had one. It was an uncomfortable feeling for me.

However, I knew the ONE thing I was not going to do: push her. I would not suggest, lead, force, cajole, ask, pressure, or demand an answer from her about the subject, as I had known of many other eligible suitors to do with her. If she wanted to spend the rest of her life with me, then that was going to be HER choice - not mine. I wanted to be the ONLY person she knew who didn't want to possess all of her:  body, mind, soul, heart. I also wanted her to always have her freedom: of choice, of movement, of future options, of life, of love - like a magnificent eagle you cannot chain to a perch. She, like that majestic bird, would have to return on her own volition, if she were so pleased. *Nit-Noy* was of the same character in my mind. I could clearly see she wanted her freedom more than anything else in the world. I only wanted her to be herself, not what her family or others had always projected on her. I sensed her deep rebelliousness was in direct opposition to those continual outside projections and influences.

But I also wanted to be the ONLY person who didn't ask her to marry. I knew she had other countless, serious proposals. If she saw I was, or going to be, the one 'special person' in her life, then she would let me know. If our relationship was going anywhere, then she was the one who was going to direct it, no matter what the future would bring us. And if she decided to walk away, now, or at any time in the future, then as much as that would utterly shatter my heart, I would accept it, no matter how hard I knew that would be. If that was what was going to make her truly happy. I would sacrifice my own happiness for hers if I could make sure she got it. I loved her very much. It was all I could do for her. The only real gift I could give her. Maybe she would see my true love one day. I would wait and see what happened. I promised myself I would be patient.

I smiled at her; she smiled back at me.

Then she covered her petite mouth with the back of her hand and loudly yawned.

"*Mung-nawn!*" she said. Then she languorously raised her arms above her head in a sinuous manner and stretched her body out like a supple cat. She yawned again and giggled. I imagined she'd gotten up very early this morning as well.

"*By ab-nam*," she added. "*By-nawn!*"

Yes, I agreed with her. It was time to take a bath and go to sleep.

-

**CORNER OF 'A' AVENUE AND 9TH STREET, SHIFT SUPERVISOR'S OFFICE, CSC, 365th SPS, *U-TAPAO* RTNAB, *CHONBURI/RAYONG* PROVINCES, THAILAND, 1400, 22 NOVEMBER 1975.**

We'd just posted-out when SGT Perryman stuck his head around the door frame of the on-duty Shift Supervisor's office with the same grim look on his face when he always had bad news to pass along to me.

"1LT Legere, see the CO in his office."

There was no comedy or comedy shtick from SGT Perryman this time. Maybe his favorite joke writer had the day off. I thought: Now what?

I only knew one thing. 'Spraybelly' was not going to give me a Letter of Commendation or an AFCM for successfully escorting the BX semi-trailer back to the base safely.

The trip back to *U-T* was as uneventful as the trip up was. At 0445 I was back at the *Klong Toey* Port loading yard by the BX loading dock with the Thai National Police and RTN security escorts ready to roll-out back to *U-T*. The BX Manager there broke two large brass, keyless padlocks and several serialized aluminum-strip locking straps that were on the back door of the semi-trailer with a large set of bolt cutters. He opened the doors, took out a Polaroid instant-photo camera from his bag and took several pictures of the goods inside from different angles. He took all the photos and placed them into a large manila envelope. The manager then sealed it with strong clear tape all around and wrote his signature across the back of it with a large marker pen. Also printing his name on the front, he handed me the envelope with instructions to give this to the BX Manager when I arrived back on base. Then the semi-trailer doors were sealed in the identical manner with a new set of keyless locks and serialized straps.

On our arrival the BX Manager cut everything off with bolt cutters; then opened the back door. He took the pictures out of the envelope, compared them with what he saw inside the trailer was the exact same thing. When he was completely satisfied that nothing inside had been pilfered or stolen, he nodded. We were then all released. I went back to the BOQ for a long nap before going over to the O-Club for dinner.

Now I was standing at attention in front of 'Spraybelly's' desk.

"Who told you that you could see *Nit-Noy* up in *Bangkok,* 1LT Legere?"

I was stunned. Who told this son-of-a-bitch I was meeting *Nit-Noy* in *Bangkok*?"

"No one, sir," I replied. I strained to hold back my quickly exploding temper. It was on my off-duty time. I had already completed my mission to *Bangkok*. I was free to see anyone I liked or go anywhere I pleased there, sir."

I didn't need anyone's God-damn 'permission,' especially his, to see *Nit-Noy* there, or anywhere else in the world. What's with this total BS?

"You needed my permission, 1LT Legere. You didn't get it and I wouldn't have given it to you in any case. Next time you make sure you tell me what you are going to be doing off-duty first before you go pulling any stunts like this again. You are dismissed!"

I saluted and walked out.

I was incandescently white hot. First, it was absolutely none of his fucking business, sticking his nose into my personal life again. Second, who in the hell told him I was with *Nit-Noy* up in *Bangkok?* She wouldn't. If she'd told any Thai, then it would have been all over the whole country in two seconds flat. I didn't. It was absolutely no one's damn business in the squadron or anywhere else anyway.

Then it hit me hard, right in the face! OH SHIT! I DID! DAMN IT! Vogelesgang! I wanted to keep him out of my room and away from *Nit-Noy* for three days. That bastard went straight into 'Spraybelly's' office and told him, of course. That sneaky, back-stabbing bastard! I screwed myself up!

-

**CORNER OF AVENUE 'C' AND 13TH STREET, DETACHMENT #7, OSI FIELD OFFICE, *U-TAPAO* RTNAB, *CHONBURI/RAYONG* PROVINCES, THAILAND, 1500, 24 NOVEMBER 1975.**

My final destination on this afternoon's little errand was going to be Det #7, OSI Field Office. The Det was housed in a small, simple, and non-descript, wooden, white-painted building near CBPO. But I had to stop by SPS HQs first. An order had come down through the CO's secretary to take some files and deliver them to the OSI Det office for the CO. Plus the CSC On-Duty SGT asked me to get him some blank incident report forms if I was going in that direction. I told him I was.

I noticed the icy stares of almost everyone (and deliberately ignored by the rest, except the Thai secretaries who all smiled at me), when I walked in there. Like I was the big, bad 'bogeyman' of legend, or had contracted some fatal, contagious disease. I'd had just grabbed a big pile of blank incident report forms in the basket from on top of the filing cabinet where I was told they always were for CSC first, when the CO's secretary walked over and was ready to hand me a big armful of thick documents in very large, sealed brown envelopes for hand-delivery. They were copies of routine OSI Initial or Updated Reports from the front cover page routing markings. I'd handled enough of them when I was pinch-hitting for both SPS Commanders I worked under at Maxwell during their many leaves, schools, and conferences. They were just SPS CO's 'courtesy copies' of routine progress reports on whatever investigations OSI were conducting. I signed the transmittal slips for them first, counted them again making sure everything jived correctly on the transmittal sheet, took them from her arms and left.

The Det was just a few minutes away. I walked right into the middle of an animated, on-going conversation between four fairly young-looking guys in single-colored safari suits sitting behind desks.

"Bullshit, asshole! I got FOUR Thai 'mafia' contracts out on me out in town!"

"Kiss muh' weenie, dickwad! There're FIVE Thai 'mafia' contracts out on my ass. So, screw you!"

"You guys are both total losers. I got you beat hands-down. I got SIX, baby, SIX! Count 'um!"

"Screw you guys and the horses you rode in on! SEVEN! SEVEN OF THEM!"

They went back-and-forth loudly arguing, like macho 10-year-olds to see who had the best marbles, the biggest bicycle, or largest comic book collection at home. I was as unnoticeable as bib overalls at a large Nebraska family reunion. I had one of them sign the forms that he received the reports. He did it absent-mindedly. I dropped the records off on the desk in-box closest to the doorway, took the transmittal sheets and walked out.

Those conversations didn't make any sense. I didn't remember hearing much about Thailand while I was back in Maxwell. I was headed to Korea until right at the very end when my orders got changed. Actually when anything that anyone told me about Thailand (that could have been a lot in hindsight, I wasn't paying any attention to it), I had just simply ignored or tuned-out. But I did remember one specific thing. It had always stuck in the back of my mind for some strange reason. I was informed that if you were in OSI anywhere in Thailand and got one creditable 'contract' on your life by the Thais or Thai 'mafia,' you were transferred out 'immediately.' No hesitation, no questions! BANG! Gone! So what were they talking about?

And why would they joke about something as important, even life-threatening, as that?

-

**CORNER OF AVENUE 'A' AND 9TH STREET, SNACK BAR, BEHIND THE SPS ARMORY, NEAR CSC, 365TH SPS, *U-TAPAO* RTNAB, *CHONBURI/ RAYONG* PROVINCES, THAILAND, 1825, 25 NOVEMBER 1975.**

There was a published news report in THE BANGKOK POST today of local interest. It explained there'd been an initial report coming from the US (as shown on some NBC Nightly News 'Special Expose') that supposedly abandoned, local *dek-deks* were being sold off for cash. (I guessed half-Thai/half-*farang* off-spring of bar girls too dumb to use contraceptives or have their 'partners' use them. Or maybe they were just being crafty and the *dek-deks* were being used as 'bargaining chips' to get the GI 'fathers' to marry them, if they knew they'd made their 'girlfriends' pregnant. Who knew?)

Anyway - the news report said these *dek-chais* and *dek-yings* were being sold to anyone who wanted one for some ready cash, stuffed in a room over a shop somewhere in Kilo *Sip*. I guessed for a couple of hundred dollars (or tens of thousands of *Baht*) you could have yourself 'instant' children, or maybe even have an 'instant' family - there were plenty of *poo-yings* dying to get married to GIs and fly to the 'Land of the Big BX.' Probably you could mix-and-match them. I seriously doubted there'd be a shortage of *dek-deks* any time soon with all the GI *poo-chais* and Thai *poo-yings* constantly banging their bodies together.

I decided to forgo chow at the O-Club and went for a quick grease-burger and fries at the little snack bar right behind the Armory. The owner, an older Thai woman - the Mama-san - with her pre-teen daughter, handled all the action slinging burgers and anything else on the grill; the young girl worked the cash register. The menu was sparse - basic stomach-fillers. They did a roaring trade in US and Thai fast food amongst the shifts. The good thing was it never closed - her husband and their other young daughter handled the second 12-hour shift. The food was lousy - barely edible, but it was very hot, very fast, and very cheap. It was also good enough if you were hungry - especially if you either didn't have time to go to the chow hall or club, or when they were closed. The little place was completely built out of scrap lumber from large AF packing crates and discarded wooden pallets.

I decided to rib the Mama-san about the *dek-deks* while I waited in line to place my order along with a few other troops on duty who were also on their dinner break.

"I heard you can buy some nice *dek-deks* down at Kilo *Sip* very 'su-pah' cheap-cheap!"

She laughed and gave it right back to me: "Why pay!? Can make for free!!"

We all broke up laughing.

-

**CORNER OF 'A' AVENUE AND 9TH STREET, PARKING LOT, OUTSIDE THE ARMORY, CSC, 365th SPS, *U-TAPAO* RTNAB, *CHONBURI/RAYONG* PROVINCES, THAILAND, 0035, 26 NOVEMBER 1975.**

"1LT LEGERE, WE'VE GOT A BIG PROBLEM, SIR!"

"What's up, TSGT Waring?"

"One of the stray dogs ran in and bit the little girl working in the Snack Bar! The dog's probably rabid! We need to get it fast before it gets off base!"

The 1LT on Mids had already relieved me. I had just turned in all of my gear, just waiting by the Armory for the final deuce-and-a-half to bring in the last troops so we could call it a night.

I started sprinting towards the Snack Bar.

"Show me where the dog went!" I yelled.

We ran around the Armory to the snack bar. I asked the handwringing, obviously distraught, girl's father did he see which way the dog ran? He wordlessly pointed towards the Main Gate. I didn't have time to check on the girl. I was sure she was being well-attended to by others. I knew exactly where the dog was heading to straight to the largest fence hole next to Pass & ID.

I ran back to the Armory, quickly signed out an M-870 shot gun and half a dozen shells (the on-duty Armorer had them in his hands and the forms signed and ready for me, already anticipating my next move). I rapidly loaded the weapon at the clearing barrel; then jumped into TSGT Waring's jeep. He was waiting with the motor running beside the clearing barrels for me.

"LET'S ROLL!"

We left rubber marks in tearing out of the parking lot, turned sharply right and shot over to 'C' Avenue, turned sharply right again and sped down the road. At this hour there was no traffic.

"WE'LL HEAD HIM OFF AT 3RD STREET WHEN HE COMES OUT PAST THE OLD BX!" I shouted.

TSGT Waring shouted back at me: "DONT HIT THE DOG IN THE HEAD WITH THE SHOTGUN, 1LT. THE VET AT THE HOSPITAL NEEDS IT INTACT TO TEST THE DOG FOR RABIES! AIM FOR THE DOG'S CENTER!"

"GOT IT!"

We whipped around onto 3RD Street in front of the bank and stopped. Kennedy cut the vehicle lights but kept the engine idling. We waited.

It didn't take long. A miserable-looking, scrawny, mangy, half-starved, black cur came trotting around the corner of the old BX and was heading in the direction of the fence opening. He was panting hard. Kennedy released his foot off the brakes, and we started our roll. The dog suddenly came to a stop at the sound of tires on pavement, looked right at us, quickly turned and began trotting back the way he came.

We continued east down 3RD Street, turned right on 'B' Avenue to 6th Street. We could see the dog was rapidly tiring. We left the road and trailed after it. We went cross-country over a wide, low grass-and-gravel strewn, abandoned parking lot between 'A' and 'B' Avenues, both of us heading straight back to the Snack Bar. The dog must have been starving. It looked like skin-and-bones; hard, sinewy muscles were about the only thing keep it from coming apart at the seams. The dog looked exhausted. As we bumpily rolled on, the dog slowly came to a halt in the middle of the field. We circled it and stopped, maybe five meters away from the now stationery, completely exhausted, mutt. It had given up the fight. This was the end, and the dog knew it. It kept staring at us.

I snapped the shotgun to my shoulder and kept the muzzle pointed directly at the dog's center.

"1LT Legere, you've got to avoid shooting it in the head! The vet will need it to see if the dog is rabid!"

I nodded my understanding, never taking my eyes, or the shotgun muzzle, off the dog.

I slowly exited the vehicle and closed within two meters. I put my cheek to the shotgun, aimed it at the dog's center, braced myself for the re-coil and pulled the trigger. The blast of 20-gauge pellets caught the dog square in the middle. It immediately toppled over. I still kept the muzzle trained on the now inert dog, walked the few steps to where I stood directly over it, pumped the shotgun's action and fired again.

TSGT Waring exited the jeep and came to stand next to me. We inspected the carcass.

"Great shot, 1LT! You missed the head!"

Just then, the Mids Assistant Supervisor for Security pulled up in his jeep with his Assistant.

"We'll take it from here, 1LT Legere. Good job, sir!"

The Supervisor directed the other NCOs to get the cardboard piece and rags out of the back of his jeep to grab the carcass, using them to avoid getting animal blood or intestines on their uniforms. They placed the dog into the back of their jeep for the trip to the Hospital.

I didn't feel anything - numbness really. I did my job, but I drew no joy from the incident. I just felt emotionally drained. I never did find out if the dog was rabid. And I never saw the little girl in the Snack Bar again.

-

**CORNER OF 'C' AVENUE AND 15TH STREET, COMMANDING OFFICER'S OFFICE, 365TH CES HQs, *U-TAPAO* RTNAB, *CHONBURI/RAYONG* PROVINCES, THAILAND, 0900, 27 NOVEMBER 1975.**

The Commander of the 365th CES, COL John Berryman, sat frowning behind his desk. He was angry. That was something he rarely did, if ever - lose his temper and become upset. But he could not help it this time.

He was born in England, while his father was attending a training course with the RAF. His Mother was of fine, old English stock, College-of-Herald's listed family coat-of-arms and the rest, from London. He mainly grew up in Boston, MA, with his mother and extended relatives when his father was posted to various overseas AAF bases as a pilot, as she declined to follow him. (She greatly disliked hot weather, so that meant traveling to ABs in the Philippines, Hawaii and Panama were out.) So, his accent was both a mixture of very proper Bostonian and British English. By the time he was 20 he had completed three years of mechanical engineering at some reputable stateside university when he decided to enlist in the AAF in the summer of 1944 before the war had ended.

The US Army, in its infinite wisdom, gave him a direct commission in the Corps of Engineers and posted him to the 8th AF, now based in England, where his father (a long-serving CAPT at the out-break of WWII) was now a full-bird COL and CO of a B-17 Bombardment Group, also based in England. After hostilities ceased the US Army gave him some time off so he could go back to finish his final year of college. He used his new GI Bill. When the AAF was magically transformed into the USAF in 1947, he transferred over and was posted to a newly constituted CES at March AFB.

An MS degree in Mechanical Engineering followed, as did positions of increasing responsibility and authority all over the world. He was on wife number three now. Wife #1 wife ran off with some 'young buck' (as he called him) not too long into their marriage. That union also did last long, as he already knew. Wife #2 died of lingering cancer a number of years ago - very sad. Wife #3 was an older, classy Thai lady who worked for the UN in Bangkok. They were very happy together.

COL Berryman was of average height, excellent build, in good health and always displayed a friendly (if proper) demeanor. Unfortunately, he looked much older than his 51 years, as his hair had prematurely turned snow white. However, that was not a bad occurrence, as he now looked exactly like distinguished, erudite professors, scientists and doctors do on popular TV shows. But beneath his positive, friendly exterior, should you try to slip something 'dodgy' past him (a British English word meaning something 'very illegal,' sometimes the COL forgot he was speaking British English to Americans) then the perpetrators would find that just about 1/100 of a millimeter below Berryman's surface was steel (high-carbon/tungsten/chromium/titanium-alloy, case-hardened). Now in his 31st year of active duty (he knew he could do one final follow-on tour back stateside and retire) he thought he had seen everything to date. Not so.

First, everything was being stolen on base (and out of the CES and REDHORSE yards) to where he couldn't perform his mission properly. He was upset about that. And the SPs weren't helping at all, in that they couldn't find the 'dodgy' culprits or slow the level of thievery down. He strongly suspected that some of the Thai workers inside the CES were aiding and abetting the criminals.

Second, the SPS had always complained that the CES didn't move fast enough to replace the cyclone fencing around the base perimeter. Well, now! Only 30-bloody-(damn)-miles of perimeter fencing to repair/replace/maintain and sometimes hundreds of meters of fencing disappearing every night with SP or TSG guards in sight of it happening. You'd have thought, according to the SPS, it was the only 'blooming' thing he had to do all day long was replace 'nicked' (stolen) fencing. But with the

RTMC troops being posted, the fence thievery had finally stopped. Now the task was simply replacing missing fence line.

And third, was this 'blasted' move to the new SP building. Or rather no 'bloody' move at all!

But I believe, he thought to himself, I have that problem now 'well in hand.' The new Base CO had done a 'right proper job' on the SPS CO at the base staff meeting, giving him a 'right proper dressing down' for his nonsensical refusal to move. As he might have said, in a flat tone, to someone British: "Not bad."

-

**BETWEEN 'B' AND 'C' AVENUES, 10th STREET, THE NEW 365TH SPS HQs BUILDING, *U-TAPAO* RTNAB, *CHONBURI/RAYONG* PROVINCES, THAILAND, 1500, 27 NOVEMBER 1975.**

Even well prior to my arrival in June, a move was afoot to get the SPS out of their old, cramped, firetrap, wooden hooch cluster into more spacious quarters. The 365th CES had already been inside the newly constructed building next to the Base Finance Office making final preparations for the transfer from earlier in the year. The final move-in was scheduled back in late April. But various delays, problems and screw-ups by the SPS kept postponing the final 'day of reckoning.' Everyone (well, almost everyone) greatly anticipated the move. Now, with the turmoil of the changes in SPS Commanders and Ops Officers finally over, the move was finally set for COB, 31 August 1975.

Spraybelly' refused. He was absolutely adamant. He came up every 'reason' in the book, plus a few that weren't, not to go. And none of those reasons made any sense, of course. He would not budge.

The new SPS home was in a new, large, simple, fireproof, rectangular cinder block and concrete-constructed building. It was well-lit, very spacious (similar to a small college gymnasium in size), had central a/c unit and a high ceiling, with many plug-in outlets, plenty of floor space for anyone who wanted some impressive office acreage, a large conference room so no one would have to stand. It was, in short, everything the old buildings weren't. Everything in there: furniture, desks, chairs, partitions, telephones, office equipment, desk lamps, and electric typewriters and filing cabinets, was right-out-of-cellophane brand new. It wouldn't have been out of place as a NASA Mission Control Launch Center, except the new building has no windows.

'Spraybelly' still said no. He would not move. Finally, after many months of back-and-forth endless wrangling between him and the 365TH CES CO, the new Base CO gave 'Spraybelly' a-direct-under-penalty-of-Special-Courts-Martial-order: Be in the new SPS HQ office building by COB Thanksgiving Day, 27 November 1975, or else I'll file charges.

The SPS moved, or almost all of them moved, by 26 November. But 'Spraybelly' and two other die-hard fanatics: Slattermann and CMSGT Lynch - inexplicably stayed in their offices even after the deadline. It was complete insanity! You'd have thought they were holding the Alamo against Santa Ana, fighting to the death. Only at the sight of CE bulldozers the very next day (at 0805) rumbling down the street did they all hastily pack-up everything they could grab and got out only a few minutes prior to the dozers unceremoniously demolishing the old SPS buildings. COL Berryman was in absolutely NO mood for further simple-minded foolishness or rank idiocy. He had a limit to his civility and professionalism, but Sprayberry had badly crossed it. No more. The base commander ordered him to start bulldozing the structures by 0830, on 27 November 1975. And he damn-well was going to carry that order out. If some people were stupid enough (or brainless enough) to remain inside the hooches, then they were going to get bulldozed under.

But the CES was saved a lot of time and effort in the aftermath's clean-up. By the following morning anything left in the rubble that was either useable or salvageable: piping, ventilation ducting, corrugated roofing materials or metal side sheeting, wood, whatever, had been stripped out and quietly removed off the base.

**BETWEEN 'C' AND 'D' AVENUES, 7TH STREET, BOQ #1, ROOM #6,  *U-TAPAO*  RTNAB,  *CHONBURI/RAYONG*  PROVINCES, THAILAND, 0045, 28 NOVEMBER 1975.**

I had just walked into my room after taking a well-earned shower to hear the phone ringing. I thought it strange for two reasons. One - the room phone never rang. And two - if it was something important about work, then the Mids Shift Supervisor would've jumped in his jeep and come over to get me.

It was neither. It sounded like CDR *Sawasdiyothin's* Deputy Security Commander: one LT(JG) *Vuttichai.* I finally caught his name after some confusion on who exactly was ringing me up this early in the morning, due to his barely past-minimal-English and thick Thai accent in speaking it. I remembered him now. Tall for a Thai, built like a sumo wrestler or a Mongolian Warlord, bald headed, had huge mole on the side of his nose and friendly. He probably had a Thai father and a Chinese mother due to his white skin, hairless body (not that Thais sprouted much body hair anyway) and more slanted eyes. I'd seen him around and we had a nodding acquaintance.

It was hard to hear him on the phone. He spoke in almost a low whisper; his minimal English and my definitely poor Thai didn't help the conversation along any. I gathered that he wanted to speak to me in total secrecy and in complete privacy. I was not to speak to him at the Pass & ID office where he kept his office.

I also finally gathered the gist of the conversation after several attempts. It was that some *gigolos* were *ka-moying* three a/c units in two more nights and spirit them past the gate guard at ECP #4 along the flight line. He wanted me to either catch them or have them caught by the SPs.

ECP #4. That struck a raw nerve.

Back in July all three shift supervisors wanted to close down most of the little used flight line ECPs (#1-#4) and other vehicle checkpoints around

204

the base. We all felt that one ECP on the flight line after normal working hours was enough. With the departure of the B-52s and KC-135s, their crews, plus the steady depletion of ordnance from the bomb dump and other flight line and support personnel being cut-back in large numbers, there was little activity on, in or out of the flight line. (Plus we wanted more troops to have more time off to enjoy themselves on their tour of duty. It was 100 times better to be out in 'Freeland' having fun than sitting at some useless checkpoint doing nothing for eight or 10 hours.)

After 1700 nothing moved on the flight line anyway. It was as dead as Dodge City is on a Sunday morning after all the cowboys off of a cattle drive in town had moseyed along to another trail drive. Dentonville made a quick decision on the whole issue. He dumped the entire problem onto the lap of the newly arrived senior NCO advisor for the SPS, CMSGT Lynch.

Lynch was a legend in his own time, or so it was explained. He was as slick as a carnival side-show snake-oil salesman, as oily as a Hollywood lounge-lizard, as seamless as a hell's-fire fundamentalist preacher, and as glib as a Chicago 'political machine' ward-heeler. Supposedly he went into the SAC Commander's 'inner-of-the-innermost,' most 'sacred-of-the-sacred-sanctums' office as a lowly junior SGT 'cup-bearer' at the gilded foot of the throne of the 'Highest-Of-All-Highest' and came out of there 10 years later as the NCOIC of the whole enlisted personnel support section running the 'whole nine yards'. Lynch was the only NCO in the entire history of the USAF to make E-9 that fast. Now he was coming up on only 14 years of service and looking to go for 40. As his 'reward' he was sent straight to *U-Tapao*.

All three shift supervisors (Jake let me sit in for him) were adamant on closing the now useless guard posts at the first 1500 meeting held in the back office, the only time all of us were awake. Lynch flat-out said "No." He wanted a proper, written 'study' done of the problem. A formal 'traffic survey' had to be conducted.

So, we had every ECP and check-point count exactly how many vehicles passed through on each shift for one full week. For example, ECPs #2 and #4 had one vehicle pass through between them every evening from

1700-0600; the other outer checkpoints had none (not counting SP vehicles). ECPs #1 and #3 had from one to not even five vehicles pass by each Swing and Mid-shift.

Lynch still said no. They were 'too important' to close down. We argued and re-argued in the weekly meetings for over a month. Finally, he relented and let us shut down ECP #2 between the hours of 1700-0600, pending no one in any other organization complained about it. No one did. No other checkpoints were closed, even though the vehicle counts all went to zero. None of this made any sense. The solution was obvious, but the back office was being absolutely dunderheaded. It was totally idiotic. I didn't understand and they couldn't (and wouldn't) explain it to me. After the final decision, CMSGT Lynch kept smiling like some venerable, small state politician who had won an overwhelming landslide victory over feeble opposition in some backwater bayou. Everything was back to normal on the shifts in his mind.

I reassured LT(JG) *Vuttichai* I'd let the proper people to know to be ready to catch the *gigolos*. In two more nights, he said. Three a/c units' *ka-moyed* out of ECP #4. I confirmed I got it.

I picked up the phone, dialed the LE Desk and spoke to the Mids Desk SGT. He acted like I was calling him about some barking stray mutt down in the middle of *Ban Chang,* almost even not caring what I was reporting. I grew irritated at his attitude and became insistent he take this all more seriously. He said he'd pass along the information to the Mids LE Supervisor. I repeated the same information twice so he would remember. I wasn't even sure he wrote what I had said down, or paid attention to it. I hung the phone up and reflected that this wasn't right.

-

**BETWEEN 'C' AND 'D' AVENUES, 7TH STREET, BOQ #1, ROOM #6, *U-TAPAO* RTNAB, *CHONBURI/RAYONG* PROVINCES, THAILAND, 0050, 29 NOVEMBER 1975.**

LT(JG) *Vuttichai* called me again. He was confirming it was 'on' for tomorrow night. The three a/c units would be *ka-moyed* on Mids, for sure, between 2400 and 0500. I thanked him again for confirming the information.

I called the LE Desk again. This time the Desk SGT's attitude was very much changed. He wasn't interested in hearing the information again, but he was very interested in knowing where I got this information from. I said it didn't matter where I got the information from. I said I believed the information to be credible and Mids LE needed to act on it. Make sure, I said, that the ECP #4 guards, other ECP gates, outer check points roving patrols, mobile supervisors and Main, Back and RTN Gates were especially attentive about looking for the *ka-moyed* a/c units. Again the Desk SGT was very curious about who gave me the information. I repeated that if the information turned out to be bogus, then nothing got hurt or changed. We just went to a higher state of vigilance for no reason. But I wasn't telling him who told me. We let it go at that. Again I reflected this doesn't sound right. Usually anyone else in LE and Security would be happy to have the information about a potential theft and act on it accordingly, not bust-my-buns about where I got the information from.

-

**CORNER OF 'A' AVENUE AND 9<sup>TH</sup> STREET, PARKING LOT, OUTSIDE CSC, 365<sup>th</sup> SPS, *U-TAPAO* RTNAB, *CHONBURI/RAYONG* PROVINCES, THAILAND, 2335, 29 NOVEMBER 1975.**

I briefed Mids Shift Supervisor on the possibility of three a/c units being spirited out past ECP #4 on his shift between midnight and 0500. He told me he had been duly informed by the LE Shift Supervisor, who had been passed the information by the Desk SGT. I expressed my irritation his total lack real of interest. But the Shift Supervisor said he'd take care of it. It was all I could do; my part was over. Now all I could hope was that Mids would be ready and watchful for whenever the *gigolos* made their move. Maybe we'd catch them red-handed just this one time.

## BETWEEN 'C' AND 'D' AVENUES, 7TH STREET, BOQ #1, ROOM #6, *U-TAPAO* RTNAB, *CHONBURI/RAYONG* PROVINCES, THAILAND, 0045, 30 NOVEMBER 1975.

LTJG *Vuttichai* didn't call again. But I called the LE Desk one last time to see if everything was being done to stop the impending thievery. The Desk SGT confirmed that LE would be ready, but was insistent, almost demanding in wanting to know who my informant was. This was making me get upset, angry actually. I refused to say; then our words became heated. Our conversation went back-and-forth like a hard-slapped Chinese ping-pong ball, growing only more strident. Finally I began to really be very concerned that Mids would take no action on the matter unless they had an independent confirmation of the information. Maybe they'd dismiss it as 'unsubstantiated' with only me being the informant and do nothing. Although I became extremely irritated at the exchanges, I had a rapidly growing suspicion he, or they, didn't believe me at all. They wanted some proof, or they'd just sit and do nothing. But this was too strange - the Desk SGT was spending all his energy on the wrong subject.

Finally, in great frustration and at the end limit to my exasperation, not wanting to lose this opportunity to do something, I blurted out:

"Listen to me SGT!" I probably said much more loudly than I had intended. "Just have someone go down to the RTN Security Office right now and either see the Commander, the Deputy Commander, or the RTN Duty Officer to confirm what I've told you! Just do it now if it's THAT important!"

That quickly ended our conversation.

**CORNER OF 'A' AVENUE AND 9TH STREET, PARKING LOT, OUTSIDE CSC, 365th SPS, *U-TAPAO* RTNAB, *CHONBURI/RAYONG* PROVINCES, THAILAND, 1315, 30 NOVEMBER 1975.**

Guillory picked me up at the BOQ and drove me to CSC. I finally had to ask him were there any reports of any a/c thefts anywhere along the flight line last night on Mids.

"Yah, sport," Guillory drolled. "Three a/c units got *ka-moyed* sometime either late last night or early this morning, not sure what time. The 703rd FMS people called it in to the LE Desk this morning when they came to work at 0800 and discovered the holes in the walls where the a/c units had been. They said the units came from one of their buildings over near ECP #4. No one saw anything at the flight line ECPs last night according to Smith when I relieved him this morning. Another clean, quick-in-and-out-*ka-moy*-job I'd say. I already turned in the incident report on it, sport."

SON-OF-A-BITCH! I almost screamed, but clamped my mouth shut, keeping it to myself. I was completely fuming, like Mount Vesuvius, ready to detonate. This was *Sip-loy mach-mach!*

After Swings posted-out, I jumped in my jeep and tore-ass straight down to Pass & ID.

"Is CDR *Sawasdiyothin* here?" I asked the RTN First Class Petty Officer manning the office next to CDR's who I remembered spoke some fair English.

"*Mai, Loi-to, kup.* He in big meeting all day. Thai Navy HQs."

"What about LT(JG) *Vuttichai?*"

"He gone. Transfer out this morning, *Loi-to, kup. Bi-lay-o!*"

"Transferred where?!"

"*Moo-loo-see Loi-to,* doan' know. He gone - transfer out. No come back."

I strained to hold back an explosion of great, mountain-sized, endless profanities.

-

**CORNER OF 'C' AVENUE AND 3RD STREET, FRONT INTERVIEW ROOM, 365TH SPS LE STAFF BUILDING, *U-TAPAO* RTNAB, *CHONBURI/RAYONG* PROVINCES, THAILAND, 1500, 30 NOVEMBER 1975.**

The LE Desk SGT called on the radio and directed me to meet with Slattermann at the SP LE Staff Building. I'd never been in there before mainly due to the fact I never had any reason to. I also rarely had spoken to him since his arrival over two months prior.

The rooms in the building were usually employed for formal interviews of LE incidents, or sometimes someone on the shift just wanted some privacy and quiet (away from the constant noise and bustle near the LE Desk SGT's area) to write out a report or speak to witness.

I was cooling off now finally. I had to deeply think about what was happening out here. But now I had another thing to be concerned about first - seeing what Slattermann wanted me for.

I walked up to the covered porch's front door, rapped a few times, walked in, came to attention and saluted.

The room had a sturdy rattan desk with matching chairs, several side tables and one coffee table that were placed on a Teakwood floor. Several inexpensive carved black-and-gold painted Thai art ware (seen in every souvenir shop) hung on the large, half-split bamboo tube walls. The ceiling was also overlain with half-split bamboo tubes. I half-expected to see Trader Vic sitting inside sipping Mai Tai's with some dark café-au-lait skinned, buxom, sarong-wearing, Tahitian hot beach-babe.

Slattermann returned my salute; then motioned for me to sit down in the room he temporarily commandeered for the session. He came right to point without preamble.

"We're moving you off shift work to the back office, 1LT Legere."

"Why's that, MAJ? I don't understand."

I'd an immediate sinking, queasy feeling in the bottom of his stomach I was being punished for something. But I couldn't put my finger on the reason. To my knowledge I had done a good job so far.

"We need you back there to help out with the paperwork, 1LT."

I considered this statement. That didn't sound right. There were plenty of qualified NCOs and Airmen in the back office, their manpower strengthened by several Thai secretaries plus two dedicated Admin officers, all to handle SPS's less-than-stupendous 'paperwork.' In fact, nothing much was getting done in any event, from I was told through the SP 'grapevine.' They were always busy working hard trying to keep their feet from falling off the edges of their desks.

As I thought more about it, if anything, they were badly over-manned with senior NCOs, all of them tripping all over themselves and just as badly under-worked big time from all reports. And not one of them looked like they were dying of less-than-slavery-like conditions. In fact, there was no cushier job on base than in the SP back office. Plus, I hadn't heard any of them needing or asking for any assistance.

"So, I can't stay on shift anymore, sir? I like it where I'm working now. It's great being outside and I really enjoy what I'm doing, MAJ Slattermann."

"No."

"So, then there's no chance MAJ?"

"We like the way you write, 1LT," Slattermann said, smoothly grinning - with finality. "1LT Vogelesgang will take over Swings effective tomorrow."

I departed without shaking hands or saluting.

I thought back to when I first had arrived on base. Even with my suppressed ego and lower sense of self-esteem than most people, I had to admit to myself that: Yes, I WAS a good writer, very good in fact. Over the years assorted people had complimented me on my unique, highly (or easily) readable, writing style and encouraged me to write something publishable. Everyone said they very much enjoyed when I put pen-to-paper and composed. However, I'd always shelved these suggestions away for some nebulous, future date.

But I'd never written anything while I was here. And I had never done any EERs either, as you might have thought with so many troops. Actually, other people wrote them. And I just usually 'chopped-off' on the prepared endorsements on the troops PCS-ing or DEROS-ing out of there, but rarely made more than a slight correction. But every EER was all 'canned' anyway, stock verbiage or phrases mixed-and-matched; everyone was a real 'water-walker,' outstanding this, superlative that, etc. Or if you were 'really special,' you were said to have 'created water and walked 10 feet above it'. But the next evals were for MSGTs. That deadline was over a month away.

Even further, I hadn't written any incident reports yet. Jake, now gone, had corrected some of them as I watched over his shoulder, since he was the still the Shift Supervisor at the time. But we really didn't have many incidents. On any I had received, again, they were written by others. I'd just correct any factual or grammatical mistakes I found and returned them for re-typing before chopping them off for the higher-ups. They were always written by the person investigating or reporting the incident, usually MSGT Veeres or MSGT Wozniak - for the most part. I just endorsed it, made small corrections, and sent it forward - all routine stuff.

I thought about this more deeply now. I had penned no official or unofficial letters. No memorandums. No drafts. No proposals. No suggestions to improve anything. No requests to do or have anything. No endorsements on anything up the chain-of-command to higher headquarters. No forms filled out. No safety reports done, or accident mishap reports completed. No investigations. Not even a leave form for R&R. Nothing. Complete zero. I had signed my name to many pieces of paper. But slapping more than two words together past my first and last name on any document? No.

Slattermann had never read anything I had written. And I would have to tell Guillory I would not be picking up his wife at the Emergency Room again.

(To be continued in THAILAND.)

<u>**THAI-ENGLISH DICTIONARY**</u>

AB-NAM: (LITERALLY) 'TAKE WATER;' I.E., TAKE A BATH/SHOWER.
ALAI-WAH (VULGAR SLANG): WHAT THE HELL/FUCK!?
ALLOY: DELICIOUS.
BA: CRAZY.
BA-BA BA-BOR: VERY CRAZY IN THE HEAD.
BAHT: BASIC UNIT OF MONEY LIKE THE US DOLLAR OR BRITISH POUND STERLING. LIKE
    MANY CURRENCIES THE BAHT WAS ORIGINALLY A WEIGHT, BUT REMAINS A WEIGHT
    FOR GOLD CHAINS. A ONE BAHT CHAIN IS ALMOST ONE-HALF OUNCE OF GOLD. IN
1975
    ONE BAHT WAS EQUAL TO ABOUT FIVE US CENTS.
BAHT BUS (MIXED THAI/ENGLISH SLANG): JAPANESE-MADE LIGHT PICK-UP TRUCK
    MODIFIED TO CARRY PAYING PASSENGERS ALONG A SET ROUTE. THE BACK IS
    COVERED WITH AN LOW METAL TOP AND HAS PLASTIC COVERED BENCH SEATS
    ALONG BOTH SIDES. THERE ARE METAL STEP(S) FOR BOARDING IN THE BACK. THE
    FARE IS USUALLY ONE BAHT (OR ABOUT FIVE US CENTS). TO STOP/EXIT THE BUS ONE
    PUSHES AN ELECTRIC BUZZER IN THE BACK.
B.E.: BUDDHIST ERA. THE BUDDHIST ERA STARTED WITH THE DEATH OF BUDDHA IN 542
    B.C. THAI YEARS ARE DATED FROM THAT DATE. SO, BY SUBTRACTING 542 FROM B.E.
    2517 WILL GIVE YOU 1975 A.D.
BUTTERFLY (MIXED THAI/ENGLISH SLANG): THE ACT OF SEX OR SOMEONE WHO WANTS
    OR DOES THE ACT OF SEX (THAIS ALWAYS SAY: 'BUTTERFLIES' DO IT WITH
ANYONE').
BUTTERFLY-ED/ING (MIXED THAI/ENGLISH SLANG): THE ACT OF HAVING/OR HAD SEX.
BY-LAY-O: GO VERY QUICKLY OR FAST; LIKE RUN, WALK, MOVE, LEAVE OR DRIVE A
CAR.
BY-NAWN: GO TO SLEEP.
CHAI: YES.
CHAI-MAI: YES OR NO?
CHANG YET (VULGAR SLANG): ELEPHANT FUCKS/IS FUCKING YOU.
CHEAP CHA-LEE (MIXED THAI/ENGLISH SLANG): CHEAP CHARLIE - A MISER OR
SOMEONE
    (USUALLY A FOREIGNER) WHO DOESN'T TIP WELL OR NOT AT ALL. (ALL THAIS HATE
    'CHEAP CHARLIES').
CHING: TRUE.
CHING-CHING: VERY TRUE.
CHOKE-DEE: GOOD LUCK.
DEE: GOOD.
DEK-DEK: A TINY BABY/INFANT.
DEK-CHAI(S): SMALL MALE CHILD/CHILDREN.
DEK-YING(S): SMALL FEMALE CHILD/CHILDREN.
FARANG: ANY WHITE NON-ASIAN FOREIGNER; I.E.; NORMALLY ANY (WHITE)
    WESTERNER.

FUN-TOKE: RAIN.
GARAUDA: MYTHICAL BIRD OF HINDU RELIGIOUS ORIGIN AND NATIONAL SYMBOL OF
    THAILAND.
GIGOLO (MIXED THAI/ENGLISH HYBRID SLANG): A THIEF. (IN THAI 'JIG' IS 'TO STEAL.')
GIGOLO-ED (MIXED THAI/ENGLISH HYBRID SLANG): STOLEN.
GIGOLO-ING (MIXED THAI/ENGLISH HYBRID SLANG): STEALING.
GO-HOKE: LIE OR LYING.
HONG-NAM: (LITERALLY) 'WATER ROOM, I.E., TOILET, LATINE OR BATHROOM.
H.R.H.: HIS (OR HER) ROYAL HIGHNESS.
ISAN: NORTHEASTERN REGION OF THAILAND; CONSIDERED THE MOST RURAL PART OF
    THE COUNTRY.
KA: INDIACTES A FEMALE IS SPEAKING, USED AT THE END OF HER SENTENCE.
KA-MOY: TO STEAL.
KA-MOYED: STOLEN.
KA-MOYING: STEALING.
KA-TOEY(S): MALE TRANSVESTITES(S); I.E., MEN DRESSED AS WOMEN, SOME HAVE SEX
    CHANGES.
KEE-MAU: DRUNK.
KHAO PAD: FRIED RICE. (VIRTUALLY THE FAVORITE NATIONAL DISH).
KHUN: POLITE WORD FOR 'YOU;' ALSO A TITLE: MISS, MRS., MR., AND MS.
KHUN SABAI DEE: ARE YOU FINE? ARE YOU WELL? HOW ARE YOU?
KILO (BORROWED WORD FROM ENGLISH): ROADWAY KILOMETER MARKER USED TO
    INDICATE WHERE A SMALL LOCATION IS BETWEEN LARGER PLACES FROM THE
START
    OF THE PARTICULAR ROADWAY IN QUESTION. FOR EXAMPLE, KILO 'SIP' IS LOCATED
    AT KILOMETER MARKER TEN ALONG NATIONAL HIGHWAY NUMBER THREE, AS
    MEASURED FROM THE ZERO KILOMETER MARKER OUTSIDE SATTAHIP.
KLONG: ANY SMALL BODY OF MOVING WATER LIKE A STREAM, CREEK, DRAINAGE
    DITCH, CANAL OR WATERWAY.
KIN KHAO (LITERALLY): 'EAT RICE'; I.E., LET'S GO EAT SOME FOOD.
KOP: THANK(S).
KOP KHUN: THANK YOU.
KOP KHUN MACH: THANK YOU (VERY) MUCH.
KOR-TOEDT: EXCUSE ME, PARDON ME, I'M SORRY.
KUP: INDICATES A MALE IS SPEAKING, USED AT THE END OF HIS SENTENCE.
LAWN: HOT (AS IN TEMPERATURE).
LEK: SMALL.
LOI-TO: USAF FIRST LIEUTENANT/PAYGRADE O-2.
LOY: 100.
LUB-LOY: HANDSOME, AS IN A MAN.
MACH: MANY, MUCH.
MACH-MACH: VERY MANY, VERY MUCH.
MAI: NO.
MAI DEE (LITERALLY): 'NO GOOD;' ALSO NOT GOOD OR BAD.
MAI LOO SEE: I DON'T KNOW.

MAI MEE BAN HAN: I DON'T WORRY ABOUT IT. I DON'T HAVE A PROBLEM WITH IT.
MAI PEN LAI: I AM NOT WORRIED OR DON'T WORRY (ABOUT IT).
MAI SABAI (LITERALLY): 'NOT HAPPY;' I.E., FEELING BAD, SICK OR ILL.
MAI SA-MONG (LITERALLY): 'NO BRAIN;' I.E., EXTREMELY STUPID.
MANG-DA: GIANT WATER BUG THE THAIS CONSIDER A REAL CULINARY DELICACY.
   (ALSO THAI SLANG FOR A PIMP.)
MIA-NOY: 'MINOR' WIFE WITH NO LEGAL PROTECTION.
MO-HO: ANGRY.
MUANG NAWN: GET SLEEPY OR TIRED.
MUANG THAI: LAND OF THAIS, OR THAILAND.
NAM: WATER.
NAM-KANG (LITERALLY): 'HARD WATER;' I.E., ICE.
NIT: A BIT.
NIT-NOY (LITERALLY): 'A LITTLE BIT;' I.E., TINY.
NOK: BIRD.
NOW: COLD.
NOY: LITTLE.
NUN-BAH ONE (MIXED THAI/ENGLISH SLANG): NUMBER ONE; I.E., THE BEST.
NUM-BAH TEN (MIXED THAI/ENGLISH SLANG): NUMBER TEN; I.E., THE WORST.
PET: HOT (AS IN EXTREMELY SPICY).
PICKENOOS: TINY GREEN AND RED CHILI PEPPERS-LIKE CONDIMENT. EXTREMELY
SPICY.
   (ALSO SEE 'PET.')
PLA TALAY: ANY (USUALLY LARGE) EDIBLE SALTWATER FISH.
POO-CHAI(S): ADULT MALE(S).
POO-YING(S): ADULT FEMALE(S).
PRATET THAI (LITERALLY): COUNTRY OF THAIS, OR THAILAND.
RTG: ROYAL THAI GUARDS.
SABAI (LITERALLY): 'HAPPY;' I.E., I'M FINE.
SABAI DEE: (LITERALLY) GOOD AND HAPPY, I.E., GOOD HAPPINESS OR VERY FINE.
SABAI DEE MACH (LITERALLY): 'VERY GOOD AND VERY HAPPY;' I.E., GREAT HAPPINESS.
SAPPALOTE: PINEAPPLE.
SANUK: FUN, OR ANYTHING THE THAIS CONSIDER AS FUN.
SATANG: 100 SATANG = ONE BAHT. THAI MONETARY UNIT EQUIVALENT TO ONE US
CENT.
SA-TAY: CHICKEN, PORK OR BEEF ROASTED ON A STICK. USUALLY SERVED WITH A
   PEANUT OR SWEET CUCUMBER SAUCE.
SAWASDEE: GREETINGS OR HELLO.
SAWADEEE BEE-MAI: HAPPY NEW YEAR.
SINGHA: LOCAL MADE, VERY POPULAR THAI BEER. ('SINGHA' ALSO MEANS 'AUGUST.')
SIP: 10.
SIP-LOY (AMERICAN-INVENTED WORD FROM THAI): 'SIP' = 10 x 'LOY'= 100 or 1,000; I.E.,
THE
   ULTIMATE WORST. ACTUALLY 1,000 IN THAI IS 'PAAN.' SIP-LOY WAS NOT
GENERALLY

USED OR UNDERSTOOD BY THAIS, ONLY USED BY AMERICANS.
SOI: ANY SIZED ROAD FROM A NARROW ALLEYWAY TO A WIDE STREET.
SUE-WAY OR SUAY: BEAUTIFUL, AS IN A WOMAN.
SUN-TEEN (VULGAR SLANG, LITERALLY): 'MY FOOT;' I.E., A TERRIBLE INSULT.
TALAY TONG: SEA GOLD.
TEE-LOCK (LITERALLY): 'DARLING;' I.E., SOMETIMES TRANSLATED INTO ENGLISH AS 'A
    HIRED OR TEMPORARY WIFE FOR MORE THAN ONE NIGHT.'
TOOT: ASS, BACKSIDES, BUTT OR BUTTOCKS.
UNG-ANG: A TINY GREEN, RED AND PURPLE FROG.
WAI: TRADITIONAL GREETING. THE PALMS ARE PRESSED TOGETHER AS IN PRAYER. THE
    HIGHER THE PALMS ARE SITUATED MEANS THE HIGHER IN PRESTIEGE THE PERSON
    BEING GREETED IS. A LOWER RANKING PERSON ALWAYS WAI'S TO A HIGHER
    RANKING PERSON, BUT NOT THE REVERSE.
WAT: THAI BUDDHIST TEMPLE OR BUILDING WITH A LARGE, USUALLY BRASS, SEATED
    STATUE OF BUDDHA IS HOUSED. NORMALLY CONSIDERED TO BE THE WHOLE
TEMPLE
    COMPLEX.
YAI: BIG, LARGE, HUGE, A LOT, LARGE QUANTITY.
YAI-YAI: VERY BIG, VERY LARGE, VERY HUGE, A VERY LOT, A VERY LARGE QUANTITY.
YEN: COOL (AS IN TEMPERATURE).

## US AIR FORCE DICTIONARY

AAF: ARMY AIR FORCE (DESIGNATION DURING WWII AND PRECEEDED THE US AIR
    FORCE'S FORMATION IN 1947).
AB(S): AIR BASE(S).
A/C: AIR-CONDITIONING.
ACSC: AF AIR COMMAND AND STAFF COLLEGE, MAXWELL AFB, AL.
ADMIN: ADMINISTRATION OR ADMINISTRATIVE SECTION OF A UNIT.
AF: AIR FORCE.
AFB(S): AIR FORCE BASE(S).
AFCM: AIR FORCE COMMENDATION MEDAL.
AFM(S): AIR FORCE MANUAL(S).
AFMPC: AIR FORCE MILITARY PERSONNEL CENTER.
AFN: ARMED FORCES NETWORK (RADIO AND TELEVISION).
AFR(S): AIR FORCE REGULATION(S).
AFROTC: AIR FORCE RESERVE OFFICER TRAINING CORPS.
AIR BASES, THAILAND:
    DON MUANG AB, NORTH OF BANGKOK.
    KORAT (SOMETIMES SPELLED KHORAT) AB, NAKHON RATCHASIMA.
    NAKHON PHANOM (USUALLY CALLD 'NKP') AB, NAKHON PHANOM.
    TAKHLI AB, NAKHON SAWAN.
    UBON AB, UBON RATCHATHANI.
    UDORN AB, UDON THANI.
    U-TAPAO AB, NEAR SATTAHIP.

AIR FORCE BASES/AIR BASES, OTHER LOCATIONS:
   ANDERSEN AFB, GUAM.
   BIEN HOA AB, BIEN HOA, SOUTH VIETNAM.
   CHING CHUAN KANG (C.C.K.) AB, TAICHUNG, TAIWAN.
   CLARK AB, ANGELES CITY, THE PHILIPPINES.
   ELLSWORTH AFB, RAPID CITY, SD.
   F.E. WARREN AFB, CHEYENNE, WY.
   GRAND FORKS AFB, GRAND FORKS, ND.
   HICKAM AFB, HONOLULU, HI.
   LACKLAND AFB, SAN ANTONIO, TX.
   MALMSTROM AFB, GREAT FALLS, MT.
   MARCH AFB, RIVERSIDE, CA.
   MATHER, AFB, SACRAMENTO, CA.
   MAXWELL AFB, MONTGOMERY, AL.
   MINOT AFB, MINOT, ND.
   OSAN AB, OSAN, SOUTH KOREA.
   TAN SON NHUT AB, SAIGON, SOUTH VIETNAM.
   TRAVIS AFB, FAIRFIELD, CA.
AIRMEN: USUALLY E-1 TO E-3 PAYGRADES, BUT CAN INCLUDE ALL AIR FORCE ENLISTED PERSONNEL WHEN SPOKEN ABOUT IN GENERAL.
AL: ALABAMA.
AO UDOM: SMALL TOWN JUST NORTH OF PATTAYA BEACH.
AP: AIR POLICE. (SEE SECURITY POLICE).
APOE: AERIAL PORT OF EMBARKATION.
ARTICLE 15: NON-JUDICIAL PUNISHMENT AS OUTLINED IN THE UCMJ.
APS: AERIAL PORT SQUADRON.
ASAP: AS SOON AS POSSIBLE.
AUSSIE (SLANG): AUSTRALIAN.
AWC: AIR WAR COLLEGE, MAXWELL AFB, AL.
BA: BACHELOR OF ARTS DEGREE.
B-52: USAF LARGE, FOUR-ENGINED, INTERCONTINENTAL STRATEGIC BOMBER AIRCRAFT.
BAG-DRAG (SLANG): FINAL DAY ON-BASE, I.E., DATE OF DEPARTURE. (ALSO SEE 'WAKE -UP.')
(WHEN THE) BALLOON GOES UP (SLANG): SOMETHING BIG OR IMPORTANT IS GOING TO START
   HAPPENING VERY SHORTLY PHRASE DATES FROM WWI TRENCH WARFARE WHEN OBSERVATION BALOONS WERE LIFTED PRIOR TO A HEAVY BOMBARDMENT OF THE ENEMY FOR ARTILLERY SPOTTING.
BEAUCOUP (FRENCH, FROM VIETNAM): MANY, MUCH.
BEQ: BACHELOR ENLISTED QUARTERS.
(THE) BIG WAR (SLANG): THE VIETNAM WAR.
BINJO (OR BENJO) DITCH (JAPANESE): DRAINAGE DITCH OR CANAL ALONG EITHER SIDE OF A ROAD, USUALLY FILLED WITH HUMAN WASTE OR EFFLUENT AND WATER.
BIRTHDAY BOY (SLANG): THAI PROSTITUTES WILL GIVE YOU A FREE SCREW IF YOU SAY

IT'S YOUR BIRTHDAY.
BOONDOGGLE (SLANG): US GOVERNMENT FUNDED PROJECT, USUALLY A WASTE OF TIME
   AND MONEY.
BOQ: BACHELOR OFFICER'S QUARTERS.
BROWN-BAR (SLANG): AF SECOND LIEUTENANT/O-1 PAYGRADE. (ALSO SEE 'BUTTER
   -BAR.')
BS (SLANG): BULL-SHIT.
BS-ED: BULL-SHITTED.
BS-ING: BULL-SHITTING.
BSM: BRONZE STAR MEDAL.
BUNGALOW(S) (BENGALI, SLANG): ONE-STORY, THATCH-COVERED, SIMPLE BUILDING(S)
   USED AS A HOME OR BUSINESS.
BUTT-SKIS (SLANG): ASS, BUTTOCKS, READ END.
BUTTER-BAR (SLANG): SECOND LIEUTENANT/O-1 PAYGRADE. (ALSO SEE 'BROWN BAR.')
B-T-Z: BELOW-THE-ZONE, I.E., ELIGIBLE, CONSIDERED FOR EARLY PROMOTION OR WAS
   PROMOTED TO THE NEXT HIGHER GRADE AS AN OFFICER.
BUFF (SLANG): (MULTIPLE MEANINGS) BIG UGLY FAT FELLOW, BIG UGLY FAT FUCKER;
   BIG UGLY FLYING FUCKER; (MOST POLITELY) BIG UGLY FLYING FELLOW, I.E., B-52.
   (ALSO SEE B-52.)
BOUGHT (OR BUY) THE FARM (SLANG): DO SOMETHING FATAL TO YOUR CAREER TO GET
   THROWN OUT OF THE AIR FORCE; ORIGINALLY MEANT GET YOURSELF KILLED IN AN
   ACCIDENT.
BX: BASE EXCHANGE.
CA: CALIFORNIA.
CAMMO(S) OR CAMMIES (SLANG): US MILITARY CAMOFLAGE JUNGLE UNIFORM(S).
CANNED (SLANG): FIRED.
CBPO: CONSOLIDATED BASE PERSONNEL OFFICE.
C.C.K. AB: CHING CHUAN KANG AB, TAICHUNG, TAIWAN.
CE: CIVIL ENGINEERING.
CES: CIVIL ENGINEERING SQUADRON.
CHECK-OUT (SLANG): STOP WORK AND START OUT-PROCESSING FROM THE BASE.
CHERRY-BOY (SLANG): A VIRGIN. THAI PROSTITUTES WILL GIVE YOU A FREE SCREW IF
   YOU SAY YOU ARE A VIRGIN.
CHIT (FROM THE HINDI WORD 'CHITTY'): USUALLY A SMALL REQUEST OR NOTE NEEDING
   AN ENDORSEMENT.
CHOPPED OR CHOPPED-OFF (ON) (SLANG): APPROVED OR ENDORSED IN WRITING.
CLASS A UNIFORM (OR CLASS A's): US MILITARY VERSION OF CIVILIAN BUSINESS DRESS.
CLASS 'VI' STORE: BX-OPERATED STORE THAT SELLS ALCOHOLIC BEVERAGES WITHOUT
   LOCAL RESTRICTIONS: I.E., LIKE BEING OPEN ON A SUNDAY WHEN OFF-BASE STORES
   ARE CLOSED.

CO(S): COMMANDING OFFICER(S).
COB: CLOSE OF BUSINESS.
COJONES (SPANISH): TESTICLES OR BALLS; I.E., LITERALLY COURAGE OR BRAVERY.
COMMO: COMMUNICATIONS.
CSC: CENTRAL SECURITY CONTROL.
CSG: COMBAT SUPPORT GROUP.
CT: CONNECTICUT.
C&W: COUNTRY AND WESTERN (MUSIC).
DAP (SLANG): ELABORATE GEETING USED BY MAINLY BLACK TROOPS THAT INVOLVES
    A RAPID SERIES OF HANDSHAKES, FINGER GRIPS AND SQUEEZES PLUS ARM
    TOUCHINGS AS A WORDLESS GREETING OR EXPRESSION OF SOLIDARITY.
DAY(S): SP DAY SHIFT; I.E., ON-DUTY 0800-1400.
DC-8: MCDONNELL-DOUGLAS CIVILIAN COMMERCIAL FOUR-ENGINE, FIXED-WING
    PASSENGER AIRCRAFT.
DEROS: DATE EARLY RETURN FROM OVERSEAS; I.E., THE EARLIEST SOMEONE CAN
    RETURN FROM AN OVERSEAS ASSIGNMENT AND STILL GET CREDIT FOR THAT
    ASSIGNMENT.
DET: DETACHMENT.
DEUCE-AND-HALF (TRUCK) (SLANG): TWO-AND-HALF TON ALL-PURPOSE MILITARY
    TRUCK.
DIGGER-STYLE (AUSTRALIAN, SLANG): WIDE-BRIMMED SOFT HAT WORN WITH ONE
BRIM
    SIDE ATTACHED TO THE CROWN.
DJ (SLANG): DISC JOCKEY.
DOD: DEPARTMENT OF DEFENSE.
DOR: DATE OF RELEASE FROM ACTIVE DUTY.
DPDO: (DEPARTMENT OF) DEFENSE PROPERTY DISPOSAL OFFICE.
DR.: DOCTOR.
DREAM SHEET(S) (SLANG): FORM(S) WHICH ALL PERSONNEL LIST THEIR DESIRES OR
    REQUESTS FOR FUTURE ASSIGNMENTS IN A RANK ORDER OF PREFERENCES.
    SUBMITTED TO AFMPC. NO DREAM SHEET SUBMITTED MEANS THE INDIVIDUAL WILL
    ACCEPT ANY FUTURE ASSIGNMENT.
ECP(S): ENTRY CONTROL POINT(S).
EVAL(S): WRITTEN PERFORMANCE EVALUATION(S).
FAST-BURNER (SLANG): USUALLY AN OFFICER SLATED FOR BELOW-THE-ZONE
    PROMOTIONS AND IS EXPECTED TO QUICKLY ADVANCE TO MUCH HIGHER RANK.
    (ALSO SEE 'B-T-Z.')
.50 CAL.: .50 CALIBER HEAVY MACHINE GUN.
FIGMO (SLANG): FUCK IT, GOT MY ORDERS, I.E., APATHY TOWARDS WORK. (ALSO SEE
    'SHORT-TIMER'S ATTITUDE,' 'SHORT-TIMER' AND 'SHORT.')
FL: FLORIDA.
FMS: FIELD MAINTENANCE SQUADRON.
FNG (SLANG): FUCKING NEW GUY; I.E., NEWEST PERSON IN THE UNIT OR
ORGANIZATION.
    (ALSO SEE 'NEWBIE.')

FOUR-STAR(S) (SLANG): GENERAL/O-10 PAYGRADE.
FREEDOM BIRD (SLANG): MILITARY CHARTERED AIRCRAFT TAKING PEOPLE TO AND
  FROM US AIR BASES IN THAILAND OR THAILAND'S COMMERCIAL AIRPORTS.
FREQ: RADIO FREQUENCY.
FRUIT SALAD: RIBBONS ON A UNIFORM.
FUBAR (SLANG): FUCKED UP BEYOND ALL RECOGNITION. (SOMETIMES CALLED
  FUBAR'ED.)
FULL-BIRD COLONEL (SLANG): COLONEL/O-6 PAY GRADE.
FULL-BULL COLONEL (SLANG): COLONEL/O-6 PAYGRADE.
FULL-CHICKEN COLONEL (SLANG): COLONEL/O-6 PAY GRADE.
GA: GEORGIA.
GARRISON CAP: FOLDABLE CAP WITH STRAIGHT SIDE AND WITH CREASE DOWN THE
  MIDDLE. EASILY TUCKED UNDER A BELT OR A SHOULDER STRAP.
GAU OR GAU-5: SHORT, COMPACT VERSION OF THE M-16 RIFLE.
GI(S): GOVERNMENT-ISSUE; I.E., GENERAL TERM FOR US SOLDIERS OR US MILITARY
  MEMBERS.
GO-SLOWS (BRITISH): TRAFFIC JAMS.
GREEN BEANIES (SLANG): US ARMY SPECIAL FORCES MEMBER(S); I.E., 'GREEN BERETS.'
GREEN-HORN (SLANG): ANY NEW PERSON, USUALLY AN A SECOND
  LIEUTENANT/PAYGRADE O-1. (ALSO SEE 'SHAVE TAIL.')
GROUND-POUNDING (SLANG): BEING A US ARMY INFANTRYMAN.
GRUNT(S) (SLANG): US ARMY INFANTRYMAN (MEN).
GUARD MOUNT: MEETING HELD AT THE BEGINNING OF EVERY AF SP SHIFT TO DISCUSS
  PROBLEMS, PAST ACTIONS, OR INCIDENTS ON THE RELIEVED OR OFF-GOING SHIFT,
  ANY UPCOMING EVENTS AND OTHER GENERAL INFORMATION.
HARD-COPY (SLANG): WRITTEN OFFICIAL DOCUMENT, LIKE PCS ORDERS, AS OPPOSED
TO
  'VERBAL' ORDERS.
HEAD-SHED (SLANG): ANY HQs.
HH-53: SEARCH-AND-AIR-RESCUE HELIOPTER; ALSO CALLED 'SUPER JOLLY GREEN
  GIANT.'
HHG: HOUSEHOLD GOODS.
HI: HAWAII.
HOOCHES: ONE-STORY, LONG, WOODEN, ALUMINUM OR SHEET METAL-COVERED
SIMPLE
  CONSTRUCTED HEMI-SPHERICAL BUILDING.
HOSED (SLANG): TOTALLY SCREWED UP. (ALSO SEE 'FUBAR.')
ID: IDAHO.
ID: IDENTIFICATION.
IL: ILLINOIS.
INC: INCORPORATED.
JAG: JUDGE ADVOCATE GENERAL.
JCRC: JOINT CASUALTY RECOVERY CENTER.
JD: DOCTOR OF JURISPRUDENCE, I.E., FIRST-LEVEL LAW DEGREE.
JP-4: TYPE OF MILITARY JET ENGINE FUEL.

K: KARAT. (FINESSS OF GOLD, I.E., 24K IS 100% PURE GOLD, 18K IS 75% PURE GOLD).

KC-135: USAF FOUR-ENGINE, FIXED-WING TANKER AIRCRAFT.

KGB: RUSSIAN INTELLIGENCE SERVICE.

KIM-CHEE (KOREAN): FERMENTED CABBAGE AND SPICY PEPPER CONCOTION THAT IS THE NATIONAL DISH OR KOREA; (SLANG) SOMETIMES USED BY GIs TO MEAN 'DEEP TROUBLE' SINCE KIM-CHEE IS USUALLY BURIED UNDERGROUND TO ALLOW IT TO PROPERLY FERMENT.

KLONG MONSTER: (SLANG) LARGE, RARELY (OR NEVER) SEEN (DEPENDING ON WHO'S TELLING THE STORY), MYTHICAL LIZARD ABOUT THE SIZE OF A LARGE CROCODILE.

KLICKS (SLANG): KILOMETERS. (ALSO SEE 'KILOS.')

K-9 (SLANG): CANINE, I.E., SP MILITARY WORKING-DOG SECTION.

KNOBBER (SLANG): FELLATIO OR BLOW-JOB.

KISS-OF-DEATH (SLANG): DOING SOMETHING FATAL TO YOUR MILITARY CAREER. (ALSO SEE 'BOUGHT (OR BUY) THE FARM.')

KS: KANSAS.

LAND OF THE BIG BX (SLANG): THE USA.

LB(S): POUND(S).

LBFM(S) (SLANG): LITTLE BROWN FUCKING MACHINE(S); I.E., THAI PROSTITUTE(S).

LE: LAW ENFORCEMENT.

LEAVENWORTH: US MILITARY DISCIPLINARY BARRACKS, FORT LEAVENWORTH, KS. WHERE US MILITARY PRISIONERS ARE HELD FOR LONG-TERM CONFINEMENT FOR SERIOUS CRIMES.

LIGHT COLONEL (SLANG): LIEUTENANT COLONEL/O-5 PAY GRADE.

LIGHT-BIRD COLONEL (SLANG): LIEUTENANT COLONEL/O-5 PAYGRADE.

LIGHT-CHICKEN COLONEL (SLANG): LIEUTENANT COLONEL/O-5 PAYGRADE.

LLM: MASTER'S DEGREE IN LAWS AND LETTERS, I.E., SECOND LEVEL LAW DEGREE.

LITTLE SATTAHIP (SLANG): SMALL, POPULAR SHOPPING ARCADE NEAR THE U-TAPAO RTNAB SPORT'S FIELD, ALSO VERY CLOSE TO THE BEQs.

LOE: LETTER OF EVALUATION, I.E., IF AN OFFICER OR SUPERVISOR DEPARTS PRIOR TO THE END OF THE NEXT RATING PERIOD, THEN AN LOE IS WRITTEN TO COVER THAT PEROD. IT IS MERGED WITH THE OFFICER'S NEXT REGULAR OER.

L.T. (SLANG): SECOND OR FIRST LIEUTENANT/O-1 OR O-2 PAYGRADE.

M-16: FIREARM, COLT INDUSTRIES-MADE, .223 CALIBER, SEMI-AUTOMATIC ASSAULT RIFLE CARRIED BY SP TROOPS.

M-113: TRACKED VEHICLE USED AS AN SP ROVING QRF; AN ARMORED PERSONNEL CARRIER (APC).

M-870: FIREARM, REMINGTON CO.-MADE, 20-GAUGE, SIX-SHELL MAGAZINE, STANDARD SHOTGUN, USED US MILITARY-WIDE.

MA: MASSACHUSETTS.

MAITRE D' (FRENCH): PERSON WHO GREETS CUSTOMERS AT A RESTAURANT AND ESCORTS THEM TO THEIR TABLE.

MAJCOM: MAJOR COMMAND, I.E., SAC, PACAF, TAC, ETC.

MAMA-SAN (JAPANESE, SLANG): FEMALE SUPERVISOR OF A BAR, BROTHEL, MASSAGE PARLOR, LOUNGE, DRINKING ESTABLISHMENT OR ANY SIMILAR BUSINESS.

MIA: MISSING-IN-ACTION.
MID(S): SP MIDNIGHT SHIFT, I.E., ON-DUTY 2200-0800.
MIG: RUSSIAN-MANUFACTURED FIGHTER AIRCRAFT.
MILITARY TIME:

| | |
|---|---|
| 0000: 12:00AM/MIDNIGHT | 1200: 12:00PM OR NOON. |
| 0100: 1:00AM | 1300: 1:00PM |
| 0200: 2:00AM | 1400: 2:00PM |
| 0300: 3:00AM | 1500: 3:00PM |
| 0400: 4:00AM | 1600: 4:00PM |
| 0500: 5:00AM | 1700: 5:00PM |
| 0600: 6:00AM | 1800: 6:00PM. |
| 0700: 7:00AM | 1900: 7:00PM. |
| 0800: 8:00AM | 2000: 8:00PM. |
| 0900: 9:00AM | 2100: 9:00PM |
| 1000: 10:00AM | 2200: 10:00PM |
| 1100: 11:00AM | 2300: 11:00PM |
| 1200: 12:00PM OR NOON | 2400: 12:00PM/MIDNIGHT |

MP: MILITARY POLICE.
MPH: MILES PER HOUR.
MMS: MUNITIONS MAINTENANCE SQUADRON.
MS: MASTER OF SCIENCE DEGREE.
MSM: MERITORIOUS SERVICE MEDAL.
MT: MONTANA.
MUFTI: MILITARY OFFICER IN CIVILIAN CLOTHING.
NAF: NON-APPROPRIATED FUNDS. THE COMMISSARY, BASE EXCHANGE, BX-OPERATED CONCESSION STANDS, OFFICER'S CLUB, NCO CLUB, AIRMAN'S CLUB, ETC., WOULD BE EXAMPLES OF NAF FUNDS OR FUNDING.
NAM (SLANG): VIETNAM.
NASA: NATIONAL SPACE AND AERONAUTICS ADMINISTRATION.
NBC: NATIONAL BROADCASTING COMPANY.
NCO: NON-COMMISSIONED OFFICER (E-4 TO E-9 PAYGRADES). (ALSO SEE 'RANKS, AF.')
NCO CLUB: NON-COMMISSIONED OFFICER'S CLUB.
NCOIC: NON-COMMISSIONED OFFICER IN CHARGE.
ND: NORTH DAKOTA.
NE: NEBRASKA.
NEXT (SLANG): NEXT PERSON SCHEDULED TO LEAVE OR PCS FROM THEIR UNIT OR ORGANIZATION.
NEWBIE (SLANG): NEWEST PERSON IN THEIR UNIT OR ORGANIZATION. (ALSO SEE 'FNG.')
NJ: NEW JERSEY.
NORTHERN-TIER (SLANG): LARGE AFBs IN THE NORTHERN PART OF THE US; USUALLY CLOSE TO THE CANADIAN BORDER IN SMALLER TOWNS, CITIES AND ISOLATED COMMUNITIES.
NPRC: NATIONAL PERSONNEL RECORDS CENTER, ST. LOUIS, MO.
NVA: NORTH VIETNAMESE ARMY.
NY: NEW YORK.

O-CLUB: OFFICER'S CLUB.
O.D.: OLIVE DRAB.
OER: OFFICER EFFECTIVENESS REPORT; I.E. AF OFFICER'S 'REPORT CARD' OR
    EVALUATION DONE EVERY SIX MONTHS OR ONE YEAR.
OK: OKLAHOMA.
ONE DIGIT-MIDGIT (SLANG): 1-9 DAYS LEFT FOR DEROS/PCS. (THE BEST SITUATION.)
ONE-STAR (SLANG): BRIGADIER GENERAL/O-7 PAYGRADE.
OPS OFFICER: SP SQUADRON OPERATIONS OFFICER; SIMILAR IN DUTIES TO AN
    EXECUTIVE OFFICER IN THE US ARMY, US NAVY, AND US MARINE CORPS.
OSI: OFFICE OF SPECIAL INVESTIGATIONS.
OTS: OFFICER TRAINING SCHOOL, LACKLAND AFB, TX. SIMILAR TO US ARMY AND US
    NAVY OFFICER CANDIDATE SCHOOL (OCS).
OV-10: TWO-SEAT, PROPELLOR-DRIVEN, FORWARD AIR CONTROLLER AIRCRAFT; ALSO
    CALLED A 'BRONCO.'
PACAF: PACIFIC AIR FORCES, HQs AT HICKAM AFB, HI.
P/T: PART-TIME.
PCS: PERMANENT CHANGE OF STATION.
PCS-ED: LEFT ON PERMANENT CHANGE OF STATION ORDERS.
PCS-ING: LEAVING ON PERMANENT CHANGE OF STATION ORDERS VERY SOON OR
    SHORTLY.
PFM (SLANG): PURE FUCKING MAGIC.
POCKET-ROCKET (SLANG): AF MISSILEMAN QUALIFICATION BADGE.
POV(S): PRIVATELY OWNED (OR OPERATED) VEHICLE(S).
P-3: US NAVY FIXED-WING, FOUR-ENGINE, LONG-RANGE ANTI-SUBMARINE AIRCRAFT.
PULL-A-TRAIN (SLANG): A PROSTITUTE HAVING SEX WITH MULTIPLE PARTNERS IN
QUICK
    SUCCESSION.
QRF: QUICK REACTION FORCE; I.E., AN M-113 TRACKED VEHICLE WITH SP TROOPS
INSIDE
    TO QUICKLY RESPOND IN FORCE TO ANY ARMED ATTACKS UNTIL OTHER
MANPOWER
    ASSETS COULD BE MUSTERED.
RAF: ROYAL AIR FORCE.
RAILROAD TRACKS (SLANG): CAPTAIN/O-3 PAYGRADE RANK INSIGNIA.
RANKS/PAYGRADES, AF:
    ENLISTED:
    CMSGT: CHIEF MASTER SERGEANT/E-9 PAYGRADE.
    SMSGT: SENIOR MASTER SERGEANT/E-8 PAYGRADE.
    MSGT: MASTER SERGEANT/E-7 PAYGRADE.
    TSGT: TECHNICAL SERGEANT/E-6 PAYGRADE.
    SSGT: STAFF SERGEANT/E-5 PAYGRADE.
    SGT: SERGEANT/E-4 PAYGRADE.
    A1C: AIRMAN FIRST CLASS/E-3 PAYGRADE.
    AMN: AIRMAN/E-2 PAYGRADE.
    AB: AIRMAN BASIC/E-1 PAYGRADE.

OFFICER:
GEN: GENERAL/O-10 PAYGRADE.
LTGEN: LIEUTENANT GENERAL/O-9 PAYGRADE.
MAJGEN: MAJOR GENERAL/O-8 PAYGRADE.
BGEN: BRIGADIER GENERAL/O-7 PAYGRADE.
COL: COLONEL/O-6 PAYGRADE.
LTC: LIEUTENANT COLONEL/O-5 PAYGRADE.
MAJ: MAJOR/O-4 PAYGRADE.
CAPT: CAPTAIN/O-3 PAYGRADE.
1LT: FIRST LIEUTENANT/O-2 PAYGRADE.
2LT: SECOND LIEUTENANT/O-1 PAYGRADE.
RECON: RECONNAISSANCE.
RED HORSE: RAPID ENGINEER DEPLOYMENT, HEAVY OPERATIONAL REPAIR SQUADRON
ENGINEERS.
REPAIR(ING): GO(ING) TO A LOCATION.
RI: RHODE ISLAND.
RON: REMAIN OVER NIGHT, I.E., TRANSIENT STOP ON A TDY OR AIRCRAFT FLIGHT. (ALSO
SEE 'RON-ED.')
RON-ED: REMAINED OVER NIGHT. (ALSO SEE 'RON.')
R&R: REST AND RECREATION.
RTG: ROYAL THAI GUARD(S).
RTMC: ROYAL THAI MARINE CORPS.
RTN: ROYAL THAI NAVY.
RTNAB: ROYAL THAI NAVAL AIR BASE.
RTNB: ROYAL THAI NAVAL BASE.
SAC: STRATEGIC AIR COMMAND, HQS AT OFFUT AFB, NE.
SAM: SURFACE-TO-AIR MISSILE.
SC: SOUTH CAROLINA.
SCOOP-FROM-GROUP (SLANG): THE LATEST INSIDE GOSSIP FROM HIGHER HQS.
SD: SOUTH DAKOTA.
SGLI: SERVICEMAN'S GROUP LIFE INSURANCE, I.E., US GOVERNMENT USD$20,000 LIFE
INSURANCE POLICY FOR ALL MILITARY MEMBERS ON ACTIVE DUTY.
SHAVE-TAIL (SLANG): AF SECOND LIEUTENANT/O-1 PAYGRADE. (ALSO SEE 'GREEN
HORN.') PHRASE DATES FROM THE AMERICAN CIVIL WAR.
SHORT (SLANG): USUALLY THIRTY DAYS OR LESS FOR DEPARTURE FROM THAT
ASSIGNMENT. ALSO MEANS HAVING A TOTALLY APATHETIC ATTITUDE TOWARDS
WORK. (ALSO SEE 'FIGMO' AND 'SHORT-TIMER'S ATTITUDE.')
SHORT-TIME (SLANG): QUICKLY HAVING SEX WITH A PROSTITUTE THEN LEAVING.
SHORT-TIMER (SLANG): SEE 'SHORT.' (ALSO SEE 'FIGMO.')
SHORT-TIMER'S ATTITUDE (SLANG): APATHY AGAINST DOING ANY WORK DUE TO PSC
-ING SOON OR IN RECEIPT OF PCS ORDERS. (ALSO SEE 'SHORT' AND 'FIGMO.')
SILVER STAR(S) (SLANG): GENERAL(S)/O-7 TO O-10 PAYGRADES.
SOP: STANDARD OPERATIONG PROCEDURE. WRITTEN RULES ON EXACTLY THE STEPS

TO TAKE FOR ROUTINE TASKS, I.E., LIKE WRITING A TRAFFIC TICKET OR FILLING OUT AN INCIDENT REPORT THAT IS NOT COVERED UNDER USAF REGULATIONS OR IN THE MANUALS.

SOS: SQUADRON OFFICERS SCHOOL, MAXWELL AFB, AL.

SP: SECURITY POLICE.

SPS: SECURITY POLICE SQUADRON.

SS (GERMAN): SCHUTZSTAFFEL; I.E., ELITE GERMAN MILITARY ORGANIZATION.

SSAN: SOCIAL SECURITY NUMBER.

STRAT (SLANG): STRATEGIC.

SVN: SOUTH VIETNAM.

SW: STRATEGIC WING.

SWINGS: SP SWING SHIFT, I.E., ON-DUTY 1400-2400.

TAC: TACTICAL AIR COMMAND, HQs AT LANGLEY AFB, VA.

TDY: TEMPORARY DUTY ASSIGNMENT. (FROM 1 TO 89 DAYS.)

10-4 (RADIO SHORT-HAND): YOUR MESSAGE IS RECEIVED AND ACKNOWLEDGED.

TEQ: TRANSIENT ENLISTED QUARTERS.

31ST AF: 31ST (NUMBERED) AIR FORCE, HQs AT CLARK AB, THE PHILIPPINES.

.38: SIDEARM; SMITH & WESSON-MADE .38 CALIBER SIX-SHOT REVOLVER CARRIED BY SP
TROOPS.

THREE DIGIT-MIDGIT (SLANG): 100 OR MORE DAYS LEFT TO DEROS/PCS. (THE WORST SITUATION.)

THREE-STAR(S) (SLANG): AF LIEUTENANT GENERAL/O-9 PAYGRADE.

T.O.: TASK ORDER(S).

TOQ: TRANSIENT OFFICERS QUARTERS.

TOUR-OF-DUTY: ANY CURRENT ASSIGNMENT.

TSG(S): THAI SECURITY GUARD(S).

TV: TELEVISION.

TWO DIGIT-MIDGIT (SLANG): 10-99 DAYS LEFT FOR DEROS/PCS. (A BETTER SITUATION.)

TX: TEXAS.

UCLA: UNIVERSITY OF CALIFORNIA, LOS ANGELES.

UCMJ: UNIFORM CODE OF MILITARY JUSTICE; I.E., MILITARY LAWS AND REGULATIONS CONCERNING THE ADMINISTRATION OF PUNISHMENT, DISCIPLINE AND JUSTICE. (ALSO SEE 'ARTICLE 15'.)

UFO: UNIDENTIFIED FLYING OBJECT.

UN: UNITED NATIONS.

US: UNITED STATES.

USAF: UNITED STATES AIR FORCE.

USD: US DOLLAR(S).

USO: UNITED SERVICES ORGANIZATION. CIVILIAN VOLUNTEER ORGANIZATION THAT PROVIDES FREE ENTERTAINMENT, FOOD, RECREATION AND OTHER ACTIVITIES FOR MILITARY MEMBERS AT BASES AND LOCATIONS WORLD-WIDE.

U-T (SLANG): U-TAPAO (ROYAL THAI NAVAL AIR BASE).

U-2: USAF TWO-ENGINE, FIXED-WING, HIGH-ALTITUDE RECONNAISSANCE AIRCRAFT.

'V' DEVICE: DENOTES 'VALOR' ON SOME DECORATIONS. (ONLY AWARDED FOR COMBAT.)
VA: VIRGINIA.
VC: VIET CONG.
VD: VENEREAL DISEASE.
VIP: VERY IMPORTANT PERSON(AGE).
VIS (SLANG): VISIBILITY, I.E., TO BE SEEN BY OTHERS DOING SOMETHING IMPORTANT. HIGH 'VIS' IS BEST.
VN: VIETNAM. (ALSO SEE 'NAM.)
VOQ: VISITING OFFICERS QUARTERS.
WAKE-UP (SLANG): FINAL DAY ON-BASE, I.E., DATE OF DEPARTURE. (ALSO SEE 'BAG DRAG.')
(THE) WHOLE NINE YARDS (SLANG): EVERYTHING.
(THE) WORLD (SLANG): ANYWHERE OTHER THAN SOUTHEAST ASIA; USUALLY MEANS THE USA.
WWI: WORLD WAR I.
WWII: WORLD WAR II.
WY: WYOMING.


## US NAVY/US MARINE CORPS/ROYAL THAI NAVY/ROYAL THAI MARINE CORPS DICTIONARY

LINE OFFICER: US NAVY OFFICER AUTHORIZED TO COMMAND UNITS IN A WARFARE SPECIALITY: SURFACE SHIPS, AVIATION, SUBMARINES, SPECIAL OPERATIONS OR SPECIAL WARFARE.
MCRD: US MARINE CORPS RECRUIT DEPOT, SAN DIEGO, CA, I.E., WHERE US MARINE CORPS
    BASIC TRAINING IS CONDUCTED.
NAB: NAVAL AMPHIBIOUS BASE.
NRD: US NAVY RECRUIT DEPOT; I.E., WHERE US NAVY BASIC TRAINING IS CONDUCTED.
P-3: US NAVY FIXED-WING, FOUR-PROPELLER ENGINE, LONG-RANGE, ANTI-SUBMARINE DUTY, LAND-BASED AIRCRAFT.
RANKS/PAYGRADES, USN/RTN/RTMC:
    ENLISTED:
    MASTER CHIEF PETTY OFFICER/E-9 PAY GRADE.
    SENIOR CHIEF PETTY OFFICER/E-8 PAYGRADE.
    CHIEF PETTY OFFICER/E-7 PAYGRADE.
    PETTY OFFICER FIRST CLASS/E-6 PAYGRADE.
    PETTY OFFICER SECOND CLASS/E-5 PAYGRADE.
    PETTY OFFICER THIRD CLASS/E-4 PAYGRADE.
    SEAMAN FIRST CLASS/E-3 PAYGRADE.
    SEAMAN/E-2 PAYGRADE.
    SEAMAN BASIC/E-1 PAYGRADE.

    OFFICER:

ADM: ADMIRAL/O-10 PAYGRADE.
VADM: VICE ADMIRAL/O-9 PAYGRADE.
RADM: REAR ADMIRAL/O-7 PAYGRADE.
CAPT: CAPTAIN/O-6 PAYGRADE.
CDR: COMMANDER/O-5 PAYGRADE.
LCDR: LIEUTENANT COMMANDER/O-4 PAYGRADE.
LT: LIEUTENANT/O-3 PAYGRADE.
LT(JG): LIEUTENANT (JUNIOR GRADE)/O-2 PAYGRADE.
ENS: ENSIGN/O-1 PAYGRADE.
RTMC: ROYAL THAI MARINE CORPS.
RTN: ROYAL THAI NAVY.
RTNAB: ROYAL THAI NAVAL AIR BASE.
RTNB: ROYAL THAI NAVAL BASE.
TSG(S): THAI SECURITY GUARD(S).
SWOS: US NAVY SURFACE WARFARE OFFICERS SCHOOL, NAB CORONADO, CA.
USMC: UNITED STATES MARINE CORPS.
USS: UNITED STATES SHIP.
WESTPAC WIVES & WIDOWS CLUB (SLANG): US MARINE CORPS NCO CLUB, MCRD, SAN DIEGO, CA; WHERE MAINLY SINGLE ORIENTAL WOMEN, WIDOWS AND DIVORCEES PLUS 'WESTPAC WIVES, I.E., WIVES WHO'S HUSBANDS (OR GIRLFRIENDS WHOSE BOYFRIENDS), ARE DEPLOYED OVERSEAS OR TEMPORARILY AWAY FROM HOME (MAINLY TO 'WESTPAC' OR THE WESTERN PACIFIC, COME TO MEET ELIGIBLE MILITARY OR EX-MILITARY MALES FOR COMPANIONSHIP, POSSIBLY MARRIAGE OR SEX.

Leonard H. Le Blanc III was born in San Antonio, TX in 1951. He grew up in Danbury, CT. He graduated from Kansas State University with a BS in Geography and two MA degrees from Webster University in Management and International Relations. Leonard also graduated from the University of the State of New York (now Regents College) with a BA in History and from Charter Oak State College with a BS in Individualized Studies (English, History and Psychology). Leonard honorably served in the US Air Force and US Navy. He has lived and worked overseas in military and civilian jobs for over 25 years in Nigeria, Japan, Thailand, Kuwait, Bosnia, Iraq and Afghanistan. Leonard has resided in Bangkok, Thailand since 1991 when he is not working on overseas defense contracts. His next historical novel about U-Tapao Royal Thai Naval Air Base will be called THAILAND will be for sale on www.amazon.com as a Kindle eBook along with AFGHANISTAN - LASHKAR GAH: HOME OF THE WARRIORS. (One Year in Taliban Country Book 1 and 2). He has also been a freelance reporter for THE BANGKOK POST, and English Language Advisor to THE NATION GROUP and a volunteer advisor on Peace and Human Security issues in South and Southeast Asia plus an editor and proofreader for UNESCO Regional HQs-Bangkok. He is married to the former Lana Adnan Issa al-Shareeda of Basra, Iraq and they have two children, Lujane Jasmin (L. J.) and Leonard IV (J. L. or 'Yusef').